PROOF OF LIFE

KAREN CAMPBELL

PROOF OF LIFE

HODDER &
STOUGHTON

First published in Great Britain in 2011 by Hodder & Stoughton
An Hachette UK company

1

Copyright © Karen Campbell 2011

The right of Karen Campbell to be identified as the Author
of the Work has been asserted by her in accordance with
the Copyright, Designs and Patents Act 1988.

A CIP catalogue record for this title is available from the British Library

Hardback ISBN 978 1444 70045 9

Typeset in Plantin Light by Hewer Text UK Ltd, Edinburgh
Printed and bound in the UK by CPI Mackays, Chatham ME5 8TD

Hodder & Stoughton policy is to use papers that are natural, renewable
and recyclable products and made from wood grown in sustainable forests.
The logging and manufacturing processes are expected to conform
to the environmental regulations of the country of origin.

Hodder & Stoughton Ltd
338 Euston Road
London NW1 3BH

www.hodder.co.uk

This novel is all the better for the help and support I received from a very fine bunch of people. My thanks go to Captain Andy Goldsmith for his (fire) cracking advice; the wee tiny boy that is Garry Maximus Deans for patient, prompt (and sometimes even helpful) responses; Stuart Barrowman and Gerry MacDonald for updating my IT knowledge; Alan Porte for Tulliallan information; Tom Cassidy because he'll go in a huff if I don't; Jim Clark for his blogtastic reviewing; Ian Watson – again! – for the photos; my friend Helen MacKinven for her thoughtful advice; Mum and Dad for their indefatigable campaign of rearranging shelves in bookshops; Mrs Anne Reekie and her daughters, for generously bidding in the auction to support the Prince and Princess of Wales Hospice, Glasgow; my agent Lisa and my editor Suzie, who between them have nurtured, tweaked and midwifed these books into existence; Leni for all her PR & positivity, plus Jack, Francine and everyone else at Hodder.

Thanks also to all the cops I've served with and known over the years – your banter, your skills and your bravery have been an inspiration. A special thanks to my friends and family for supporting me at every turn. And finally, all my love, as ever, to Dougie, Eidann and Ciorstan – my ain wee clan.

This book is dedicated to the memory of Constable John Forrest.

GLASGOW FAIR

All around is smoke and mirrors. The grey whiteness opening and closing like mouths on shivered glass and shattered people and slivers that refract the boldness back at her. Bright flame and fluorescent light, in and out, artificial light and daylight and primitive, angry, licking light that smells of petrol and withered flesh. They have dragged the man away, but a blood trail smears in accusatory fingers from the Jeep to the roadway, hauling over the kerb to the pavement to the speed bumps and then it disappears. As if by magic. But the burning car remains, and the surging, shell-shocked people, pushed back by the rows of cops and airport staff, their screams and their silences becoming shrill relief.

'Jesus, Jimmy – did you see that?'

'Andrea – you alright?'

'What about our luggage?'

'Carly! I canny find Carly! Carly! Carly hen, where are you?'

A camera crew is trying to set up less than twenty feet from the simmering wreckage. A cop is dispatched to move them on.

'You need to keep back.'

'We need to get it all in shot.'

'We're evacuating the entire concourse.'

It could still go up, she wants to scream. *It's a giant bomb and it could still go up.*

Her hand moves across the front of her body, spine rounding. The action is conditioned. Concave space like the mouth of a shell, her belly hanging over air, shoulder blades wings against the jostling. It is universal. In the face of unstoppable disaster, you would literally curl up and die. Expecting the comma of bone you form to shield you, like those twisted shapes who made themselves small, so small, in Pompeii. Or the beach-imprinted bowls of resignation when the tsunami came, or the simple submission of a dog being kicked.

A superintendent comes over, says something to the reporter. Two superintendents, a chief super, escaped from Headquarters, from days off, from . . . there's an ACC now.

A camera, you say? You need a statement?

More engines arriving. Sirens. Chaos. Everyone and their granny, rushing from somewhere else to here, to the centre of the universe, which is an unassuming, one-and-a-wee-bit-which-is-really-a-Portakabin terminal airport in Abbotsinch. And she, Anna, is no different, was on her way to the shops at Braehead, heard it on the car radio. A terrorist attack? A terrorist attack? *At Glasgow Airport?* No way.

Now the camera crew are comfy, over the road. Space has been made for them on the first floor of the car park. It has a vantage point, a vista with a background pall of smoke. Other camera crews are joining them and the focus is shifting. More media arrive. Who saw it? Did you see it? Who laid hands on them? And the doughty Scottish maleness shakes itself down like a damp terrier, puffs up its chest as one and breenges over to confess.

I just seen red.

Aye me too.

I wis having none of it . . . Aye, and then I decked him . . .

Anna has no official detail, is just one of many superfluous cops who are ringing the locus and keeping folk back, or waving traffic away or holding tape. She gravitates to where the press have set up camp: there seems to be no one in charge. A sullen Scottish summer; damp air warm as bathwater; bodies colliding like bubbles. Several men are being interviewed, a baggage handler, a guy in a tracksuit. A man who is clearly a cop in part-uniform, denim jacket over cheap black combats, the polish of his Docs scuffed. He is wisely hanging back, waiting to give his statement to the detectives when they are ready. He catches Anna's eye, half smiles, ashamed at all the fuss. His hands are red and burned, and that is his job. Damping fire with his hands and saving the life of a man who would kill thousands, that is his job, the one he's paid to do every day. It is a reflex not to recoil. But the others are unaccustomed heroes; this was not their job, yet they did it. While others fled, they waded in. As a burning vehicle crashed into the sliding glass doors of Glasgow Airport, as two figures leapt out screaming, they tried to intervene. Men going their holidays or picking up their mums. Men driving taxis or shoving trolleys or shifting cars. Stunned men who are blinking before the assembled press, who will clam up or spout off to seal their place in history, no matter what it was they actually *did*. It will be the packaging of their braveness that matters, ultimately.

THEY MADE A STAND FOR GLASGOW!

As if their bravery had thwarted the attack. As if it was the collective, furious, irrepressible will of Glasgow that prevented the smoking oil drums from igniting, that blocked the path of the vehicle's tyres, physically stopping the iron-solid rubber from ramming over the pale, peeled legs of Scottish holidaymakers.

But it was brave nonetheless.

Someone has given Anna a yellow jacket marked Police. It sits uncomfortably atop her jumper and jeans, but keeps her in the inner circle. A reporter is turning towards the off-duty cop and the cop edges away but cannot escape. Too many people pressing. Anna intervenes. 'I'm sorry. We can't give any statements at present.'

And then the bloody camera is on her, all the hungry bloody cameras and it is a feeding frenzy.

'And you are?'

'Eh, Anna Cameron. Chief Inspector Cameron, A Division, Strathclyde Police.'

'But what are the police saying? Was it deliberate?'

'I'm sorry. You'll appreciate that our main concern at the moment is to ensure the safety of everyone at the airport.'

Something furry under her nose. 'Is it a bomb right enough?'

Anna searches for the ACC. He was floating here a minute ago, all silver-braid and stiff back, ready for the telly.

'It's too early to say.'

'So you're not denying it then?'

'All our officers are working hard to investigate this incident, but our priority is to make sure everyone is safe.'

'What about the man that was on fire? Is he dead?'

'Naw,' says a voice. 'He was pure squealing when the polis huckled him. I seen it all.' The faces swivel on to him; Anna sinks back, grateful, into the tumbling crowd.

There will be hell to pay for that. And her not even media-trained as well.

Chapter One

'Well, I'd always vote SNP.'

'How come? They're a bunch of arseholes. My old boy says that taxes would go through the roof.'

It was just after the holidays, and for some reason the conversation had gone from who you'd shagged in the summer to who you'd vote for when you finally turned eighteen. Joe had already turned eighteen, but knew better than to stick his oar in; and anyway, no one was aware that he'd repeated a year. Patrick would be eighteen this coming February, and was getting quite excited about the whole 'exercising his franchise' deal.

'Bullshit,' he said. 'Why shouldn't we rule our own bloody country? Why are we all so shit-scared of standing up and being a proper nation?'

'You tell 'em, Braveheart.'

'Christ,' said Brillo, 'he'll be setting off a bomb at Glasgow Airport next.'

Patrick punched the air. 'Too right I will. Free-ee Dum!'

'Typical Glasgow though, eh? Fucking kick the shit out the terrorists.'

'Fuck, man, I know. Did you see it on the telly?'

'See it?' Doug paused for dramatic effect. 'My uncle was at the bloody airport! Totally inside the concourse when the whole place went up.'

'Shi-it.'

'Well, it didn't exactly go up, did it?' Patrick winked; the way he was positioned, Doug probably couldn't have seen him. But Joe could.

'Nah. You know what I mean, though. He said he could actually smell burning flesh, you know? Like off the terrorist?'

Joe was standing at the edge of the group, listening. The games master had been round twice in the last week to check for smokers, so all the guys had been on the move, varying their haunts as well as their poses. Sometimes Joe thought he knew where they were all going to be, was sure he'd heard Brillo or Doug say where and when for lunch, then he'd get there and there'd be nobody about.

He moved closer to Doug. 'D'you think he deserved to die? That terrorist?'

Doug didn't hear him. 'So, anyway, my uncle had been heading to Bolivia – you know that jungle-run thing he was doing?'

'Borneo,' said Joe.

This time, Doug did turn his head. 'What?'

'It's Borneo. That's what you said last time. And Bolivia doesn't have any jungles.'

A small boy careered into them, swinging a thick, woody clump of evergreen.

'Oh, sorry,' he squeaked, as the stick made contact with Doug.

'You fucking will be, you little shit.'

The boy blinked, a skinny wee leveret, then loped off back to his own group of friends. Some of the second years had been on a biology trip to Kelvingrove Park, had come back wielding branches which they were currently using as weapons. Doug picked a tiny piece of leaf from his arm. The laurel green was only a shade lighter than the myrtle of his blazer.

'You know my uncle, do you?'

Joe said nothing.

'The TV producer one? Or what about my aunt, who's a screenwriter? Do you know her, Joe? Do you know any interesting folk at all, *Joe*?'

'Slowjo.' Brillo was drawing the syllables out, stretching them like chewing gum.

'Cause they both went to Bo-li-via, you fuckwit. Okay?' Doug sniffed. It was an affectation of his; he did it so folk thought he did cocaine. Joe knew that, because Patrick had told him, one night when they were all pished and Joe had been helping him home. Joe didn't drink, but he was very tall, and got served no bother.

He shrugged. 'That's not what you said before.'

'Oh, fuck off prick and gies peace.'

Doug tried to use slang all the time, but it never sounded right. His mouth was too full of the family silver. See, that was the sort of thing Joe should say to him, all that stuff he thought in his head but never articulated. Even if he just said it once, or even if he punched him, just tried to deck him once instead of counting into himself and just standing there looking at his massive big feet.

'They've got a fucking cheek though, eh?' Doug was the smallest of the group, but every inch of him was bulldog-tight. He played rugby like it was a gift from God, and, if he was to be believed, slept with a different girl every weekend. 'I mean, why don't they fuck off back to their own country instead of moaning about this one?'

'You mean the terrorists?' said Ali.

'Yeah, I mean the terrorists.'

Most other guys would temper their belligerence at this point. Not Doug. He opened out the challenge, the uplift of his voice creating an invisible parenthesis into which you could insert: *So what you gonny do about it?* or: *How, Paki-boy? You got something to say?*

A lot of folk thought it was weird, that an Asian boy should go to a Catholic school, but, good as the college was, it wasn't just here that it happened. Joe's cousin Alice went to Notre Dame, an all-girls state school nearby, and it was full of Asians. *Strong moral code, you see,* Ali had told him. It was when Ali had first started here, just after Easter. Seemed years ago, now.

The mater and pater like it, Ali had nodded sagely. *Just so long as I don't start drinking blood.*

Joe had laughed, immediately getting the transubstantiation reference, and Ali had laughed as well. Encouraged by the laughter, it had just slipped out:

You want to come round to mine after school?
Aye, sure.

And he had, and it had been brilliant. Seeing Joe's mum's face break into a quickly suppressed beam, her careful, solicitous distribution of snacks and drinks, then more snacks and more drinks. Seeing his house, his room through someone else's eyes, all his *stuff*, that was expensive and right and, ultimately, didn't matter.

After a few weeks at the college, when Ali had been absorbed more seamlessly into the gang than Joe could ever imagine, Joe had asked him round again. He'd been waiting for a reciprocal invite, but since none was forthcoming and his mum had been on and on at him about 'his friend', he'd just asked. No big deal, just what mates did all the time, did it without even thinking about it, without writing it down and working out the best way to say it so that it sounded loose but friendly. Spontaneous. He'd waited until they were going into Latin – Ali was going to be a lawyer – until the words had set dry and thick inside his mouth. Waited until they were sitting down and Mr Cross had told them to get out their books.

'You want to come round to mine after school?' He kept focused on his bag, kept his hands delving inside, though his Latin folder was right at the top.

'Eh, no. Cheers. I've got stuff on.'

'Okay.' A pause. 'What about next week?'

Ali had flicked through his book. Flicking and flicking and it didn't take that long to find the bloody page.

'Maybe leave it, yeah? I've got tons of studying.'

Feeling his face inflame, feeling his fingers crush the folders in his bag. 'Sure. No bother.'

That had been it, clean as surgery; Joe reverted to his rightful place. For the first wee while, Ali had been awkward round Joe, who would always be *there*, always on the periphery, and thus unavoidable. Ali made sure he was never even standing beside him, as if they'd been caught *in flagrante* in the gym and it was all a horrible embarrassment. Then the summer holidays had come, and eight weeks' respite from all this posturing and learning and cold stone and watch where you put your feet, your hands, watch your mouth. Now, Joe wasn't sure if the guy remembered his name. He watched Ali push the lank silk hair away from his several faces. *This* would be interesting.

'Yeah, I know what you mean. It's not like they were even born here.'

Patrick was the only one whose eyes clicked with Joe's; making sure he had Joe's attention, then his pupils rolling up so his eyes were all white space. He held them like that, like wet white globules, until it just looked creepy. They all laughed, Patrick and Ali loudest. False, harsh rags of sound, and Joe had had enough. He walked away from the group, over towards the chapel. You could spend large chunks of lunchtime in there and no one would ever bother you. All you needed to do was close your eyelids, adopt an expression of pensive piety, and they would leave you entirely alone. But before that, first, came the drinking in.

Joe closed the chapel door, closing out the light. It wasn't the sprinkle of water on skin that he relished. Nor was it the metaphysical, gulping sustenance of the Holy Spirit giving him succour or strength. This, this thing that made Joe's heart hurt, was the simple rain of dense, sharp colour that hit you when you entered the church. All the bright proofs and prayers of butter-yellow and green and gold and rose. Of eggshell-blue domed walls, a cupola full of light and brilliant jewelled glass. Of green-grey marble and toffee marble and creamy marble, with the scarlet vein of carpet running through. Of the Last Supper shining in its multitude of gold-dust curves and bevels that capped the altar.

Ad majora natus sum
I was born for greater things

Joe took his seat, shut his eyes.

Today, he would be mostly making holy water boil, by the power of telekinesis.

Chapter Two

Autumn. It was a beautiful, orange, golden name.

'They named this time of year after you, you know.'

Mary smoothed her cheek along the horse's flank. Blunt stubs of hair bristling, musty warm breath, him and her. Him and her. In the arena, a lesson was in progress; she could hear the trullumph, trullumph as another old-timer approached the two-bar jump. Dutifully schooled, these ponies would leap just the requisite height – no more, no less – no matter who was rocking on their backs. A bored, rich blonde recapturing her youth, a plump boy wearing jeans and trainers and a big daft grin. Or like now, six sets of hooves and a gaggle of schoolgirls, some with the careless, high trot of owning their own ponies, the ubiquitous *like* of hockey and privilege swinging wide as their artful ponytails.

So, like, are you going to Cara's on Sunday?

Yeah, and like, my mum, she just said . . .

Others who just closed their eyes and breathed it in. You knew their faces, not quite making it every week, but always willing, whenever they were there, to untack the ponies, or lead them to the field. Saving up birthday money, the proceeds of Saturday shelf-stacking, pennies from lemonade bottles, pounds from purloined cosmetics sold in the girls' toilets. Blackmail money, blood money, begging money. Mid-teens, early teens, all tight reins and glowing cheeks. And some who were still sufficiently pre-pubescent to enjoy the thrill of all that power vibrating between their legs, and not quite understand why. She liked that too, the sweet-sour mix of innocence and massive, slapping dicks. There weren't many geldings at Calder Riggs Equestrian Centre. The owner didn't approve of castration. *Not for animals, anyway,* she said.

Mary ran the brush up and down the horse's withers, brushing firm against the grain, then smoothing it down. Soft chestnut polished to a conker shine. Autumn wasn't a gelding either, but he was far too old, too much of a gentleman to trouble her for anything more than a wet-kissed nudge, the odd low harrumph into her neck.

'Mary, can you fill up the hay nets when you're done here, please?'

Fiona, the owner, was about thirty. Unfailingly polite, she was a rubbish teacher, let the kids walk all over her – especially the spoilt-brat ones who you wished would take a tumble more often than they did. So Fiona stuck more to the administrative side, and employed instructors to do the bulk of the work. Mary could hear Bernadette shouting, her sharp voice slicing the nose of some stuck-up wee besom who was saying how she *didn't want to* . . . something or other. Bernadette was the best of the instructors; she was brilliant. Took no snash from any of them. Her voice had a way of sliding suddenly, of losing its roundness and becoming whiplash-hard. You just wouldn't mess with her, no way José. It was Bernadette who had found her this job.

It was Bernadette who had found *her*, full stop.

This place had been Fiona's family farm, tucked away at the back of what was now the teeming Glasgow burgh of Maryhill. You'd never guess it could be secreted there, inching along the fume-clogged artery of Maryhill Road, past the high grey-brick walls and railway tunnels, the old networks of canals and docks. Past Eastpark Children's Home, where forbidding Victorian stone was making way for low-level comfort and wheelchair accessibility; past bookies' and supermarkets and bakers' shops and McDonald's; then a swift turn right, some hidden – and therefore even nicer – rows of Edwardian villas, a school; and then, all this wonder. Suddenly, in the heart of industrial, sickly Glasgow, you were in a country lane. A little rescued pocket where the fields were broad and horses neighed and a patched-up, weathered mews faced a purpose-built stable block and the smart new bungalow where Fiona and Bernadette lived. Above the old carthouse was a converted hayloft. That was Mary's house. Nearly a year she'd been here, longer than any other job she'd held down. She'd been so grateful to Bernadette. Fiona too, of course, she was the boss and everything, but it was Bernie who had given her the chance.

Mary's Hill. It was meant to be. True, not named for her; but for the Mother of God, after whom she was named, so that was just as good, really. There had to be an ancient chapel or a well or something. A vision, perhaps, seen high above the spread of open land? Fiona had chuckled; Bernie had quickly disabused her of such fancy. Not at all. It was just called after the woman who owned the land. Mary Hill, simple as that. Proprietrix of the Gairbraid Estate, who feued the plot on condition that it was forever known as Maryhill.

Mary chucked the currycomb in the bucket. 'No need. I've done it already. And I've fixed up the feeds too.'

Fiona's gilet made her look shapeless. 'Thanks, Mary.'

She was a tall, grey woman, hung about with a cloud that darkened her dirty-fair hair. The kids were spilling out from their lesson. Two Tamaras and a Sadie-Jo, wiping down their skinny thighs, and then a Kirsty, a Lalla and lovely, dumpy Jess. Leading two ponies as usual.

'Once you've untacked the ponies, would you come and see me in the office, please?' said Fiona. Too thin as well as tall: a long, lanky streak of misery is how Mary's mother would have described Fiona. And yet, she was kind, in a soulful, sorrowful way.

'Sure.'

Mary's face must have folded in on itself.

'Don't worry – it's nothing bad.'

Jess beamed at them both. 'Hey Mary. Hi, Miss Cairns. Mary – is it okay if I untack Geronimo?'

Asked as if it was a favour, as if Mary was the kind of person who could waft out permissions.

'Yes, but I'll take him up to the field. Mind the last time you took him?'

Kind wee Jess had taken the notion of untacking literally, hadn't even left on a head collar with which to grab the horse when it decided on a life of liberation, of no more sweating buttocks and vicious, jibing heels.

Jess chuckled, slapped Geronimo's neck. 'Yeah, but he had good fun running away, didn't he?'

'Just whenever you're ready, Mary. No rush.' Fiona slumped her hands inside the gilet's folds, picked her way over the potholes and puddles of the yard towards the arena. A woman less like a farmer's daughter it was hard to imagine. But then, you would be hard-pressed to encounter a woman less like a lawyer and a teacher's daughter than Mary at her lowest depths. *I had a pony once too, you wee shits.* That is what she would most like to screech at Tamaras one and two. She bolted the lower half of the stable door, gave Autumn one last ruffle of his mane.

'See you, handsome.'

Her nails were black. Horsehair clung to the arms of her fleece, and there was a healthy dollop of shite on her boots. If she could bottle it, bottle these mottled smells, the ache of muscles, this sulky sky, then she would. Over by the arena, she could see Bernadette. Small and angular, dark hair taut on her temples, held back by one of the red elastic bands the postman was forever dropping in the yard. Fiona was saying something to her, then they both laughed, fair head leaning into dark. Bernie touched Fiona's cheek. No more than a second, just a kiss of skin on skin. Mary rubbed her own cheek. It felt hot.

'That's me done with Gerry. Can I do Apollo now too?' Jess bounced on her heels, all cheeks and untamed hair. Too much energy, that one.

'You not got a home to go to?'

'Well . . . my mum's not here yet. *Please.*'

'Fine. Untack him and give him a wee rub-down – but he's not to go up the paddock. I think Bernie's using him the lesson after next.'

'Okely-dokely.'

Mary watched Fiona going into the office. Bernadette had a quick glance round the yard, then flipped her lighter round a cigarette. Always good for a tap, if you had the craving. She could wheech cigarettes from air like a magician with flowers. Thin mouth drawing the smoke in, cheekbones like scars. Mary liked hearing her laugh. It was a rare, spontaneous eruption that flashed her clamped face open. A jagged lightning scar, going as quick as it came, but that was the beauty of it. Bernie caught Mary looking, waved at her with the smoke-free hand.

She waved back, went to Geronimo's stall. Jess had flung the saddle over the edge of the stable door, rather than put it in the tack room. Wee bugger. She'd put it back when she went to the office.

'C'mon Geronimo. Let's cut you loose, boy.'

The paddock was the biggest of the three fields that ringed the riding school. Standing in the centre of it, you could be in the middle of nowhere. A long copse of trees edged the far perimeter, extending along the rise and down to where the burn ran. A smell of fresh-rotting, of goodness. Leaves were turning, falling golden red and russet. It looked like silent fire. You couldn't even hear the traffic here, or, if you did, you just pretended it was the water plashing. Middle of absolute nowhere, best place in the world. But still, folk found them. People walking dogs, boys that came at night and tried to ride the horses. Tried to hurt the horses. They'd had to rig up a makeshift CCTV camera at the start of the year, after Fiona found Starlight missing half her tail. God knows how they'd caught her – poor thing was the most nervous of the bunch to start with. Bernie had fixed the camera, got some stuff from somewhere and wired it up to work through the old video recorder in the office.

'Used to be a spy,' she'd winked at Mary.

It worked, though. Just the salutary fact of it, swaying there on its pole. A twenty-first century scarecrow, even when they stopped bothering to switch on the tape.

'Off you go, pal.' Mary patted Geronimo's rump, unwound her fingers from his mane. She was manky from brushing Autumn.

If you walked down the side of the paddock, following the line of the trees, you'd come to where the stream fell into a pebbled pond. One day, she was going to swim in there. It wasn't really big enough, but you could probably lie bath-deep, feel transparent water freeze the filaments of hair, rise the very scales of your skin up. The thought made her shiver. She would do it next spring, rinse herself clean for the year. For now, she would rinse her hands. Far more hygienic than the sour wooden loo the kids and their boots made filthy on a daily basis. Mary never used her loft in the daytime, even though it had its own wee cooker and a smart white shower room. That was home and this was work.

Aye, dirty work, Bernadette would say. *But someone's got to do it.*

Mary squatted at the edge of the pool, fibrous mud crumbling into water where her boot rested. The burn was clear and brown, then silver, splashing and invisible as she rubbed. Going rippled, then dark while the water settled, then clear and brown again. It must go underground. When it got to the road and the built-up streets. It couldn't just stop. You couldn't just disappear.

As she came out of the woods, she saw a man, fixed like he'd always been there. He was leaning on the fence, his back to her. A heavy-set man, thick wrinkles of blubber at his nape, and a tiny gold stud in his ear. He didn't look like a dog walker – forbye the fact he had no dog. He wore a loose beige raincoat, dark trousers and slip-on shoes. Not the sort of footwear for hiking across fields. Something about him, about his stance, made her hold back. He hadn't seen her, was staring over at the riding school. Mary reversed into the shadowed overhang of trees. The second lesson was a hack, she could see them coming from the arena. A line of stomping ponies ploughing up dust, then soil. Bernie was at the front, a languorous zigzag of back, thigh and femur, her neck white, corded as she turned to give instruction. The ride was coming closer to the man, but he wasn't moving, except for a slight tightening in his shoulders, a sense of coiling.

It was private property, Mary could just walk out and tell him to bugger off. Maybe he was a parent. That was it; he was a parent come to watch his wee one on the horses. She tried to relax. There were five on the ride, stolid, dumpy things. Not really horses, not except Bernie's. She was on Toronto, a beautiful bay mare who smelled of honey. All the ponies moved behind her in a looping straggle, like she was towing them. Then one horse stopped to crap, another one watching, wandering out of file. Bernie wheeled Toronto round, trotting to the side, the shepherd with her flock. Back in line again, a sinuous pilgrimage making for the trees. Mary could smell the crush of grass as they approached, could feel the bigness of their hooves vibrate through earth. One horse dropped its head to tear at grass, its panicked rider nearly shooting between its ears.

'Keep your reins tight, Peter. Elbows in, that's it.'

Sun shafting clouds, a brightness projecting her profile forwards. With her hard hat on, all you saw was Bernadette's mouth and chin. It felt dirty almost, to be spying on her through the trees. To see nothing but the pinkness of her mouth. Then Bernie pushed her hat back, high on her brow. About twenty feet from where Mary stood, she reined in the horse. Her eyes narrowed, then widened. Blinked rapidly like stutters.

Bernie had seen the man, but she had not seen Mary. The man leaned off the fence, walked deliberately to where the whole ride had halted. It *was* deliberate, Mary would say that later, when she reappraised the scene. It was like when you are small, and you play tic-tac-toe. One foot then the other in a perfect slow trail. His arms were up, raised against the light. Or not . . . no. It was more a signal, that thing they do in America, when an umpire makes a 'T' shape with his hands.

Like a gallows.

A moment hanging.

The kids were buffeting pony against pony. Too close; bunched up like that, one of them would start to kick. She waited for Bernadette to sort them out, but her gaze was fixed solely on the man. A terrible dawning on her face.

First the recoil, then the lash. Mary wasn't sure who broke first; the man flying for her reins, Bernie swinging out with her crop. Then Toronto's hooves were flailing in air, Bernie sliding, galloping, bearing down on the man like Boadicea. He slithered, half fell. Began to run into the woods. Mary jooked behind the tree she was clinging on to, but he saw her. He saw her alright, eyes locking like a camera.

Then he was gone.

Chapter Three

'You're not my mum!'

There. Essential punctuation for almost every exchange Laura deigned to lob her way. Anna had tried to develop a rhino hide, bouncing words like missiles off a public order shield. Last autumn, she had done her Bronze Commander training – disused factory site, over-zealous 'hoodlums' clanging chains and flinging stones (and scoring petty points actually, since they were cops themselves, let off the lead with the exuberance of kids dousing teachers at the school fete). Even had petrol bombs raining down, the works. But *this* was infinitely more scary. This sweet-natured child, who six months earlier had snuggled up to Anna in bed, sighing like she was releasing all her thirteen years. Who had whispered, unprompted: *Love you, Ma-Na.*

Anna had skirted round the whole issue of what to call herself – it was Laura who created the name. *Well,* she'd gone, *it was that, Anna-Mama or Evil Stepmother.* Smile, teeth, dimples, everything; a shared joke, which was now a concept so far distant as to have dropped from the horizon and slid over the edge of the world. The world of the Cameron Brown household anyway. All Anna had done was ask Laura to put away some of her shoes instead of littering the hall with discarded trainers, pumps and . . . what were these? Soft like slippers, but with laces like boots. Black-and-white chequered articles best suited to an all-in wrestler. Deep breath out, pick them up. And those ones, she snatched . . . and those ones. Chucking them all in the cupboard under the stairs, spilled in an even worse confusion than they'd been in the hall. But it was fine; she could shut the door on this mess. One of the squashy boot things began to shift, not a settling, but an unfurling. Dark movement underneath. She jumped back. Jesus, they must have mice again, coming in from that damn field of a garden. Then Alice stuck her head out of the pile. Stretched.

'Bloody hell, cat. What are you doing in there?'

The cat flicked a disdainful tail and stalked from the cupboard.

'Did someone shut you in there, baby?'

Alice sat, squeezed her eyes. Benign once more.

'Or were you hiding from that stinky dug?'

Donna the dog was getting old. And smelly. If Anna had her way she'd be in a lovely kennel in the garden. Or, better still, someone else's garden. *I mean, she craps all over the lawn, slevers all over the couch. Nobody ever walks her apart from me.*

We've got the dog walker.

Rob had not been in the mood. Donna, as always, was non-negotiable.

I'm just saying.

Well don't.

There were days when Anna felt steel bands tightening round her arms and legs, clamping them harder and smaller and deeper. And there were other days – last Sunday, for example – when the three of them were sitting on the deck outside, when it had been warm enough, with the chimenea burning (this was Scotland, so you had to take your chances) to have a barbecue, and Rob had finally lifted all the dog deposits and given the grass its last cut of the year. When the lawn looked smooth and Anna had planted up a basket of herbs.

Not flowers? said Laura.

No, herbs. Pretty and practical. Look – the sage will flower, so will the chives. Big purple pom-poms. And you can use them for cooking.

Hmm.

That had been a good day. Rosé wine, Alice lounging at Anna's bare feet. Rob skimming his lips on the top of her head as he set down a plate of burgers. Then Laura, taking a flakey because there were clothes hanging on the line and she'd noticed Anna hadn't washed her gym kit.

But you never gave me it to wash.

But I need it for tomorrow.

Well how am I supposed to know?

And Laura had cried and Anna had felt like shit. It had been so much simpler when Anna was new and exciting, a comrade-in-arms to gently mock at Rob, a girlie to giggle with, a drumskin to test. Gentle rhythms at first. Synchronised heartbeats, joyful timpani of greeting and indulgence. Then louder, more urgent. Bigger noises, deeper imprints. Pounding headaches all round, and the constant thrum of war.

She ran the kitchen tap, sluiced down a couple of Panadols. There were a pair of rugby boots on the draining board. She shoved them off with the back of her hand. Nothing surprised her in this house any more. Now her hand was muddy. Anna missed the comfort of clean lines and spaces. Of knowing that, once you've scoured the bath and shined the taps, it will stay that way until you next chose to bathe. Of going out to work and coming home to the same calm sanctuary you'd hoovered that morning.

But then Rob would come and kiss it all better and it would be worth a thousand scummy lines of hair and dirt. She'd thought it might pall, just by the fact of him *being* there. A commodity to reach over and take, the way you would an apple. No, that was wrong. it was more like stoking a fire, or building up an excellent curry, so that the flavours infused more intensely with each layer. See, some folk wouldn't get that, but Rob would. Being compared to a fine curry was praise indeed from Anna.

This constant immersion in love heightened all her senses, unlocked a rush of repressed . . . was repressed the right word? She'd not exactly been an arid spinster. Okay, of . . . bottled-up desires. But the desires weren't sexual; sex prompted them, yes, but they were slower, warmer feelings. The kindling of anticipation as his key turned in the lock, the easing back into arms that supported you like a sofa. Waking up to breakfast in bed. Waking up to a glass of water, to safe hands and someone else turning on the light.

Anna's teens had been a lonely firestorm. If someone had reached down through the smoke and offered a hand to pull her to safety, she would have grabbed it. Gladly. On paper, she and Laura had much in common. Anna had lost her dad, Laura had lost her mum. And they both loved Robert Brown. Anna loved Laura too, she really, really did. It seemed to be unconditional, this love; taking whatever batterings it was given, yet coming back for more. But she sensed the intensity was not reciprocal.

'Where are you going now?'

'Out.'

Jacket on, one hand on the front door latch. Shit, the girl was good. Anna hadn't even heard her come back down the stairs.

'Out where?'

'Just out.'

'Now you know the rules. If you don't say where you're going, I can't let you out.'

Laura slouched against the door. Facing Anna, which was good. Scowling, which was not.

'How? You gonna put me in handcuffs?'

'Don't be so bloody stupid.'

Don't swear, don't overreact. And, whatever you do, do not call your teenager stupid.

People did what Anna told them. At work, she only had to raise an eyebrow and the task was complete. In fact, people had been known to fight over *who* would do the jumping, not just how high they'd do it. It was a privilege to carry out Anna Cameron's bidding. Issue instruction, await result. She didn't know how to negotiate . . . okay, no, she did. She could do this.

'Look, I hear what you're saying, Laura. You want to go out. You need your freedom. But you've got to appreciate that we need to know where you are. So, how do you think we can sort this?'

What are your demands, you little besom? A suitcase of money and the release of four prisoners? A plane waiting at Prestwick Airport? A Burger King?

'You can let me go out?'

'You can tell me where you're going?'

'Just hanging about.'

'But hanging about *where?*'

'Park. Probably.'

Anna's legs were starting to throb. She'd noticed the beginnings of a varicose vein in the shower, an ugly purple whorl that needled the back of her knee. That's what you got for a lifetime on your feet. Cops, hairdressers, nurses – martyrs all to their veins.

'Thank you. And when will you be back?'

'I don't know,' she yelled. 'God. Stop *interrogating* me. My dad disny go on like this.'

'Your dad's not here. And it's "doesn't", not "disny". Putting on a neddy accent doesn't make you tough.'

'What does putting on a posh one do?' Laura slammed the door, not waiting for an answer.

Anna threw the door wide. Caught the kick of a chequered boot as it battered out the gate. 'Be back by nine,' she shouted into the street.

The retired accountant next door was out in his drive, washing his Volvo. 'Lovely afternoon,' he called.

Anna waved back. 'Isn't it just?' She was still in her dressing gown.

'Hope you don't mind.' He nodded at the scaffolding heaped under his front window. 'We're getting a bit of work done on the roof. It won't be up for long – couple of weeks at the most they think.'

'No, no that's fine. We should really think about getting our roof checked out before the winter. Maybe you could ask one of the guys to pop round?'

'Will do.' He flapped his chamois as she went inside.

Cup of tea, then she'd get showered. She returned to the kitchen, noticed her handbag lying open. Not the purse, but the make-up bag. Her mascara was missing; so too was her foundation. Forty-two going on twelve; Anna's chin had started breaking out in spots. She'd never worn foundation before, hated the clagging in her pores, the festering of face as the day progressed. Like wiping yourself in clay. Anna zipped the plastic wallet shut. Laura was welcome to the stuff. No point telling her it would only make her spots worse. Or perhaps it wouldn't. How would Anna know? It was not in her gift to say so, to crow *See? Just like mine. I told you it would flare up.*

You have sensitive skin. Growing up, Anna would have been delighted to shake off the sameness of her mother's skin. As her own skin expanded, pulling in curious bumps and swells, as her hormones spoke a new language of fury and lust, it felt as if everything was bursting. She was hatching, to emerge new and separately glorious. An *adult*, who need never again heed one word her mother said.

But Anna and her mum had a whole chain of DNA lacing them tight, no matter what. Anna and Laura had twenty odd months of shy exchanges and the thrust and parry of vying for one man's attention.

She loaded the dishwasher, a pool of brown spilling from an upturned bowl. Coco Pops. The wee bugger had had Coco Pops for lunch again, even though Anna had told her to have a sandwich. She shifted the bowl so it was slotted in correctly.

'Shit.'

Chocolate milk splashing through the wire dish rack, spattering her slippers, Donna galloping in with mud-smeared paws to lick the floor, lick Anna's feet.

'Get off!'

The dog's warm tongue anointed the tops of her feet with meaty love. Anna tried to move away, but Donna was a chunky girl, had settled down on top of the slippers for a good old session. Ach, she'd need to wash them now anyway. And the floor. The remains of last night's Chinese congealed on a tower of unscraped plates: puckered fowl skin, jellied black sauce.

'Here, how d'you feel about crispy aromatic duck, girl?'

She tipped the scraps on to the vinyl, rewarded by the dog's bulk shifting to follow this new and pungent source of delight. Anna patted Donna's head. Rob's wife's dog's head.

She'd been kidding herself. She had no locus here. Laura had the perfect excuse, for everything.

You are not my mum.

Chapter Four

'But it's pathetic. Haven't you noticed? I mean, she's even started dyeing her hair the same colour as yours.'

Mary stiffened, fingers at her mouth. Through the crack in the wood, a runnel of sap long since bled, she could see the back of Bernadette's head. Fiona was out of shot, but it was her doing the talking.

'Och, leave her alone. She's fine.'

'No Bernie, she's not. She's been even worse since that nutter jumped you at the paddock.'

Bernadette's head titled slightly. The circumference of her skull was perfect. It was a fortune-teller's globe, all milky shifts of light.

'She's just looking out for me, that's all.'

'She's like a dog in heat. Honestly, one night we'll wake up and she'll be standing at the window, watching us.'

'Don't be daft. The bedroom's one floor up.'

'Exactly. I mean she'll be floating there, like one of those spooky vampire kids. What was that film again? *Lost Boys*?'

'Was that no a Duran Duran video?'

Bernadette's hair trembled as they both laughed. Just a collection of notes and aspiration; a laugh could elevate you, cuddle you. Or slap you hard across the jaw.

It didn't matter. Bernie had said to leave her alone.

A long, stooping outline. Fiona's shoulders, her arms hugging Bernie. Mary held her breath.

'That's better. You've not been yourself since the mugging.'

'Fiona, I wisny mugged.'

'Well, attempted mugging. It was only a matter of time, I suppose. You hear about it on golf courses, don't you? Gangs lying in wait at the furthest hole, jumping out on women golfers.'

'Hmm. Well, he buggered off sharpish, so no harm done.'

'But what if he comes back?'

'Nah.' A hesitation. 'Well . . .'

To Mary, it sounded like Bernie was thinking. Not considering the question, more like considering the answer. Was it a good one? Would it work? The pause, then dash of thinking on your feet. Mary knew that movement well.

'Well, I didny want to say . . .'

'What? What is it?'

The cadence of their voices was like music: Fiona high and sharp, careful with her notation; Bernie, low, guttural. It was the music of horses' hooves drumming up the soil; you could feel it, here, in the dip between your breasts.

'If he does come back,' said Bernie, 'then I'll be ready for him, put it that way. And I don't want you getting involved, alright?'

'Christ, now you're scaring me.'

'Fiona, I think he was one of they men from the builder's. Bastards are really stepping it up now. And they canny keep hassling us like this, I'm no having it.'

'No, you're wrong. They—'

'Look, don't get upset, right, but I know for a fact they've already applied for outline planning permission.'

'Don't talk rubbish. How can they? They don't even own the land.'

Pins and needles in Mary's foot. She tried to move without making any sound, wiggling her toes inside her boots. What they were saying did not make sense, but the vivid rise of fear did. This was her home. *Their* home, and someone was angling to take it?

'I don't know how, but they have. Diane Rice at the school got a neighbour notification thing through. Three hundred houses, it said.'

'Och well, that's just nonsense. There's obviously been a mistake. Don't worry, Bernie, they can't build on land they haven't got.'

'Well, they'd better no fucking get it, eh?'

'No,' said Fiona. 'No way.' She sounded exhausted, not fierce like Bernie.

'Well then. I'm telling you Fi, I'll die before I let some bastard scare us off this land, no matter how many nutters they send in to put the shits up us. And I'll tell you something else – I'll take a few of the fuckers with me first.'

'Oh God, Bernie. Please don't talk like that. Please.'

Another lull. What were they doing? Mary squeezed back into her original position.

'I couldn't lose you and the land.'

'Oh, Fiona.' Bernie's head had shifted sideways. Mary could see her ear, her cheek. Tendrils of her ponytail escaping, Fiona's bony fingers stroking the hair. So? Anyone would want hair that colour. It was a beautiful colour. *Midnight Auberge.*

'You are a total fanny. You're never gonny lose me.'

And then Bernie kissed her. Mary's breath went harder into her lungs, a little bullet at the back of her throat. She *knew* they did it, plenty of women did it, but you shouldn't watch. Should never watch that press of mouth on mouth, the yield of lip to pressure pushing. The flick of tongue that searched inside . . . The feel of them, fluid inside you.

Wanting the taste of someone else.

Officially, there had been no allusions to the incident at the paddock. After the man ran away, Mary had emerged from the woods, pretended she'd only just got there.

'I was washing my hands. What happened?'

'Nothing. It's fine.' Bernie's eyes had been red. Not just the rims, like she'd been crying, but the white bits too. Or maybe it had been the brightness of the sun. One of the kids was crying, but Bernie just ignored her. She slid from Toronto's back, handed Mary the reins. 'Gonny carry on the hack, please? I need to nip back to the yard.'

'But Bernie . . . are you okay?'

'A half-hour, up to the railway line and back, yeah?'

'I . . . yes, okay. Whatever.'

Bernie had given her the crop. Pushed her head up, fierce against Mary's. 'Any problems,' she said, 'use this.'

Mary guessed that would have been it, but for one of the parents phoning Fiona on Monday there, asking *what the hell had been going on?* Clearly, Fiona had been unaware. There had been voices, raised ones; Bernie thumping a wall with the flat of her hand. A lesson left waiting in the yard with horses flicking tails and bleached, ironed mothers tapping watches. There was the click of the office door, then muffled long tones. She had heard her name mentioned, more than once. Mary, Mary.

Our little secret.

Then there was the scene she had just witnessed through the partition in the stable. But nothing was ever said, not to Mary. She was the carrier of truth. She felt some test had been passed. Bernie had needed – had wanted – her help.

'Mary – gonny check that hose please? I think there must be a kink in it.'

Bernadette was washing down the yard, Mary was shovelling shit. Just the two of them. Fiona had gone out somewhere, and there were no lessons till after the schools came out.

'Ho, you.' Bernie was squinting at her. 'Is that my jumper you've got on?'

Mary feigned surprise. 'What, this?' It was an old red sweatshirt she'd found in the laundry room, mixed up with a bale of horse blankets. There was always something waiting patiently to be claimed: jackets and sweaters, crops and boots, a kind of communal equine wardrobe. But this sweatshirt was an old favourite; she'd known it was Bernie's. And it had been cold this morning.

'Aye, that. You keep your mitts off my stuff, you.' She said it smiling, that glittering hard loveliness where she never showed her teeth.

'You sound like my big sister.'

Nothing meant by it at all, just banter. Just a slipped-out revelation offered as an opening.

So, tell me about your family, Mary.

You know nothing about my family, Bernie.
You have never asked about my family, Bernie.
Am I your family, Bernie?

'Just check the hose, will you?' Bernie turned away, twisting at the nozzle.

Mary put down the spade and bucket, followed the line of rubber back to its source. Damp squeaking on her skin, deposits of grit sticking from where the hose had slithered over the ground. Her hands were red, peeling round stunted nails. *Sign of an honest worker, that.* Bernie had offered her cold cream one night, when it was just the two of them clearing up. She'd got a paper-cut, only from straw, running straight down her lifeline. *You don't believe all that crap do you?* said Bernie. *No, no,* she'd laughed, although she did, a bit. 'No, you're right. The only thing you can tell from your hands is if you're a grafter.' She had tried to make her words reflect Bernie's, had never expected the definite shuttering of her face, the spit of: *Aye. Well there's more ways to graft than with your hands.*

The hose coiled from the yard, behind the stable block, to the outside tap on the pillar. Fashioned like an olden-day drinking fountain, but with a handsome, verdigrised tap instead of a spout; Fiona had told her this was part of the old farm. *My gran can remember when we had no plumbed-in water at all – had to get it all from here.*

You could have made it into a courtyard, put a wee iron table and some seating in. Mary had suggested it, that they could sell coffees to the mums, make some traybakes. Fiona had laughed a bit, said she didn't have the time. Bernie had simply ignored her.

Around the flagstone base, Mary could see the ground was soaking. The head of the tap, a great four-span splat of corroded metal, was lying in the mud, water pumping over it from the denuded tube at the top of the pillar. She could fix that, easily. It was a matter of seconds to screw the handle back, then turn everything off. She waited a minute, turned the water on again. No leaks, just the healthy flex of water pushing through the rubber hose.

'Sorted!'

She waited for Bernadette's grateful thanks to rise above the sloosh of water. Rounded the wall of the stable block, saw the yard was empty. Went to shout out *Bernie!* Then did not.

The air contracting. The silent space of her not being there.

You couldn't just disappear. Only you could, of course you could. That's what Mary had done. The girl with cellist's fingers, with bright, bold eyes and an even gait. All gone. The girl, who, when she was little, did nothing but make up stories. She could not even walk home from school without it being some elaborate fabrication:

Swiftly, the maiden pulled her cloak across her shoulders. Heels tapping on the cobblestones, she ran through the quadrangles … that was a beautiful word. Quadrangles. She had seen it in the prospectus for her older cousin's university, absorbed its secret, quavering whispers. Mary had a lexicon of wonders, stored for future use.

Ah, but where did stories get you, in the end?

Instead of shouting, she crept. She pulled her metaphorical cloak across her shoulders, boots slapping on the squidge of muck and hay. Bernie could be in one of the stalls. But she wasn't. Most of the horses had been turned out, their stable doors wide open for airing. She could be in the office, although why would you go there so suddenly, your feet all dripping wet? If the phone had rung, Mary would have known – they had the bell amplified so you could hear it in the yard. Another of Bernie's clevernesses. Perhaps she'd gone to the tack room, to make up feeds. You had to mix the meal with bran, and they usually did enough for the next day at least. If you did it too many days in advance, it would all turn fousty and you'd have to bin it. It would smell like sick, and you'd know. You would shake your head and try to conceal it from Fiona, hiding it under a bag of bottles and tins. You had been too organised, too smart for your own good. Sweet sickness was what it smelled of.

The tack room was locked, the key still tucked under the mounting block. Some of those leather saddles cost a fortune. She sat on the mounting block, waited. Did Bernie mean for Mary to follow her somewhere? Was that it? Her belly tightened, quick and hot. Did she *know* Mary watched through walls? She felt shame, and then excitement. Then fear. Was Bernie playing with her – or looking for payback for all that had gone before? Mary had never considered that a debt would require to be paid, had assumed, because they were here and they were happy, that time would just absorb it. Wipe her clean as her veins. She wasn't sure she *could* make reparation for what Bernie had done for her.

Her hands together, slipped between her thighs. So, so quiet here, with even the horses gone. Her cold, red, wet hands smarting in air. When would she know to begin? Not like counting to a hundred; what if she made the first move and it was wrong? The silence began to panic her; she hadn't realised how . . . strong it could be. And then she heard a man's voice, coming from inside the office. The window, an old sash, was raised slightly, propped open with a tin of travel sweets. Fiona was always crunching them; disgusting floury things. A man's voice, wisping over the sweets and out of the window. Mary crept over. *You're a creep, Mary. Mary, you're a creepy creep.*

The window was frosted; it was the old scullery and toilet once. Basic outlines, basic, blunt words:

'How did you find me?'

That was Bernie. Mary wanted to go to her. She sounded scared.

'It wisny hard.' An odd, twanging delivery, too much hissing in the 's'. And so much anger there, too, drawling low in your guts. 'Dugs aye come back to smell their own shite.'

A strangled sound, neither laugh nor cry.

'So?'

'So? It's time, doll. He's no fucking daft, and I hope you're no either.'

'Excuse me,' said a voice behind Mary.

Mary screamed, couldn't help it, it was just the feel of that hand on her shoulder, and the vicious grind of that man's voice, not this voice. This voice came in a uniform, a blue jacket piped with red.

'Excuse me. Sorry. Did I gie you a fright? I'm looking for Calder Riggs Equestrian Centre.'

'What?'

Instinctively, she shielded them both from the piercing quiet that rose, spreading from office to the air. She straightened, moving quickly from the window.

'Calder Riggs Centre. Is this it?'

'Yes, yes it is.'

The postie's voice grew louder. 'Cheers. Only, I wisny sure what an equestrian was, know?'

'Riding,' she whispered. 'It just means riding.'

'Aye. That's what I thought. I've no done this run before, you see.'

'No.'

If she kept walking, so would he. They were nearly at the stable block.

'Eh, well – can I gie you these?'

He passed her a pile of paper, letters. Mary could not focus on them, was watching all the while. Waiting for the man to appear, to come and run and get her. Of course they had heard her.

'So, can you sign for this parcel too, hen?'

'What? Aye. Sure.' She took his pen, scribbled a messy M. Looking, continually looking, back up the yard, but nobody came out. 'That it?'

'Aye. Well, you wouldny know where Lochgranan Path is, would you? I've been driving roon here in bloody circles.'

'No, sorry. Don't have a clue.'

The door to the house began to open. Mary grabbed the package from the postman, ran inside the staircase that led to her hidden loft. *Hidden it was, carved from the deepest recesses of forbidding castle walls.*

Peering through her tatty curtain, willing Bernie to come out. Was she alright? What kind of a mate was Mary, who would not batter doors and faces to save her friend? She heard an engine start, the crunch of car on stony track. Saw, at last, Bernie, leading, almost dragging Toronto from the stables and swinging herself on to his back. She cantered towards the woods, driving the horse on to leap the paddock fence rather than slow and lean down to open the gate. Going for the head-rush of flying on an animal that is bigger and better than you. Mary felt herself unclench. She knew the relief of jumping hedges higher than your head. Bernie was okay. .

Mary didn't feel okay though. She felt unaccountably afraid, in her hidden loft in her safe, secret home. *Nobody would find her here. If she locked the door twice, said her magic incantations. No one would find her here.*

Chapter Five

'And the winner is . . .'

Deacon Blue had just completed their set, a dervish dance of whoop and melody that jettisoned Anna back twenty years. *Twenty*. To a time of dubious hair, of Bezique and Midori cocktails (when flush; snakebite and blackcurrant when skint), to nights staggering up Scott Street's steepness to reach the Cotton Club, and hope you passed the style test for that week (tablecloths? perms?) and they let you in. To a time when a teenage Anna would have shaken her head at twenty-something Anna. Spitting, possibly, in disgust. And God knew what she would have made of Anna now.

Something had happened to her when she joined the police. For a while, she'd lost the sharpness that chafed her; had wanted, instead, to run with the herd. A reaction, no doubt, to becoming a pariah at the instant her warrant card was issued. You couldn't be set apart like that, then double-dare yourself to do it again. No, it was one thing to be louche and aloof in the confines of school and college, to segue from punk to slick Glasgow secrets like Orange Juice, *quick before the rest of them get into it*, chasing music and stances and beliefs *because they were different*. But not when she joined the police. Branded a misfit, you sought sanctuary in being plain. Off duty, you cleaved to what was normal and dull and you hated yourself for it. At least Anna did. Until the truth floated to the surface again, as truths often do, and Anna realised that she was who she was, she could like what she liked and that nobody, really, ever gave a stuff.

Deacon Blue were cheesy, but they made her want to dance. As did Verdi and Patti Smith. Midori was vile – and lurid green to boot. Ironed jeans were neater, she suited a classic bob and she missed making eggshell mosaics on her own.

Anna hadn't meant to end up on the stage, but it was an excellent watchtower. All the performers and officials were linked in a titanic chorus line, filling the venue's platform. She stood virtually in the wings, a massed army of Glaswegians before her: school kids, athletes, council officers and politicians, all of them punters holding flags. So many Saltires, you could have marched past Derby and seized London in a heartbeat, your feet barely touching the ground. In all the dark corners of the Old Fruitmarket, Excitement was a person in her own right, a huge, blowsy, gallus dame who was chewing gum and pumping her fists.

Wait for it . . . Wait for it . . . Wait *for it.*

Great booms of delirium surfed out from the crowd; there was a kind of savage hunger to their glee. Big Rory – a red-wigged stiltwalker who was as vital a civic presence to Glasgow as the Duke of Wellington statue and its traffic-cone hat – teetered over everyone, his tartan bunnet brushing the names of long-dead merchants. They had shifted out all the fruit and veg barrows years ago, but had kept the dusty name signs. A copperplate *J Carmichael & Sons*, painted in the faded colours of a carousel, marked the booth from which that family must have plied their trade. It and all the other booths, the wrought-iron galleries, the rafters, were decked in fairy lights, the entire Victorian hall given over to functions and concerts, saved for posterity like the Cheese Market and the Fish Market and Candleriggs over the road.

Above all the noise, Anna was aware of a beat, a steady thrum against her hip. Her mobile was vibrating. Carefully, she extracted it from her many layers, glanced down. It was home. Moving further into the wings, she held the phone up to her ear.

'Yes?'

It came like an impatient hiss; she was at work, she was *at work.*

'It's me, Laura.'

She sounded tiny, lost almost in the swell and pulse of the Fruitmarket's celebrations.

'What's up? I told you I haven't had time to go to the shops. There's some crisps behind the breadbin—'

'Anna, it's Donna.'

'What about Donna? Come on, you know it's your turn to take her out.'

'She's dead.'

'What?'

'I found her in her basket; she's all cold.'

Her voice broke, became gulps.

'Oh, pet. Oh, darling, are you sure?'

'Of course I'm sure. Her eyes are open and her tongue's all puh . . . puffy . . . and I wasn't with her. No one was with her.'

'Oh sweetheart. Look, I can't get away right now, but I can—'

'Forget it.' The tiny voice became a yelp, brutal through thick, nasal tears.

'Laura, please. Don't be silly.'

'Just forget it. I'll phone my dad.'

A cold click, a beep, and Laura was gone. Anna held the mobile against her lips, eyes shut. She had been the first person Laura had thought of to phone. Not Rob. She wanted to hold her spiky, sprouting body and kiss it better. The dog was Laura's last link with her mum, yet Anna's first reaction had been denial, followed by excuse. A proper mother would drop everything to run to her daughter's side. Immediately, she dialled home again, but it was engaged. Tried Rob next, also engaged. She couldn't do this. Be this. She didn't know how. It was like a zip ran between her and Laura, at one tug locked tight and intertwined, the next, ripped open, one end flapping lamely while the other disappeared. And it wasn't just the vicious up and down that exhausted her, it was how the momentum was gathering speed, becoming faster, more random, and how Rob didn't seem to *see*.

'Quick,' someone whispered from the body of the stage. 'That's them going to make the announcement.'

Anna blinked. Made her way back into the spotlights. She found herself standing next to Amy Macdonald.

'This is great, isn't it?' whispered the girl.

Anna gave a wide, weak smile. A whole other voice for a younger generation, who had not even been born when Deacon Blue were at their height, the young singer had not long finished entertaining the crowd. A cynical Anna had folded her arms and waited to be disappointed, yet she'd liked Amy's music as much as Deacon Blue's. The girl's plaintive folk-rock had something of the same lilt to it, a defiant Celtic candle passed from age to age. That, and the massed pipes and drums of the polis Pipe Band, had stirred everyone to a pitched, patriotic fever. Everyone except Anna and her cops, who, though expected to smile benignly, were not expected to engage in the impromptu ceilidh reels or the swigging from suspect bottles. Anna sighed out, let her breath cool her cheeks. She would phone home as soon as this was all done. Partly there for show, her cops were also present for security purposes, scanning the crowd for crush injuries, unattended bags that could be bombs, assassination attempts on the lives of the assembled big-wigs (well, apart from Rory, medium-wigs really; all the proper big-wigs were at the official announcement ceremony in Sri Lanka). This being Glasgow, they were mostly watching for guys nipping lassies' bums in the crush, and sneak-thieves dipping pockets.

That it should come to this. The City of Glasgow: a serious contender for the 2014 Commonwealth Games. It was only them and Abuja left in the competition since Halifax dropped out. The screens behind Anna's head were showing a live link-up with Colombo, where, in less than thirty seconds, the announcement would be made. The TV cameras at the Fruitmarket were sweeping the crowd, with one fixed on the woman at the on-stage microphone. She grinned hugely, her eyes a little wandered as, behind her, in slightly out-of-focus Sri Lanka, Glasgow's bid delegation leapt with delight.

'What?' the woman asked into the mic. 'Have we won it?'

Manic hugging from the Scots on the screen, their embraces edged with a row of sombre African faces, still seated in their bright array. An unsure rumble, then howls of joy from the crowd in front of Anna, all nudging and yelling and bouncing as if on springs. Only a few of the delegation on stage hesitated, searching for their BlackBerries and confirmation.

'Is that it? Yes, yes!' The presenter in the Fruitmarket hugged her earpiece, straining to co-ordinate sight and sound above the racket of the crowd. And to keep smiling. Very important that. 'Yes! I think we've won it!'

Then a rain of confetti poured from the rafters, a full minute after the official announcement had been made.

Another out-of-synch national embarrassment. It was Hogmanay '89 all over again, when big Robbie Coltrane kept talking past the Bells, and they missed the midnight countdown. Anna had been marooned at that too, a uniformed model of sobriety when all around was unfettered delight. Look at them now, all bouncing, literally, leaping for joy. School kids were rattling long orange and blue inflatables (why?); even Nicola Sturgeon and Wendy Alexander, nippy sweeties and political rivals both, were locked in a genuine embrace. A man in a tracksuit tottered towards Anna, arms outstretched, face aglow. She kept smiling. Very important that. Softly breathed: 'Keep walking, pal.'

It was mental, a truly Glasgow celebration; ruddy faces, sweaty dancing, and unnatural trysts declaring undying love – all with the lurking potential to erupt in a good-going rammy. A well-known sports presenter started jigging with the former First Minister, who wore his usual sheepish grin. And it wasn't the dancing, he always looked like that.

C'mon man. You've just won gold! We're the best wee daftie country in the world!

A council bailie, regal in purple and golden chain, held hands with athletes Yvonne Murray and Liz McColgan. The bailie was grinning fit to combust, patently unbothered that she'd missed all the jollies, the partying in Colombo.

Bright on the screens at their backs, a massive projection writ large in matching purple:

WE DID IT!

'Isn't it wonderful?' The bailie planted a kiss on Anna's cheek, a
waft of perfume following. 'Oh, isn't it wonderful, my dear?'

'Yes. Yes it is.'

Hot red-yellow spotlights, smeared by her damp lashes and the
motion of her head. Anna found herself quelling a sudden urge
to cry.

Clattering into the office, panting into her phone. She hated being
like this. Weighted. Tied. Always checking her watch.

'But you're sure she's okay, Rob?'

'She's fine,' he said. 'I told her we'd rent a movie tonight, get
some pizza.'

'Okay. She sounded terrible on the phone.'

It was a tentative way of feeling for bruises, when what she
should have asked was: *Does she hate me? Particularly at the point I
abandoned her for the revelry of one thousand strangers and the chance
to grin inanely on TV. Did she say I was an unsympathetic cow?* Anna
hoped she had. The times that Laura stood up to her, she felt a
tight pride in the region of her chest, as if she – Anna – had crafted
the riposte herself.

'Och, she's been through worse.'

Said quietly, though not in a self-pitying way, but she felt a
deeper contraction for Rob, and that faint sense of exclusion
which wound occasionally through their relationship. When
you partnered a man who had lost his wife, the past presented
itself gravely, as a vast hidden space into which you might slip,
lit occasionally by unexpected shafts of insight or revelation –
and your own bright jealousy. A past that imposed itself, and one
which you were obliged to accept. After all the stolen men she had
enjoyed, Anna reckoned it was her penance.

'Look,' he went on, 'we've decided not to bury Donna. Not here.'

'Yeah. Those foxes would have her up and mangled in no
time.'

'No, I meant because it would be too upsetting for Laura. You
know, getting reminded every time she went out into the garden?'

'Yeah. Of course.'

'So, I'm going to take Donna to the vet's.' His voice grew even more hushed. 'I think they incinerate them. Do you want me to wait till you get home? So you can say goodbye?'

'Eh, just a wee minute Rob. Alright guys?' Anna nodded to the clutch of senior officers, engaged in fierce discussion outside the commander's office. Her breathing was laboured, she slowed right down. She was too late.

'Sorry. Um, no, it's okay. It's pretty full on here. I'll see you tonight, yes?'

'Sure. Don't work too hard.'

'I won't.'

She waited to catch her breath, had taken the stairs, only one flight, but she was struggling. Holding the metal banister bought her some respite, steadying her feet for the final step. And who'd have thought it would have come to this? Back at A Division – only they called it 'City Centre' now – fat as a pig, and unable to gulp in more than shallow spoons of air.

Stewart Street office had had a slight facelift out front, but inside was much the same, including the sophisticated banter.

'Ah, here she is: the PW herself. Wotcha, gel.'

'You some kind of dinosaur, Colin?'

She drew near to where Colin was standing with two of her other colleagues. There had been a meeting with the divisional commander earlier; she'd hoped to get back in time, but clearly it hadn't lasted long.

'I've no heard that one in ages.' Head down, she thought she'd got a stitch. Jesus, she'd only walked in from the yard. But it was there. Little separations of sinew from muscle, a small ripping inside that burned and choked. Anna was afraid of fire. Anna was afraid of ripping. With one hand nursing her back, she straightened up. 'Maybe it's different in the Met, Col, but here we stopped defining officers by their gender about twenty years ago.'

'Nah love,' he grinned. 'It's just your nickname, innit?'

Colin Potter, a recent transferee from London, thought he was everyone's favourite chief inspector. As proud of his lush moustache as he was of his non-stop patter, Colin was a refreshing zephyr wending through A Division's dust. He winked, joshed and chuckled all day – and had been known to wear his slippers under his desk.

Ambitious? Me? Not a chance. Not what I told them lot, of course, but if I make it to super, I'll be happy. See, the wife's a Jock like you mob.

Colin's master plan was to buy an old house in Argyllshire, work till his thirty was in, then run a B & B when he retired. Had it all sorted. His one apparent failing so far was that he could not read subtleties. All was jokes and joshing to our Colin, and only a comedy frying-pan in the face could stop him in his tracks.

Aye. That yin'll get a sore skelp one of these days, the cleaner had observed, primly removing her mop from his office, where he'd dressed it in a police hat and raincoat and left it in his chair.

'Crime prevention,' he'd said later, when asked, never sensing that his SDO was less than amused.

Same as now, Colin nothing but profuse, hirsute grins as his buddies shifted from the coming broadside, a thin movement away from him, leaving an aura of space all round. Donald Mackinnon was all aquiver, jaw jutting at Colin, radiating the need for silence.

'It's my *what*?' said Anna.

'It's just you being daft Colin, is what it is.' Stuart Barrowman turned to Anna. 'Anyway, I got you these—'

'Nah, c'mon boys,' beamed Colin. 'You said, didn't ya?'

'Yeah, c'mon boys. What did you say?'

'Och, it's just a thing the troops say really . . .' Stuart rummaged through the folder he held. 'Any road, I took some notes for you. Wait till you hear what the new Chief's got planned.'

'Aye, but I'd rather hear the end of this conversation first.' Anna folded her hands above her belly. 'Colin, you were saying?'

'Shit, love. I thought you knew. The boys 'ere said you'd had it since you was a sergeant.'

'Had what? *PW*?' She looked at Stuart and Donald. 'Police woman? That's a bit crap, isn't it?'

'No really,' said Stuart. 'It stands for Picketty Witch. Quite ingenious when you think about it.'

Behind him, Donald snorted.

'What?'

'Och, it's after some daft old hippy band . . .'

'Yeah, no, I got that – but what does it mean?'

'Look, it was just something . . . och, d'you mind old Jimmy Black? Used to be CID clerk here?'

'Yes . . .' She had no idea where this was going, but she was enjoying stringing it out. Stuart had assumed a look of childish eagerness in his bid to convince her, both of the triviality of the whole affair and the kind good humour with which the jibe was meant. His round, milky face could almost carry it off.

'Well,' he continued, 'I was at Lochinch with a couple of mates—'

'What's Loch Inch?' asked Colin. 'That near Loch Lomond?'

'No, no,' said Stuart. 'It's the police club. In Pollok Park? Cheap beer, pies and a bowling green – you'd love it. Anyway, we were talking and he was asking me who I was working with now, and when I mentioned your name, Anna . . . he kind of laughed and went: *Sure. Picketty Witch. A lovely girl, that.*'

'D'you get it?' said Donald. 'It's good isn't it? Picketty because, well, Anna, you can be quite fussy sometimes. You know, about doing things the way you want them done. And, um, witch . . .' He tailed off, his initial burst of enthusiasm having carried him a little too far, like Wile E. Coyote's legs, scrabbling mid-air above a yawning canyon. Anna thought it was quite funny. But she bit the inside of her lip to keep from giving any sign.

'Ach I know. It's all in the hooky nose, isn't it? That and my propensity for casting hexes.' She examined her nails. 'Picketty Witch, eh? And now it's been reinstated, has it? Wonder how that happened?'

'Who knows?'

So. She'd had a nickname for years. Was that a good thing? Should she be flattered that she was unique enough, an individual sufficiently well kent to merit her own moniker? Or be angry at the obvious slight? A bit of both probably. You could earn a nickname, she thought, in one of three ways: born from pure affection; forged in the heat of hate; or arising from a grudging, communal acknowledgment that you were a bit of a nightmare sometimes, a bit of a character, but you werny really that bad.

Let's pretend it was version three. All publicity was good publicity, she supposed. But it wasn't the revelation that she was famous that gladdened Anna. It was the fact that she was still able, even now, to engender fear – well, discomfort at least – in the hearts of grown men. She had worried they would sniff her softening bones and conclude she was gently rotting. Look at them, though, shuffle-bunnies, the lot of them, heads low, humble. Waiting for the roar.

She said nothing. Simply walked up to Stuart and lifted a stray hair from his black nylon shirt.

'This,' she said, holding the hair to his nose, 'is now mine. Oh, and don't worry if you start to get stomach cramps in the night. It'll just be the magic working.' She folded a clean tissue over the hair. 'Aye, it's the pins in the head you'll need to watch out for.'

'Oh fuck,' said Colin. 'She's a Voodoo Queen – I knew it.'

The moment eased, they started laughing.

'I mean, it's only in A Division . . .' Stuart was being all cheery again.

'Yeah, but it'll go global when you're a super, mate,' said Colin.

Anna smiled at him, wondered if he knew yet about his own nickname. It had only begun to filter up from the troops, but it was sticking – despite his sunny demeanour. The wee English bastard, or 'Web' for short.

'No that that's gonny happen anytime soon. For any of us.' Donald took Stuart's folder from him. 'Read that.'

'Right now? Do I have to?' Anna really needed the toilet. 'Oh, we won by the way.'

'Won what?'

'The Commonwealth Games, ya tube.'

'Woo-hoo. Do we get a medal?'

Donald shut the folder. 'Nah, don't bother reading it, actually. It'll only depress you. In a nutshell, we've just been telt that the new Chief's commissioning a review of superintendents' posts. Word is, they've already decided how many are going to be cut.'

'Aye,' said Stuart, 'they're chucking a load out of Headquarters jobs. Plus, operations are going to get hammered as well. We'll be losing at least one super from here, every division will. There's going to be a total rejig of responsibilities.'

'Yup,' said Donald. 'Deputy SDOs are basically going to be doing the super's job, as well as their own. But without any extra pay.'

'Fucksake. How's that going to work?'

She leaned against the wall. Anna may have thought that Giffnock was busy, but since returning to the City Centre, with its marches and parades, its exhibitions, its dignitaries, tourists, clubs, shops and daily chaos, the demands on her time had been colossal. Every day's workload subsumed by the debris of the day before – and the planning for the days to come. With the amount she was needing to pee recently, she was very seriously considering the purchase of a fine device she'd seen on telly: a *Whizz Away!* Made from medical grade thermo-plastic, this little gem came complete with a lilac (self-cleansing) bag, a 'flower-inspired' lip ensuring less spillage and a 10-cm antibacterial impregnated tube designed to offer an 'eco-friendly toilet on the move'.

Ah, thank God for Bid TV, her flickering, glittery companion to insomnia.

'Anna. Are you listening?' said Stuart. 'I said one of us is likely to get bumped too.'

'You're joking? How?'

'Apparently it's the English model. Too many chiefs—'

'Aye, you're no joking,' interjected Donald.

'And no enough Indians. He's getting rid of shift inspectors too.'

'And Community Policing.'

'But Community Policing does a brilliant job. How does that make sense?'

'Apparently,' they chorused, 'it's the English model.'

Like Colin, the new Chief Constable had recently arrived from southern fields, and seemed determined to reshape Strathclyde in an Anglicised form. The biggest of all the Scottish forces,

Strathclyde had been drawn from the ranks of Scotland's western constabularies: the county forces like Ayrshire; burghs such as Lanarkshire; and from Britain's very first force, the City of Glasgow Police. All sucked in during the formation of Strathclyde Region, compressed into a single entity, then, some twenty-five years later, left high and dry when the regions retreated, forcibly reverted back to the smaller islands they'd been before. *Inefficient, you see,* some had said. *Profligate, unwieldy. Too powerful,* muttered others. But the rationale used for breaking up Strathclyde Region had been the same rationale for retaining Strathclyde Police. *More efficient, you see. Pooling resources, joined-up thinking.*

Too powerful, muttered others. Yet so it remained, a behemoth ruled by a tripartite arrangement of Chief Constable, councillors and government ministers. But even these sands were shifting. With every successive piece of tinkering, the force's separate divisions had morphed and merged, each time more closely aping the boundaries of one of the twelve local authorities in which the divisions lay. On one hand, local autonomy – on the other, some strenuous local pulling-on-the-strings. Policing was no longer about organising your resources to best patrol communities and fight crime, wherever those geographies might lie. It was being moulded, and moulded and moulded again – to suit conflicting loyalties and masters, it seemed to Anna, not to make it better.

'What happened to "if it's no broke, don't fix it?"' she said. 'Community cops are your standard bobbies on the beat. I thought that's what people wanted?'

'People might, but – ' Stuart assumed a lecturing tone – 'it's just not cost-efficient any more. No, the way ahead *apparently* is: a crack-squad of probationers, who will be given . . . oh . . . at least four days' training, kept in a central warehouse, then helicoptered in to war zones for the sole purpose of extracting a prisoner or attending a call. Only the calls that the community wardens can't handle, of course. In and out in five minutes flat, and never once lifting up their visors.'

Colin was shaking his head. 'And you call *me* a dinosaur? You lot are just a bunch of lazy, sheep-shagging Scotch bastards. You like to have your nice cuppas, chat to the old lady who's a wee bit lost. Now, in the Met—'

'Aw, fuck up you,' said Stuart. 'I've never met a Met cop who wisny an arrogant—'

'Boys! Boys,' said Donald. 'What if the diversity super heard yous?'

'*Well*. Don't you lot dare lecture us about community relations.'

'Why, thank you.' Colin scratched his moustache. 'Nah, you're right though; I thought I was escaping from all that bullshit – not being the advance bloody guard. I tell you, it'll only get worse.'

At what point did shaking things up become an act of vandalism? Anna noticed she was stroking her tummy. Noticed she didn't, actually, care that much, once the initial rush of anger subsided and they'd all stopped yabbering. Or, if she did care, it was with a resigned acceptance of her lot. Anna Cameron could no longer stem tides, and that was okay. All she could do was choose the firmest ground available and wait. Cling to the rock marked, *This too shall pass*. A satisfied warmth suffused her. It felt like feathers pushing inside, softening the hard angles of her face, hazing her eyes with calm. She was Buddha, she was a hen.

She was thirty-two weeks pregnant, and desperate to pee.

Chapter Six

They must, thought Mary, be family after all, because it was evident that nobody was going to speak of the matter again. That man had *not* returned, he had definitely *not* been threatening Bernie in a locked office, and Mary had never heard a thing. A delicate dance of three monkeys, who saw, heard and spoke nothing but the most inoffensive of banalities; that was Mary's experience of family, and it was repeating itself here. She did honest work, the horses were plain and uncompromising, needing only food, water, exercise and an occasional scratch behind the ears. The land was plain and good, simple dirt, and she had washed in fresh, good water. Was it too much to expect a discourse as well?

Bernadette must have come back at some point on Friday, because Toronto was stabled up in the evening when Mary went to check. No sign of Bernie, though. On Saturday, she and Fiona had gone to a friend's wedding, leaving Mary in charge. Yesterday, Bernie had been out of the house before Mary started work and had avoided her all day. This morning, she had made sure she was up, dressed, breakfasted before anyone else appeared. It gave her some kind of moral superiority, she thought, being here first.

See, I have nothing to hide.

And she would catch Bernie coming out of the house, at least. Fiona was up and in the office, but no Bernie. Yet. It meant there would have to be some kind of challenge, Bernie couldn't ignore the physical fact of Mary standing there. In fact, there she was now, there was Bernadette, coming from her house. Mary saw her turn in Mary's direction, then linger in the doorway, make a mime of forgetfulness; you could see her mouthing a quizzical 'now?', as in: *now where did I put that thing?*, or *now what was I going to do?* She swayed a little, a foal's legs in boots, then tugged hard on the base of her waxed jacket, set off across the yard. A kindly person would have focused on that awkward stone, would have held Starlight's ankle firm in one hand, the hoof-pick grating in the other. But kindliness, though well meant, was a blanket over fire. Mary's parents had been 'kind', not harsh. They had never faced the truth, and had watched their daughter burn.

'Oh Bernie,' she called, dropping Starlight's hoof and picking up the package. The package she had taken to her room, had squashed through its padded sides and shaken. 'Glad I caught you. This came for you. On Friday. The postman dropped it off.'

That would be the postman who had spoken out loud, had startled them all, had been there, *there* when the man was, and Mary was, and was she going to say anything at all?

'Thanks.' Bernie glanced briefly at the postmark.

'Aren't you going to open it?'

'I will do. Later. Now, did Fiona no ask you to clear up the paddock this morning? There's broken glass in it again, from they arseholes drinking.'

Fiona *had* asked her to clear the paddock, but only minutes ago. Bernie was not there, could not have heard. They must discuss her when they lay in bed. Plotting out her day like they scheduled in the horses. A reluctant, nudging thought came in, would not leave; she saw them naked. One sipping tea, the other trailing a finger up a leg and complaining of an aching back; a look of love passing between them. Mary was viewed as nothing more than a child at best. At worst, a convenience.

'Does Fiona know about that man who came round the other day?' she said, her eyes locking, deliberate, with Bernie's.

'What man?'

'The man I heard talking to you in the office.'

Without warning, Bernie dipped her head, like an angry swan, and seized Mary's face. She could feel the shock of tight-pressed fingers crushing on her jaw, could smell the horseshit beneath Bernie's ragged nails. Up close, so close they were almost kissing, Bernie's small, raw face, her ferret mouth sharp and cursive.

'You saw no man in the office.'

'But I did . . .' she was gasping, her hands on top of Bernie's. 'Please, stop it.'

Bernie gripped her tighter, blunt nails digging crescents through her flesh.

'Please,' Mary wept. 'You're hurting me.'

Bernie's voice took on the clarity of silver knives. No muddled diction, no slurred slang. 'You saw no one because there was . . . *No. One. There.* And if you ever say that there was, I will kill you, Mary. Do you understand me? I will kill you.'

And then, knives in butter, she slipped again, a quick smile wiping it all away. 'Now, how about that paddock? We don't want anyone getting hurt, eh?'

Gladly, Mary ran to the paddock would keep running if it meant shaking off that image of a face cracking. Of its covers peeling back like you would skin a skull, until it was simply black hollows and broken teeth. With bare hands, she seized the jagged lips of bottles, not caring that they cut her. There were loads of cans and bottles, beer bottles, cheap harsh vodka and something called Mad Dog, all purposefully drunk then just as purposefully shattered, so that vulnerable hooves and skin would bleed. Why else would they do it? There was no other reason, save the sound. That exhilarating high of destruction. Yes. That was good. That was plain and good and simple too.

She flung the bits of bottles into a wheelbarrow. It had been left there, someone had used it to load up shite, piling up faeces in straw-stuck clumps, but never transporting it back to the dung heap. There were still some spaces, grey metal between the hummocks of manure, and she aimed for these. More often than not, the bottles landed softly, a whump into receptive crap. But, where it hit bare metal, the glass gave with a glorious smash. It began to rain, but she kept on throwing. Breaking them smaller, taking them out then smashing them again. Glass on glass now, the manure a distant cushion and the rain slapping down. Her hair sticking to her forehead. She wore no jacket, just Bernie's red sweatshirt, which was torn and soaked. And the rain falling, constant in her eyes.

At lunchtime, you could pretty much do what you wanted, unless there was a private lesson booked. Today, Mary would go for a walk. The thought of food was anathema to her, but the air, the cold light, would be delicious now that the rain had stopped and the smell of metallic earth was rising from the damp. There was a route she took sometimes, when she had an afternoon off, that meant you could walk for miles in perfect isolation, right through Glasgow's heart. You hardly ever met a soul. She told no one she was leaving.

At the end of Caldercuilt Road, the quietness gave way to sharp blasts of car engines. Exhaust gases and morose, greasy fumes from shops wiped over lips and tongue, sinking into the sponges of your lungs. On the other side of Maryhill Road, she could see the angry red zigzags of the train-station sign. She crossed at the lights, put her head down to walk the mile or so of pavement that would take her there. There were plenty of shops and bakeries selling hot, larded bridies, or alarming pink-iced buns that had masqueraded yesterday as finger rolls, but she still had no appetite. Not even for the lurid 'lunchtime speshalls!!!' *Scotch pie and beans – on a buttered roll.* You'd never have got served anyway, thanks to the legions of school kids queuing for chips and cans of ginger.

By the time she reached Skaethorn Road, the crowds were thinning. Lunchtime must be over, the streets returning to their usual parade of litter and old ladies, of blank, leathered men, of incontinent dogs and workies who wereny working. She felt shivery, her back clammy where the sweatshirt had dried, sandwiched between her T-shirt and her coat, the press of her rucksack sealing it all in. Skaethorn was only a stump of a street, barricaded against cars, ending in a heap of rubble. A woman had killed herself here. A few years ago, she'd just driven off the road and straight into the canal. So they'd secured it against traffic – it didn't lead anywhere anyway – but pedestrians could slip by.

Breathe in, skirt the barrier and behold! The same hidden surprise as Calder Riggs, where city gave way to space. A titanic staircase of canal locks and basins opened like a gasp, smartly edged in black and white. The deep dark circles and channelled water of the canal stretched far out to distant hills, where an old gas tower stood like a Roman temple, or a folly on the horizon. Mary had been to Chatsworth once, on a school trip; its famed artificial runnels and terraced fountains were tame compared to this. There was a grim majesty in the water's oily toil; she liked that this was called the Maryhill Lock Flight, that water might soar, the whole canal taking off in fantastical flight, with the shape of it contained in a shivering liquid snake. In the sky, the water would be clear and whole, would tremble opaquely like that creature in *Predator*, like Harry Potter's invisible cloak, not be made of ink and brown scum which frothed in whorls like spittle.

Somewhere underground, a train or dragon rumbled. Mary stepped across the narrow chevron of planks that bridged the top of one of the locks. The arrowpoint at which the two opposing planks met was disjointed; your eyes dropped, fast, into the gap and to the waiting canal. Pointing it out to you, so you could not avoid that torrent which rushed beneath your feet. How deep was it here, this water on which she was walking? A person could easily slip, at any number of points along the way. You could climb under the thin white railings; you could tumble, head first, into the pummelling cataract that gushed and dropped through the lock. Or just fall, neat and clean, from anywhere on the smooth paved lip of the canal. From Maryhill Road, rows of flats overlooked the canal – not posh ones; simple flat-roofed squares of fawn and cream. Jerusalem houses; one had actual palm trees in its scrap of front garden. *Palm* trees. On Maryhill Road. That was even more absurd than flying canals.

Mary sat on one of the wooden arms which would lever the lock in and out, and the road instantly vanished. Now that she was here, she didn't know what to do. You could walk much further, follow the canal all the way to Port Dundas. This was just the beginning. Her eyelids smarted from crying, her vision smudged, slightly puffy. All she had wanted to do was help, to offer something of herself.

It's time, hen.

Delivered like a death-knell. The man's voice had been curious, on one hand mournful, as if he had no choice. But, on the other, smooth and satisfied as porridge. That was what made him frightening. Mary had seen Bernie's face when the man jumped out on her in the fields. She was petrified. He must want the land for more than houses. Bernadette never got parcels either. Or mail. Everything came addressed to Fiona. They'd joked about it once, her and Bernie. *Maybe I don't exist*, she'd said, eyes wide and laughing.

Mary wondered if they had missed her yet. If Fiona was getting flustered, if Bernie was feeling guilty. There was a riding for the disabled session booked for this afternoon, always labour-intensive. They needed one member of staff for every pony, no matter how docile the beast, or how well-secured the child. Mary loved doing it. There was no better feeling than lifting up gentle bodies, with arms that may try to hug you, but sometimes flailed instead, then easing stiff legs into stirrups and clicking your tongue. It was the magician's click that did it, when the beasts began to move and the children with them, the long, easy movement of walking, transmuted through one single form.

Maybe she should have opened the parcel. What if it was something bad? Too wee for a horse's head, too big for a poison-pen letter, it had probably been a catalogue for riding clothes. Mary looked down at the red sweatshirt. Bernie could do with some new clothes. Brown smears and grass stains slabbered all down the front, the patch pocket, snug like a muff in the middle, torn and frayed at either side. She used the back of her hand to brush the worst of the mud off. There was something white inside the pocket; she could see it poke through the feathered hole in the fabric, feel it crinkle.

It was a leaflet. Something to read. When she was little, Mary used to read everything – cornflake packets, sauce bottles, *A Child's Garden of Verses*, her mum's *Guardian*, her dad's dry, dry books.

They'd smile fondly at their little prodigy, nod at one another. *Following in your footsteps, then.* Mary smoothed the leaflet over her knee.

The Glasgow Citicard Is Here!

Fed up with endless paperwork and bureaucracy? Want to deal with officialdom, but can never find the right form or reference number or phone number when you need it? Want to take the kids out, but you just don't know what shows are on in the city?

We are delighted to inform you that Glasgow City Council, in conjunction with Strathclyde Passenger Transport, Culture & Sport Glasgow and Glasgow Community Safety Services, have voted to introduce the fantastic new Glasgow Citicard – opening up a one-stop portal to a world of services and benefits for you.

The Glasgow Citicard will allow you to store all your important details in one handy credit-card-sized 'community passport', which you can use to gain user bonus points in the city's museums, theatres and recreation centres, to access discount travel on the city's bus, rail and subway networks and, of course, to pay for services like your Council Tax, special refuse uplifts, car parking, travel cards and so on.

While the scheme is totally voluntary at present, our aim is to extend the use of the Glasgow Citicard to enable access to services like Jobcentre Plus, Community Mediation Services, Customer Services, Housing Allocation and Glasgow's Citizens' Opinion Panel. Eventually, we even hope the benefits will extend to NHS Greater Glasgow, allowing you to use your Citicard to let accredited professionals access your full medical records anywhere in the UK, saving time, paperwork and, ultimately, saving lives.

All agencies involved agree that the Citicard will also greatly help us in future planning, throwing up patterns of service usage across the city, and making sure we provide the right services for the people of Glasgow – when and where YOU need them. This is why our plans to extend the Citicard to NHS Greater Glasgow Services will be so beneficial, as it may in fact help to slash hospital waiting times, too.

We hope you will be impressed by the benefits the Glasgow Citicard will bring. We'll even be able to send you details of events and information we think you may be interested in hearing about – and it's absolutely free! If you're aged sixteen or over, all you need to do now is fill in the attached form, and send it, along with a passport-sized photograph of yourself, to the address at the bottom of the form.

Citizens of Glasgow – here comes the Citicard! Glasgow truly does belong to you!

That was what she'd heard a couple of the yummy mummies talking about. *They'll be wanting our bloody fingerprints next.* It was the word 'fingerprints' that had caught Mary's ear. Well, she'd not be applying for one any time soon. She balled the leaflet in her fist, lobbed it across the towpath. Hard air slicing, her hands stinging where the glass had cut. She blew on them. She should go back. And maybe, for the sake of visitors, they'd all put on a happy face and she could . . . Mary sighed, tore up a chunk of long grass. Make a fresh start. How many of them did you get? The soil from the grass roots fell on to her thighs, on to the cuts in her cupping hand. Then she thought of Bernie's werewolf face and she shuddered. This jumper was disgusting, adhering beneath her armpits and breasts. She took off her coat, peeled off the sweatshirt, her right hand tugging at the left sleeve. A magpie was watching her, its black-masked head tilted to one side. She looked around for another one, it was bad luck if you didn't see a pair, but there were only wee brown birds in the trees.

She crossed her fingers.

Good morning Mr Magpie. Even though it was afternoon.

No, Mary would not return to Calder Riggs. Mary would go into the town. She would buy some sandwiches, sit in George Square and feed the pigeons. Queen Street Station was right beside the square. She could study the train timetables at least, see where she went from there.

Maryhill Road was a Quality Bus Corridor. It had said so on the many leaflets strewn over their top field last spring. Like the weekly newssheets that were often deposited there, some kid must have got fed up posting leaflets through doors, and had tossed them instead to the disinterested horses.

See that Dobbin? Thon's a Quality *Bus Corridor thon.*

Is that right Red Rum? Quality, eh? And do they do an equine bus pass?

Well, aye. But only if you're over sixty.

What it meant, though, was that buses got priority over cars, and you never waited more than two minutes for one to trundle by. Now that Mary had decided what she would do, she felt a little lighter. Not that she'd decided anything really, except to disassociate herself by degrees. From today, only. For now.

The bus stop was directly in front of the beige flats. Several people were waiting; there was an impatient jangle in the air.

'S'terrible, hen.'

Mary smiled at the elderly man next to her, not quite catching his eye. 'What's that?'

'Been waiting near ten minutes here. Piece a bloody nonsense, so it is.'

She doubted much that he was in a hurry to get anywhere, but she nodded.

'I know.'

A flash of scarlet, as the paper flower on his lapel wobbled in indignation. 'See me, I'm only aff tae get batteries for my magnifier, but still. It's bloody chittering.'

Of course. Yesterday had been Poppy Day, the eleventh. The old boy must have forgotten to take his poppy off. She felt a sudden guilt that she had never even bought one, that she couldn't stand with equanimity alongside this bent wee soul in his bunnet and scarf.

'What's a magnifier?' she asked by way of apology.

'One of they looking-glass things. You know, it lights up so you can read your paper.'

'A magnifying glass? Och, that can't take very big batteries. Why don't you get batteries in the newsagent then?' She pointed to the shop less than a hundred yards away. 'Save you waiting.'

'Aye, but the ones fae the eye clinic are free.' He clasped his hands behind his back, like there was nothing more to be said.

Eventually, a double-decker could be seen, inching its way through the mess of traffic.

'Whit one's that, hen?'

Seems she was back in favour. Mary looked up to see the number, although they probably all went into town.

'It's a . . .'

Above the numbers, on the top deck, a harsh pale shape of inverted triangles, nose, cheekbones, chin all pointing down. The eyes in the face were black and unseeing. It was Bernadette.

'What's that? I canny hear you, lass.'

She didn't know.

'It's a forty, pal,' said the boy on the other side of the old man.

'Aye, that'll dae me. Thanks son.' He hauled himself up on to the step of the bus, Mary right behind him.

'One into town please.'

The driver was one of those creepy ones, no conversation, but plenty of lingering fingers as he passed her the ticket. She chose a seat downstairs, near the back of the bus. The old man sat at the front, but she could still hear him. 'Piece a bloody nonsense,' he said to his neighbour. 'Twenty minutes that's me had tae wait . . .'

Why was Bernadette heading into town? They definitely had a special needs booking in the diary, Mary had seen it this morning. On any other day, this would have been a happy coincidence, the kind that would have had you running up the stairs to laugh and go: 'Hiya. What are *you* doing here?' It would have been the sort of unasked-for good fortune that gave you proprietorial rights, budging up so you could share a seat and chatter happily about the unlikeliness of it all. Instead, she found herself shrinking into the window. It felt wrong. Mary down here hiding, Bernie upstairs with her secrets and her unknown face.

The bus made its long way up congested Maryhill Road, a stop-start shunt and grind. At almost every weary stop, passengers were deposited or got on, the bus stuttering back into traffic five cars further behind where it had been. She wanted to close her eyes, wished she had never come. But, at each hiccup of the doors, she would hold her breath in case Bernadette alighted. They had passed St George's Cross, were going towards Charing Cross before Mary realised that Bernadette was indeed moving. First, skinny, dark legs appearing, then the grasping hand, the thin, determined curve of her back as she picked her way down from the upper deck. Face turned towards the door and her future destination.

Keep staring out. Mary picked up a *Metro* that was discarded on the seat beside her, held it like a fan.

The sharp ponytail swung against the hood of Bernadette's jacket, black on khaki, bone-white bumps of knuckles clutching the metal rod as her body swayed with the movement of the bus. This was the final point, where Mary could wave, call out, get up and go *oh, hi Bernie – what are* you *doing here?* Once that point was passed, she must either let her go, or creep off the bus behind her, shielded by the bulk of the middle-aged woman who was also alighting, and then skirt and duck her way along the day-lit, open street like some B-movie spy.

The bus had slowed, had stopped. Both women got off, Bernie striding, the middle-aged woman fumbling with shopping, her gloves. If she dashed off to the front right now, she could still make it, and then the middle-aged woman was off and the doors were squeezing shut and it didn't feel like relief. It did not feel like she had done something noble – refusing a fag, say, or that other slice of cake – and now the bus was moving, chugging on, and it was turning the corner, and it was the same corner that Bernie was turning. Mary could see her, looking behind. Sudden. Shrewish. Thank God she'd not got off there; something had held her back, that same something which was now telling her it was *meant*, that she should get off, now, at the next stop, which you could see just down there, on this same road. It had a bus shelter, with bold adverts for Primark's new lingerie range, a sultry teenager with enormous breasts held in a wisp of scratchy nylon lace.

She rang the little bell, got up before she decided that she would just stay put after all. Made her way to the front, ribs fluttering like they were on a cord; a Venetian blind of flat, wide, clinking bones.

The vehicle slowed, spitting open its doors in a compressed sigh of air. She got off the bus. 'Thanks driver.'

Everyone said thanks to Glasgow bus drivers. Even the most obnoxious of drunks, or harried of mothers.

Mary's eyes were level with the bra model's cleavage. She stayed where she was, in the shelter. Peeking her head out, up the length of the street, dipping in and out like a drinking bird until she could see Bernie striding, arms almost in a march. It was the walk of a confident woman, a woman who would not be messed with. Do not mug me, said the set of her shoulders; do not approach me, do not get in my path. Although her arms were scissoring back and forth, her hands were not moving freely. The left one was wide and open, not folded in determination like you'd expect from such a walk, while the right one held a package. A brown-wrapped parcel that you could not be sure of from here, but it was definitely brown, in the same paper, the same size, as the one from yesterday.

Mary had been right to follow Bernie, she knew that now. It wasn't creepy. She waited in the bus shelter, pretending to study the timetable printed under Perspex in which she could see her reflection, eyelashes dancing like tiny flies. Mary could also see the street behind her, she could see the woman walking on the other side of the street; Bernie in reverse, a shadow puppet jerking along the road.

This part was called Argyle Street, which was absurd, because everyone knew that Argyle Street was in the town, proper. It was the busy, half-pedestrianised artery that formed part of the Golden Zed: Argyle Street, Buchanan Street, Sauchiehall Street. Full of Glasgow's finest glories, the firm foundations on which this post-industrial city was now built: shops. All the big names; you had your Marks and Sparks, your Accessorize (two of, plus a Monsoon), River Island, Top Shop, Debenhams, Hobbs – those unique, quirky outlets that gave a city centre its individual identity.

That was Argyle Street, not this sad wee dog-end which was a legacy of life before the motorway. If you plotted it all the way back, though, if you could simply grab a giant rubber and erase the monstrosity that ground its massive pillars, its slabs of asphalt and concrete and pebble-dashed momentum deep into Glasgow's heart, then you could see the logic. Argyle Street began with shops, loads of them, down in the town. Running from the mediaeval

Trongate, where fourteenth-century Glaswegians would come to weigh their market goods at the public scales, running all the way along the same path as the River Clyde, but a few, less important, streets back. Running under the Hielanman's Umbrella, which was really just a railway bridge, though a huge, thick, dirty dark one at that, whose shadows and nooks had sheltered Highland immigrants to the city, those poor buggers who had planned on making it to America. Running through the Red Light district – the Drag, which was *never* mentioned in the tourist brochures, and then . . . yes . . . where the motorway cut through now, you could see how this street here, this scuffle of high-rise flats and brick-built newish apartments, this street that rejuvenated a little once it got past the turn-off to Finnieston, becoming terraces of tenements again, broader, wider, with some nice wee bistros and a fish shop, and there it was, opening out to take in the grand, sweeping vista of the Art Gallery at Kelvingrove – yes, you could see how this would have been the same street, once.

Bernie had walked right past her. Granted she was on the other side of the road, but *still*. Part of Mary had wanted her to see, to sense her, as Mary had been acutely aware of the defined shape of Bernie's head, even from the top deck, even through smeary glass. If it had been Fiona standing here, would Bernie have noticed her?

It was probably safe to turn round; her heart was still guttering, like she was doing something wrong. In front of Mary, the Anderston flats loomed, prison-grey. A concrete rack for storing people. Busy road to the front, motorway to their left, and behind . . . behind was that church, where a mad bastard had slain a young girl, and secreted her under the altar.

The sky hung in pleats, towering, increasing in bulk, the light shifting again. It had been doing it all day, breathing in and out in purple eddies and whorls, intermittent cold brightness flaring briefly, defining the world in dark and light flames. She felt the air lapping at her feet, pressing on her. Bernie's shape was growing smaller; it would be best if Mary started moving. How long and for what distance, she wasn't sure. Until something happened, she supposed.

A double-decker pulled up at the stop, blocking her view. Mary started walking down Argyle Street, in the same direction as Bernie, but remaining on the opposite side of the street. A police car rolled by in the other direction, no hurry, a cone of pale sunlight spotlighting its progress. She watched it turn into a lane at the back of the low, brick police station over the road. *Anderston,* it said above the door. The door through which Bernadette appeared to be walking.

She was no longer just holding the parcel, she was clutching it under her breast. Whatever it was, it seemed grievous heavy and very, very precious. If that package had caused her grief, if it had made her go hard and freaky; if it was connected in any way with that man, then Mary was happy. Bernie was taking it to a police station. She was doing the right thing, the thing which would mean that *something would be done.* And if something was done, then they would all be safe. They need not talk of it again. Life could go on at Calder Riggs as it always did, quiet, a little strained, but essentially good. Mary would settle for good. She'd settle for good enough.

She was aware that she had stopped walking, aware of the breath in her lungs being a little sore and tired. She became aware that the sun had slipped again, and perceived, more sharply, the sensation of an unknown breath at her ear. Of a moist damp hand thumbing her nape, fingering the cartilage of her neck.

'Alright doll?'

His voice, familiar. Chilling.

'How about you and me going for a wee walk?'

There was a smell of sweat, of meat and sweat and a strange sweet perfume that rose from drapes of skin fermenting under the weight of yet more skin. At the cusp of her down-turned eye, a broad, grained finger, the nail yellowed, ridged. It was the hand of a fat man.

How fast could a fat man go?

She thrust her hand deep in his chest. Started to run.

Chapter Seven

'Now just let your knees relax. *Relax,* Mrs Cameron.'

A hand pressed on Anna's inner, naked, thigh.

'It's *Ms.*'

'I'm sorry. Ms.'

Her mouth tasted of stale coffee. 'Are you sure it's okay to do this when I'm pregnant?'

'I just want a quick look at your cervix.'

'That's what all the boys say.'

'I'm sorry?'

'Nothing.' Anna pinned her eyes on the ceiling, concentrating on the porous, spidery patterns of the polystyrene tiles as cold air passed across her overstretched labia and shame sucked all the colour from the room. Pressure pushing on her lower back, a heavy, solid mass was bearing down, it was her bowels, oh God it was her bowels. She tried to squeeze her buttocks while the young, male doctor kept insisting on opening her thighs. This was beyond mortification, this was why she ignored her smear-test reminders. The weight of the baby's head was relentless in its assault. How in God's name do you hold it in when everything is hinging out? And they wanted *students* to come in and watch this?

'So, other than this, are we keeping well?' Cold metal, clinking somewhere in a dish. This was like an evil, inverted trip to the dentist's. Soon she'd hear a drill.

'Mm.'

'Still working?' His palm on her vulva. He was *leaning* on her vulva.

'Mm.'

'And what is it you do?' A slow insertion, water in her eyes.

'I'm a police officer.'

'Ah.' A pause. His head descending lower. Then a quick slide out, relief of pressure. 'Did I tell you I got a parking ticket the other day?'

Anna slammed her eyes shut, the same way she wanted to slam her thighs. *Oh Jesus God.*

'Yeah. Thought they were going to tow me.'

The doctor's voice was lilting; he thought he was being *funny.* And then she realised, this was the same guy the girl in the waiting room had been talking about. *I saw the young one last time, you know, thon fit one? But, my God, see his patter? My name's Tracey Rumbles, right? I know, shite name, but it didny stop me fae marrying him. Any road, the bold doc introduces hisself, then goes: Ah. I see you have a little rumble in your tummy.* The girl had smiled, then tutted. *I mean to say.*

Anna opened her eyes. Could see the top of the doctor's head. He was still *looking.* 'Sometimes when you have bleeding at this stage in the pregnancy it suggests your cervix may have opened slightly. But everything looks fine.' He turned away, she could hear the sticky-ping of Latex gloves being tugged off. 'Most likely it's your piles.' Kept talking as she lay on the high, thin bed, distorted kneecaps flopped wide on the paper sheet, the splay-legs of a dissected frog. 'There is a little cluster there, I'm sure you've noticed.'

Only her belly protecting her. If it wasn't for the draught, you could pretend all of this was happening to some other poor sod; the furthest Anna could see was her distended belly-button.

'Dr Carroll.' A nurse stuck her head into the cubicle, 'Can you check this sample when you're done?' She smiled at Anna as if they were meeting at the coffee machine. 'Alright there?' And was gone. Was the doctor gone too? Anna wasn't sure.

'Excuse me, can I move yet?'

'Oh, sorry,' came the doctor's disembodied voice. 'Yes, up you get. Just pop your clothes on and we'll have a little chat.'

He was lucky if he was twenty-five, this boy, but already he'd adopted the mien of the consultant at her initial appointment, who had not actually addressed his statements to Anna at all, but via an accompanying midwife. *So. She thinks she's pregnant, does she?* and *Let's get mother up on the couch then,* and on and on until Anna had gone: *Ho. Mother has two ears, a mouth and an actual brain. Do feel free to avail yourself of them.*

The consultant hadn't asked to see her again. But she minded less now, the further down the conveyor belt she passed. All these people; the unshockable nurse, the rude and erudite consultant, the auxiliary who squeezed her shoulder as she took away Anna's pinkish urine sample; this lad who was probably juggling two clinics and several weeks' studying: they were all components of the same skilful machine. And they all shared Anna's goal – for her baby to come out healthy.

Running water outside – he must be washing his hands. Anna's bladder pinged, as conditioned as one of Pavlov's dogs. Oh, oh, turn it off. She heaved herself from the bed, bare from the waist down. Crouched to fumble for socks and knickers in the little basin beneath the bed. Her trousers were heaped on the floor beside. It was getting tricky to hook clothes round her feet, but she managed; terror of the curtains opening as her full-moon arse glowed for all the world to see lent her actions some speed. Yes, yes, he'd seen it all already, but it seemed worse when you were standing up.

She zipped up her trousers and emerged from behind her curtain. The doctor was tapping on a keyboard.

'Now, sister's taken your blood pressure, you're booked in for your next clinic. Is there anything else you'd like to ask?'

Where's the nearest toilet? Anna shook her head. Sitting down might help.

'Don't worry about the bleeding,' he smiled. 'It's just spotting really. Just take it easy for the next few days – and, obviously, come straight back in if you're worried at all.'

'Okay. Thanks.' She wouldn't bother saying to Rob, he'd only get upset. For a doctor he was remarkably susceptible to baby-related panic.

'Now, I notice that you've elected not to have any amniocentesis test?'

'That's right.'

'You realise that, as an elderly primagravida, your risk of genetic abnormalities increases?'

'Yes.'

Each new face had told her this. Then told her that the option was hers, kept reiterating this while they explained all the other options that this option might lead to. Which mostly involved counselling and hand-wringing and the potential to have your insides flushed away. Inside her, the baby rippled.

'Yes, we've discussed all the implications. I – my partner's a doctor.'

'I see.' He smiled again. 'Well, I think that's us.'

Partner ... It sounded too sterile, here in this sterile place. 'Husband' was round and pleasant. She picked up her bag to leave. Paraded the notion round her head again. *Husband.* Maybe the patient, moulding pressure of pregnancy changed more than the shape of your body.

'One other thing,' said the doctor. 'What about our parentcraft classes? Have you signed up for them?'

'When are they?'

'Mondays three to five. With two partners' evenings nearer the end.'

'Doubt it then,' she said. 'I'm planning on working right to the bitter end.'

That's what she had told her boss this morning, too. Mrs Reekie was the A Division commander. Yet another female gaffer, but a woman less like Marion Hamilton you could not hope to find. Where Anna's previous boss had been a foul-mouthed Weegie bully, Mrs Reekie was shaped from placid Falkirk loam – albeit with gravel running through. Her dark-waved hair crinkled like the lines round her eyes, and her uniform never seemed to sit quite right on her solid shoulders. Mrs Reekie bemoaned the day she had to swap from shirts, and don a T-shirt which exposed soft arms. *I've just not got the definition any more, have I?* Her arms were pale and freckled, like her work-worn hands which took no nonsense. But they were kindly hands too. In her office, earlier, she had reached over to pat Anna's hand.

'Dinny you be daft. You take all the time you're entitled to.'

'Yes, but I worry that I'll get left behind, ma'am. Especially now they're cutting so many supers' posts.'

'Och away. You're young, you're smart – you'll get on fine in this job. And mind, the job's not your life.'

She had folded her hands inwards, like cat's paws. Mrs Reekie's first name was Anne, and, throughout the division – though never to her face – she was known as 'Grannie Annie'. Anna pretended that their almost-shared name gave them an affinity, but the truth was, Mrs Reekie was like this with everyone. She had a knack of fixing problems simply by listening, or by pre-empting conversations you didn't know you needed to have.

'I know that, ma'am. But you still want to do the best job you can, don't you? For yourself I mean. And I don't want to see everything that I've worked for just slide away.'

'Aye, but there's more than one way to skin a cat.' Mrs Reekie had picked up a picture frame that was propped on her desk. 'Look. See that?' A photo of four blonde, handsome women in their thirties, each raising a champagne flute for the camera.

'Your daughters, ma'am.'

'My girls. Lynda, Fiona, Dorothy and Gillian.'

'I met Lynda last year, at the Open Day.'

'That's right, so you did. Well, Anna, my girls are my life, not my work. And that doesn't mean I don't love my job, because I do. I love it with a passion. But I love my family more.'

She put the photo back down, angled so it was facing her again.

'I was thinking,' she said. 'Now that Glasgow's won the Commonwealth Games, there's going to be an awfy lot of planning required. I've been asked to identify a chief inspector to head up a team looking at all the security implications for a start. Now, that's not likely to happen for the next six to eight months, but I was thinking: might be a job for you, eh?'

'Babysitting shot-putters and runners?'

'Now Anna, you know that's not what I mean. We're talking massive strategic planning, inter-agency liaison, emergencies planning, VIP security . . .'

'Nine to five and weekends off? No thanks, ma'am. I'd rather go straight back to operational duties when I return.'

'Why? Because you're feart they'll say you canny hack it?'

'No. It's just—'

'Anna. Do you ever wonder why I've no pictures of my husband up?'

Anna didn't answer. There was a set to Mrs Reekie's jaw that suggested this was a rhetorical question.

'My husband died when my girls were tiny. There was me, four mouths to feed, sick with grief, night shift looming and me worrying about childcare. But I was *determined* the polis would give me no quarter. Was back at work within a month – only to find they'd transferred me to the Courts Branch.' A sad wee smile. 'Nine to *four*, mind, and weekends off. I was mortified, argued with my sergeant till I was blue in the face, but he said I'd to go, and that was that. And look at me now. I have four healthy, happy daughters, seven grandchildren, and I'm commander of the most prestigious division in Strathclyde Police.' She leaned forward, opening up her hands like she was receiving a blessing.

'I earned the right for them to cut me some slack, Anna – and I've paid it back a hundredfold. You will too, I know that. And this isn't a mickey-mouse job I'm talking about. So you think about it, alright?'

Anna nodded. 'Alright. I will. Thank you.'

'Good.' Mrs Reekie was rummaging in a Boots the Chemist plastic bag that was lying on her desk. 'You want a wee biscuit for your coffee? I've some of those Shapers ones – hardly any calories at all.'

'No thanks, ma'am. I've got antenatal today, and they keep chinning me about my weight as it is.'

'Fair enough.' Mrs Reekie brought out two bottles of perfume, then the packet of biscuits, then another two bottles of perfume. 'Buy one get one free. Och, they'll keep till Christmas. Cost me a fortune that lot, so they do.' She shrugged. 'You'll never get those early days back. When your bairns are wee and they need you.

It's what I tell my own girls: My today is your tomorrow. And I'm always right. So you listen to Grannie Annie.'

Anna's coffee had spilled out of her nose.

'Aye, that's one of the nicer names they call me, eh? Far better than Auld Reekie.' The divisional commander had squirted some Chanel No 5 into the air. 'Cheek of it! Reekie by name maybe, but no by nature.'

Anna wasn't in the market for another mum, but having Mrs Reekie behind you was like having a firm, comfy cushion at your back. Which she could be doing with now. Why were hospital chairs – the very place you visited when you were sore, unwieldy or destined for an interminable wait – so unyieldingly hard?

The doctor stood up. Unshockable Nurse had reappeared with a large glass bottle and a slightly tighter face, and was waiting by the opened door.

'Well, if there's nothing else, Ms Cameron, that's you free to go. As I'm sure you tell all *your* customers,' he grinned.

'Cheers,' said Anna, hoisting herself to upright. 'Oh, and by the way – you need to update your material.'

The doctor pushed his designer glasses up into his hair. 'I'm not with you?'

'Yeah, parking offences were decriminalised ages ago. Next cop you get in the stirrups, say something about getting done for speeding. Or better still, for telling wholly unfunny jokes.'

She nodded at the nurse on her way out, walking briskly until she reached the lift. Bra-straps sawing through her shoulders; could her breasts get any heavier? Her car was parked miles away. This out-of-town, all-purpose 'super hospital' had replaced the local maternity unit, which would have been ten minutes from Anna's door; and while there were hundreds of disabled parking bays, no one had thought to earmark any for fat, breathless breeders. Anna's vein twinged.

Driving back into the city, she deliberately kept her mobile off. She refused to be on duty until she'd had a nice long pee and a decent cup of tea. At least at Crannyhill she had her own parking space. She had to stop calling it that; it had been renamed Anderston Subdivision years ago. But old names stuck. She pulled into her parking bay. What if Picketty Witch stuck? It was horrible. At least 'Grannie Annie' had some warmth about it.

'Alright, wee yin. I hear you.'

Her coat was open. Well, it could no longer be buttoned up, and the material had fallen back so that her black-smocked belly was on full view. Through thin fabric, Anna could see a spectre shifting, flesh within her flesh that was stretching awake. It began almost as soon as she'd taken the key from the ignition. Engine noise always lulled the baby: the car, the washing machine, even the Hoover seemed to rock her – or him – to sleep. Rob was convinced it was a boy, but not Anna. No, this determined wee midden with the needle-sharp knees was definitely a girl.

She entered the code into the back-door keypad, went inside. Her station assistant, Jean, was watering the crisp-tipped spider plant she insisted brought 'good vibes' to the office.

'Hi, ma'am, how you doing?'

'Hanging on, thanks. Much been happening?'

'No really. That mannie from the City Centre Traders dropped off the report you were looking for, the Pipe Band want to know if they can practise in here at the weekend . . . em,' she bit her lip, 'oh, yes. And Mark Guthrie's had to go home sick – drunk female attacking him with a stiletto shoe.'

Anna checked her watch. 'At four o'clock on a Monday?'

'Hmm. Think her work was having a birthday lunch for her, and she'd been tanking it since then.'

'Is Mark okay?'

'Och *aye*. Big wean so he is, ma'am. It was only a wee bit blood above his eye. Jesus, I'd wee Tracey at the dentist this morning for two fillings and she didny make half as much fuss.'

'Oh yeah – how'd it go? She alright?'

'Aye, she's fine thanks. And thanks again, ma'am, for giving me the time off.'

'No probs.'

'I tell you, it's fair handy, working so close to the wean's school. Really makes a difference. Oh, and there's a woman here to see you by the way. She's been waiting a while, but she won't say what it is.'

'Okay, Jean.' Anna tried not to jog on the spot, but it was getting desperate. 'Two ticks while I nip to the loo – is that her there?'

On the CCTV screen that monitored the front foyer, Anna could discern a long, dark ponytail, white hands clutching a package on her knee.

'Hope that's no a bomb,' she joked.

Jean screwed up her nose. 'I know. It's like Paranoid City now, isn't it?'

The girl in the foyer could not hear them, could not possibly have heard Anna, or know that she was there through two thick doors, but her pale neck flexed and her head came up, longer and higher as her profile turned, as her face took form to stare directly at the camera.

And Anna's life, her future, froze.

Chapter Eight

Mary wasn't sure how long she had been pressed into this doorway. She raised her head up, trying to grab some mouthfuls of air. It was all bruises: the sky, her lungs. Breathing in a panicked continuum, crushing, crushing herself into the mouth of the close. They were secure-entries – you couldn't just run into the lobby. Panting, trying to fade into the safety-glass door as the length of her crushed against its hard, transparent hopelessness. Legs hurting, all the tiny bones in her feet felt like splinters.

All this because he wanted to build some houses? That guy was a maniac. She was shaking still. It must be fine to move now. You would have to be a total stalker-psycho to wait this long and not give up. As slowly as she could, Mary let her body bleed out from the doorway. The street was clear, only a boy on a motorcycle pulling up to park.

It was fine, fine. But as soon as she got back home, she was going to have it out with Bernie. Fiona too, if needs be. There had to be a way they could get this guy off their backs. Did Bernie have any idea he was following her? Was he after that parcel? And when was someone going to tell her about the threat to the bloody farm? It was her home too, folk seemed to forget that. There needed to be some honesty at Calder Riggs. They had to start treating her like an equal. She wasn't some wee stable girl. She was. She was . . .

And then she saw it. The sludge-grey of the fat man's coat appearing from the side of an Indian restaurant, and she was running again, *must keep running*, round another corner, towards a bank of looming statues that were music and painting and all the arts. Beneath them were four mighty Atlantes, necks drooping,

arms beseeching the pediment above to stop being so heavy, so
relentlessly hard and heavy and she was running to them, past
their blank stone faces that had seen it all, had seen their edifice
grow and blossom from the burnt remains of a concert hall to
this: the Mitchell Library. A massive, soaring building and there
was her one last chance. A door she could go through, Mary
running inside, into the light, bright surprise of fawn marble, of
Internet pods, glass tables, sofas. And was he still behind her, this
fat bastard who never gave up?

People were staring. She stopped in the foyer, flung her spine
against the wall, and let her breath catch up with her heart. Let
her limbs slow down to the ponderous page-turning and scone-
munching tempo of the library café she was in. Looked to the
door, to the people coming through. Not him, not him. Two
students, then a lady and her child. Then just an empty expanse
of glass and the street beyond with another Indian restaurant and
rows of tenement flats.

But he had been so close, so very close to laying hands on her
neck again. She moved further into the building, past the toilets
and the café and the computers, up a short flight of stairs to a
mezzanine. Beyond the mezzanine, a wood and glass door. There
was no sign that said 'Private', no 'Staff Only' or red silk rope.
She went through. On the other side, she hesitated; she was in a
different world. Stark modernity had reverted to dark mahogany
panels, to black-white chequered floors and the sweeping marble
staircase and the beautiful smell of dust-imbued leather and print.
Crackling air of all the thousands and thousands of words that
whispered. On any other day, she would have relished this.

The staircase twisted up and away. Mary laid her hand on the
smoothness of the balustrade. A uniformed attendant sitting at a
nearby desk smiled. This must be okay, it must be okay to go up
these stairs. Her leg muscles were tight, the same glute-ache as
after riding. As she began to climb, the urge to run again increased.
The attendant was watching her, she knew it. Taking in her tear-
stained face, her sweat. The tatty rucksack, the lack of briefcase or
books. She kept it steady, got to the next landing. A long marble

corridor stretched either side of the stairs. She picked the left one, and, at that moment, heard his voice below.

It was the same rasp, but library-lite. He was modulating the volume, and the forced control of his ragged, quiet expletives was even more terrifying. Her feet wouldn't move, just listening, listening to his snake-hiss with the one strong thought: *At least it's me. At least he's come after me, not Bernie.*

'Naw, I'll no be long,' he rattled. 'Aye, I know you telt me that, but I canny be in two fucking places at once, can I?'

His voice got lower. It sounded like he was talking to someone on the phone.

'I know that. But that's three times she's turned up like the proverbial, know? She's getting in ma fucking road. And if we're gonny come the heavy with the hoor, I canny—'

Mary crouched by the banister, tried to see down the stairs without her head poking out. She thought she could make out the crook of a rumpled elbow. Leaned a little further to catch his drifting words.

'Aye, aye. I'm sorry pal. That was outa order. Alright? I'm just pure . . . ach. Right. Okay, fair dos, Gee. Right, I'll *deal* with it. Okay? I'll gie you a bell, alright? Soon as—'

Another voice broke in.

'Excuse me sir. I've already told you you canny use a mobile phone in here. This is a library. If you need to make a call, away through to the café.'

'Away and kiss ma big fat erse.'

'Ho. That's it, pal. You're out of here.'

From her squashed-up vantage point, Mary could see the man's elbow jerk back, then his head. His great fat head and his eyeballs, staring up at her through sinuous marble curves and there was saliva on his chin. She scrambled to her feet, hitting the stairs with her hands first, on all fours like a crawling, scrabbling animal, running up the next flight, him behind, bawling at her.

'C'mere you, ya wee boot!'

Her feet slipping on the stairs, one shoe twisting in a sliding T and her on her knees again, her knees bleeding, his feet slapping close. He was at the outside of her vision, like some primitive memory of fear and the need to run, his black bulk flying, gaining on her, almost on this set of stairs as she chucked herself round the marble newel at the top, on to the second floor. In this corridor, same layout, options left and right and the most stunning windows, glorious arches of coloured glass what was she doing what was she doing this wasn't a fucking art trip, left, just go left beyond the stairs, a little niche. Pale green tiles through a swinging door, a hidden corridor into which she ran. Some presence of mind that was not conscious made her grab at the door, made her stop it swinging so it was still as he ran past, her wedged in the corner behind door and wall. She could hear feet clattering up the next flight of stairs, could hear men's voices, several men, then a crash. Some kind of dragging noise, one voice saying: 'That's the polis coming.' There was a shout, more like a cry but she couldn't look out. Could only cramp in her little corner, eyes shut, buried in her knees.

'Ho, Rodge. Bloody grab him!'

The running again, getting closer. Her mouth was over her kneecap, sobbing.

The running, getting closer.

Going past.

Keep going, keep going she prayed into her knees. She sat there, praying, and no one came near the room. No one came near it for ages. If she was foolish, she could let herself believe she had woven some charm, but, clearly, this was an orphan room, as unwanted as Mary. She sat until her neck ached and the light through the windows softened into thick, fat purple. Its drape was comforting.

Holding on tight, flesh and mind. She was anonymous Mary, had constructed a soft and secret nest. She did not want that nest to be disturbed. Hours and hours, as sculpted as the sad Victorian caryatids outside. Reassuring herself that her increasing hopelessness was proof that she was sane. Could feel the creeping, tugging low that tingled at her toes. It would penetrate and seep like water again, if she let it.

More feet moving. A voice calling, *that's us closing up, folks.* The harsh lights in the building stammered off like abrupt applause, and Mary had a choice. Either she hid here, and they locked her up, or she took her chances and went back outside.

No choice really. Mary never wanted to be locked up again.

Chapter Nine

'Ho! You'll never guess. Thurr's bin a murr-der!'

'Ha ha. Very funny.'

Alex Patterson flicked the pages of the book he was reading. *Lost Voices of the Somme*. It was heartbreaking, this stuff. A collection of reminiscences, documents, letters. Boys just out of school or off the farm, trying to articulate with stubs of pencil and limited space how they felt about having no clean socks, when what they really meant was how they felt about lying in a pool of mud and faeces, watching rats eat their dead colleagues while a constant barrage of noise and death fell thicker than the flies. Hundreds of miles from home, telling your loved ones that everything was fine when all you wanted was to weep in your sweetheart's arms. Ach, Alex would have been good at that.

'No seriously, there has. And you, my friend, are it.'

Alex took his feet off the desk. One finger smoothing down a triangular corner, one hand closing the book. Approach everything slow. Give the adrenalin time to surge. He always imagined it to be navy blue, a high wash of panic and thrill in which it was impossible to see. You just had to go with the flow, like surfing in Belhaven Bay; wait till you thud the shore, then shake your head clear and stand up.

'Where?'

'Up by the canal.'

Well, it would be. Depository for stolen motors, shopping trolleys, careless drunks and deid things.

'Aye, you can near see it from the office. It's just up at the Stocks.'

In its glory days, Maryhill had been the hub of Glasgow's canal system, the industrial pivot at which the Forth and Clyde Canal split. At Stockingfield Junction, one watery arm reached for Bowling, while another branched off towards Glasgow and Port Dundas. Maryhill had been a Very Important Place, once upon a time. The world's first ever steamboat was tested here. It had been a West Coast Venice, with its own glass industry, and a proud flotilla of craft bobbing in the Maryhill Docks. Sadly, that had been two hundred years ago, and the only memories remaining now were a street called Murano and the scar-faced legacy of the Maryhill Fleet – no longer an armada, but a nasty wee gang of the 1960s, whose erstwhile, aged members could still be seen on occasion, propping up the bookies and the bars.

'Who, when, why? Answers to any or all of the above will be much appreciated.'

Ian Morrison put his hands in his pockets. 'Who: a wumman. When: pretty recent – she's only a wee bit green. And why? I reckon sexual – she's nae clothes on and a pair of fishies wrapped round her neck.'

'Classy. You got the motor?'

'Aye.'

Maryhill Police Office was four floors of squat brown brick to the front, then a rise of windowless tower behind. It could have been a brutal, post-modernist chapel, or a castle made from cardboard boxes, save for the blue and white cop-shop sign. They headed into the yard. It was getting dark, but the streetlights hadn't yet come on.

Alex let Ian take the wheel. Another awkward step in the dance of who was king. Ian had been a DS for seven years, Alex for two. Six months after he was promoted sergeant, they put Alex back into CID. He'd been an aide at Stewart Street, then a DC for a year, but he'd never felt wholly comfortable. Too many sharp-suited wide boys for his liking. *He* was the only sharp-suited wide boy in the village. Anyway, uniforms suited him. Brought out the colour of his eyes. Piqued the interest of the ladies, too. But a move was a move, B Division was only down the road. And, bloody hell, hadn't they loved him there? The SDO was a girl called Hayley, thought the sun shone out his arse (or somewhere in the region of his trousers). Alex had smiled and quipped and charmed his way through every job they'd flung at him, with a massive daud of luck at the start of his second year there. He'd been coming out of the bookies when he'd seen a car parked up on the pavement. Three boys with hats on, and ants in their jittering pants. Grand National on in fifteen minutes. *Everyone* bet on the National, ergo, Christmas time at Barrett's Bookmakers. It was a matter of minutes to shout for reinforcements, circle the building and scoop up the neds as they came out. The raid alarm had only just begun to ring.

'But how did you *know*?' breathed Hayley.

'Local contacts, ma'am. I make sure I get around.'

Result. A performance review note and another six. He'd had 'six' appraisals every time – which was ten out of ten in polis-speak. When the gnarled old stick that was DI Angus Grant had finally succumbed to woodworm (and don't let anyone tell you it was stress-related urticaria), it had been Alex, not Ian, that was chosen to act up in his stead.

'Just for the time being, you understand?' said the lovely Hayley. 'Let me see what you can do, eh?'

'Oh, you'd be surprised ma'am,' said Alex. Resisting the urge to wink.

In the space between open door and car, Ian took a draw of his thrice-smoked fag.

'Times that hard, pal?'

'Naw. I've a whole bloody packet here, but I canny get anywhere to smoke them. Two quick puffs, then I've to nip it and put it back. Tell you, I must've cut down to about four a day.'

'So, who's down there at the moment?'

Another suck. 'Eh, Shirley Clark, wee Tube and the lovely Doctor Jaconelli.'

'She there already?' Alex clicked on his seatbelt. 'So, is that me the last to know then?'

Ian flicked his fag on to the tarmac, tugged the door of their crappy wee Fiesta shut. 'Fucksake Alex. Is there a problem? Do you need me to run it by you before I scratch my arse now?'

'No.'

'Sorry if I've fucked your wee tick list.'

He had to be referring to the scrap of paper Alex kept in his inside pocket. *Major Incident Enquiry: DI's duties.* It had grown like a flower, petals unfolding as he had added another loop. Keep it in the loop. Keep everything in the loop. He could see it, bubbled in his head:

Set up MI Team … Crime Scene … Notify …Witness ID …

Each heading with a subsection, then a jumbling foliage of words: *Consider request for HOLMES … Crime Scene Manager … Media … Intelligence Cell … Support Unit … PF …ANPR.*

It was how he'd studied for his tickets. Like notes for a speech, it was just a crib, he knew it all, of course he did. But it was a comfort to have the solidity of paper pressed against his heart. Just for the time being. He hadn't realised anyone else knew it was there.

'You contacted the Fiscal too?'

'Of course.'

The barrier raised, they drove outside. On the pavement, a drunk was reeling, an old jakey with his arms flung wide, cackling at seagulls. His manky tweed coat sucked out like sails, wind nudging, him grinning. Just going with the flow. A wifie trundled past, expertly swerving her shopping trolley to avoid the old man's feet.

'So – is she inside or out?'

'Of what?' Ian checked his rear-view mirror, pulled into the evening traffic. This road was never quiet. 'The water?'

'Well … no. I meant, is she in the open air or not?'

'That's what I said to you, Alex. She's at Stockingfield Junction.'

'Yes, but there are still buildings there. Well, in the street going up to it.'

Ian sighed. 'Yes, but *that*'s no the junction. Anyway, I told you she was a wee bit green. Does that no suggest to you that she was in the actual water? But now she's oot.' A tightening of his hands upon the wheel. 'The woman is lying in the open air. By the side of the canal. At Stockingfield Junction. *Boss.*'

'And did someone find her like that, *Ian*, or was she pulled out?'

'She was pulled out, *sir*. By the uniform that got the call.'

A terse few minutes until they got there. The locus was only streets from the office; turn right up Lochburn Avenue, then breathe in. A narrow street, always packed with cars, although, now that rush hour was over, there were pockets where you could see the pavement. A squeeze past industrial units, dull offices, the odd scrapyard, until the road bent, apparently ending in a massive stone wall. Then you saw it was not a wall, but a tunnel, open and arched as a desperate mouth. Access to Stockbridge Junction was directly in front of this tunnel. The junction itself was up in the air, resting on the bridge of stone above their heads. Ian went to pull into an inshot at the side of the road. You could reach the canal by two paths – one that ran from this inshot up the land on the right-hand side of the bridge, the other a set of steps across the road, which curved up the left-hand side.

'No wait, Ian. Don't stop here.'

'How no? If I stick the car anywhere else it's gonny block the road.'

'Well, we'll need to close the whole road anyway – both ends. But I just . . . look, you're right. This *is* the most obvious place to stop a car. That's why. If we think that, so might anyone else who'd business here. Just go through the tunnel and park up the other side.'

Ian kept the engine idling, still centre in the sliver of road. 'Aye, and what if they came through from that side – all we're doing is disturbing the locus there.'

'I know, but . . . it seems less likely. Just humour me, eh? Just until I get Scenes of Crime to look at it.'

'You're the boss.'

Alex smoothed the fabric of his suit. Could feel his knee beneath, a singing electricity in the joint. This was going to seep for miles and days and miles. Al fresco bodies were always problematic. For a start, they weren't at home, or at work, or at their friend's house – so you were starting from an augmented position of ignorance. Unless the deceased was good enough to be wearing nametapes on their undies, or have their driving licence in their bag, before you began the 'why', you had to solve the 'who'. And if this girl was in the scud, the 'who' might take a while. You also had to consider the possibility that this lonely dumpsite was not, in fact, the crime scene; that the murder had been committed elsewhere, and this was only a bus stop on the way to her final resting place. So, no blood-spray to show the struggle or force. No witnesses to go: *Aye, there was some weird guy with her. But you don't like tae get involved, know?* No scraps of paper or last numbers dialled on her phone. Scant physical evidence to link time and rhyme and crime, and what there was would be scattered over Glasgow like breadcrumbs in the woods.

'I take it Shirley's the crime scene manager?'

'Well, we've both been trained.'

'Yes, but it's her that's been there all the time.'

'I only came up to get you.'

'Yes, no, I appreciate that, Ian, but the point is, I'm assuming that's why she was left here. To manage the scene?'

'You should never assume anything, boss. Anyway, it's no up to me. It's your call.'

The car crunched on to a patch of stony verge, and Ian ratcheted the handbrake.

'That's us then.' He got out, not waiting for Alex. Then, jettisoned as an afterthought: 'Do you mind which path I use, or have you a sixth sense about that and all?'

Alex ignored him. It was a moot point. By this time, Shirley should have secured one sole point of access in any case. He left his coat in the back seat. It was chilly now that the sun was easing down, but he found he was sweating. He crossed the road, Ian striding on ahead. Good. Shirley *had* sealed off one of the paths. Same thinking as Alex – keep the obvious vehicular access intact; use the path with the steps. A probationer stood there, clutching a clipboard.

'Eh. 'Scuse me. I've to . . .'

'DI Patterson, and DS Morrison. Maryhill CID.'

'Can I see your warrant cards . . . ?'

'Oh for fucksake,' grunted Ian.

'Sure.' Alex held his wallet out. 'There you go, son.'

The boy let them past.

Roll up, roll up. Free admission granted to the greatest game on earth. See the monkey-god bringing order to chaos, see him draw the threads of truth from the very fabric of the earth. Mud will cling, taproots of prevarication and false starts will drag it back. But the monkey-god will prevail. He must, or chaos wins. And what will old piggy do then, poor thing?

'Ian. D'you remember that programme? Monkey?'

'Naw.'

Ian's sports jacket was getting shiny where it fell across his backside. A wee visit to Burton's menswear was called for. Alex could hear him wheezing as they neared the top of the path. Maybe a wee visit to the gym and all.

Alex paused at the head of the stairs, the wind fair slapping his face.

Amazing.

Standing on the bridge, back to the parapet; a vast expanse of water lay flat and low like Everglades.

Oh, he knew there was a body waiting for him. But he was allowed a space of seconds, just four or five blinks to reacknowledge this wonderful construct that slid and lapped in secret at the back of city streets. He'd lived in Glasgow all his life, and never known it was here. Not until he came to Maryhill and Ian had 'wanted to get some air'. Ian had in reality wanted to have a fag, but it was in the days when they were still equals and friends, and so they'd got burgers from McDonald's and come out to the Stocks.

Here, high in the sky, the canal broke free from its bonds of straight lines and rigid sides. Loose, slack water, yawning in a massive Y, in tantalising estuaries where time was slow, horizons fixed. A heaviness settled in his chest. He used to like it here.

Over by the widest stretch of water, a huddle of uniformed cops was shuffling to and fro, their breaths beginning to shimmer. Alex could also see the DC they all called Tube; partly on account of his initials – Terry Baird – but mostly because he was one. A wee, daft, irritating tube. From the motley crew, a figure in brogues and M & S slacks emerged. It was Shirley. She raised a hand. 'Alright boss. Over here.'

Nearly fifty, Shirley Clark was a superlative DS. Brightest cop he'd ever met, with mad grey-blonde hair and a full twenty-five years steeped in Maryhill. Pass a twelve-year-old loitering in the park and she could riff out his family history going back three generations. Had a mouth on her like a packet of razor blades, though, which frequently nicked at Hayley.

Nice lipstick, ma'am. You going up the dancing after work?

And *there* was another wee dab of toilet paper on the tracery of cuts that would forever sever Shirley from further advancement. Shirley, however, could not give a toss. Shirley had no time for Hayley. Neither had she time for arse-lickers, lazy bastards, lassies who cried (particularly policewomen) or neds. Any neds, but lippy neds were the worst. God help the deluded chav who tried to chance their arm with Shirley.

She strode to meet him, her raincoat flapping miserably in the wind.

'Shirley,' said Alex. 'I'm appointing you crime scene manager.'

She looked puzzled. 'Aye, I know. Me and Ian divvied it up already.'

Ian, head down, fag in mouth, was already approaching the main cordon.

'Ho! Put that fag out, you,' shouted Shirley. 'And stay out of my crime scene. So,' she smiled at Alex, 'you want to see wur wumman? It's okay,' she added cheerfully, 'she's no a minger or anything. Quite a pretty lassie, actually, apart fae the bloating.'

She handed Alex a pair of white paper slippers, to tug on over his boots. Led him to the inner cordon. 'No further boss, eh? Not till Scenes of Crime have finished.'

They were right by the edge of the canal, where thick reeds grew, their hollow ochre stems like so many straws. A low stone wall, which seemed to be ballast for the earth behind it, separated the patchy grass meadow from an overgrown path. Two white-suited forensic officers floated over the body, one snapping, the other scraping. Papery wraiths from the netherworld, come to see how these strange creatures work. Not very well, as a rule.

Humans you call them? Hmm. But we do not understand. From humanus*? Meaning genial, merciful and kind?*

Through twilight and tape, Alex could make out a pale, soft outline. Belly and breasts, one nipple lolling directly at him. Thin girl, white. Very white. Medium height – five three, five four maybe. Keep the face till last ... up ... up ... there it was, in profile. Chiselled chin above the black-net ligature, below the straight nose, the gloss black hair. Wet, of course, like the rest of her. One distant, open eye.

It was getting dark. Up here, there was little in the way of illumination; no streetlights, no headlamps, only the glow from their torches, and refracted water-light playing tricks.

'We'll need to get some proper lighting in. Ian, will you get on to Emergencies Planning, please, and ask them for some portable lamps. Get an incident caravan off them too.' He looked directly at his DS. 'If you put it in that inshot by the path down there – *after* we've had the ground searched – we can use it as a rendezvous. Plus it might attract some witnesses over. What is the position with witnesses, Shirley?'

'Just the two that found her. A couple of lovebirds, winching. They were having a good-going snogging session, sitting on that wee wall, when the lassie's shoe fell off. Loverboy climbed down to get it, and seen a pair of legs floating in amongst all that crap.' She gestured to the tangle of rubbish that had been dragged out with the girl. Alex thought he saw a cycle wheel in with the tree branches and poly bags. Had she come by bike? A naked cyclist; was there a circus in town?

'So the shoe was on the other foot, eh?' said Ian. 'Classic.'

'Ian.' Shirley's face was deathly serious. 'Please stop your unrelenting banter. I think I've just soiled myself.'

'Some amount of junk there,' said Alex.

'I know. She was all tangled up in it – that's what kept her afloat.'

'Thank fuck for the fly-tippers of Glasgow, eh? They really are performing a civic duty, bunging their old fridges in the canal rather than hauling them to the dump.'

Shirley frowned at him. 'You alright, Alex?'

'Aye. How?'

'No reason.

Alex looked round the periphery. Empty, barren land; in the distance, the pseudo Art Deco of a half-done block of flats. *Canalside living! See the sewage floating by!* Even if the apartments had been occupied, you wouldn't see anything from there. Shapes like ants, a darkened scuttle; you'd never even hear the splash. A rusted lock-gate hung by a thread on the approach to the stretch marked *Falkirk*. They actually had signposts, sticking out of the water. Who *came* here? In the foreground, a nest of beer cans, festive in their red, white and gold. Drinkers came here. Winchers came here. And a murderer had come here.

'So, who was first on the scene?'

'They two over there – eh, Frank something-or-other and Emma Taylor.'

You couldn't fault the cops that found her. Doing everything possible to preserve unlikely life. Even this, a floater in a canal, deserved that fleeting hope, where you would jump in or chuck a rope or . . . in this case it looked like drag with branches to the side, pulling and heaving until you got the body ashore. Checking for any vital signs, and praying a swollen arm didn't come off in your hand.

But it all meant scene-shifting. Literally: the scene was no longer intact. The forensic chappies were conversing now, big white hoods bobbing. What if they missed something? How do you know which twig or lump of stone rubbed past the body, which frond of weed, which crisp packet possessed some crucial speck?

Another white-clad maiden hove into view.

'Dr Jaconelli. How the hell are you?'

She grinned. Wiped a long blonde tress from her face, nudging it back inside her hood. 'DS Patterson. Looking good.'

'Ach, this old thing?' Alex tweaked his suit lapel. Dark grey, with a subtle blue weave. Well, new job, new gear. No wee pips to put on your shoulder when you were in civvies. 'Had it for ages.' He didn't correct her about the rank. 'So? What about our Lady in the Lake?'

'Female. Twenty, twenty-two maybe. Nice hair, bad teeth. Been in there less than a day.'

'Deid then dumped?' asked Ian.

'I reckon so. Need to wait till the PM obviously, check the lungs.'

'Right,' said Alex. 'Shirley, when Scenes of Crime are done there I want them to extend their examination out, looking at any evidence of recent vehicular access. There's no way someone's carried her all the way up – it's too public, whatever way you come in. In fact, get the Traffic down here too, see what they can see, tyre marks or whatever. And check all available CCTV for the last twenty-four hours, any number-plate recognition we have in the area. I also want the Support Unit to come out and do a ground search. This entire basin will need to be scrutinised – we're looking for clothes, personal effects . . .'

Take your time, son. Slow it down and look around. It was the mantra of Derek, his mentor in the Flexi Unit. Always letting the air from Alex's youthful exuberance. He was right, though. You only got one chance at any crime scene. Like goods in a sale, when it's gone, it's gone. *Stop, look and listen.* Meditate on the picture before you. It is a rebus; there will be something there.

'Underwater too?'

'Of course.'

'Excellent.' Shirley clapped her hands. 'Bring on the boys in rubber. Is that big lad Stevie still in the Unit?'

Dr Jaconelli laughed. 'Oh, yes. I saw him when I was at that drowning on Glasgow Green. You should see the arse on him.'

'I know. You could just bite it, couldn't you?'

'Ladies, do you mind?' Alex addressed the casualty surgeon. 'Dr Jaconelli: sex?'

The doctor glanced over her shoulder at the collective of cops. 'Well, it's a wee bit public the now. But maybe later . . . ?'

'Marisa Jaconelli. I'm surprised at you.' Alex shook his head, clocked Ian watching him; this young buck bantering with the birds. 'Right. Come on now. Sensible heads on, please.'

You couldn't help it sometimes. There was a high about a murder scene, a defiance that made you want to grab at life. You, who could still savour it, even if the poor bastard lying before you could not.

'*Doctor* Jaconelli,' he said. 'Does your initial examination suggest that the victim has been sexually assaulted?'

'Other than her lack of clothing; no. I'll take all the usual swabs, of course, but there's no obvious evidence of any bleeds or contusions.'

'Thank you.'

He'd start with sexual offenders anyway. Just because you look but don't touch disny mean you're not a pervert. Divisional Intelligence could work on any similar crimes forcewide and nationally, and MAPPA would provide details of sex offenders living in the area. He'd need to set up an incident room, a full MI Team. Contact the divisional commander and chief super Crime, too. No show without Punch.

'What about Missing Persons, boss? D'you want me to start with that?' Ian blew a cloud of smoke across the navy sky. It coiled like fingers, faded, was gone.

'If you would, Ian. Thanks.'

Whose daughter had not come home tonight? What mother was glumly stirring a pot of something over-boiled, her annoyance congealing to that slow, cold knot of fear? *Gone eight o'clock now; she's never this late.* Whose wife or girlfriend had got all dolled up to meet her pals, had said she'd phone when she wanted a lift home? Chances are the girl had not even been reported yet. He peered again at the body. Unless she was a proper waif, a runaway living on the streets. Hard to tell in this light, and without the façade of clothes. You could tell a lot about someone from their clothes. Naked, we're all just meat.

'Do canals have currents?' The Tube had wandered over, was snuffling into a tissue.

'Whit?'

'Well, I'm just thinking,' he sniffed. 'Could she have drifted here from somewhere else? I mean, it's a kind of crossroad for canals. Or . . . what about a boat. Could someone have chucked her off a boat?'

Ian exhaled a smoke ring. 'There's nae boats come up here now, ya daft prick.'

'Aye there is. All that Forth and Clyde regeneration – I'm sure you can get a trip in a barge; all the way fae Kirkie to the coast now.'

'Away. What happens when you get to Drumchapel and the wee shites start chucking stones at you?'

'You duck,' said Alex. 'I doubt there's any currents, Terry, but we'll ask the Underwater Unit when they get here.'

'*I'll* ask them,' said Shirley.

'Gies a loan of your torch, Terry.'

Alex crouched down, so he could see under the tape. The girl's left arm was less than three feet from his knees. A remnant of cobbles glistened beneath holes in the tarmac, humped spines pushing like fossils from an industrial past. You could feel the coldness down here, a marsh-damp unfurling from the ground. He held the torchlight steady, then circled it out, the beam's pale neck rooting through all the dark places, sweeping the thickness of her hair, catching her crying eye, which was bloodshot. Seeing her smile – they did, they always did; the mouth dropped back when you lay supine. His light brushed a scarf of latticed black. The pair of tights had been knotted, her skin puckered above and below. Down the slope of her breast, her arm. The white blueness where her elbow curved. The faint, scarred ladderwork of angry blades. All up her forearm, from her wrist to elbow-joint.

Alex must have been about twelve, first time he'd seen marks like these. His sister in the bathroom, him walking in to go to the loo. She was slashing herself, fucking sticking these scissors into her arms, right in through the flesh and him screaming and her screaming. His mum was out, he didn't know what to do. Didn't know what to do. She was bigger than him, fifteen. Flung him out and locked the door. He didn't know what to do.

All he *could* do was watch her, every day. Check her room for sharps when she was out. Throw out razors, tweezers, her compasses for maths. He would spy on her at the swimming, see tiny, precise zigzags raised on arms and legs, and wonder why no one else could see them.

This girl here had been full of anger: at life, or herself, or someone. Alex raised his head. 'D'you think there's any chance that she could have done this to herself?'

'Sorry?'

The Underwater Unit had just pulled up, and neither Dr Jaconelli nor Shirley's attentions were focused wholly on Alex any more. A fine mist of rain began to fall; its washing of the scene the last thing he wanted.

'Marisa. Look at her arms, will you? She's clearly been a self-harmer at one time. Is there any possibility our girl could have committed suicide?'

'Suicide? By self-strangulated drowning? Aye, right. Away and bile your heid Alex. Now, if you'll excuse me, I'm off to say hi to the men in skintight latex.'

Alex stayed in his crouch. Watching over the fragile cage that once contained a person. Her eye, remote. A liquid disk. What was the last thing it saw?

What is that final succession of after-images, multiplying into infinity?

Above him, the monkey-god snickers.

Chapter Ten

For an instant, when she pushed the door and silence met her, Anna thought she was alone. Truly alone, as if they had abandoned her, cleared out all the vital bustle of life. It wasn't just the absence of Donna's feeble, friendly bound, which, four days on, was even louder; it was the calm neatness of everything. The hall was suspiciously clear and new-swept, the floorboards fully visible, coat tree pruned. She hung her wet jacket on one of the empty pegs and let the stillness wrap around, holding her head like a cool soft hand. In a minute, surely, noise would burst, a door would slam upstairs, feet gallumphing. The kitchen door would open and disgorge TV noise, her keys, even, falling on the hallstand, would shatter this sphere of nothing; her still, unkeepable secret.

Then the baby tumbled inside her.

She saw her knuckles tremble, tighten over the keys. Fought to swallow nausea, averted her face from its mirrored twin. Perhaps they had gone out for tea. Yes, that was it – shit, it had been her turn to cook as well, but she was so late now, they must have got too hungry, had probably called her, if only she'd had her phone switched on. She put her keys down, one soft, tinny chink absorbed by the wood. Halfway up the stairs, a pair of eyes blinked.

'Hey beautiful,' she whispered to Alice. 'How's my girl?'

Even though Donna had gone, Alice continued to flaunt her fury at having been compelled to share a home, share *Anna*, with a dog. She skulked upstairs for hours at a time, positioned on the bedroom windowsill, gaze fixed outside, tail a malevolent pendulum. Anna hoped that as the days became weeks, Alice would forgive her, revert to the cheeky, playful bundle of before.

Occasionally, she would allow Anna to lift her up, but would never stay on her lap for long. This evening, she graciously permitted contact as Anna knelt on the stairs, pushed her face into soft, knowing fur.

'Baby girl,' she whispered. 'What have I done?'

A pain like ice cream in her head, the thick force of her throat swelling. Alice there, unmoving and quiet, Anna mouthing on her fur. Wet pelt on her lips as the cat began to purr. It was a little engine burning, a small, bright proof of life, like the baby turning, like the empty coats that belonged in this hall. Where were they? An irrational fear constricted her throat, pressing like a cormorant's ring. It made her breathless how much she loved them.

Her family.

This morning had seemed so light. Sky open and vast. Then the clouds had started scudding, she'd seen them rush above her office window, a fury of movement, gathering like spreading news, like bruised, knitted brows and puffed-out cheeks. She could smell their fretfulness on the wind, on the coat the girl wore as she entered the office.

And Anna's life, her future, froze.

It had sealed itself like ice, transparent so the world went on about her, and she in it. Cold too, unbearably cold, the kind of cold that roots you, deadens all response until there is only your eyes left, panicking in your head, and your leaden limbs going through the motions. This hand, spanning that fur, your face so close that the stripes and mottles are single blades of grass and you can see each tremble of their separate movements, the whorl of the fur settling after you have swept it.

She was in shock. Once she'd had time to think, to rationalise, Anna would, Anna would—

'Where've *you* been?'

Laura clattered down to the landing, Alice leaping to the hall floor.

'Oh. I thought you were out.' Anna held the banister, pulled herself straight.

'*No.*'

How could a single word sound so defiant?

'Where's Dad?' said Anna.

'My dad's getting Chinese. Again. *You* were supposed to be making dinner.'

Laura carried on downstairs. She was holding a stack of glasses, the first cupped in her palm, the rest balanced up the length of her arm like a seasoned barmaid. Was she frequenting pubs already?

'I know, I know. I got caught up at work. Hey,' Anna held her hand over her belly. The baby had unfurled again, a rounded bump pushing firmly from her navel. 'Hey, the baby's moving. D'you want to feel?' She reached out to touch Laura's shoulder. Laura flinched.

'*Pshw*. That's gross?' Her every utterance was an inflection of scorn or boredom. 'Anyway, I've to tidy up.'

'Have you? Wow, that's great. Thanks. You know, I'm really, really knackered . . .'

'Yeah. Dad says my Auntie Liz is coming.'

'When? Tonight?'

'Mmm.' Laura was inspecting her chin in the hall mirror. 'He's picking her up before he gets the carry-out.'

'Oh for f—'

A sharp, shrewd pivot. 'Were you going to swear there?'

'No. The baby just kicked me.'

'You were so. You were going to say *fuck*. Or *for fucksake*.'

'Laura! Don't you dare use language like that.'

'Or you'll what? *Smack* me? Grass me to my dad?'

'I . . .' Anna leaned against the newel post, the sweat of effort, of confrontation, beading on her lip. 'Please just don't swear Laura, okay?'

'How not? *You* do it. All the time.'

'No I don't.'

'Aye you do so. And not just *bloody* like my dad does. You say *fuck* and *bugger* and *shit* – I even heard you say *cu*—'

'That is *enough*. You get to your room right this minute, you hear me?'

Before she realised, they were chin to chin. Who had moved first, faster? However it happened, they were facing, Anna slumped and bell-shaped, Laura *en pointe*, a furious exclamation mark that quivered, swayed and then raised itself even higher. For a bitter second, Anna thought Laura was going to strike her. Instead, the girl opened her hand and the glass she was holding scudded to the floor. It smashed in gleeful, hearty chunks.

'*Fine.*'

She could see tears on her stepdaughter's cheek before Laura turned, fled back upstairs. Anna went to the kitchen to get the brush. The tremble in her hand was growing progressively worse. She put the big light on, began to sweep up all the glass. A nice, steady rhythm of drag and swish. Drag and swish.

Drag.

'Hello, hello!'

There was Rob in the open front door, a white carrier bag in either hand. Dark hair damp against his forehead, and that small deep kick whenever he smiled at her. It was the smile and it was him of course, but it was the *downness* of it too – the way he was taller than her and that made her feel safe; how he tilted it slightly, his head and the smile, so the beam was directed straight to her and no one else.

'There's a wee man just accosted me, says he's had a look and we've a few slates missing. Mean anything to you?'

'Oh, yeah – next door are getting their roof done, and I asked for a quote . . . is that okay?' It was still technically Rob's house.

'Of course it is. I've told them just to go ahead. It's not that much—'

'What's not that much?'

Elizabeth, Rob's sister-in-law, appeared directly behind him, no, now she was in front, bustling past without invitation. Every step proclaiming *I was here first*. Anna nodded at the floor.

'Mind out, there's been a spillage.'

It was a long-handled brush she was using, fortunately, or they'd have witnessed her bearing down in an inelegant squat. All good practice for the Big Day.

Elizabeth hung her coat on the hallstand. Tutted as she raised the vase of flowers from the little shelf there. From Anna's hallstand.

'Och look, you've made a mark. You need to put coasters underneath, Rob, I keep telling you that.' She slid a letter under the vase, placed it back down. 'Never thought I'd see you as Mrs Mop, Anna.'

So that was the hellos out the road then.

'Liz, lovely to see you. How *are* things?'

'Oh, you know. Busy, busy. I'm hardly ever in – Rob was lucky he caught me.'

'Ah – just a spontaneous gesture was it, Rob?'

She knew this visit had never been mentioned.

'Well . . .' Rob smiled benignly, like the gentle, generous man he was, carrying the bags through to the kitchen. 'Are we hungry now, ladies, or will I get us a drink first? I'll stick these in the oven. Liz, how about some wine?'

'Oh,' she giggled. 'You know me, Rob. I get all silly with wine.'

'*You're bloody silly without.*' Anna's head was low, scrabbling with the daft wee shovel. And she barely even muttered it.

'Pardon?'

'I said it's very windy outside.'

Looked like she'd got it all. She didn't want Alice cutting a paw on some stray shard.

Elizabeth waited until Anna had heaved herself and the shovel back to upright.

'Oh Anna, silly, you should have *said*. I could have done that for you.'

'So you could.'

'I'm sorry.'

'No problems. It's done now anyway. Come on through to the lounge.'

'Och away, the kitchen's fine for me. It's not like I'm company or anything.' And she was gone, straight after Rob. 'Shall I get the plates out, Robster? Oh God, is that cat in here again? They're *so* unhygienic . . .'

Robster.

'Auntie Liz!' Laura yelled. 'Wassap, Big L?' She ran past Anna, straight into the kitchen, where all the best parties happened.

'Wassap, Wee L!'

Aunt and niece embraced, Anna edging past to shake the shovel into the pedal bin.

'How are you, darling? I'm so sorry about poor Donna.' Elizabeth kissed her niece's head.

'Thank you.'

Anna was not permitted to mention Donna, had tried holding Laura to her breast and been told she was too fat to cuddle anyone.

'You know Laurie-lee, I swear you've got bigger since last month.' Elizabeth winked and lowered her voice. 'Boobs have got bigger too!'

Laura's face was a wash of coy delight. Only yesterday, Anna had mentioned about getting her measured for a new bra, and Laura freaked. *It's none of your business. It's my body; I'll decide.*

'Dyed your hair too? It's *nice.*'

No, no it's not. You had to be honest with kids, surely. They looked to you for guidance, not soft, white fibs that would leave their bellies exposed. Anna had found the hair dye in advance of finding Laura. Well, she had found a trail of angry spatters on the bathroom lino and the bathmat. Seen the brownish rim around the sink, the ruined towel. Seen another ruined towel, then Laura's half-shut door. She had pushed it open, shouting about the mess before she'd even seen the result. Then, she had started screeching about the hair.

'Yeah.' Elizabeth was running idle fingers through her niece's curls. 'You look just like your mum.'

Anna felt herself vanish, go small inside until she was a little twist of air.

'Doesn't she Rob? Doesn't she look like Amy?'

Rob smiled. 'She looks beautiful, so she does. Laura can you get the glasses down, please? Anna, do you want some wine, darling?'

'She can't have wine Rob, don't be daft.'

Anna held out a glass. 'Yes, please. I'll have some white.'

The thought of pouring acid into her already burning gullet was quite an unpleasant one. But necessary.

'Cheers.'

Elizabeth clattered open the cutlery drawer. 'I really don't think that's a good idea, Anna.'

'Don't you?' Anna took another sip.

'I mean, you don't want it having foetal alcohol syndrome or something.'

'Liz, for goodness' sake. It's fine,' said Rob. 'The odd glass is okay. Amy got a real taste for beer when she was expecting Laura.'

'Ah, but beer's different – it's got . . . hops and stuff. It's all quite healthy.'

'Wine's made of grapes,' said Laura.

'Aye. Sour grapes.' Anna's mouth was half inside her glass.

Elizabeth heard it fine. 'Meaning?'

Carefully, Anna placed her glass on the kitchen table. 'Elizabeth, it's very nice that Rob invited you over. And you know you're always welcome as a guest in our house. And I'm sure you don't realise that you're doing it, but—'

'Auntie Liz !' squeaked Laura. 'D'you want to come up and see my room? I've moved all the furniture round – the bed's over by the window now and—'

'Yes, in a minute. Anna, you were saying?'

Rob caught her eye. Laura too, their tight, bright smiles unbearable.

'Nothing. I was saying nothing. Why don't you go up and see Laura's room? She's got it looking really great. You know that turquoise throw you brought her back from France? Well, she's used that as the theme. New blinds to match and everything.'

Elizabeth nodded. Stood, put her hand on Laura's shoulder. 'Sounds nice. Okay madam, let's have the guided tour.'

As she left, Elizabeth's elbow brushed against the curtains, and Anna could see outside. Twilight; those curious clouds again, moving in open mouths. Heavy curled smoke against the sky, the light split like oil on water. Every purple, from palest mauve to damson, in breathing, shifting layers. Even the moon was lilac. Then the curtain fell back, and she and Rob were alone.

'Oh honey,' Rob kissed the top of Anna's head. He smelled of fresh air, his chin digging, resting on her as he spoke. 'I'm sorry. How did you get on at the clinic today?'

'Fine. Everything's good. But ... Elizabeth? Did I miss something?'

'Och, she phoned me at work again, asked if I could pop in and fix her dishwasher.'

'Can she not get a wee man to come and do that? I gave her the name of that odd-job guy Elaine and Pete use.'

'I know, I know. But I went. And then I couldn't get away. I thought the best thing to do was to ask her over here for tea, or I'd be stuck there all bloody night.'

'Your soul is too noble, you realise that?'

Rob moved to kiss her belly. 'That's it. You think nothing but good thoughts. No poisonous effluent for my wee boy to float in.'

'It might not be a boy.'

'Trust me, I'm a doctor. And that ring on a string trick never lies.' His hair was softer than Alice's fur. She loved him so much. The weight of his head, skimming her breasts, pressing on their baby.

'Although it does work best if it's your own wedding ring you use.'

His voice was muffled by the drumskin of her stomach. She could pretend not to hear him as usual, just keep stroking his hair. Or she could go: *Okay then, you're on,* and see him drop with shock. But he was already moving away, his face above her now, no longer stooping, his hand lingering on the side of her face.

'Just remember how good Elizabeth was to me and Laura when Amy died. I couldn't have managed without her, no way.'

'I know that. It's just . . .'

Laura and Elizabeth came back in, Laura heading directly to the oven. 'Can we eat now? I'm starving.'

'Her room's lovely, Anna,' said Elizabeth. To a spot somewhere above Anna's head.

'Och, it was all Laura's designs . . .'

'Yes, but she said you painted it. That can't have been easy.' Elizabeth passed round the plates. 'In your condition.'

'Thank you.'

The crockery was a mix of what Anna had brought from her flat in Shawlands and what Rob had owned before. Soft creams and blues – the stripes were Anna's. The floral must have been Amy's choice, but they all kind of matched. Anna took the chipped plate, three wee bite marks along one side. *Vintage distressed*; you read about it in the house magazines she'd begun to sneak indoors, insinuating themselves amongst the glossy shames of *Good Food* and *Parenting Today*.

'So. What do you make of this new Citicard scheme?' said Liz. 'Have you had your letters in yet?'

'Yeah. Piece of nonsense,' said Rob. 'All that crap about how it'll streamline services, but really, all they're doing is recording our every bloody move: where we go and how we get there, if we've ever had to complain about our bins not being emptied or had hassle with noisy neighbours. Talk about Big Brother.'

'I bet you disagree, eh Anna? Council loyalty cards providing surveillance on the cheap – must be right up your street!'

'Actually, no. I think it's a terrible idea.'

'Really?'

'Absolutely. Thin end of the wedge. Why the hell should some wee lassie in the cooncil know all my business? And if they do extend it to the NHS as well—'

'They won't,' said Rob. 'No way. Laura – what *are* you doing?'

Before she'd even got her plate, Laura had reached across the table, grabbed four battered balls of chicken. Anna opened her mouth to remonstrate as well, Laura opened hers, stuffing two balls into each cheek until she resembled an angry hamster. Like a curve-ball, Anna's words changed direction. Their velocity evaporated, and she started laughing.

'It's the amazing expanding rodent-girl!'

First Anna, then Rob laughing, then Laura, spraying masticated chicken down her front. Elizabeth was there too, of course, and she was laughing as well, but she was their audience, there for them to perform to.

'Chipmunk Laura!' Rob puffed up his face, then hit his cheeks. The air expelled in a pop.

'Shut up, Dad!'

'Oh, God, yes,' laughed Anna. 'Do you remember Disney, Laura? Remember Chip'n'Dale and you screaming about their teeth? That they were going to eat you—'

'Oh, oh,' Rob waved his fork, 'and then you tripped over Chip's tail! Mind?'

More chicken flew from Laura's overstuffed mouth.

'You lot are mad.' Elizabeth shook her head, her smile vague and floating.

They were just doing the same mundane things, enacting the same tired quibbles and the same silly jokes they always did, but Elizabeth being here changed the dimension, reflecting them through a different light, this lilac, laughing light that lay behind the curtains. In Elizabeth's eyes, Anna saw her family defined, and felt happy. Then she felt small and mean. There was always room for more.

'More rice, Liz?'

'No, I won't, thanks.'

Anna helped herself, budging up the prawn crackers to make more space.

''Scuse me, ladies.' Rob pushed his chair back. 'I'm just nipping to the loo. Save me some rice, gorgeous.'

'No, I was saying to Rob on the way over,' Elizabeth poured herself some more wine, 'it must be so liberating not to have to worry about your waist. Has the doctor said how much weight you should be putting on?'

'No. Why?'

'It's just . . . well, it's going to be awful hard to lose it at the other end.'

Anna dropped her spoon into the dish of rice. It struck the concave gap her digging had left, metallic crack on ceramic glaze. A starter's pistol.

'For fucksake Liz. Will you give it a bloody rest? I'm fat because I'm pregnant. I have a full-grown otter leaping in my stomach, ankles that would do an elephant proud and the biggest, most pendulous tits I have ever had – or am likely to have again – in my life. Plus I could fart for Scotland, the amount of wind bagged up inside me. So cut me some slack, eh? Two spoonfuls of rice is hardly going to make much difference.'

Elizabeth sniffed, wiped her mouth with her napkin. 'I was only saying. And I really don't think there's any need to swear like that in front of my niece. You're not at your work now, you know.'

'No, I'm in my house. My own house, Liz, and Laura is my daughter—'

'No she's not. She's not even your stepdaughter. But I *am* her aunt, and I won't have you using profanities—'

Anna hit the table. 'Where do you get off, you sanctimonious cow?'

'Stop it!' screamed Laura. 'Just stop it!' She ran from the room; Anna could hear her feet pounding on the stairs. Liz got up to follow her, Anna too. Both hit the doorway at the same instant, Anna winning the advantage on account of her girth.

'*I'll* deal with it, Liz.'

'Don't worry, I'm leaving anyway. I'm not going to stay and get cursed at by you.'

'You do that, doll.'

'Hey, what's going on?' Rob emerged from the downstairs loo, still buckling his belt.

'Oh, SuperLiz'll fill you in, *Robster.*'

Anna went up to Laura's room. There was no point in knocking; it would only be ignored.

'Laura.'

'*Go* away.' Her head was under her pillow.

'No. And you can't make me. Not even you would push a pregnant woman down the stairs.'

Anna lowered herself on to the edge of the bed. The displacement of Laura's sharp-angled legs was exaggerated, deliberate.

'Plus, all this stress is making me want to pee, so if you're about to kick me, I'll probably wet my pants.'

One eye keeked out.

'Just leave me alone.'

'Can't do that, Laura. You know me. I'm like a dug with a bone.'

And then the sobs started. Terrible, tremulous ebbs and flows of grief.

'I miss Donna,' she cried. 'And I *hate* your stupid cat.' Her face twisted, then disappeared again into the folds of her duvet. Anna's hand went out, cupped the air above Laura's shivering knees, fingers open and yearning to caress. Her stepdaughter, weeping in a cat-shaped curl. Touch and she might yield to loving pressure. Or might arch, and turn, and bite.

Well then. Anna would deserve it.

She laid her hand on Laura's leg, feeling the sobs beat and pass from Laura's skin to hers. Laura didn't move. Anna's other hand rested in its common place, on the bridge of her belly where a smooth, spherical hardness of head or haunch would surface regularly, like a porpoise coming up for air. At night, when she couldn't sleep, Anna would trace her baby's movements, darting in shoals and dips. Would know the big curves from the little dents, the knobs and ripples that pulled and poked and nudged out her flesh. And she would be amazed.

'Talk to me Laura-lee.'

'Go away.'

'It's not just Donna, is it? There's your new hairdo—'

'Isnota *do*!'

'And you've been a wee bit touchy lately—'

'You're one to talk.'

'True. But we're talking about you just now, aren't we?' She stroked hot hair away from Laura's brow. 'What's his name?'

Laura bolted upright. 'What?'

'I just wondered if there was a boy on the scene . . .'

'Oh, for God's sake.' She shrank down again, even tighter-curled than before.

'But is there?' Anna persisted. 'You know, it's fine to like a boy. Or a girl . . . But is it a boy?'

Shoulders shaking until a strangulated '*Yes*' emerged.

'Oh, pet lamb. And does he like you back?'

'No . . . yes, I thought he did. He's always carrying on with me in the class, and he's been asking me to dance all the time at PE.'

Practising the Dashing White Sergeant and the Gay Gordons for the Christmas Dance was a rite of passage for all Scots school kids. Anna remembered well the indignity of waiting, lined up against the wall bars in the gym, while the boys on the other side of the hall eyed up who they might pick.

'Well, that's good.'

'But then . . . but then he asked Tanya Graham to get off with him at the wee . . .' the tears began once more, 'at the weekend. And I feel . . . I feel . . .'

'You feel like you just want to die, don't you?'

'Uh-huh. I *do*. I really like him.'

'Ssh.' She drew her stepdaughter into her arms, began to rock her. 'I know you do . . . Look, I'll let you into a secret. Before I met your dad, there was this boy I really, really liked.'

'Did you love him?'

She considered the question for a moment. 'Yeah. I did. I loved him very much. I loved him that way that you think your heart is going to burst out of your chest when he comes into the room.'

'And you get all stupid and your face goes red?'

'Exactly.'

'So what happened?'

'Oh, we went out for a while.'

Mouth slowing as her brain revved up, flooding with colours and the flash-flash of intermittent memories. Wandering down them, trying them on for size; it was a nice meander. Her eyes anchored on the mundane boxiness of Laura's bookshelf.

'In fact, that's my old dictionary you've got there, isn't it? Wait till I show you this. But you've got to promise never to tell your father, okay?'

'Okay.'

Anna pushed herself half off the bed, reached over to the bookshelf. As she bounced back down on the mattress, Laura wobbled too.

'Whoa,' said Anna, unable to balance herself on the uneven surface. 'Watch out for the shock-waves.' She opened the dictionary at the back. 'I won this at police college, for coming top in all the exams.'

'Yeah?'

'Uh-huh. I'm actually quite clever you know. Anyway, look.' She opened out the fly-leaf. It had been so long since Anna looked at it that she wondered if it was still there. But it was. A pen-and-ink sketch of a thin-faced girl gazing through a window. She and Jamie had been fighting; she was in the huff, ignoring him, and he'd drawn it in just a few quick strokes. Underneath was written: *I love you, Anna Smart-Arse*, and a single, swirly J.

'He drew that for me.'

'Wow. That's really good. He must have loved you too, then.'

'Yeah, I thought so. But it turned out he didn't – he went off with someone else, just like . . . ?'

'Ross.'

'*Ross*. And d'you know what – I'm glad that he did.'

'How?'

'Because if he hadn't, then I wouldn't have met your dad. And I'll tell you this, Laura-lee, there's two types of love. There's all that flashy fireworks stuff – lots of bright light that looks like it might take you to heaven – and there's the type that . . . well, you know that feeling when you get into a warm bath and the heat just soaks up right inside you? That's the best kind.'

'Is that what you and Dad are like?'

She kissed Laura's head. 'Mm-hm.'

'But what if I never get that? What if . . . but I *can't* not be with him. And I *hate* Tanya Graham.' Her face buried into Anna's breast. 'It really hurts.'

'I know, baby. I know.'

'Anna!' yelled Rob from downstairs.

'What?'

'That's Liz away.'

'Just a minute,' she called back. 'Hey you.' She ran her hand along Laura's shin, against the grain of stubby hairs. Wee soul must have started shaving. Anna could have bought her Immac or Ladyshave or something. If she'd said.

'You coming down to say goodbye to your auntie?'

Laura shrugged.

'Please?'

'Don't feel like it.'

'Och, c'mon. She's got her coat on.'

Laura's lip was trembling.

'Oh, come on, darling. I'm so sorry. I'm sorry about Ross and I'm sorry I was horrible to you earlier. I hate it when we fight.'

'So do I.'

'And I'm sorry I shouted at your Auntie Liz.'

'Did you tell her that?'

'Eh . . . no. But I will. I promise.'

'Good.'

'So will you come down then?'

Laura shook her head, a timid gesture, like a little shrew.

'Why not?'

'Because you'll get upset.'

'*I'll* get upset? No I won't, don't be daft.'

'But you *do*. You hate my Auntie Liz, I know you do. And you're always watching me when she's here.'

'Oh Laura.'

Anna drew the child who was not a child back into her arms, warm wavy head beneath her chin. Stroking coarse hair, the sunshine scarlet that had been rinsed brown, that did not suit her at all. The colour was too harsh for Laura's chalky skin. It made her look older, drawn. Just like the girl who came to Anna's office today.

No.

Who had stood by the window, refused a chair, and let the stark dull light illuminate her face.

Who had let her mouth drop open and begun to tell her tale of old hurts and threatened revenge, and the bogeyman coming to get you.

But that girl was a ghost. An icy, distant past. And ghosts are not real.

This, this scratchy dye-plumped hair grazing her chin, was real. Anna had enough to be dealing with here.

This morning it had been sunny. It was sunny and Anna was full of joy. She had a man she loved, a teenage daughter and a baby on the way. She was blessed beyond everything she'd ever hoped for. For once in nearly four decades she had stopped fretting about the 'ah, but' always guaranteed to befall her. No more; she was making up for lost time. Each day was perfect enough. To focus on the day ahead, enjoy the day she was in, that was all she needed.

That girl in her office today had been frightened; she had garbled out her fears. *Her* fears. They were not Anna's, never Anna's. Lost time could not come back and bite you: it was gone. You deal with the now, then you move on, confident you've done your best. That's what Anna was going to do.

She would kiss her daughter's tear-blotched face, then go down and plead insanity to Liz, be rewarded with another smirk. As far as that girl in her office was concerned, Anna would do nothing. It would not be her future that was frozen, but her past. It would seal itself like ice. Transparent so the world went on about her, and she in it.

And she would not, would never, consider how the ice might already be melting.

Chapter Eleven

Joe finished eating his sandwich. He liked this quiet part at the end of his shift, when it was just you and the dark and the shielded-off safety of your cabin. All the punters gone away. Mum-made and predictable, Monday night was Cheddar cheese. The texture of lithium was the same as cheese. That's what the teacher had said this morning; that's what had started it all.

If he let it, the shaking might begin again. He made himself think of chewing, just his jaws and his chin, his teeth just working on the pappy white bread. The smell of burned cloth still clung to him, despite the accumulations of fag-breath and booze and cheap perfumes and sweat that coated him as his shift progressed.

Science was about *proof*, you see, and the teacher wasn't letting them prove that; was insisting that they all stand back, that nobody could touch it, only him, and even then, with neat tongs and a little steel knife, cutting through the greyness and going: *See?*

Joe could not see, not properly. They were in sixth year, they weren't kids. He had wanted to feel the substance in his fingers, to squeeze the small grey lump and see what kind of cheese it felt like. Was it feta which crumbles, or the rubber-bounce of mozzarella? Squeaky, sweaty Cheddar? What? 'Cheese' was not specific.

'Any moisture at all, even the dampness from my hands, will cause lithium to react.' The teacher laid down his knife. 'Now, if you could all stand back a little more . . .'

If Joe had stood any further back he'd be out of the lab entirely. But more than that, he was not content to stand back. He was always at the back, he wanted to see this, to have heat on his face and confirmation of the texture. Was it layered or porous?

How bright would it flame? They had done magnesium, loads of times, that painful, blue, instant flash, but *this* stuff burned. The sense of theatre was immaculate; the teacher had arranged it like Communion. Slowly, ponderously, he had taken the dark brown bottle from inside a plastic box, had poured the oil from the bottle and extracted the element from within. A glass cup of water waited, a small dropper resting inside.

Just at the point where Mr Gilroy was lifting the dropper, the classroom door opened, and a wee first year squeaked:

'Please sir. Mrs Humphries says you've to remind everyone who hasn't that they've to hand in their Citicard forms into the office today, by four o'clock today.'

'And did she furnish you with that grammatically painful message herself, Alasdair?'

'Sorry sir?'

'Was that it verbatim, or did you choose to embellish it yourself?'

The child looked utterly confused. Gilroy waved a weary hand. 'Och, off you go, sonny. And knock next time you come into my classroom,' he bawled as an afterthought, picking up his discarded dropper at the same time. 'Right. Got that? Anyone not in possession of a completed Citicard form by four this afternoon will be lined up against the gymnasium wall and shot.'

'Police state or what?' muttered Ali.

'No, I heard you got free swimming.'

'Can you say no?'

'Bloody right you can,' said Patrick. 'It's a total invasion of your privacy—'

'Quieten down now people.'

'Check out Rambo's nips,' whispered Doug. 'No way was that bra built to handle her.'

Joe saw Doug bump against Lorna Ramsay, purposely shoving her nearer to the teacher's workbench.

'Beat it, you,' she squealed.

'Right guys, that's enough!'

'It's the dilithium crystals, Captain. They canna handle it!'

An utter void of sound. The dull silence of after-blast.

Joe realised these last words had come from him, that he had bawled them out and that the entire class, in unison, had swivelled to face him.

Mr Gilroy clinked the dropper against the side of the beaker. 'Joseph Grier. We are not at some Star Trek convention now.'

That was what fractured the shock, caused his classmates to laugh. Why had they not laughed at what Joe said? It was funny. If Doug had said it, or Patrick, everyone would have laughed.

'Kindly leave my classroom, please.'

Gilroy had liked that they had laughed at his joke. You could tell from the way his posture altered, he was more upright and generous with his gestures. A languid arm stretched to indicate where the door was. Gilroy was playing to the mood of crowd, a big, lanky jester.

'No.' Again, the offering of words, of resistance that felt alien. 'I haven't done anything wrong.'

He heard a female voice say: 'Klingon.'

'Are you arguing with me, boy? Away into the corridor and ask Scotty to beam you up.'

'But I want to see the experiment.'

'Then you shouldn't behave like a moron.'

'Aye, *Slowjo*,' said a male voice. Then another, and another, taking up the chant.

Slowjo! Slowjo! On you go, Slowjo!

There was a smell of gas. He could see Doug, making wanking signs, his arm behind a bench, below the teacher's line of vision, people milling, chanting.

'Shit, man!'

Patrick's face by his, his hand striking Joe on the arm. 'Shit – Mr Gilroy. Look at his arm!'

The gas smelled sour and hot. Joe raised his arm, saw gold and orange and a pale tick of blue eating up the green.

'My blazer's on fire. *Sir*. My blazer is on fire.'

Then Patrick was rolling him on the ground, it was all feet and grey tights and trousers flash-flash-flash and perhaps his head hit the wooden leg of the trestle once, and then it was fine. He was in the medical room and Patrick was handing him a cup of water.

'You sure you're okay?'

Joe glanced at his arm. His blazer, lying beside him, had taken the worst of it, but his jumper, shirt, skin smelled funny too. 'Yep. No harm done. The mother ship must've put up a defensive shield.' He tried to smile, but his lips were numb, just numb and rubbery like mozzarella.

'You know it was a Bunsen burner? Gilroy's making out you did it yourself.'

'But I didn't.'

The water was nice and cool; Patrick must have gone and got it out of the water dispenser, not from the tap in here. Just gone and got it for him.

'You know, you don't have to take this shit, Joe.'

'What do you mean?' He noticed the water ripple; his hand, the hand holding the cup, was jittering of its own volition. It would seem he could no longer control his own words *or* movement.

'You could just leave.'

'Leave?'

'Yeah, leave. Christ, you're a total brainbox, you got six As in your Highers – why you even doing a sixth year anyway?'

Joe winced as the water from his cup splashed on to his arm. Someone had rolled up his sleeve; it was just bare flesh and it was fine, it didn't hurt, but it was like his body was primed ready to feel the hurt anyway. He looked away. 'I don't know,' he said.

'D'you not want to go to uni?'

'I don't know. I don't know what I'd study.'

'Jesus, you could study anything man. What about maths? You're ace at that. Or history? You won that essay prize last year, didn't you?'

'That's right. *The Dear Green Place.*'

'Well, there you go? Why not go and become an Oxford don and write the definitive history of Glasgow. Christ, O'Dowd said you knew more about the city than he did.'

Oxford was 360 miles away, Joe had looked it up on Autoroute. His mother, too, had suggested it after his Higher results came in.

Talking of the self-contained colleges and how he could meet new people but that it would still be like a home from home. Nobody looked out of place there, she said. There was a mellowness that soaked into your joints, made them swing. Mum and Uncle Euan had gone there as teenagers, to visit a friend, and she'd loved it.

And Joe had wondered at the fact that Oxford was almost as far from Glasgow as you could get and still be on the same island. That would be some drive, all the way down there. Especially if it was raining. Yes, he would love that; him streaming past the world, alone in his big tin box with a mass of clear chainmail cascading on the windscreen. The best thing ever was driving in the rain. Patterns of water running silver races, and you, swiping windscreen wipers and seeing it all come back again. Rain was resilient.

The stupid thing was, everyone talked of going 'up' to Oxford – which was plainly wrong. It was patronising, in the same way it was patronising when newsreaders referred to 'The North', when they meant somewhere like Newcastle, which was very firmly south; as if nothing existed beyond Hadrian's Wall.

Joe's belly was tight; there was an energy there that tingled.

'Maybe I could help *you*,' he said.

'What?'

'You said you were a nationalist. That day, when the guys were talking about Glasgow Airport. They called you Braveheart.'

'So?'

It was enough the way he said it; he didn't need to bunch his nose and mouth up like that. Face concentrating into a caricature: the Mask of Tragedy, hanging in the drama studio. Joe wanted to say, *Aye alright, pal. You've made your point*, thereby making *his* point about the obviousness with which Patrick was closing himself off – did folk think he didn't *see* these things? – but still, he drove on. It would make him more uncomfortable to stop. It would be like constipation.

'You need to know history to be a nationalist. Maybe I could help you? I could write leaflets and stuff. I mean, people don't know anything about the history of their own nation. We think we're a crap wee country, but folk just don't know, do they? They don't know that we were never conquered, that it was a Scottish king who joined with England, or that we invented the phone and the television, or about the Enlightenment. Or – I know! We could start off by burning our Citicard forms, and get the papers to come and—'

'Aye, alright Joe. Chillax.'

Patrick was fully gone now, his body drawn up into itself, one hand on the doorknob and his expression a mix of desperate and bored. Joe knew he had lost it, all the vestiges of Patrick's sympathy, just by offering some help. How was that fair?

'Could I come to one of your meetings, though? Do you go to meetings; do they plan stuff like campaigns?'

'Aye, well, no really. I've been at an SNP social once. But seriously, Joe, why don't you just leave?'

'Leave school?' he echoed. 'You think I should?'

Patrick shrugged. 'I dunno. Surprise us all.' He allowed Joe a final smile, was in the mood, once more, for concession, seeing as he had already opened the door and could smell the sweet escape of school dinners. Tomato and garlic. It would be bolognese. 'I'd better go.'

Bolognese. Again. Joe, looking at his feet, just looking at his feet and the blackened-lace sleeve of his blazer. It had made him late for work.

Chapter Twelve

The water lapped reed-spiked earth. A dark curve as a cormorant slid by; its long black body languid, there was no discernible movement save for the regal swivel of its neck, yet underneath that water, frantic yellow legs would be going like the clappers, pistoning and pumping to maintain a sure slow progress.

A bit like him. Alex picked up a stone, turned it two times, three times until he had the feel for it. The stone matched the water, flat and smooth. He waited for the bird to drift away, drawn by the water's flow, then, when it had sailed out of sight, he skimmed the stone across the canal. Two bounces and a stutter, before it sank with a sad wee *ploop*. The post mortem was being held this morning, for that girl they had found last night, but Alex didn't have to be there. Any two stalwart representatives of Strathclyde's finest would do, and he didn't understand the alacrity, the hunger almost, that some of his colleagues displayed to fulfil this duty.

He had no desire to be there at all. Why would anyone go there if you didn't have to? Standing in a cold silver room, shallow-breathing into your collar as unobtrusively as you can. The squeak of wheels or the clang of a drawer as the body is rolled out, the camera switched on. They weigh it and they scrutinise it, examining for the tiniest wounds, the presence of hairs or fibres or specks. They are like Aslan's fastidious mice, pouring over the corpse with nibbling, careful teeth. Then they clip its extremities, swab all its holes, noting, always noting, every lesion, nick and blue-blooded patch.

And then the fun begins.

Out with the saw. *Shzzrr. Shzzrr.* The pathologist never really revs it like a manic lumberjack, but Alex is ever-hopeful that he will. *That* way, it would break the ice, would slice through the thick, anticipatory air that hangs like sea haar in a mortuary until the moment they slice through the breastbone and start cracking out spare ribs.

He picked up another stone. No, Ian Morrison had gone to the post mortem, along with Lesley Sneddon, whom Shirley had just dubbed 'Jigsaw'. *After that last bloody performance at the Sheriff? No way, Alex, no way do I want her giving evidence for anything I'm involved in again. She's a fucking jigsaw, so she is.*

Alex had laughed at Shirley's pain-filled face. *A what?*

A jigsaw. As in: she aye goes to pieces in the box?

They didn't have any name yet for the girl who was naked and unclaimed.

Alex lobbed the stone; it wasn't a skimmer, this one, just a big hard lump that made a satisfying splash. Round about now, they'd be peeling off her scalp, having sorted her offal into neat, bloody piles. One sharp noise, which is worse than all the rest in its nursery simplicity, you wait for it, tensing, and you don't look but fix on a point to the left or the right and here it comes: the swift crack of chisel. Then the top comes off, neat as an eggshell, and the brain is exposed.

Butchered and bagged, and they didn't know her name. He watched the concentric water-rings flowering out, travelling wider and wider until they simply disappeared. Even in daytime, the water was ink-thick impenetrable. Like baleful eyes in a face that rarely spoke, a head that would not let you in.

Alex carried on along the canal bank, a can of Coke in one hand, Dictaphone in the other. Scenes of Crime were still working round the locus, but already his scope was moving out from there. If the girl hadn't arrived at the scene by vehicle or boat, then she must have come on foot. And if she'd come on foot, the chances were that she'd been alive. The old towpath was narrow, the water deep – you wouldn't heft a body along here. Plus there were too many possibilities for being seen. Although the Forth and Clyde was a glorious vein of nature, it didn't flow in splendid isolation. Dotted all along its banks were flats, factories, or luxury homes like these ones right here; a little enclave of what looked like posh wood cabins. Closer up, you could see they were really solid houses, clad in that cunning timber effect that would fade to pale silver over time. Alex's sister was an architect now, she used that kind of stuff all the time: *modern lines with an eco-twist.*

A woman's hand twitched one of the full, thick curtains framing the patio door. She was spying on him spying on her pots of dull-burning autumn flowers that lined her lush garden by the water. Alex looked away. Who'd have thought it, up here in the skies above Maryhill? Barbecues on wooden decking, and cormorants floating by.

He took a swig of Coke, hoping the sugar would jettison some energy, spark some sharp-witted perception that would lift him up and give him wings and let him see the whole long dark undulation from above. Alex hadn't slept much last night. Part of him was expecting to be called back out anyway. But most of his fitful dozes had been interrupted by a carousel of things he should be doing, had done, had he done them right, should he do them tomorrow?, getting faster and faster and impinging on his chest. He was no longer a cop or a sergeant who could feed in and take out only those chunks of an investigation that he thought he could manage, offloading or dyking the tricky, dirty, boring bits on to someone else. His wage slip said he was a detective inspector, and his colleagues said he was a boy.

As he walked, Alex's head constantly swivelled, searching for clothing or a phone, fresh, uncrushed litter, even, that might stand out like spoor. A little further along, heading back in the direction of the office, the path became a grid-iron bridge, which stretched hugely over the busy road below. The buzz and rev of traffic had been echoing this change of pace for some minutes; his ears had been aware of this, but his brain had not quite registered it. When you couldn't see an actual 'thing', Alex found – when the fact of it was not evident or spelled out to you, and it was not your work, so you didn't have to be always scraping back the veneers – then 'things' were quite easy to ignore.

The 'thing' from this morning, for example, when he'd got up quietly, made himself a coffee, gone into the lounge with the paper and an empty, dull head. Heard the grimness of the tap being rattled, the water run, the kettle reboiled as Sandra came down five minutes later and made her own, and never once said anything. They had eaten their breakfast, her sniffing, him reading, her eventually saying, 'So what time did you get in last night?' and him rippling his paper, then answering, 'Late.' Then that was them done, the requisite motions gone through and her sad dark eyes had repositioned themselves somewhere to the left of him. But it was grim all the same. It was a *thing*.

To Alex's left, the grimy stone of Gairbraid Church towered on its hill above the road, almost on the level with the bridge and canal that had come after it, its centuries-old walls wrapping arms round ancient graves. Alex drained the last of his Coke, shaking metallic dregs on to his tongue. Bet that was a bummer, thinking you've been laid to rest in the perfect elegy of a country churchyard, then discovering you're actually keeping watch over the A81. At least they hadn't been dug up and repositioned, not like some of the graves in that war book he was reading. He wished the writer hadn't done that, added a coda at the end about what had become of some of the boys he'd been reading about. How the powers-that-be had waited a considerate period of time, then shifted whole grave-pits in industrial clods, to make way for essentials like *hypermarché* car parks.

When you move a body from the locus of a crime, everything has to stay intact, so it arrives at the mortuary exactly how it left the scene. Until the post mortem has examined every millimetre of skin, that body is sacrosanct. It's a reverent, fleeting courtesy, one that is mocked by the untrammelled invasion of what has gone before, and that does not really mediate the forensic disassembly that comes after. But once that is over, once they've put all your bits back together and quick-stitched you up, then they can poke freely at your teeth, check dental records against fillings. Pinch some fingerprints, swipe your DNA. Put all these things in the cocktail shaker and see what colours pour out. The girl was only in her twenties, but, at some time, Alex hoped, one part of her or another would have had a history.

It was growing quieter again, as the canal wound down to Maryhill Locks. The noise of the road was fading, or his ears were tuning it out, but either way, he relaxed a little; feeling the swing of his arms, one slightly unbalanced by the gripping of his empty can, feeling the swivel of his head and the steady progress of his feet through damp, dying grass. As the canal spread itself into the waiting basins of the locks, he slowed. It felt like a hiatus here, a scoop out of time. The water falling in steps and stairs, Nature and Man edging one in front of the other, and back again. The wee gates on the top of the locks were painted like sergeant's stripes, quite cheerful in their stern, smiley lines. A weird place, this. On the one side of the canal you had a valley, with perspective and easy hills. The other was truncated by Maryhill Road and the squat cubes of mediocre buildings.

Alex sat on the edge of one of the lock gates. There was a lock-keeper's cottage that looked as if it was still occupied; it had newish windows and a black wheelie bin outside. He pushed his legs straight, let his feet slide across the grass as his calf muscles tightened and his back eased off. He'd need to get back to the five-a-sides soon; he loved that feeling when your muscles were hard and ready. Stretched again, a slight resistance at his feet. A mass that was not grass – it had better not be dogshit. He withdrew his feet, checked them for muck. Looked down at the ground and saw a splash of crimson fabric, a sweatshirt that was still bright. He picked it up, sniffed. He had smelled shit, but it was horse muck, he knew that as soon as he breathed it in and started sneezing. Alex was allergic to horses.

The sweatshirt had not been lying there long, the dirt on it was clean, if that made sense. He turned it over. It was from Gap. It was a woman's.

It was, perhaps, a start.

Chapter Thirteen

No way was she having it. No way. It didn't matter how much Calder Riggs was worth. You couldn't terrorise people like that, not over some piece of land. Not over anything.

Mary took a bite of croissant, swilled the coffee round her mouth. She hadn't gone home last night. There was no one clear reason; part of her thought the man might follow her there, or be waiting for her – he knew that's where she lived. Part of her just didn't want to be swaddled in walls and duvets. And part of her wanted to spite Bernie. She wanted her to fret, wanted to see if she came looking. But she hadn't even phoned. Mary had checked her mobile, many times, as she had stoated round the city, eschewing dark corners for riotous lights and noise. Train stations were busy places, so she hung about Central for a while; then there was Burger King, and that pub near the Barras that served nightshift workers. When all else failed, there was the basement door which opened out to reveal a hot, bright night-kitchen. But Mary had only stayed there as long as it took to drink a bowl of soup; it was always full of grotty alkies, and Christians trying to convert you. Then she had wandered towards Queen Street and Glasgow's second train station. Found an early opening bakery, got herself breakfast. Mary had managed; she had not forgotten the niches and warm vents concealed in Glasgow's nightgown. Mary had been fine. Mary had been many things, before Bernie rescued her.

She brushed the last of the crumbs from her breasts and dropped the paper cup in the bin. The city had her morning face on now, night-wrinkles smoothed into colours of bustling businessfolk; students struggling with an early rise and the trauchle up the hill to uni; hopeful tourists in windcheaters and cropped trousers; private school kids wearing expensive blazers; council workers watering hanging baskets of burnished flowers or making clean sweeps in their motorised buggies, their wide, fat brushes swishing all the night's debris under Glasgow's carpet. In a city, so they said, you were never more than six feet away from a rat.

What now? From the station, a tannoy-twang announced that the nine-oh-twelve was off to somewhere indecipherable. That sounded like a nice place to go. She could just say *bugger them all*, and jump on the next train out of Glasgow. That would serve them all right.

A woman in a fitted suit clipped past, document case under one arm, a cone of rolled-up parchment protruding from the crook of her elbow below. On the other side, nearest to Mary, her cheek and ear were clamped to a mobile – *ya, we're submitting the plans right now*. Pale nails caught a wisp of hair, tucked it behind phone and ruby-studded ear. Mary glanced down at her own dirty, horse-stained jeans.

This is not who you are.

Mary could never walk away from Bernie; Bernie had never walked away from her. Alright, she'd had a wee flakey, roughed her up a bit, but that only showed how much Bernie cared, how passionate she was – and how scared she was about losing Calder Riggs. What hold did that man have over her? All the wide-awake night, Mary had struggled to think of what she could do to stymie him and regain Bernie's favour, a magnificent masterstroke that would see her ride home triumphant, having saved the day. With ticker tape and bunting, and a banquet in the upper field. Of course, a wimple would be best, with a mediaeval drop-waisted dress . . .

The woman who had passed her was making her way into the City Chambers on the east of the square. She was so elegant – her red shoes matched her earrings. Two bright slashes clipping up the stairs, past a straggle of folk with placards, who moved respectfully to let her past. People should not be ranked according to their clothes, but they were. She'd thought that often, usually as she was mentally disparaging a cream-clad riding mum in Ugg boots and shades. Yet she would still stop sluicing or brushing to let them pass splat-free. The woman's bum wiggled as she negotiated briefcase, plans and the revolving City Chambers door, and one of the placard-men rushed over to help. His placard dipped as he leaned over to push the door.

No to ID Cards on the Cheap!!

The writing was sloped and urgent, scarlet as the woman's shoes. A final flash of red, imprinting itself on Mary's retina. Her body felt light, surprised at itself. Yes, yes, yes! Why had she been so slow? A wee bit of hustle; of course she could do that. She grew more excited, creating the narrative in her head. *The woman entered the portals of local government, lips primed with bubbles of eloquence, her cashmere trench coat drawn tightly against the bitter chill of the approaching winter. An official rose to his feet as she presented a lengthy petition . . .*

But not – Mary wiped a crust of dried mud from her kneecap – looking like this.

If she could kid on she was some kind of official . . . She tried to recall her father's preparation, how he would sit at the kitchen table, spread his papers out and pick up the phone. As his career had slid – due in part, as he never stopped bitching, to Mary and her 'problems' (although in truth it was a chicken and egg of drink and disappointments to which he was a fair old contributor himself) but, anyway – as his legal light had dimmed, Dad had taken on any old crap. And he'd definitely advised on a few 'fight the mobile masts' campaigns. This wasn't much different, surely? Was Mary a competent objector, someone who could legitimately lodge her protest against building on Calder Riggs land? Who could protest, again? Neighbours, community council – the Church kept nudging at her too, or was that licensing law? She could say she was a community representative at least, or something about kids. Disabled kids, and how they needed the equestrian centre for therapeutic purposes. Threaten the council with the press as well – her dad had always used that tactic, although usually with an unnecessary degree of belligerence after his legalese had failed him and he was worried about not getting paid.

Legs all bouncy with caffeine and fine ideas, Mary turned into Ingram Street, where several upmarket clothes shops populated the ground floor of what used to be the main Post Office building. That forgotten, delicious anticipation was fully roused, her head ten leaps ahead of her body. It felt like she was waking up after a long, unsatisfying sleep. First things first. What, where and how? Oh but she could, she could do this and win Bernadette back. It was a busy street, full of buses and commuting cars. Across the road, through the gaps in the traffic, Mary could see another designer store, this one housed in a splendid old bank, with stone lintels and curlicues and crests abounding. A lorry, hazards flashing, was parked half on the kerb outside the store, and she could see the driver climbing out of the cab, a Range Rover tooting at his backside as it swerved past. Carefully, Mary bundled up her jacket, pushed it, and her rucksack, behind the open storm-door of the office block she was standing beside. Then she strode towards the lorry, approaching it from the far side, so it would seem as if she was looking for the driver, who was now pressing on the service bell of the shop.

'Excuse me,' she called. 'Is that our delivery?'

'Aye, hen.' He came away from the door, over to where Mary stood. 'I'll need to be sharp though; they traffic wardens are out in force this morning.'

'I know,' she said. 'I just came from round the back – we've opened up there so you can bring the gear straight in. Want me to give you a hand?'

The driver breathed out heavily. 'Christ on a bike. That's a new one. You lot are aye telling me to bring it in the front.'

Mary proffered a sympathetic smile, all the while watching to see if anyone was coming out from the shop. 'New manager,' she shrugged. 'If you just open up the back we can take a load each, eh?'

The man hurried to the rear of his lorry. 'Och, you're some lassie, so you are. Most of that lot in there are far too stuck-up tae get their hands dirty.' A *scrwush* as the metal shutter rolled up, then a grunting heave and he was up inside the lorry. Mary's eyes swept over the interior. She could see bales of pale woollens cased in bubble-wrap, and a row of dark suits on rails, each one hung inside a polythene sheath.

'These all ours?' she asked.

'Aye. You're my last drop-off.'

'Okay – hand me down a bunch of those suits.'

'Right you are.' He scraped all the coat hangers together, bundled them over his arm until the pile was so high that he could barely see. He leaned forward, blindly offering his armfuls. 'Got them?'

Mary stretched up, panting as the weight of the fabric began to fall into her arms. 'Yup. Oh, shit,' she shouted, 'that's the wardens back. You'd better move – they've already done two lorries here this morning.'

'*For fucksake*,' buried under his breath. 'Sorry, hen – it's no your fault.'

'Look . . .' She dropped some of the suits back on to the floor of the lorry. 'I can't manage all of these. You just nip round the block and I'll take what I can carry in; then I'll come back out for the next lot. Oh, quick,' Mary off-loaded another pile of suits, this time returning them to the panicking driver's arms. 'It's that big hefty one. You canny argue with her.' She extricated one hand from under her prize, banged the side of his lorry. 'See you in five.'

She reckoned she had about thirty seconds before he would have put down the suits, jumped to the ground, pulled down the roller shutter and realised there were no wardens at all. Between the old stone bank building that was now the shop and the old stone High Court building that was now a pub, a narrow lane slid quietly from the hubbub. Mary knew it well; it dog-legged round and down to Virginia Street, another forgotten backwater, with few occupied buildings, and fewer visitors. It was to this lane that she walked, briskly at first – because it could just be, to the casual observer, that this was indeed where the rear entrance was, and experience had taught her that the less suspicious you acted, the better – and then – when the pummelling in her chest got too much, for by God she was out of practice – running. Three sprints in two days, not good; not bloody good at all, the five or six suits she carried were bouncing against her chin. Halfway down Virginia Street, nobody around; she slowed again, flicking through the collars inside each wad of slippy plastic.

Size 8; Size 8; Size 8.

Shit. Trust her to have stolen all the skinny-midget selection.

Size 10; Size 10; Size 12.

That was the one. She let the others slide to the ground, kicked them in to the shade of a doorstep and kept walking, shrugging the jacket over her T-shirt. The T-shirt was red, the jacket a dark, charcoal grey. It looked fine, buttoned up; these buttons were too wee, her thick fingers slipping, trembling; she felt exhausted, and exhilarated. And free. They charged extortionate prices in these shops anyway. This wasn't theft, it was merely redistribution of wealth.

To her left was a broad, empty loading bay for a nearby department store. She nicked into it, unzipping her jeans, peeling them over her dirty boots, ach, boots – whoever looked at them? She could swish them in a puddle. One leg hopping, one leg bent up, and her jeans were off. A boot came with them, all scrunched in puckered denim; she let it fall. Ripped off more plastic, pulled on her new, grey-wool trousers. Tight, tight, *breathe in.* Oh. They fastened; just, but she left the zip part undone. Tugged the jacket down. Perfect: the jacket covered a multitude of sins. She shook out her discarded jeans until the boot dropped out, stuffed her wet foot back inside. Then stiffened, as a round of applause broke out from a window up above.

'Nice arse, doll. Do we get an encore?'

Keep your face turned down. Just walk away. She kept repeating the words as she carried on down the street. Give it five minutes and she could probably go back round the block for her rucksack.

Walk away. Just walk away. *This* is who you are.

Chapter Fourteen

The farm opened out before him, one more surprise gift in the contradictory parcel that was Maryhill. Rolling, abundant green; stables, house and fields, all jolly smoke curls and bales of hay one hundred metres from a housing scheme.

Alex had shouted in for someone to come down to the Locks and bag the sweatshirt. It wasn't as if he carried all the accoutrements in his smart wool Crombie. Almost immediately, the dispatcher had come back, asked if he was still there.

What did the lad think? That Alex had left the jumper lying in a puddle and skipped off? The old Force Control, manned by streetwise cops and experienced comms ops, was gone, had been replaced by call centres full of eager kids with limited nous – and the odd retired cop who could keep them right, when he had a moment. Alex felt suddenly old.

'It's just, if you are,' the boy had said, 'we've a report of a missing person very close to where you are; a female, who would appear to fit the description of last night's Code . . .' He hesitated at the unfamiliar ciphers. 'Eh, the suspicious death? The place is called Calder Riggs Equestrian Centre. Stations are at the locus now.'

And so, at last, was Alex. He'd hitched a lift from the patrol car that came to uplift the sweatshirt, and was currently rocking and bouncing its way back down the pot-holed drive. Another marked car was parked outside the farmhouse; the shift cops who'd been dispatched to take the missing persons report. Excellent. If they really had found their woman already, then that was about three days' work done and dusted. A body with a name, a home and a set of last-known movements was a giant, spiky coat rack with numerous hooks on which could be pegged all manner of illuminating scraps: phone calls, visitors, arguments, diaries, enemies, friends. Mind, the last two were often interchangeable.

In the distance, he could hear a horse neighing. Alex breathed the fresh sharp air, tried to imagine what it would have been like once, when all the lands of Gairbraid had looked like this. No sandy-coloured houses, no Maryhill Road, no massive stone walls of the Barracks – where the ghosts of soldiers marched, and Rudolph Hess had once been held. Just a vista of pure elemental green and brown, and the sound of running water. He breathed in again. The whole farmyard stank of horses, same as the jumper he'd found. This place was indeed a gift.

The front door of the farmhouse was weathered-blue. The details he had were sketchy – a young woman who'd gone out yesterday afternoon and had not yet come home. He smiled at the young cop who opened the door. Mandy? Susie? A cute name, he remembered that; one which suited her elfin features.

'In here, sir.'

She led him through a small, damp lobby, towards the rear of the house, then paused outside a panelled door. An old barometer hung above a Bakelite phone, stationed on a triangle of purpose-built shelf. The barometer insisted there was change ahead. Maybe outside. Inside, though, it didn't look like much had changed in over forty years. The faded trellis wallpaper and the smell of animals and mould reminded Alex of his granny's.

'We've taken all the details already,' said the cop. 'The missing person's name is Bernadette Murphy, she's aged twenty-five, and she runs the riding school here, along with Fiona Cairns.'

'Is that who reported her missing?'

'Yes sir.' She bobbed a dainty head. 'She's in there.'

Mandy. It was definitely Mandy. 'And is someone with Ms Cairns at the moment?'

'My neighbour, Mark. She's pretty upset, sir.'

'You haven't said about the body we found, I take it?'

'No, of course not. But she'd already heard something on the news this morning – I think that's why she phoned us in the first place.'

'And what do you reckon, Mandy?'

The girl's pupils dilated. More dimples at the fact of him knowing her name. Ah, the power, the power. He felt his shirt rub against his chest. Sandra never bloody bobbed at anything.

'Is she "putting it on" upset, or "roaring and greeting" upset?'

'Utterly devastated and trying to hold it together upset, I'd say.'

'So, what is she – Bernadette's sister, her pal?'

'Em, I think she's her partner, sir.'

'*Partner* partner?

'Partner partner.'

He liked this girl. They were talking in knowing shorthand, she was quick and small and pretty. And her perfume was the nicest thing in this moist and grubby hall.

'Oh, but there's another thing you should know – Bernadette's not the only missing person. One of the stable hands didn't come home last night either. A girl called Mary Brown.' She moved a little closer to him. 'Between me and you sir, I think there might be a wee bit of a triangle going on here. Fiona Cairns never even mentioned Mary to me – it was one of the other girls that said. I . . . em, I haven't said anything to Mark yet. I thought you could maybe bring it up with Fiona? You know, see what her response is to the suggestion?'

'You've got a very devious mind, Mandy.'

'Not at all, sir. I didn't want to overreach myself. Thought I'd learn the art of interrogation from a professional.'

Alex leaned against the wedge of table. 'I presume you know we've a vacancy for a CID aide coming up?'

'Really? No, I had no idea.'

The panelled door opened; another cop's head appeared.

'Oh, hullo sir. Thought I heard voices out here.' He dipped his head back inside the door. 'Excuse me a minute, Fiona.' Then he closed the door over, ingratiated himself into the huddle.

'Should we get her down to the mortuary, sir?' he whispered.

'What for?' Alex whispered back.

'To identify the body? I'm positive it'll be the same woman. Long black hair, slight build.'

'You may well be right – Mark?'

The cop nodded.

'Only problem is – what about specialist knowledge? Your woman in there might well be my front-runner suspect. We take her down for a nosey at the body, and then she'll know exactly what lumps, bumps and scars are on it. Then she can either start explaining them away or sending us off on some wild goose chase.'

The cop frowned.

'Look, what I want you to do is get some up-to-date photos of both women.'

'Both women, sir?' said the cop. 'You mean Fiona too?'

'Oh, no. Sorry. Apparently one of the stable hands has gone missing too. A girl called Mary. Amanda here has all the gen.'

A brusque tut from Mandy, then a careful solidifying of her posture.

'So I want you to get me pictures of them both, and some recently worn items of clothing. If all else fails, we can try and get some DNA off their clothes, match it up with the body and see who fits what. Do we have a description for the second girl, Mandy?'

She read from her digital unit, didn't look at him. 'Mid-twenties, medium build. Pasty, thin face – and long black hair.'

'Ooh. The plot thickens.' He winked at her, but she remained aloof. *Och weel.* The Lord giveth and the Lord taketh away. 'Right troops,' he said. 'Go to it.'

Alex watched the easy sway of Mandy's backside as she followed Mark up the stairs. Shame, that. Then he chapped the door in front of him, let himself in.

It was a wee office, barely enough room for the shelves and desk and chair and cabinet to all jostle for their place along one of the whitewashed walls. In the corner of the room, facing the window, a woman occupied the only chair. Her hands were gripping the seat, purple-pressing fingers that seemed to want to push through solid wood.

'Fiona?'

She half turned; was what you would call a handsome woman, loose and rangy, with a strong jaw and raw, pulsing eyes. He felt instantly sorry for her, for the journey on which she was embarking and for the panic and terror and hope that would be lacing her insides. For all her days to come, that would be defined by this day.

If, that was, she was for real.

'Hi there. I'm Detective Inspector Alex Patterson, from Maryhill. I understand that one of your employees didn't return home last night?'

Her voice was barely audible. 'She's not an employee. She's my wife.'

'I see. I'm sorry. I know you've already been asked a whole load of questions by my colleagues, but would you mind if I asked you a few more?'

A lacklustre movement of her shoulders. 'If you want.'

'It would probably be better if we went into the office. My office, I mean.'

'Why?'

Because I want to interview you at length, under controlled conditions, where everything you say will be corroborated and scrutinised, and I don't know you from Adam. Because this is the first time I have been a senior investigating officer and I want to do it slowly, carefully, correctly.

Alex smiled. Sympathetic, open. He had many smiles.

'It just makes things easier. Plus, if there's any news at all, it means you'd be the first to hear it.'

'News? You mean like that body they said they'd found in the canal? That was "news".' The bitterness, the word itself, was barely audible.

'Ms Cairns, at this stage, we have no idea who that person was. What's important to us is that we find out all there is to know about Bernadette, so that we can establish exactly where she might have gone, or who she might be with.' He paused. '*Is* there anyone you think she could be with at the moment?'

'Do you not think it's her then?' There was a desperate wildness in her voice.

'Like I said, until we've had time to have a proper chat about Bernadette, about what's been happening in her life, then it's far too early to say. Now, do you want to grab your coat? It's a bit nippy out there.'

Slowly, she raised herself from the chair. 'Is it cold? I don't think Bernie had a jacket with her.'

'No? When did you last see her then?'

'Yesterday morning. She was working in the yard.'

Alex helped her on with the waxed jacket she was struggling to find an armhole in.

'Remind me. What did she have on then?'

'I . . . I don't remember – a jumper maybe? I told that girl it was her Barbour, but that's hanging up in the stables.'

Briefly, she shut her eyes. 'It was . . . there was definitely her jumper in the pile there too, and it's gone. I got her it.' Opened them again. 'Did she have that on, do you think?'

'I don't know. What colour was the jumper Fiona?'

'No. Not a jumper, I mean a sweatshirt. Just a red sweatshirt. I got her it, you see.'

'Oh, okay. Let's get you in the car.'

He held her arm as they were leaving.

Chapter Fifteen

Mary took the stairs two at a time, a force of nature, a volatile little businesswoman who knew what she wanted and would not take rebuttal lightly. She entered the City Chambers by a side door, one where she had observed a few members of staff going in and out. That way lay fewer barriers to be surmounted, particularly as a kind chap actually held the door for her as he was going in, so she didn't need to produce her swipe card. Which, of course she was rummaging for in her bag as he shuffled in, his back propping the door open, and Mary smiling gratefully.

'Pain in the arse, isn't it?' he said.

'Yeah,' she smiled, not sure if he meant swipe cards, or the weather, or the simple fact of being at work. The rucksack, which had been waiting for her in its urine-smelling alcove, was a bit of a problem – it definitely said 'student' not 'professional', and, also, it had a vague tang of dung about it. But she had nothing else, and for a woman to progress through life without a bag would be more noteworthy than being seen lugging this grubby sack. Women were not like men, they could not carry all their baggage in a pair of trouser pockets and one thin satin slit inside their jacket. The bag and the boots would just have to say *funky young professional* and be done with it.

She was standing in a little hallway, dark wooden doors to her left and a wall of arched, frosted-glass windows on her right. Before her, another door, more wood and old-fashioned glass, the kind you might get in a pub, with *Town Clerk's Office* painted in ornate yellow on an oval lozenge. The guy who had let her in was now clicking his card into a wall-mounted box, a beige tin thing with digital numbers glowing in a little rectangle. Clocking in. He shook his head. 'Brilliant. That's me going to lose about four hours again.'

Mary gave a kind of hmm noise, concurring but noncommittal. Now she was through the door, her momentum had faltered a little. She had to phrase her next statement carefully.

'I'm here about Planning? I've got an appointment.'

He put his card back into his wallet. 'Planning? Picked the wrong person to ask, I'm afraid – I've only been brought in to work on the Commonwealth Games. I'm not too sure they're in here, actually; I think you want the building in George Street—'

As he spoke, one of the wooden doors on Mary's left burst open, and a young girl scuttled out, her colour high. An older woman appeared behind her. She raised her voice, obviously continuing a conversation begun on the other side of the door, '. . . and tell him, if I can't get the staff, then this just isn't happening. Alright?' She was still shouting as the glass door swung shut, and the girl disappeared into whatever was on the obverse of *Town Clerk's Office*. The woman folded her arms. She was of indeterminate age, with ash-blonde hair piled up at the sides, revealing fluff and loose clinging hairs on the shoulders of her black cardigan. 'I *said* this would happen,' she told the door. Then she turned, scowling at Mary and the guy at the machine. 'Yes?'

'Em, Ms Riley, this girl's got an appointment. She's here to see—'

'About bloody time.' The woman's eyebrows rose, softening her face in relief, then quickly stiffening again. 'You from the agency? You're late.'

'That's right.'

Later, Mary would wonder why she had agreed so readily. It was instinctive; she was in the zone, seizing whatever this freely offered assumption was as merely another open door, one that could usher her a little deeper in. And with each step forward, you become more embedded, less obtrusive, as you merge and blend into what folk thought you were. She saw it a bit like hitchhiking. Unless the guy had one eye and blood-spatters on his face, you should never hesitate when offered a lift. If you weren't too bothered about how and where you were going, you tended to get there much quicker. At least, that's what Mary had usually found. She spoke more slowly, made a bit of eye contact. Agency-schmagency. She would weave a pretty tale.

'I'm sorry I'm late. The traffic was bad.'

'Right, well you're here now. In you come.'

Mary gave a little wave to the guy at the machine, ignoring his parted lips, and followed Ms Riley into her office. The room was pleasantly bright, a corner office, with two large plate-glass windows, one of which looked on to the street Mary had come in from, the other giving on to George Square. She felt sharp and effervescent; it was in her knees, her belly. Outside, she could see the arm of a cherry-picker angled high at a streetlight, a single figure, a man, silhouetted against dull November sky. Beside the man, a filigree angel soared. The angel was the same size as him, and they were dancing, the man holding her silver fretwork wings as she bucked and dipped. Then she realised they weren't dancing at all: he was wrestling with her, Jacob and the angel, who apparently did not want to be dangled from a Glasgow lamppost. Other, more obedient, angels had already been put in their places, interspersed with snowmen and peacocks – which were bound to look lovely and iridescent when all lit up, but were hardly what you would call seasonal.

'Have a seat, have a seat. Okay, we're running *very* late here, so . . . I have all the . . . just inside . . . oh bugger,' muttered the woman, wading through a pile of papers, knocking a folder to the floor. 'Ah. Here we are.' She picked up a sheet of paper. 'As you know, I'm Margaret Riley. And you are . . .' She peered at the form, 'Charlotte Deans?'

'Yes, but I prefer Charlie.'

Where was this coming from? The cheek of her; she loved it! She was a secret agent, she was a crusader. She was a Greek climbing into a wooden horse, and all the time she was scanning the room. It was definitely an inner council sanctum of some kind. Now what? There was a paper knife on the desk. Take hostages? Demand the head of Planning on a plate and an immediate reprieve for Calder Riggs?

The woman's head was angled like a bird's. 'Sorry, I should have asked. Coffee?'

'No. Thanks.'

'Well, okay, Charlie. I'm in charge of PR here – press, advertising, marketing, et al. I'm sure the agency's briefed you, but this department is under severe pressure. We've just lost several key members of staff to the Commonwealth Games, my assistant has gone on maternity leave, and we're also launching *and* managing a major new initiative for the Glasgow Citicard. You are aware of the Citicard, aren't you?'

The shape of the word was familiar, the way the woman said it, how the syllables all ran together like the 'i's were simply tuts and not letters in their own right. Mary could picture the word, she had read it recently, had held it in her hand. She watched Margaret place her fist under her chin; waiting for an answer. Adrenalin quickening, enlarging all the room, her hand seemed huge, her nails hard-packed with screaming-black mud, Mary saw – briefly – a piece of crumpled paper: that leaflet she'd found yesterday in Bernie's jumper – that had said Citicard on it. Something about joined-up services, what bloody services? It didn't matter.

She nodded. Assumed what she hoped was a thoughtful expression, and pushed her grubby hands beneath her thighs. 'Offering a single access point to a range of joined-up services. Bound to be controversial, isn't it?'

'Exactly.' Margaret's lips curled to reveal squint canines. 'Good to see you've got a handle on the bigger picture. Often, in PR, we have to endorse and promote schemes that we may not actually . . . well. You'll know all about that.' Her eyes returned to the form. 'I see you were at . . . Barker's, wasn't it?'

What was Barkers? It could be a dog-food factory for all Mary knew.

'That's right. Do you know it?'

'Of course. One of the top ad agencies in the country. We used them quite a bit, to get various campaigns off the ground—'

'Of course. There was that one quite recently, wasn't there?'

'The TV jingle? Yes . . . I mean, there was a time when we did everything in-house here, but what with cutbacks . . .' She flapped a hand. 'So, after Barker's, where did you go? How come you're temping at the moment?'

Mary let her body drop forward, creating an intimate little triangle formed of her and the desk and Margaret. 'I know what you mean about cutbacks. It's happening everywhere, isn't it? And when it's about saving money, you tend to find that creativity's one of the first things to go, don't you?'

She was playing Margaret like she would any dupe. You could do it with most scams. Fraud, bogus callers, even fortune telling. Just pick up on some innocuous statement and reflect it back to them, the subtle mimic of their words or gestures. Or their moods. Margaret Riley oozed all the signs of being underappreciated and under siege. Mary could relate to that, in copious spades. She noticed, too, the staccato movements; how Margaret's attention always seemed fixed elsewhere, her ears straining for some other conversation. Her colours were decidedly muddied.

But none of this game, exhilarating as it was, was of any practical use.

'Absolutely. So, we really need you to hit the ground running, Charlie. To be honest, I've never used agency staff before. Goes against the public service ethos and all that. But needs must. Of course, you won't be leading on anything, just providing general support to our press officers.'

The phone on Margaret's desk began to ring. 'Um . . .' her nose wrinkled as she looked at the incoming number. 'Shit . . . better get that. Excuse me a minute.' She picked up the receiver. 'Harold?'

Mary looked at the door. She should just get up and shuffle sideways. This was a waste of time. Public relations was not going to save Calder Riggs. What she needed was to find out the name and address of whoever had submitted these plans Fiona was talking about. Actually track them down and confront them. At the end of that trail, she might well find the fat man waiting, but she would be less scared then, because she, Mary, would be prepared and in control. And she'd have formed some plan by then, to discredit the man or bankrupt him. Or she could just torch his house . . .

'Yes, well, that's not the point.' Margaret was getting agitated again. 'She's here now, so they obviously don't have a clue what they're doing either. Like I said to Elaine, this is what happens when you farm stuff out.' She lowered her voice. 'No, Harold, I will not apologise. If you didn't have so many bloody job-sharers working for you, we might get a bit of coherence in Personnel now and again.' She paused. 'Oh, *sorry*. Human Resources. And don't bother contacting that agency again either. This one will do meantime. Look, I have to go – I've got a Planning pre-agenda in ten.'

She terminated the call as it had begun, without pleasantry.

'There. Sorry about that. Your agency apparently thought you couldn't make it. Now look, ideally I'd like to have had more time to show you round—'

'Um, I noticed you mentioned—'

Margaret's phone rang again. Two fingers raised to silence Mary. Perhaps it was a blessing, for she had been about to say 'Planning'. And then what? *Oh, please, miss. I have a particular interest in planning. Can I come to your meeting too?*

Sitting in a plush leather chair, issuing staccato instructions down the phone. Margaret Riley, with her mad hair and librarian cardi, didn't fit the picture of a slick PR. But she was doing the job alright, a job that would appear to straddle every aspect of the council's business, with access to all the meetings and papers and privileges that entailed.

'Look, Greg, I told you all this yesterday. Our position has not changed. We are confident there's no danger whatsoever to . . . I'm sorry . . . the tests show what? Well, why didn't you say that? Now, don't take that tone with me, or I'll be on to your editor before . . . Yes, right, I'll see what I can find out. I'll call you back.'

Margaret slammed down the phone.

'Un-bloody–believable! This place. It's peopled by morons.' She tugged her hair, more tendrils escaping from her ponytail. 'They think if they just fib to the Press Office, then the papers will never find out. But,' she added darkly, 'they don't know the bastards like I do.'

Mary wasn't sure if she meant journalists or council staff.

'Two more minutes,' Margaret mouthed, thumping in a number.

'Bill, Mags. Get on to Environmental Health and find out the results of those asbestos tests. Yes, the ones at the nursery school . . . Yeah, well not according to Greg at the *Glaswegian*. I don't care if you're busy – just do it.'

The handset cracked into its cradle. 'Don't worry,' she beamed. 'We'll be gentle with you – for the first few days at least. Ha!'

There was an awkward lull, which Mary wondered if she should fill. *I'm sorry but I think you're mad and there's been a terrible mistake* would be a start. But this was akin to being on a playground chute. She'd climbed up, was pushing off and seemed to be meeting no resistance. Why not then? If this woman was stupid enough to let her in, why shouldn't Mary spend the day wandering and poking? It would just be for today, see what she could find. Or better still, see if she could . . . Mary's imagination was in florid torrent now . . . she could maybe access some computer, delete the Calder Riggs planning application, or . . . blacklist the fat guy and his company forever, or . . . well, she could do it, secretly, then slip off home, no damage done. And imagine Bernie and Fiona's faces if she—

Margaret belted the table and bellowed: 'Okay, let's get you a desk and get cracking!'

Mary jumped up, followed her to the door, only to have Margaret mutter she'd forgotten something, and would be *back in a tick*. For the second time in twenty minutes, Mary hung about the little corridor by the clocking-in machine, before Margaret re-emerged, wearing a completely different top.

'That's better,' she whispered, pulling at her jumper, as if that explained everything. They walked past several more ornate mahogany doors, numbered with gold paint, until they reached number 42.

'This is you, here. Let's go and meet the troops.'

Like the Tardis, the room beyond belied its entrance. Once through the heavy portal, all was light, blonde wood and computer screens. And the room seemed to go on forever. Mary heard someone shout: 'Where do we file murders again? It's been so long since I've done this.'

'Community Safety and Joint Police Board,' yelled another.

'Police *Authority*,' said a third. 'Remember they changed the name?'

'Oh, yeah.'

Mary was paraded round, introduced to several people; names and faces blurred.

'Cilla, Kate and Lisa – they do public information.'

Two giggly girls, and one dour middle-aged woman glanced up from their PCs and phones. Mary didn't know who was which; guessed the older one was Cilla.

'Bill and Ali do press. We've two others, but I think they're out on a job just now. Are they? Where's Rachel and Celine, anyone? In fact, where's Bill?' called Margaret.

Everyone ignored her. They nodded and smiled at Mary though; she nodded and smiled back.

'Oh, there's Bill, through by.'

Margaret pointed at a small, glass-partitioned office at the far end of the room. 'This is actually several rooms knocked into one. Most of the other doors are blocked off. I call this Bill's little bus shelter.' She tapped the glazed door, pushing it open as she did so, then went to stand directly over Bill.

'Did you get Environmental Health? Is that them? You tell them it's a bloody ridiculous way to run an outfit. We should be the first to know, not the last.'

Bill broke off the conversation he was trying to have and handed her the phone.

'I've got the Director here, Margaret. Would you like to tell him yourself?'

'No. No, you follow it through. I can't get myself involved in every little thing. I'm far too busy. Speaking of which; got to go. This is our new temp – get her sorted, will you?'

And with that, she left, Bill still on the phone, Mary hovering. A period of unease and inelegant miming followed, Bill signalling at a chair, Mary indicating that she would wait outside, Bill shaking his head, and finally going, 'I know, I know. Let me get right back on to the *Glaswegian* and we'll sort this out. Bye now. Bye, bye.' His beige, thin-haired head followed the journey of the receiver, nodding lower with each 'bye', closer and closer until the receiver was replaced and his cheek was almost alongside the phone. He let out an exaggerated sigh. 'And rest.' Then he raised his head, extended his right hand. 'Bill Murray – no, not *the* Bill Murray. But I am just as funny, actually.'

'Ma . . . Charlie. Charlotte Deans.'

'So, welcome to the madhouse, Ma Charlie.' When he smiled, properly, his face transformed from grey to golden. He had lovely straight teeth.

'Just Charlie.'

'Okay, just Charlie. Mags filled you in on what's what, then?'

'Um, pretty much. She says you've to find me a desk, give me a pay rise, oh, and she wanted me to look out some planning papers for her?'

Mary had no idea how long it would be before someone sussed her out, so she was as well starting now. Once, when shoplifting in Fraser's department store, she and he-who-shall-not-be-named simply walked straight in, took the goods lift to the first floor and wheeled out an entire, chained-up rail of leather coats. The secret was to be so blasé that you were virtually untouchable. Plus it helped that she was well-spoken and articulate; not your average thieving ned. People didn't like to cause a fuss, or make fools of themselves by acting on some loose instinct, and so, invariably, if you looked them in the eye and went robustly about your business, you were fireproof. Well, not invariably, obviously. The days when bliss was singing in your veins and you had that high-eyed jitterbug of a walk, you got clumsy. Objects slipped from your too-many fingers, and you'd laugh, or get the itches, be clawing at your head or your arse. Then you wouldn't look the part, and it was like the whole façade would disintegrate, the good part of you with it, all crumbling into junkie dust just because of the wideness of your eyes, or the way someone saw you shuffle from foot to foot. So you'd get the jail, or get a fine and, either way, your card would be marked. The store detectives would print off your photo from their CCTV and stick it up in their wee security room, or, worse still, punt it round their goonish mates. And your mother would find out where you were again, because the police always checked your address, and she would come down and weep and all you had bloody wanted was to score. So, again, you swore that you would only do it clean. Clean and acute, as she was this instant – Mary was a professional.

She wondered if it should appal her that she would return so readily to her former ways. Was it different because *this* was for a noble cause?

'She did, did she?' Bill was smiling at her. 'And did she tell you that she was only *acting* head of Corporate Comms?'

'No.'

'Hmm. You look like a smart girl, Charlie. You'll learn soon enough what questions to ask in here – and who to ask them of. And, quite frankly, I don't have the time or the resources to babysit you. Desk, I can do. Pay rise – you can get behind me in the queue for that, my dear, and Planning? Why Planning? She's got all the papers she needs for the pre-agenda on her desk. I bloody put them there myself.'

Mary shrugged. Behind her back, her hands were slippy. 'Some query about an application? I wrote it all down. I just need to know where the records would be kept.'

'Depends how far back it goes – this year or earlier?'

'This year.'

'See that woman! Just remember Charlie, the reason you've been brought in here is to act as a general press assistant, not as Margaret Riley's new PA. I think her last PA's still in her office, actually, buried under all that breeding paperwork.'

Bill stood up. Oh shit, shit, shit – he was going to take her through to Margaret.

'Oh, you don't need to show me. Just tell me where to get them. Have you not got to phone the *Glaswegian* back anyway?'

'Did Margaret ask you to supervise me too?'

She had gone too far. 'Oh, sorry. I didn't mean—'

'I'm kidding you on. You're quite right, of course, I do indeed have to phone the *Glaswegian*. However, the thing is, that story they called about will already have been written; the paper will only have contacted us for a comment at the end, and the fact we're now going to refute the comment we already gave them means it's far better just to say nothing else at all.' He let his hand float and dip like a bird in flight, his voice growing slower, soporific. 'Just let the deadline slip on by . . . oops, there it goes. Because you can rest assured there'll be another one along in five minutes.'

His PC gave a little two-tone ping. 'Make that four. Incoming – ooh red flag and an exclamation mark . . .' He looked up again at Mary. 'Right, sorry. Desk: take the empty one over there – see the one beside the two filing cabinets? Get Cilla to show you where the press cuts and newspapers are filed, because that's the first thing I want you to do tomorrow, once you're settled in. I want you to focus on the Citicard in particular – that's one of the main areas you'll be working on – not fetching and carrying papers for Margaret.'

'But should I get them anyway? Since she asked?'

'Your call. But you'll either have to go round to George Street and get Development and Regen to call them up, or you'll need to go down to the basement. They're all supposed to be available online, but there's a massive backlog and they've not been properly indexed yet. They're lying in alphabetical order – supposedly – but, as far as I know, none of this year's have been put on computer at all. *That*'s why Ms Riley wants you to dig them out rather than her.'

This was all good.

'How do I get to the basement?'

'See the door at the far end of the office, the one that looks like it's from a bank vault?' Bill was pointing at a green door, studded round the border, and with a wheel-like handle in the middle. 'That'll take you down the steps and into the basement. There's a light switch on the right just as you go in. Planning, Roads and Environmental Health are all in room two.'

'There's whole rooms in your basement?'

'Not just rooms, dear; vaults. Lots of vaults – and spiders, secret tunnels, ghosts, the works. A twisty labyrinth that stretches right under George Square, so I'm told. So don't forget your ball of twine.'

A coldness had entered his voice; he was plainly not happy that Mary was basement-bound.

She made her way through the buzzy room, where everyone had at least one phone grafted to their ear, a couple talking in stereo on mobiles as well. There was a charged immediacy to each movement, whether it was reaching for a pen or grabbing a coffee cup, scratching a head or leaning up to pull down a file. On adjacent walls, Sky News and BBC 24 rolled in subtitled silence over two large screens. They were single-minded jugglers, these folk. To them, Mary was a flitting ghost. She probably could have walked directly into their midst without any introduction at all, and not one would have challenged her presence.

She went over to the green door and turned the wheel. Expected it to creak but it moved smoothly, the weight of the iron door falling in on itself when released. The light from the general office shone far enough in for her to see the light switch inside; one of those old button-shaped ones. She flicked it down, and a pale, dull yellow illuminated a set of stairs. Mary closed the door behind her, then descended, ducking her head. Safe in the shadows, she allowed herself to relax. These people were in charge of PR for the council. Worse than that, they were masterminding this ID card thing, and yet, here was she, a total stranger off the street, given the right to roam. *Let Glasgow Flourish* indeed. She ducked under another arch and found herself in a narrow corridor, with a low ceiling and silvery, fat pipes gurgling at picture-rail height. A series of numbered doors stretched before her. You see, it had been he-who-shall-not-be-named, the bastard who told her if you *smoked* heroin then it was 'only a bit of fun', who'd taught her that normal people were not suspicious. They took all the stuff you said at face value because they had no reason to think otherwise. Number four, number seven? This numbering made no sense. Hopefully the bastard was dead by now. Up ahead, two intersecting corridors. She wheeled left. Number six, number . . . two. Another button switch, another weak light.

On one side of the room were wooden shelves, warped like hammocks and laden with boxes. On the floor, neatly tied bundles of paper, baled and piled on top of one another. She looked at the report headings that lay face-up on top of each stack. Roads . . . Roads . . . Land Services . . . Roads. No piles of planning. But there was also a row of old-fashioned filing cabinets at the back. Mary started at one side, opened a drawer. The first sheaf were all outline planning applications, and the second, and the third. Good. She pulled up a box to sit on, and began working her way through. She would be methodical and calm – as far as the Press Office were concerned, she had every right to be here. Bill had said the papers were alphabetical, but did that mean the name of the applicant or the place? First few weren't much help, they seemed to be filed by code numbers. As she got more au fait with the system, she realised the papers had all been filed differently, some under the name of the applicant, some relating to the site and others by these numbers. This was going to take forever.

A sudden bang, like a distant door-slam, reverberated through the basement. Several papers leapt from Mary's hand. She looked at her watch. She'd been down here fifteen minutes, had no idea how long Margaret would be at her meeting. All it needed was for her to come back and ask Bill where the new temp was. Fuck, if they really started to check her out— Oh, this was hugely, crushingly stupid. She'd been conscientious for so, so long, brushing and sluicing and doing her penance, keeping low and straight. Bernadette had held Mary's cracked, sore hands in hers, had told her she was doing fine, that she had a home, a second chance here, and it was like all the vertebrae on her spine had unclenched.

She wanted to go home. Her eyes hurt, all the dust and pale light, the streaks on her face that were stiffening into threads. She was hungry, tired. She wanted to hug Bernie and tell Fiona how grateful she was, to just *be* grateful, not covetous. Five more minutes, one final drawer, then she'd better go. She retrieved the fallen papers, went to replace them in their file. *Carling Construction, Court Knowe Gardens, Cruachan Builders.*

Calder Riggs Farm.

Mary kissed the frontispiece, opened the report.

Planning Application
TOWN & COUNTRY PLANNING (SCOTLAND) ACTS
Please read the guidance notes before completing this form.
I/WE APPLY TO THE COUNCIL FOR:
Planning Permission in Principle
Have there been any pre-application discussions NO
APPLICANT
(Please print) Name: Robert Crilley & Co. . . . .
Address: 14 Dungavel Crescent, Barlanark, Glasgow . . . .

Robert Crilley. She shifted the syllables around her tongue. Did the fat man who chased her look like a Robert? A Bob, maybe? No, Fatso would just be the hired muscle. 'Bob' would be the man she had overheard him talking to, in the Mitchell.

ADDRESS OR LOCATION OF PROPOSED
DEVELOPMENT
Calder Riggs Farm,
Calder Riggs Road, Maryhill, Glasgow . . . .
EXISTING USE OF LAND AND/OR BUILDINGS (if
vacant please state last known use) Equestrian Centre (2 acres
only) General/ brown field for remainder of site . . . .

Well, that was a lie. The big paddock alone was an acre and a half. She tore off the page, folded it and folded it again, each angry crease trapping the name of *Robert Crilley* in tighter and tighter squares. Barlanark was to the east of the city centre, out Ballieston way. She could get there in under an hour. The next page, which was now the front page, began:

DETAILED DESCRIPTION OF PROPOSED DEVELOPMENT

Outline application for residential development at 500 habitable rooms per hectare with primary access off Calder Riggs Road with some other matters reserved . . . .

Five hundred rooms per *hectare?* The steady thud of her blood rose like waves, at the enormity of the plans and the seeing of it, there in official black and white. She sat for a second, staring only at her knees. She didn't think she could bear to read any more, the details were too oppressive, the words too full of complacence. Mary rubbed her hand across her eyes, sending flecks of starlight into her brain. Composed herself. A brief skim-read, and then it would be over:

I have completed and enclosed the land ownership certificate.
I enclose the necessary fee, including the advertisement fee if required.

Quickly, she turned the pages, looking for the stuff about ownership. It had to be a fraud: Fiona owned the land, there were warnings all over the application about fines and prosecutions if details were knowingly incorrect. Maybe this was all she needed . . . here it was.

IF YOU DO NOT OWN ALL OF THE LAND OR PROPERTY TO WHICH THIS APPLICATION RELATES, YOU MUST NOTIFY ALL THE OWNERS AT THE SAME TIME AS SUBMITTING THIS FORM USING THE NOTICE PROVIDED.
A I hereby certify that (please tick one box)
1. 21 days before the date of this planning application, the applicant owned all of the land to which the application relates.
OR
2. The applicant has given notice of this planning application to every person who, 21 days before the date of this planning application, owned any part of the land to which it relates.

Box one had been ticked. Mary could feel the outrage building; her feet were all pins and needles, jigging on the ground like she was on withdrawal. This guy Crilley was saying *he* owned the farm. The square of folded paper jagged into her palm. *Patience, Mary, Saviour of Calder Riggs.* She had to harness this energy until she found him. Found a massive machine gun. There was another clunk, this time overhead. People or plumbing? Mary stood up. She'd better get back to the office. One further paragraph, which she almost didn't read. And then she did.

B I hereby certify that (please tick one box)
1. 21 days before the date of this planning application, none of the land to which this application relates formed part of an agricultural holding.
OR
2. The applicant has given notice of this planning application to every person who, 21 days before the date of this application, was a tenant of an agricultural holding.

This time, it was box two, not one that had been ticked. With the following detail filled in:

Name of Tenant: Fiona Cairns . . . .

The thick basement air caught in Mary's throat. She had lied. That bitch Fiona had lied. She didn't own Calder Riggs at all. Mary's fingers felt like they didn't belong to her. She flexed them, made one slow, sharp crease to fold the application in half, then put the whole thing under her arm. She had been going to return the file to the drawer. Not now. Wait till Bernie saw this.

As she turned towards the door, there was another bang. Then all the lights snapped off, the room flooding with instant black, disorientating her. Sending her turning and turning in search of the exit. Hand out blindly before her, she felt her way forward, running her fingers over shelving and brick, carefully inching until she relocated the doorway. Tried to remember, had she gone left or right when she came in? Like snow, the density of the blackness muffled everything, there was nothing for her senses to fix on. Nothing except a slow scuffling sound. Rats? She went to cry out, then stopped. With the thin, frantic clarity of terror, she realised what the shuffling was.

Footsteps.

It was him; Jesus it had to be him, had he been following her all this time? How did he *know*? Mustn't run, mustn't run. *I am not afraid of him, he's just a bloody builder* but her pace was hurried, hand swinging blind from side to side, trying to stay quiet and find the stairs and dodge the footsteps. She was doing well – was nearly at the stairs – although she didn't know that, before her hand made contact with a warm human chest.

Then she screamed.

Chapter Sixteen

Shirley put three cups of coffee down on the desk. It was a protest thump, a definite distinction in emphasis that sent the liquid swilling out of Alex's mug only, and on to the wooden surface.

'Cheers, Shirley.'

She ignored him. She hadn't even made the coffee, the Tube had done it, but Alex had let her carry the tray in, had sat and watched her hand round the mugs, and, evidently, that was wrong. He dabbed the milky ring with a paper hanky. Was Shirley pissed off that he was pulling rank, or pissed off he was demeaning her sex? He gave her a grade-three grin, crinkled-up eyes, the lot. Shirley helped herself to a digestive.

It was very close in the interview room; heavy air and a smell of socks that permeated the thin partition walls between them and the adjacent male locker room. They'd need to be finished by the change of shift, or all you'd hear was a melange of clanging lockers, farts and filthy jokes.

They'd already done the first round of studied nods and frowns as Fiona related how, when and where she'd last seen Bernadette. She had been very calm, very quiet, and Alex still couldn't get the measure of her. Was she a woman who could be roused to fierce and jealous rages? They had not yet mentioned Mary Brown, interested to see if Fiona would. Plus the results of the PM were imminent, so it suited Alex to string this out with tea and sympathy for a bit longer. Till he had some more meat on the bones, so to speak. Despite what he'd said to the cop out at Calder Riggs, there was no suggestion at this stage that Fiona was anything other than a distraught partner. She was here on a purely voluntary basis, and you could take as long as you liked with those kinds of interviews.

'Okay, Ms Cairns,' Shirley said, pausing for a quick biscuit-dunk. 'What we'd like now is for you just to tell us all about Bernadette.'

She eased into her chair, the solid set of her relaxing into a slump. Shirley dressed in the manner of a Sunday School teacher, eschewing the stylish for the comfy. Jumpers were her all-time favourite attire – long, short, bobbly, striped and – today – a wrinkled polo neck in vicious red which sketched her fat, heavy breasts, the low curve of her shoulders. You could lie on those breasts for hours, their generous swell just rocking you off to sleep.

He breathed in, breathed out. Alex was scared he'd fuck this all up. Shirley made him feel safe; he should not wind her up. Yet, because Alex was deemed to be (by whatever benchmark, he wasn't sure) smarter than her, Alex had become Shirley's boss. They were interviewing a woman who had either just lost her life-partner, or had recently committed a passion-fuelled murder, and Alex was mulling over Shirley's breasts. Could you be both smart and shallow? What would that make you? It would make you wide, his fond mother's favourite appellation for him. *See you Alex, son. You're as wide as the Clyde, you.* He had tried explaining this accolade to an English girlfriend, years ago. *Well, she means I've always got an eye on the main chance, you know?*

What?

Em . . . that I'd sell my granny down the river to get on? But I'd be gallus with it.

She had blinked, blank, and he'd given up. Gorgeous lassie, though.

'Please, Fiona,' Shirley was saying, 'I'm just looking for general stuff, the kind of person she is. Just so we can build up a picture of her.'

'Do you think it might not be her then?' Fiona looked to Alex for confirmation, then, when none was forthcoming, returned to Shirley. 'Do you really think she's still alive?'

'I promise you, as soon as we know anything at all, we'll let you know. Now – Bernie? Start at the beginning. You know, how long you've known her, where you first met . . .'

Alex let Shirley do the talking. Often, it worked best when a woman interviewed another woman. They could do the sister act, but they could also ask those most direct, straight-for-the-jugular questions that you were frightened to ask lest you made the lassie greet.

'We've been together for five years.'

'And how did you meet?'

Fiona clasped her hands around her mug. 'Um . . . we met in a club in town. I . . . she asked me to dance.'

'I see.'

Alex could 'see' it too; see exactly what Shirley was thinking. Miss Fiona, of the green Barbour and grubby jeans, giving it laldy, all sparkly in a gay club? That was what five years of marriage must do to you; dim you down a wee bit duller every year, until all the lights finally went out.

Alex had been married for two.

Shirley slid off her jacket, hung it on the chair-back behind. Ah, here we go. This was her just warming up.

'Does Bernie go clubbing a lot, Ms Cairns?'

'No.'

'But she *did*, clearly. Do you think she gets bored, cooped up at the stables day in, day out?'

'I don't know quite what you're getting at.'

'Does she have other lovers, Ms Cairns?'

'No!'

'Are you sure about that?'

'Of course I am. I live with her!'

'And yet you don't know where she went after you saw her last. I mean, she was missing for almost a full day before you bothered to contact us.'

'I . . .'

A knock on the door. The Tube poked his face through the half-crack he'd opened.

Either come in or stay out, man. Don't hang about like an apology.

''Scuse me, boss. Can I have a word? PM,' he mouthed, nodding his big wobbly heid.

Alex rose. 'Fiona, I'm just stepping out for a second. Why don't you drink your coffee before it gets cold?'

He closed the door tight behind him, made sure they'd walked a few feet away before he spoke again.

'Well?'

'Well it's no her, that body we've found.'

'*Fuck.*' Alex's hands made a little prayer-shape over his nose. He tasted the warm breath cupped in his palm. Coffee breath. Lowered his hands, found his pockets. 'Right. Is it the other one then? This Mary Brown lassie?'

'Nope.'

The Tube looked almost happy at this latest development. He was clutching a buff folder, like he was a kid with a special secret.

'Well who the fuck is it then, Terence?'

'A lassie by the name of Francine Gallagher.' There was an imperceptible bounce to the man, little gleeful tremors that made him rock on the balls of his feet. 'Aye, we had her fingerprints on file. She's been done hunners of times, as well.'

'For what?'

'Hooring. In fact, I'm surprised you don't know her, boss. Did you no work in the Vice Squad in the Central?'

'Flexi,' he said dully.

'Pardon? You saying they were flexy, boss?' The Tube had wet, grinning lips. Always wet.

'It was called the Flexi Unit.'

Alex leaned against the wall, remembering a scabby council flat and a baby who was blue with cold. Seeing a teenage lassie with red-raw eyes, her big sister a zombie. Yes, Alex remembered Francine Gallagher, remembered how she'd disappeared, just slipped off the radar after her sister's baby had died, and how he and Jenny Heath, his neighbour in the Flexi, had both noticed. Jenny had checked Francine's flat, found it empty. They'd PNC-ed her, to see if she was working some other town, perhaps been jailed elsewhere. No trace. Alex had always hoped Francine had been one of the lassies who'd made it out.

'Yes. I do know her, actually.'

'Surprised you didny recognise her with her clothes off then, boss!'

'What did you say?'

The Tube stopped his bouncing, but did not have the intelligence to disengage his mouth from the offensiveness that was spilling out. 'Well, she was in the scud when we found her. No bad tits as I remember, either.'

'Terence. Gonny do me a favour, pal?'

'Sure boss.'

'Gonny take yourself up to DS Morrison and tell him that you're applying for a transfer to Road Policing.'

'Ha! Nice one, boss.'

He truly was like rubber.

'Just fuck off, will you, Tube? And if you ever talk about a deceased person like that again, I will personally see to it that you are on the very next transfer list to anywhere that isn't here. Got me?'

'Aye . . . aye boss. Sorry. I didny realise you had a . . . connection with the lassie.' He sniggered as he said it, a soft, subtle sound that you could choose to ignore.

Alex let his head rest a little deeper into the wall. Francine Gallagher. Shit. Where had Francine Gallagher been all these years? Hiding in Glasgow, keeping her head down, face averted? Some girls did find routes out of prostitution, but it necessitated an incredible effort, a physical and mental move away from their pushers, their pimps, the easy money they knew was so accessible. Even if they did get clean, and dissociate themselves from their old lives and connections, there was still the massive hurdle of trying to find decent work with a string of convictions to your name. Most of them ended up drifting back to the game – that, or dead, or both. Was that what had happened to Francine – had she come back to work, got picked up by some slap-happy punter? The Tube had begun to wander back up the corridor.

'Ho, wait up.'

He turned. 'Boss?'

'I take it you checked to see when she was last arrested?'

'Years ago, boss. Looks like she was a right wee goer back in the day, then, whump. Nothing for about six year until she turns up deid.'

'And her last known address?'

'Some flat in Townhead?'

The flat Francine had shared with her sister. Angela Gallagher was long dead, had been found with a needle protruding from her groin, but Alex couldn't remember if that had been before or after Francine disappeared. Maybe Jenny would know.

'Right, okay. Get as many of the team reassembled in the incident room, and I'll just finish up with Fiona here. Shirley can allocate the missing persons report back to uniform for the time being, if it's nothing to do with this enquiry.'

The Tube nodded. 'Do you want this report the now, boss, or will I just take it up the stair with me?'

Alex hesitated for a moment, allowing his thoughts to stack, to slide like toast into waiting slots. He wanted to see the body again, now he knew it was Francine. Would her features become familiar, would he pause and lower his head, offer up a silent goodbye because he'd *known* her, he'd known the person inside the husk? Aye right. If he'd passed Francine in the street last week, would he have even noticed? Just another hoor, who gave him a bit of cheek whenever she got the jail, then had skipped off into the sunset. Set in death, though, their casual, adversarial acquaintance would assume a status it never had in life, and it made him feel stupid and guilty and sad.

'Aye – no, gie me it the now, and I'll have a quick shuftie through before I speak to the troops. Tell them five minutes, yeah?'

'Right you are boss.' The Tube handed over the file and wobbled away. His head was definitely too big for his shambling frame. *Thunderbirds*; that was what he reminded Alex of. He was too young to have seen the original broadcasts, but his big cousin was a cult TV buff, had collected the entire series, along with stuff like *Monkey* and *Marine Boy*, and some creepy East German thing called *The Singing Ringing Tree,* whose black and white horrors had infiltrated many of Alex's dreams.

He returned to the interview room, fixed on a thin-lipped smile. At least it was good news, of a sort, for Fiona.

'Sorry about that.' Sat down, slid the report over to Shirley. 'How are we getting on?'

'We're just about done boss,' said Shirley, opening the file.

'Good,' he said. 'Well, I don't see any reason to detain you any further at this stage, Ms Cairns. We've got all the information we need at the moment—'

'Wait.' Fiona reached over, gripped his hand, her touch papery, rough with bales of hay and chafing reins, with tautened muscles and jittery nerves. 'Are you telling me that that woman you found isn't Bernie?'

It was too early to give out any information at all. Much as he'd like to reassure the hunted, haunted woman in front of him, he could say nothing until it was all confirmed, until he was a hundred per cent sure of his facts and he'd read the PM report in full and the body had been formally ID-ed. That would mean tracking down one of Francine's relatives, or, failing that, a friend. Or someone else that had known her. Someone like him.

He pulled his hand away. Already, in his head, he had moved on from this woman's anguish. It was a shame, but it was no longer anything to do with him. He had a murder enquiry waiting, and a room full of hairy-arsed detectives champing at the bit.

'You'll appreciate, at the moment, that we can't really—'

'Excuse me, sorry.' Shirley looked up from what she was reading. Her eyebrows were dancing at him, pushing themselves up into the thickness of her curly fringe. 'DI Patterson, would you mind if I just asked Ms Cairns another couple of questions?'

'No, not at all – if that's okay with you Ms Cairns?'

Fiona said nothing.

Shirley had moved the file so it was between her and Alex, was tapping a page with her painted thumbnail. For as long as Alex had known Shirley, she had never worn make-up, and yet she always had immaculate nails.

'Has Bernadette ever talked to you about her past, Fiona?' she said.

'You make it sound like she's a spy or something.'

'Just answer the question, please. Say if she had some secret, for example, something that would make you jealous – how do you think you would react? Would you get angry, d'you think?'

'I don't know . . .'

'Och, I think you do, Fiona. For example, one of the girls at the stables said you got angry about Mary Brown. The way she was hanging round Bernie all the time . . .'

'For heaven's sake. That's ridiculous.'

'You know that Mary's gone missing too, don't you?'

'Well, I was aware she hadn't come in last night—'

'But you didn't think that was an important thing to tell us?'

'Not really, no. She's a big girl, she can look after herself—'

'But Bernadette can't, is that it?'

Fiona started to cry.

'Em, I think we should take a wee break here,' said Alex. 'Let Ms Cairns compose herself.'

He had no idea what track Shirley was careering along, but whatever it was, they were going to have to formalise this interview. Fiona's head was down, shoulders heaving

He leaned into Shirley. 'What are you doing?'

'Have you actually read this?'

'No, I've no had time.'

'Well, read the DNA report for Christsake,' she whispered. 'Here.' She passed Fiona a paper hanky. Probably the same one he'd wiped up the coffee with.

'Fiona, what was Bernadette's job before she started working in the stables?'

'She was a hairdresser.'

'Is that right? And where did she work?'

'I don't know. Some salon in town.'

Alex scanned the page. They never put this stuff in bullet points, it was always lardy, dense text that you had to carry out your own post mortem on, cutting away layers to get to the point. In the background, Shirley hammered on.

'Did you ever see her there? Pick her up after work? Get a free haircut maybe?'

'No, I . . .'

There it was. The results of the DNA matches:

'Samples had been taken from . . .'

'Would it surprise you to know that Bernie was a prostitute, Fiona?'

Alex heard the words, heard a chair scrape back. He stopped reading, looked at Shirley, at Fiona, her body recoiling. One arm pushing on the desk, independent, fighting it like she was being electrocuted. 'Of course she wasn't a bloody prostitute! I know my own wife. How dare you? She doesn't even like men.'

'I'm sorry, Fiona,' said Shirley, 'but you need to understand. Bernie had a whole other life before she met you.'

Alex was going to have to stop this interview, but his brain was way ahead of him, knowing, now, where it was going, wanting to be sure.

'Yes, but not like that,' sobbed Fiona. 'How can you say these things? How *can* you?'

'I can because they're true, I'm afraid. You need to know this. Bernadette isn't even her real name.'

'*No*. No!'

Shirley's voice was growing softer. 'Fiona, I need you to look at me.'

Alex was at the bottom of the page.

. . . found that the samples obtained from both Item 4(b) (pair of pants taken from the washing basket within Bernadette Murphy/ Fiona Cairns's bedroom) and from item 4(f) (used sanitary towel taken from the bin within en-suite bathroom adjacent to bedroom of Bernadette Murphy/Fiona Cairns) matched that of the deceased.

A final double-check that the facts were there, were making sense as Shirley slipped out a photograph of the face. It was a close-up, in repose, of Francine. Definitely Francine now he *saw* it, clearly. Now he knew. The image was in profile, and he was there again, his torch easing back the darkness round the black wet hair and the dead wet eye.

'Is this Bernie?' Shirley asked.

'Oh God yes.' Fiona grasped at her mouth, the way Alex had held his own face, moments earlier.

'Fiona. This woman's real name is Francine Gallagher. She's known to us, as a prostitute. We have her fingerprints on file. And I'm so, so sorry to tell you this, but she *is* the woman we found in the canal.'

Chapter Seventeen

'Here, drink this.'

Mary shook her head. 'I'm fine, honestly.'

'Hot sweet tea when you've had a fright.'

'Och, the lassie would rather have a big gin, wouldn't you, hen?'

Several of the Press Office staff were gathered round, pressing Mary with drinks and curious, concerned frowns. So much for staying inconspicuous as she slipped about the office. Bill had his arms folded, was staring down with his long, sad face. 'Are you sure you don't want to go home?'

'No! No, I told you. Really, truly, I'm okay. I just got a bit disorientated down there.'

'I'm awful sorry. I should have shouted out first – I never thought. I just knew that the lights would be on their timer and you'd end up in the pitch black. I should have told you.'

Mary touched the space beneath her breast, checking for the reassuring crinkle of paper. Yes, the planning document was still there, she hadn't dropped it. Good thing the waistband of those trousers was a wee bit tight. Okay, a big bit tight. She had to get these people to go away before Margaret came back and asked why they were crowded round her, and then someone would say, 'Charlie near shat herself in the basement', and then Margaret would go 'but why were you down there anyway?'

'Please, honestly, it's absolutely cool.' Her heart had stopped galloping now; it was more of a gentle canter. Just a shrivel of after-shock and a deep mortification. She shook her hair back, pushing the blackness from her face, the cuticles dye-swollen and heavy. Fiona was right, the colour didn't suit her at all.

'Anyway, I guess that's me officially made my contribution to Corporate Communications. Just call me Charlotte the Screamer from now on, eh?' She stood up, forcing the huddle to part. Someone laughed, and then a phone rang, and then another and it was business resumed, the sideshow over. Bill gave her one last mournful lip-twitch, and returned to his half-office.

The rest of the day was flat. There was a bit more screaming, this time about the asbestos scare, with Margaret stomping and Bill being very silent, but nothing to trouble Mary. She sat quietly and admired her desk, feeling a thrill of ownership as she ran her hand across its surface. She'd never had a desk before, not since school. She could bring in a little plant, a wee pot for her pens. Photos. If she'd been staying, that was.

Cilla came over, showed her where the press cuts and newspapers were filed, told her that she'd need to be in early next morning to sort them.

'We use a media monitoring service,' she explained, 'so it's not like you have to scrutinise all the papers yourself. The duty press officer will come in early too, and tick the wee boxes on the back.' She turned one of the pages over. 'See – there, depending on what service they want it allocated to.'

'Right.'

Cilla swung her head round to glance behind her, then lowered her voice. 'Just watch if Celine does it, though – she disny really have a clue. Aye,' she continued, 'we used to have a lot more services, but half of them have been hived off, plus they've got rid of a lot of the committees too.'

'How come?'

'Oh, we're run by an Executive now, you see. It's the chosen few who make all the decisions.'

'That's democracy, is it?'

'No. But it's efficient.' Cilla gave a pinched wee smile.

Another girl walked past. Lisa? Laura? Mary was no good with names. 'Anyway,' said Cilla, 'back to the cuts.'

'Oh yeah. The cuts.'

This was dull. Mary would much rather be out in the fields, the wind brushing her face with the sweet smell of horse dirt. It was the only time she felt really clean, there at The Riggs with the hot quick blood of the beasts and all those acres of sky. It was lunchtime; she would go and phone Bernie, tell her the news. Instantly, she saw the sky diminish, the gauzed layers of blue suck back like a plug had been pulled. As soon as Mary opened her mouth, Calder Riggs would be spoiled. Either she would be ejected, an anguished Eve full of knowledge nobody wanted, or Bernie would turn on Fiona, they'd fight and it would all come crashing to an end. But if Mary said nothing, Calder Riggs would slip into asphalt oblivion. And where would the horses go, and the kids? It had to be done. She would tell Bernie to meet her, somewhere away from The Riggs, just so they could talk. She'd have to word it carefully – forceful enough so Bernie knew it was important, that Mary was not winding her up or being needy, but not so scary that she was afraid to come. God – did Mary really freak people out? Did Bernie honestly think she was a burden, instead of a boon?

Cilla was lecturing her again. Mary nodded, tried to pay attention, but she wouldn't be here tomorrow morning, so all the abbreviations and instructions could just bounce off her skin.

'So we're clear?'

'Yeah. No problems. Tick, tick, file.'

Everyone seemed to do their own thing at lunch, none of which included Mary. Folk air-kissing, arranging to meet in restaurants, floating in, floating out. No one told her what time to take lunch, so she sat, waiting for instruction. Public information girl two came over. Kate?

'Hiya. What you doing for lunch?'

'Hadn't really thought. Go for a wander round the shops, probably. When can I go?'

'Pretty much any time between twelve and two, as long as someone's here to man the phones – just use your flexi-card,' she replied.

'I don't think I have one of them.'

'Well, just take a note of when you clock out and in, then you can put in an exceptions report once you're all computerised. Make sure you don't lose any vital minutes that you're owed.'

'Right. Thanks.'

The girl hoisted a sports bag on to her shoulder. 'I'm only asking because some lunchtimes me and a few of the lassies go to an exercise class. Wondered if you fancied it?'

'Oh . . . I don't have any gear with me . . .'

'No? Well, maybe another day? Day after tomorrow?'

Mary pushed her legs further under the desk. Sitting down all morning, the unfamiliar tightness of tailored trousers had compressed her legs, making her more and more uncomfortable. It was the horse riding, you see, not the burgers. Gave you massive thighs.

'Well, yeah, I suppose . . .'

'Look, you don't have to, just a thought.' The girl made to walk away.

'No, it's just . . .' She could think of no convincing answer. The girl's face was round and expectant . She looked like a nice person. Fresh. The sort of girl who might ride horses.

'Yeah, okay. That would be great. Thanks.'

'Great. See you later.'

Mary waited five minutes, so she wouldn't catch up with the girl and have to fall into conversation with her. She was getting too settled, believing her own hype. Every exchange was potentially damning; the best scams were those that involved an initial convincing intrigue, then a quick in, out and away. With the planning application stuffed down her breeks, Mary had got what she came for. She picked up her rucksack, tapped the door of Bill's den.

'Bill, I'm going out for lunch now.'

He nodded without looking up from his computer screen. He was battering out a media release before the Director of Environmental Health held a press conference. Mary felt suddenly sorry for him.

'Can I bring you back a sandwich?'

He stopped typing.

'Eh, yeah, thanks. Anything except egg, ta.'

Why had she said that? She wasn't planning to come back after lunch at all. Ach, she didn't know where her head was, awash with the slurry of Fiona's duplicity, then getting scared shitless in the basement. Oh yeah, and she'd stolen a designer trouser suit . . . All she had meant to do was come into town and skulk for a while. Maybe feed the pigeons. Well, she'd phone Bernadette, grab a sandwich and take it to Bill, then make some excuse and leave. In fact, she'd just leave. Talking only entrenched you deeper.

At the same time Mary was heading out of the Press Office, a long, thin man was coming in. He looked like an adult version of Harry Potter, but without the scar. In one hand, he carried what looked like a homemade Bakewell tart. With the other, he held the door for her.

'Well, he-llo. Is this new blood for me to suck?'

'I beg your pardon?'

'Gordon Thomson. Your friendly local government correspondent. I would shake hands, but I come bearing gifts instead. And you are?'

'Charlie.'

'Charlie? You don't look like a Charlie to me.'

'Well I am. A proper one.'

'Ooh, I like her, Celine.'

'Mm.' Celine, whose desk was nearest to the door, kept typing.

'Hallo darleengs,' he called to the office in general. 'I've brought you some sustenance.'

A few muted *Thanks Gordon*s came back. 'I'll just leave it here, shall I? So, Charlie, what is it you do?'

'Bit of this, bit of that.'

'Beautiful *and* enigmatic. Wonderful. Well, let me tell you, anything you want – front page headlines, exclusive coverage – I'm your man.' He slipped a card from his inside pocket, presented it as a magician would an apparated bouquet. Then he lowered his voice. Up close, his breath smelled lightly of onions. 'Seriously. You're new, I'm ambitious. You scratch my back, I'll scratch yours.

I'll not be at the *Times* forever. What I'm really looking to do is move into investigative journalism, so if you ever—'

At this, Celine began to tut loudly. 'Oh for goodness sake . . .'

'Oh, there's Bill. Must have a chat with Big Bill. Laters, Charlie.' And off he strolled.

'Watch him,' whispered Celine. 'He steals stories: stands behind your computer while you're working. Plus he poisons all his cakes.'

The queue for Greggs the bakers trailed from the door on Queen Street right round the corner into St Vincent. Hungry office workers squidged up against the plate-glass windows to let pedestrians shuffle by. But the women of Greggs had the Great Glasgow Lunchtime down to an extremely fine art. Trays of bridies and sausage rolls were continually rotated from the tiers of metal ovens – baked ones out, raw ones in. Piles of cellophane-wrapped Softees and sandwiches were replenished constantly, and banks of pink-armed staff kept the crowds rolling along, barking orders, dishing out change and polystyrene cartons of tomato soup.

Mind yir hauns, hen. It's roastin'.

Mair mutton pies on, Cissie. I'm doon tae ma last wee lamb.

Of course, you could go to some other place and avoid the queues, but why would you, when Greggs was pumping out hot-wrapped bags of steaming pastry goodness? As she waited in line, Mary took out her mobile, pressed Bernie's number. It went instantly to messages.

Just leave your number, please, and I'll catch you later. Cheers now.

All said in a hurry, like she was about to laugh or something. Mary could visualise Bernie rolling her eyes, trying to emulate the posh phone-voice Fiona used. She hesitated, enjoying the happy sound of Bernie being Bernie, but unsure of what message to leave. The blank after Bernie's voice stretched on. Mary had been all psyched up to say she was sorry, but you had to say that to a person, not a tinny silence.

'What can I get you, hen?'

Mary checked her purse. She had about a fiver. 'Em, two cheese and onion pasties and a cheese ploughman's, ta.'

As she returned to the City Chambers, she became aware that the protest she had seen by the front door this morning had grown bigger. There were at least thirty folk now, and they were all chanting:

No ID! No ID! No way, no way, no ID!

One man had a megaphone, and was on the top step, leading the shouts. Two men in green blazers flanked the revolving door, barring him from coming any further. They looked official, had their arms folded. One was sucking on his bottom lip, whether from mirth or fear, Mary wasn't sure. The other, older one had a face of stony resolve. The protest was spilling into the road, vehicles blasting angry horns as people shouted and stamped. A young guy with a multicoloured hat on was attempting to clamber on to the Cenotaph, which faced the City Chambers. Quickly, a police officer emerged from inside the Chambers, shoving his way through the protesters.

'Right you. Down now, or you're getting the jail.'

'On what charge, *cunt*-stable?' The young man was on the low grey wall at the rear of the monument, one hand clamped round a black metal flagpole. Mary was only a few feet away. At the base of the pole, a wreath of iron-black leaves, woven in Victorian mourning-style, signified exactly what it was he was scaling.

'This is desecration. You're committing a breach of the peace.'

'Really? I don't think so. Nobody here thinks I am, do you, guys?' He let his arm elongate, so he was virtually swinging from the pole.

'You go for it, Patrick!'

Another boy, a kid really, jostled against Mary, his brown donkey jacket brushing her arm as he raised his fist and shouted: 'A paean to imperialist warmongers, that's all this is.' Tall and angry, he put out his other hand to touch the Cenotaph.

The policeman jerked his thumb, indicating again that Patrick should come down. 'I said off. *Now.* This is the equivalent of a gravestone—'

'Actually, no,' said the swinging boy. 'Cenotaph comes from

the Greek for "empty tomb", signifying that this is a memorial to people who have died elsewhere.'

'I'll no tell you again son—'

As the policeman advanced, Mary moved away, skirting the mob and going round the side of the building to the door she'd first gone in this morning. She felt the same daft thrill as when she'd sat at her desk. *I have privileges here. I know things.* But the door was locked. Fine. Well, she'd tried to give Bill his stupid sandwich. She turned to go, bashed straight into Cilla.

'Charlie! Sorry hen, I near knocked you down there.' Cilla unzipped her handbag. 'Nightmare this, isn't it? Were you trying to get back in?'

'I—'

'Wee tip for you. Any time there's a hoo-hah outside the building – and it's no *that* infrequent, let me tell you – you just come in through the Gatehouse, right? It's twenty-four-hour access, so if you're ever called out—'

'Would I be?'

'Well, it's usually the duty press officer, but I've seen the times it's been all hands to the pump. See just there, when we won the Commonwealth bid? Oh man, we had calls from India, Japan. I don't think any of us slept at all that night.' Cilla beamed at Mary. 'Rare fun though, so it was.' She opened her purse, took out a credit card. 'Come on, this way.'

Mary followed her. 'What is it that's happening? Why are all those folk there?'

'Och, the place is going mental, so it is. That's the Health Board agreed they're to consult on its adoption now, too.'

'Adopting what?'

'That bloody Citicard. Folk don't like it, you know. They're saying it's the same thing as a national identity card.'

'Is it?'

Cilla paused, took Mary's arm. 'C'mon hen. Let's get in out the cold.'

Together, they walked a short way along Cochrane Street, until they came to a gap in the pavement. A huge double gate stood half open, allowing them to slip into an open courtyard, hidden between two arms of the building.

'This is it. In you come.'

They passed through a kind of porters' lodge, Cilla holding up her card to another of the green-jacketed men, who stood behind the wooden counter. Mary could see now that it had Cilla's photograph on it, along with the council crest.

'What about your pal, Miss Black?'

Cilla giggled. 'He aye calls me that. Because of Cilla, get it? Show him your security pass.'

'I don't have one.'

'Och, I can vouch for the lassie, Stan.'

'Well, she'll need to get one – especially with all they nutters outside. I canny just have anyone traipsing in here—'

'Alright Stanley, cool it! I'll see that she gets one the day, alright?'

'You mind you do, Miss Black. Or I'll hold you personally responsible for any security breaches to the premises—'

'Now don't you go stressing me, boy, or I might never sing again.'

Cilla began to trill the opening bars of 'Downtown'. Stan joined in as Cilla waved at him, steering Mary down the corridor towards the Press Office.

'Eh, I think that was Petula Clark,' whispered Mary.

'Was it? Ach well – he's as daft as me, then!' She put her arm round Mary's shoulder, gave a squeeze. Her breath smelled of peppermint and coffee, and it was like a soft sweet punch to the side of Mary's head. She gulped, but it emerged as a sob.

'Och, pet. What is it?'

'No, I'm fine, I'm fine.' Mary pulled away. 'First day, stress . . . and my mum used to sing that song.'

Another lie. She didn't want to lie to these folk any more. 'She's not been well, you know?'

'Fair dos.' Cilla patted her on the cheek. 'Well missy. Shall we go and get that security pass sorted? Or you'll no get back in tomorrow.'

Of course, Mary wouldn't be back in tomorrow at all. Shame, that.

Chapter Eighteen

There was too much sugar in Anna's ginger beer. First you felt the numb-chink of ice, then the serrating fizz of acid and sugar washing over your front teeth. It was real organic ginger beer, with grainy amber chunks and a thick sediment at the bottom, which gave the drink a layered effect. Like a dull cocktail, thought Anna, raising the glass to the light.

'Do you not like it?' Her friend Elaine was shoogling her baby son with one arm, attempting to lift both her sandwich and a tissue with the other. 'C'mon Ralphie. *Blow.*' She smudged his runny nose with the hanky. 'Ginger's meant to be good for the stomach. Calming.'

Anna regarded her belly. 'Yeah? Will it flatten down this humongous bulge then?'

'Will you quit moaning?'

'I'm not moaning. I'm merely remarking on the fact that I feel like someone has stuck a bicycle pump up my arse and is inflating me a wee bit more each day. Did you never worry that you would just . . . burst?' She dropped her hands aimlessly to her sides. 'And I'm not even that hungry any more.'

'Could've fooled me.'

The remains of Anna's lunch lay before her, a bowl slicked with thick, bright Borscht (but basically empty), a slab of wholemeal loaf (crumbs) and a goat's cheese salad (thin rind and a piece of radish remaining). The salad had caused much consternation in both the waitress and Elaine, who had engaged in a circuitous debate for several minutes on whether goat's cheese was pasteurised, and did it matter anyway, when you were in the last trimester? Anna had been adamant. 'Ho. That's what I want. And it's me that's eating it, ladies.'

It hadn't even tasted that nice when it came. Everything in this cream-painted, wood-floored, Art Deco-postered and heavily notice-boarded café was organic, woven from hemp or nettles, pressed through a hair shirt for added consistency. And it was full of nibbling, flustered, encumbered women and weans. Everywhere, there were children: being held in arms, restrained in high chairs – or sporadically, you got the odd escaped and fully mobile one being let loose in the *Find Out and Have Fun Corner!!* Which didn't look like a whole lot of fun, what with the chipped wooden blocks and creepy-faced glove puppets. It was a room full of life, certainly, but a slow, different life.

She felt like she was being swallowed, even though the room was wide and full of windows.

'You okay, Anna?'

'Me? Yeah, I'm fine. Why?'

Elaine shrugged. 'You just look a bit . . . pensive.'

'Pensive? Ooh, that's a big word to be using at this time of day. Well seen you've gone back to work.'

'Absolutely. My brain has returned to pre-pregnancy size and pertness, even if my tits havny. But, seriously, is everything alright? It feels like I've been doing all the blethering, and you've just been munching away like a mournful sheep.'

'Sounds like a normal lunch to me.'

If she wasn't allowed to be quiet, Anna was determined to remain flippant. Friendships should have an easy currency about them – a movement of shore and sea, the one investigating the other so that each time they meet, they are smudged, a little shared, but with essentially the same shape. And the shape of Anna and Elaine had always been light. Theirs was a work relationship that had trickled into friendship; the friendship of two initially single women with shared interests and separate lives. Elaine was by nature open and garrulous, Anna reticent. While Elaine liked to delve deep and download, spraying indiscretions, expletives, outrage and angst with a cheerful equanimity, Anna was happy to listen, offer the occasional snippet and offload superficial moans. But neither gave any more than they were willing to. Only once had Anna genuinely bared her soul, when she'd told Elaine about Jamie Worth: married, beautiful and Anna's secret. She had been desperate, in need of a sounding board, of purging. But even then, she'd only told her the half of it.

How could Anna begin to articulate what she was feeling now? How could she describe the gradual flaring panic, her pulse tattooing through the night? Clear terror, washed new each morning, then a slackening of the tension as her daily business drowned it out; then, when there was a space again, a pause that allowed the panic to flood back in, more terror, and all the while, her with her blankest smile, her most ambivalent eyes. She was a hostage with a knife at her neck, unable to speak or signal. No matter how she battled it, the old, constricting fear was claiming her again. Even on her way here, she had felt observed, was sure the same car had circumnavigated her twice. Kept seeing shapes now, smeared across her peripheral vision; shapes that, when you spun to challenge them, were not actually there.

'Anna, forgive me for saying this, but is it Rob?'

'Is what Rob?'

Elaine placed her sandwich on the plate. 'Look, I never said anything when you two got together, and, don't get me wrong, I was really pleased for you—'

'But?'

Here was a place to put her fear. She could project it as aggression, because it was evident that whatever Elaine was polishing, she was considering the shine of what she was about to say with a saviour's fervour. Yes indeed; here came the vapid smile.

'Well, it was all really sudden wasn't it? Just after your mum dying, him with a ready-made wee family . . .'

'What are you suggesting?'

Anna thought she may as well play the game for a while. It was a glad distraction, one she could toy with and digest without actually tasting, just as she had eaten her insipid lunch.

'I'm not *suggesting* anything, Anna. I'm your pal and I'm just stating some facts here. I mean, Rob *is* a lovely guy, don't get me wrong. But he's not the standard Anna Cameron catch, is he? He's skinny, quiet, clever . . . maybe a wee bit tame?'

She stopped, raised an encouraging eyebrow. Presumably Anna was meant to dive in and spill all the deviant beans. She said nothing, but she could feel the pulse at her wrist, was aware of the shush of blood coursing on its double journey and an absolute, shocked indignation at what Elaine was saying.

It made her breathless, but she shouldn't be surprised. Pregnancy was the oddest state. You became one massive, fat, amorphous open season. Your very walking, bulbous presence informed the world that you were fecund, that you had spread your legs and indulged in sex (which was absolutely *nobody*'s business but your own), and that you would soon be exposing yourself again, giving over your vulnerable, splitting body to sterile strangers. Your bump said you were a public service incubator, which gave the world permission to pronounce on your weight, your drinking, your eating, smoking, sitting, standing, fitness, sharpness, bluntness. And, apparently, allowed it to offer insights into your most private relationships too. Pregnancy was the most visible indicator that you were an adult functioning woman, yet it was when you were treated most like a child. Who the hell was Elaine to decide what kind of partner Anna should have?

Her silence had offered a vacuum which Elaine, slightly less sure now, continued to fill. 'And I'm just wondering if, you know, you were maybe looking for someone safe . . . a wee haven after you lost your mum. And that's all very well and good, but now you're pregnant, well, there's no going back, is there?' Her diction was speeding up, becoming a little manic as words strained through her teeth. 'This is it, for better or for worse, whether you do finally tie the knot or not. So, I'm just thinking, maybe you're feeling a wee bit trapped, yeah?'

The uplift in her inflection was a plea for Anna to join in and make this monologue less lonely. To desist from her silent, baleful admonition. Anna let it roll and roll. Elaine set off on another tack.

'And that's perfectly natural, I felt that way too, you know, before Ralphie was born. But I mean, I'm sure . . . Rob clearly loves you. Anyone can see that. And you *know* that he's a great dad, so . . .'

So. What a circuitous, awkward road to nowhere. Here they were, back to where Elaine had first intruded. The status quo resumed in the knowledge that Rob was a great guy and everything was swell and smooth. Except perhaps the fragile surface of their friendship. Anna could, at this point, advise Elaine to fuck off and leave the café, could launch into a hearty defence of her husband's honour, which would sound manufactured and shrill, could tell Elaine that her wean was showing signs of ginger furze in its hair . . .

But Rob wasn't Anna's husband.

He should be, of course he should. That *was* a public statement worth making – one she should have embraced months ago, a year ago, when he had first asked her. Why had she seen it as some form of entrapment? No, no, that's what Rob thought she thought – see, even he, even the person you slept with and, beside, the one person who was allowed access to your most intimate self could not climb inside your head. It had nothing to do with being trapped and everything to do with being unworthy. Slowly, Anna had drawn love into her world, had tended it, amazed, as it quietly grew. Causing some big obvious fuss about this, sanctifying and formalising it, would be arrogant. Fraught with danger. It would be akin to creeping through a field of bulls and then, just in sight of the fence, waving a great red rag. *Wooh! Look at me. I made it. Amn't I clever and safe and oh fuck, here they come. Run!*

She looked at Elaine, at her puckered brow and wriggling child who fixed her to the world. She looked at the belly that weighted her own world, that made her sit still and grounded because she had no other option than to wait. Felt a calmness drift over her, perfect and round as a seed head. It was simple. She would ask Rob to marry her, and she would rescue her friend.

'Elaine, just cause you're my pal doesn't give you carte blanche to run your snotty fingers through my life. Cheers for the psychoanalysis, though. Oh, and, for your information, Rob has a massive dong.'

She lifted the steel teapot that sat between them. 'More tea vicar?'

'You're terrible, you are.'

'I know.'

High, false laughter. A visible loosening of Elaine's jaw.

'So,' she said, 'have you decided if you're going back full time or not?'

'Christ, I haven't even had the baby yet.'

'Since when did that matter? Knowing you, you'll have planned your whole pregnancy, maternity leave and return to work the moment the wee line went blue. I bet you've got a pregnancy folder, with coloured page dividers sorting out each month.'

It was a box file, actually, full of appointment cards, sheaves of papers on the risks to older mothers and their children, the Headquarters policy document on family-friendly working, a concertinaed strip of ghostly ultrasonic shapes, a graph of weeks and payments and permutations of leave and benefits and a cartoon-drawn booklet concerning perineum oiling and nipple-cracking. Called – seriously – 'All Dried Up and Nowhere to Go?' Everything jumbled in no order or sense, much like the contents of Anna's head. She may look calmer, reduced as she was to immobility, her swollen face 'blooming', but inside she flailed more than her baby did. Oh, she hoped it was beautiful, and smart, and that it never, ever got the cold. From the confines of his mother's arms, Elaine's son Ralphie explored his squat wet nose.

'Elaine – he's doing it again.'

'Well just don't look at him then.'

'I can't help it. It's like watching a car crash. Lainey, please.'

'Oh, for God's sake.'

Anna watched as Elaine pushed the child's worrying fingers away, going *Ditee-boy* and wiping his fingers with her own, before she retrieved her sandwich from the plate and started munching again. Eating it with the same hand.

'Oh Jesus.'

'What? What now? Did he give you a "funny look" again? Honest to God, Anna, you need to get over this. All babies are full of shit and piss and snot and slevers.' Elaine lifted her boy high into the air, revelling in his mirthful shrieks, in the smiling, fellow-mother-approved glances. 'But they are also full of gorgeous, beautiful smiles – ' she arced the baby back down, bringing her lips into contact with his corduroy-clad tummy – 'and cuddles, and . . .' A further kiss, then a rapid sniff of air, 'kisses and . . . hmm, yeah, and shit.' She sniffed again. 'Yup, he's definitely done a pooh-pooh. Haven't you, Ralphelicious? Haven't you done a pooh-pooh in your panties for your Auntie Anna?'

'Piss off, Elaine. I told you—'

'And *I* told *you*. If you're determined not to go to those parentcraft classes—'

'They're on too early.'

'Whatever. If you're not going to learn from the professionals, then you can bloody well learn from me. You've seen me do it loads of times.' She swung Ralphie over the table top, held him out like an offering. 'Now it's your turn. Go. Quick. Before it starts leaking out.'

She was tired of arguing. Which, for Anna, was akin to being tired of life. She took child, changing bag and self and lumbered her way to the toilets. At least nobody would be talking at her in there. *Hurry up,* bleated her brain, projecting forward to the horror of spillage, then back to the urgency of negotiating the packed, hot room. Once her heart would have skittered in tandem, at the panic of dripping human fluids and the need to be rid of them. But she had no speed left, no part of her physical body that was unfettered. Not her swollen thighs, nor her spreading, spongy arse. Not the taut convex walls of her belly, stretched beyond elasticity. Not the tight, breathless grind of her bones. Even her heart was sluggish, while, clenched inside her, another heart quickened. She never thought pregnancy would be so voracious. It was natural she felt jittery; this was a transition only. A metamorphosis for the baby, yes, but for her, just a staging post, and then a return to self.

'Okay you.' She laid the baby on the pull-down mat. Ha. First test passed – knowing that the yellow plastic ironing board clipped against the wall was in fact a changing table. 'Let's see if it's true what little boys are made of.'

It was. Carefully, head turned as far to the side as was possible while still being able to observe little Ralphie's nether regions, she held his kicking heels in her right hand, as she'd seen Elaine do, and raised his bottom off the mat, her left hand extracting the soiled nappy beneath. Sorted. Bundled up and taped, the smell was almost bearable. Quick wipe with the wet-ones, rummage for another nappy . . . oh . . . cream. Elaine normally put cream on his bum . . . a search for cream and a warm sprinkle of urine as the baby, glorying in the liberty of finding himself *en plein air*, shot a jet of pee directly on to her hand and hip.

'Oh, fuck! Stop it! Stop it, you wee . . .' She grabbed a wad of paper towels, held it over him until the peeing stopped, a pungent warmth growing in her hand. Ralphie gave a beatific smile, and she started to laugh.

'Feel better now, do you?' One elbow on his belly to hold him in place, she crouched so she could wash her hands under the tap, then lifted the baby and dried his back with more paper towels. The rim of his vest was damp, but his wee top was fine. Ish. Elaine need never know.

She started as the door banged next to her, and a man's head and shoulder appeared. Fat shoulders, topped with a baseball cap and small, downturned head.

He stared at her feet. 'Oh.'

Kept on staring, like he couldn't believe she was there. Either that, or he was dumbfounded by the size of her spilling ankles. She scooped up the baby, held him close to her breast. There was something unnerving in the man's stance, a delicate pause in this rotund body that suggested he was poised. To go forward or go back, she wasn't sure.

'Excuse me. I think you'll find this is the Ladies.'

'Oh right, hen. My apologies.'

He backed out, face still concealed by the tilt of his head and his hat. Softly drawing the door shut, he apologised again.

'So sorry.'

Anna waited a moment, letting her breathing regulate, which was difficult through squashed, thin lungs. She had to control this stupid panic; it was oozing into every part of her life. In one day she had gone from mellow earth mother to a woman who was feart of public toilets. Threat dripped from leaky taps and cisterns. Her breath began to mist the mirror. In and out. In and out. After a minute, the shiveriness abated.

'See me, I'm just a daftie. This is the only threatening thing here, isn't it Ralphie-boy?' Anna picked up his soiled, bagged nappy and dumped it in the plastic bin. 'Well, that and your hair maybe.'

As the fluorescent light fuzzed over Ralphie's wiry head, it was obvious. He was not to be soft, burnished copper like her Laura. No. This child was definitely a ginger.

Chapter Nineteen

It was growing dark by the time Mary returned to Calder Riggs. She was exhausted; her night without sleep had combined with the nonstop jigging of her manufactured day to send her brain into a kind of gentle fuzz, where she knew she was walking and looking and digging out change for the bus, but was registering little except the obligation to tramp forward until she reached home.

The princess, impeded by the weight of her waterlogged gown, trudged relentlessly through the snow, drawn like a homing pigeon—

Oh for God's sake. She wasn't a child.

If Bernie wasn't answering her phone, there was nothing else for it but to return to The Riggs. Mary had spent the day considering the permutations of what she would say; would she wait until they were alone, or confront Fiona with an audience? And now, with the clear white security light above the farmhouse door bleaching out her eyes, so that she had to blink and walk and think all at once, her resolve abandoned her.

She squeezed her eyelids together, trying to see past the glare. Two upstairs windows were lit, the rest of the house a charcoal sketch. Then a scuffling sound to her left. 'Mary,' whispered an urgent voice. 'Mary, ohmigod, is that you?'

A figure emerged from the nearest loosebox. Wee Jessie, covered in muck, her face all streaked and damp. Mary felt a swell of happiness at seeing her, of joy at her world, this world of dirty flanks and simplicity which was still turning with or without Mary's presence. Calder Riggs was a permanent, rooted network; it was solid. Jess lurched towards her, arms all primed to hug.

'Jesus! You gave me a fright, so you did,' said Mary.

The child pressed her cheek into Mary's breast.

'Hey, should you not be at home, madam? It's getting late.'

Jess whimpered, then out came a slew of tears. 'I can't believe it's you. You didn't do it, did you? Please say you didn't do it, please. I said you couldn't—'

'Jess, honey. What are you on about?'

Had one of those wee rich kids been bullying her? Jess was worth ten of them, with their posh hand-stitched saddles and teen-glossed lips. Mary pushed her away, gently, so she could see her face.

'Calm down, you. What on earth are you getting so upset about?'

'Oh, it's terrible. They've stopped all the lessons already, and she says she's going to sell the horses ... Oh Mary,' whispered Jess, 'tell me you didn't do it.'

'Do what?'

There was a chill hand inside her, turning. Mary was no longer made of water but of cold, cold premonition; Jess's face scarlet, the bare bright glare of the security light accentuating each patch of red.

'Oh, oh, the police are saying you did, they've been here all day, questioning us and that you've run away and – are you gay? They're saying that you're all gay – and Bernie *and Miss Cairns too*—'

Mary seized her arms, shook her until all the runaway words stopped. 'Jessie! For fucksake, what is it? What's wrong?'

Jess swallowed, her round sweet face becoming settled like a mask.

'She's dead, Mary. Bernie's dead.'

For several hours now, Mary has worn that phrase around her neck. Occasionally, when the weight grows too great and she can no longer feel it, she fingers the knot, pulls it a little tighter until the pain comes back and it is real again. If you held your hand in snow, the same thing would happen, or like when you wash your hands in the burn and the cold is just cold, then it becomes unbearable and then, after you can bear it no longer, it begins to hurt so much that it stops, until you move position, and its intensity reappears.

Strange, that she should have come back here. All the world to choose from, and she runs to a place she hardly knows. But today, after they had gone to get Mary's security card, and they had been coming back down the stairs from Personnel, Cilla had told her that there were actually two different staircases: one fawn-gold marble, the other grey, workaday.

Typical Glasgow, she had smiled. *Fancy marble one for show, and this one for actually using. All fur coat an nae knickers, that's us.*

She had stopped in the foyer. The protesters from earlier had gone; it was the quiet winter twilight when people are making tea or thinking about packing up early and heading for home.

D'you want to see my most favourite thing in the whole place? Cilla had asked, pushing the revolving door into a single spin. Outside, she had taken Mary's arm, directing her to a spot about halfway into George Square. It was freezing cold, glowing fog suspended like iced cobwebs above the ground, and the Christmas lights not yet lit.

Right, turn round.

The City Chambers was a massive, intricate wedding cake. From this perspective, you could see the whole panoramic vista of domes and spires and statues, softened by the glow of spotlights. Come Christmas, they'd change the yellow illuminations to pink and blue.

See, up there? Cilla had pointed to a spot on the apex of the pediment that sat dead-centre of the building, directly in front of its largest tower. A group of three women, two seated, one resplendently tall, gazed sightless over Glasgow. The standing figure had her right arm raised, wielding a burning torch. On her head was carved a diadem of sun rays, at her feet, the darkening city.

Tour guides'll tell you she's Glasgow's Statue of Liberty, but she's not. There's three of them up there: Truth, Riches and Honour. And that one standing is Truth. Beautiful, isn't she? Cilla had winked at Mary. *Just so you know I do know something about the place.*

Truth at the centre of her city.

It had been easy enough to return here tonight. Still sufficiently early in the evening that Mary's excuse of work had seemed plausible to the man in the Gatehouse, her brand-new proof of identity card acting like a magic key.

Press Office? Ach, I don't know why yous lot don't just sleep in there and be done with it.

If he had challenged her at all, she would have crumbled. Even now, she does not know what is holding all the pieces in place. Thin wire, perhaps, cutting into her flesh.

With the lights out and her head down, there are no flitting shadows to alert anyone that she is here. Shifts will have changed, that man gone home, another now sipping from his flask or munching sandwiches. Her neck aches from where her bundled jacket prods her, and she shifts on to her side, her arms cuddling her shoulders. Smells of nylon and dust trailing.

Lying in her space on the City Chambers floor, between the legs of her desk and the wastepaper bin, Mary can see the door that leads to the basement. There are ghosts down there, and black things – bales of secrets and files and passages; and the door does not lock, she has found. The wheel-like handle is just for show, it is not a safe at all. Just a clumsy pastiche that cannot even lock. And because of that, Mary cannot sleep. Who knows what might slither through the pointless door? There is no one to watch over her, not cold Truth above her, nor the wrestling angel outside.

There is nothing and no one except the utterance round her neck.

'She's dead, Mary. Bernie's dead.'

Chapter Twenty

Strangulation. You would think that, wouldn't you, mused Alex, what with the tights round her neck and the post mortem report citing an abrasion, brownish-black in colour, of size 9 centimetres by 1.5 centimetres, situated on the left anterolateral aspect of neck extending slightly upwards and to the left from the middle of front of neck. Telling you that there were four more similar-sized abrasions running in a gradated pattern from the middle to front of neck and another abrasion of size 3 centimetres by 2 centimetres on the left side of her lower lip. Illustrating how he'd been playing a concertina round her neck, then had gubbed her in the face for good measure. Telling you that a contusion with clotted blood was present in the anterior neck muscles. That both lungs were found congested. And then it tells you that there was evidence of apnoea, when the oxygen in the body is used up by cells. Well, fine. You'd do that, wouldn't you, if you were being choked to death? You'd suck the very air from your spongy cells and blood, not realising that you were excreting carbon dioxide as you did so, and that it was that very carbon dioxide that was pushing you to a stronger and stronger breathing reflex, right up to the breath-hold breakpoint, at which you can no longer voluntarily hold your breath.

And that's when you get drowned.

'So she wasn't throttled then?' said Shirley. They were in the incident room, eating the Tunnock's teacakes and a pile of muffins that Mandy had brought in for breakfast. Alex had relented. He needed extra bodies; she seemed smart and keen. Okay, she was a wee bit sulky, but she was trying hard, the lassie. Cakes constituted an apology, or an acknowledgement, at least, that she had been a huffy besom up at Calder Riggs. Eager young cops worked twice as hard as seasoned detectives too. Granted, you spent an equivalent amount of time checking that they'd done it right and undoing the knots they got themselves tied in but, well supervised, they were an energetic and obedient resource. Alex glanced round the room, absorbing the various expressions of fixed concentration, of shrill excitement at being *here* in the thick of it, of fatigue, puzzlement, seen-it-all ennui.

'She was throttled, partially,' said Alex. 'And then she was drowned. Partially.'

'My heid hurts,' said the Tube. 'How "partially"?'

'Dry drowning. It happens when your larynx seals up.'

Marisa Jaconelli had explained it to him: how when a certain amount of water is present in the lungs, the laryngeal cords compress as they detect the water coming in. But by doing this, they block the oxygen getting into the lungs as well as water. Nevertheless, the heart keeps pumping blood into the lungs.

'It's called laryngospasm. It can happen during drowning – when the water starts pouring in, the victim will either try to cough it up or swallow it, causing the airway to close up, like a defence mechanism. Or it can be induced by torture. You know, like waterboarding or repeated submersions in liquid. Basically you drown in your own fluids, not the water.'

'But it's a no brainer,' said the Tube. 'She was floating in the canal.'

'I know – but there's very little in the way of canal debris or water in her stomach or her lungs. The pathologist says that water in the lungs tends to indicate the victim was still alive at the point of submersion. Because they'd been panicking and gulping it in, you know? An absence of water in the lungs can indicate a dry drowning or a death before submersion, and that's what we've got here.' Alex read over his notes again. 'Yeah. Definitely dry drowning. However, what they're also saying is that no water in the lungs can also indicate a very rapid drowning, so it's not a hundred per cent conclusive.'

'It never is,' said Shirley.

Alex scratched his head. 'Right, let me finish people.' He'd read this three times already, but talking out loud sometimes helped to clarify his thoughts, as if the act of forming and arranging the words caused the various clots of facts to separate and set. On occasion, certain phrases just sounded right when you actually heard them, while others seemed clumsy and insubstantial. Of course, that system was not a hundred per cent conclusive either.

'Yeah,' he continued, 'if water enters the airways of a conscious victim, they tend to inhale even more as they try to cough it up or swallow it – which can also cause laryngospasm. Either way, water enters the stomach in the initial phase of drowning rather than the lungs. But Francine didn't have much water in her stomach either.'

Shirley helped herself to the last muffin.

'Alex, I'm confused. So what are we saying?'

'Well, if I was taking bets I'd say it was dry drowning before she went in the canal.'

'Why drown someone outside the water when you've frigging gallons of the stuff slooshing about in a dirty great canal in front of you?'

A gentle, consensual fidgeting suggested the troops were all in agreement with Shirley.

'Well, one because she wasn't drowned there at all, just dumped afterwards. Or two, yes she was killed there, but she was tortured first.'

Ian Morrison looked set to speak, but Alex made sure he was quicker off the mark.

'It's just a theory, but look at it all together: the lack of clothing, the ligature, the location. Quiet, so you'd have plenty of time. Near to a road, though, for quick access and egress as required. The fact he stripped her clothes, but there was no obvious sexual assault.'

'That could just be to make identification more difficult.'

'True, but there was no attempt to mutilate the face in any way.'

'No, but he did chuck her in the Forth and Clyde canal,' Shirley took a big bite of muffin. 'Couple of days in there and you'd be nicely green and puffy.'

'Aye,' said the Tube, 'like the creature fae the swamp. I mind this one time, I was hoicking a boy out the Clyde. Been in a week or two at least. Well, did his whole arm no come off in my hand? Started fucking floating doon the watter again and we couldny catch him. Had to get the divers out.'

The Mexican wave of nods and shuffles was starting again. Alex raised his voice. 'Hear me out. I think he was upping the ante, drawing it out for maximum effect. I think Francine was half choked, then her head was held under water just as the ligature was loosened. Going by the array of striped bruising on her neck, this could have happened several times. The thing about dry drowning is it doesn't always happen right away, so he could keep it going for a while and she'd still be conscious.'

'Sick bastard,' Shirley muttered.

'But why?' asked the Tube. 'Some form of coercion?'

Ian shook his head. 'There's still no sexual motive evident.'

'What about the fishies then?' said the Tube.

'There's nae fish in the canal, ya twat.'

'Aye, there is actually,' said Shirley.

'Naw, the tights he used? Why use fishnets? The lassie worked in a stable, she wisny wearing any fish—'

'No wait,' said Alex. 'Go back. Torture – why do people torture?'

'Like I said, because they're sick bastards.' Shirley stirred her coffee, the spoon tinging two delicate taps on the edge of the cup before she dropped it into the matching saucer. Blowsy, rose-painted china with a golden trim. She kept both cup and saucer in her desk drawer when she went home, rather than piling them up on the tray like everyone else's. As if any of the boys would be seen dead sipping from a Granny-cup.

The Tube frowned. 'Yes, but why dress it up to look like a pervy sex killing?'

'Maybe it was a pervy sex killing,' said Ian. 'Maybe he just gets his rocks off watching folk drown.'

Alex didn't think so. He couldn't say why exactly, it was still just clouds. That was how he always saw it – clouds and clouds and a hand that held hundreds of colourful kites. And he was the clouds and the kites, and the hand keeping everything together. And the other hand was hidden, but it was working too. At the start of every investigation you would split in two – one part permitting each hunch and clue and potentially useless or diverting scrap of information to bob and fly. That must be your creative side – was that the left brain? And you had to keep all these possibilities flying in nonjudgemental parallel lines. But, concurrent with this, the opposite side of you, the analytical problem-solving sculptor, was mentally chopping away, trying to cut to the one solid lead you had as quickly as you could. At some point, you had to decide which of your options looked strongest, and let the rest go. Let them fly up into the air.

For some reason, this notion of torture kept tugging him. Maybe it was that war book he'd been reading, the plain graphic accounts of genocide and mutilation that came after the soldiers' wistful letters home. When he'd finished reading the factual narrative, he'd go back and reread the letters. See if he could find the subtext of screaming woven through the mundane.

Alex sighed. 'Maybe he does. But what if he *was* using coercion. You know, trying to extract something from her – information, a name, an apology? He could have been an ex-punter—'

'Exactly!' said the Tube. 'That's how he used the fishies. Do yous no see that? He *knew* she was a hoor, and he was punishing her for it.'

'You mean he's a wronged lover then—'

Ian interrupted him. 'The lassie was gay.'

'Okay then, *she* could have been a wronged lover.' Alex clasped his hands together. He saw politicians do it all the time; it said status and certainty. It said: *Listen to me.*

'Which brings me neatly to another significant finding. Evidence of DNA from the fingernail scrapings, which appears to match that of Mary Brown. Plus, there is evidence of both Mary and Francine's DNA on the jumper that I found near the lock-keeper's cottage. Shirley – still no joy in tracing Mary?'

'Nope. She's no been back to Calder Riggs since Francine went missing. No one there has seen or been in contact with her.'

'Tried her mobile?'

'Aye, but it's switched off.'

'Former addresses?'

'Don't have any as yet. I'm working on it, though.'

'PNC?'

'No trace. No one at The Riggs knows that much about her – she seems to have got in tow with Francine about a year ago. Fiona Cairns says that Francine just turned up with her one day, said Mary needed a job and a place to stay.'

'And Fiona just accepted that, did she?'

'I don't think Fiona refuses Francine much. She said they did have words about it, later. Francine wouldny tell her how she knew Mary, just that she was a friend of a friend, and that she was good with horses. But as we've gathered, Francine didny tell Miss Fiona much about anything.'

'I get the impression . . .' started Mandy. 'Oh, sorry. Is it okay if I chip in? I've never done this before.'

Her hint-of-ingénue had the effect of making all the guys round the table go limp, and of causing Shirley to blow her nose, examine the hanky and then blow again. Shirley often acted like that when bright young things abounded. It was as if she sought ways of making herself as unfeminine and unattractive as she could. Alex didn't understand it; he would have got it if she'd sucked in her belly or tidied up her hair.

Shirley crumpled up the hanky, stuffed it back up her sleeve. 'You chip away, doll. Show us what you're made of.'

'No, it's just . . . I think Fiona really, really loves Francine. I think she's one of these people who knows how lucky she is to have found her partner, you know, that it's a kind of unequal relationship, where you'd give them anything they wanted and never question them, just because you feel so fortunate to be with them at all.'

Mandy had a beautiful heart-shaped face. Blank and clean. She reminded Alex a little of Sandra a few years ago. A swift, dark beat of melancholy winged over him.

'And what makes you think that, Amanda?' said Shirley.

'Oh, you know.' Mandy focused directly on Alex. He watched her tongue come out, damp her lip in preface to her smile. 'Just experience.'

Shirley picked some muffin from her teeth. 'And in your . . . experience, Amanda, do you think Fiona Cairns is *so* besotted that she could flip and murder her beloved? *If* she felt she'd been betrayed?'

Mandy shook her head. 'Nah. I don't think so. She doesn't seem like a bunny-boiler to me. In my humble experience, that is.' She smiled. 'Sergeant.'

The Tube gave a funny wee snigger, which became a cough and then an excruciating chasm of nobody talking or making eye contact. Some days Alex felt he was a ringmaster, not a marvellous kite flyer at all. There's the trapeze twins: Ian and Shirley – one swings while the other catches; both steady, sure hands, but each with one eye on the spotlight and the other on the crowd. In bimbles Tubey the clown, with his nodding-dog head and his inarticulate limbs. Oh look – there's Mandy, the freshly trimmed poodle come to strut her stuff.

Shirley was staring at him. Alex stuck his tongue out, a rapid dart that might have seemed lewd, but was meant to say: *I'm on your side, doll* or, *Kids, eh?* or something more profound. But he said none of those things. Instead, he resorted to corporate-speak, the sort of stuff that was anodyne and good for motivation and building your team.

'Focus, people. Focus. Look, I know it's early in the morning—'

'Early?' said Ian. 'It's still bloody last night for some of us.'

'Well, just think of all your overtime, Ian.'

That was one advantage Ian retained over Alex. Inspectors and above had sold their rights to overtime years ago. So, by the end of this week, Ian – in fact, the whole of Alex's team – would be clearing more cash than him. Still, what greater incentive did a man need than the love of a good team and a grateful public? He took a quick gulp of coffee. Yeah, well, he'd not encountered much of either.

'Right. As I was saying: when and where exactly was Francine last seen?'

Ian turned the pages of his A4 pad. 'One of the lassies at the stables said she left around three p.m. Apparently she was going to get a bus into town.'

'Do we know where to?'

'No.'

'Right. Find out what buses run along Maryhill Road—'

'Already done that,' sighed Ian.

'Right.' He had to stop saying 'right'. 'Good. Great. Well, can you get in touch with the depot and see what buses have got CCTV installed, and, if so, how long they retain the film? Failing that, make a start on interviewing any drivers who were working that day.'

Ian raised a languid hand. 'Already under way.'

'You're some man, Ian.' Alex forced himself to smile. 'And when will we have any feedback?'

'I'm sending wee Darren back down there this afternoon, boss.'

'Right. Well, keep me posted. Shirley – what about the latest search of locus? Door-to-doors in the vicinity, too – what's that pulled up?'

Shirley examined her fingernails. Exhaled slowly. 'I was wondering when you were going to ask me that.' She leaned her bountiful breasts on the rim of the table. 'Well, as you know, there's very few houses in Lochburn Avenue, and most of the business premises close up around five, five thirty. But there is a scrappy at the bottom end.'

'Milton's?'

'That's the one. Wee jakey with the checked bunnet and the red nose?'

'Aye. Reginald . . . ?'

'Reginald McPhee. Well, some nights, when Mr McPhee isny talking to Mrs McPhee, or he's maybe had more than a wee swally or two, he bunks down in his Portakabin rather than going home. And, luckily for us, he happened to be there night before last. Around six thirty, he's heading out to the chippy for his dinner, has one foot off the pavement to cross the road—'

'This is on Lochburn itself?' said Alex.

'Aye. Next thing he says this car damn near takes his toes off. It was heading north—'

'Towards the Stocks?'

'Aye. So, anyway, he kicks it.'

'He kicked it?'

'Aye. When he says it "damn near took his toes off", I think what Reggie means is that he was pished as a fart, and thereby wandered into the path of an oncoming vehicle. Which clearly wasn't going very fast if Pie-eyed Reggie was able to focus his thoughts, keep his balance and swing his tackety boot all at the same time.'

Alex went over to the whiteboard that took up most of the far wall. 'Right, okay.' He started writing:

CAR?

'So we have a vehicle in the vicinity, on the evening of Monday 12 November, about thirty minutes before the possible time of death. Anything significant about this car?'

COLOUR/MAKE?

Shirley shrugged. 'Fuck knows. Reggie thinks it was blue, or maybe green. Possibly brown. And it definitely had a driver, who was definitely a man. Although the description has changed three times already. He's been dark-haired, bald and wearing a hat. So I'm all set for him to decide it was a wumman next.'

'Great.'

MALE – DESCRIPTION? FEMALE?

Alex clicked the lid on the marker pen, returned to his chair. 'Mandy, there's something you can do. Find out if either Fiona Cairns, Mary Brown or Francine own a motor vehicle, or have hired a motor vehicle in the last wee while, and if so, what type it is, yeah? In fact, find out if any of them possess driving licences at all.' He stopped. 'Sorry Shirley. Carry on. Did the driver stop or get out?'

'No. And that, to me, is the crucial thing. Auld Reggie is a joke – someone like that blooters your motor, you're hardly going to be scared to confront him, are you? Tea time, street's empty. Well, you'd get out and remonstrate, wouldn't you?'

'We're not all as feisty as you, detective sergeant.' Ian had affected a Kelvinside drawl, the sort a well-heeled lady would adopt as she sipped Earl Grey in the Willow Tea Rooms.

Shirley gave him the finger. 'Piss off. Course you would. Some old dosser kicks lumps out your car, and you just drive off? Don't even roll down your window to shout something as you pass?'

'Yes, but all we have is Reggie's account,' said Alex. 'He could have dreamt the whole thing in a whisky-induced haze. And even if it did happen, how do we know he's got the day and time right?'

'Because, one – ' Shirley struck her left index finger with her right – 'he bought a lottery ticket at Zaffar's and the time and date is on it—'

'Wait the now, Alex,' said Ian, slightly more animated than before. 'Shirley's right. Mind we saw him, outside the office? When we were heading up to the Stocks?'

Alex had a vague recollection of a bag of rags blowing in the wind. 'Was that Reggie?'

'Pretty sure it was.'

'Well, there you go then,' said Shirley. 'When was that – hour and a half later? Was he limping?'

'How the hell would I know?' said Ian. 'He was that pished he could barely stand.'

'Okay. So we know he was definitely on the move around that time – from Zaffar's to the chippy to Maryhill Police Office, stopping en route no doubt at various hostelries for some anaesthetising alcohol. Because, two: he also presented at the Western yesterday, complaining of a broken toe. Swollen so bad he couldn't get his boot on. Minging old goat turned up in his stocking soles. So I sent someone back down to the Portakabin to check his boots.'

'And?'

'Traces of green car paint on right toecap and inner side.' She lifted her bosom from its perch on the desk and sat back, satisfied.

'That's brilliant, sergeant.' Mandy's smooth face was lively now; she looked genuinely impressed.

'Guy works in a scrapyard,' said Ian. 'Could be from any one of a hundred vehicles.'

'And,' said Shirley, 'I also spoke very nicely to Scenes of Crime and the Traffic, both of whom have concluded their searches of the locus. Interestingly, two flakes of metallic green paint were found in the grass at that wee inshot on the right, just before the steps up to the Stocks.'

Quickening pulse of a glad, glad heart. His fingertips blue, Alex fiddling with the marker pen. The smell was chemical. He resisted the desire to dance over to the whiteboard and scrawl *Get it up you, Ian.*

'So,' he said. 'If the paint on Reggie's boot matches the paint found near the locus . . . ?'

Shirley continued her one-woman show. 'We have evidence of a vehicle travelling up Lochburn Avenue at approximately six thirty p.m. on the evening of Francine Gallagher's murder and, more significantly, stopping directly below the pedestrian access to Stockingfield Junction. The Traffic have identified a partial tyre track which peters out, then picks up again on the other side of the bridge, heading north away from the scene.'

'Can they match the tyre with a specific vehicle type?' asked Mandy.

'No, not unless it was a brand-new motor,' said Ian. 'You think how often folk change their tyres.'

'Aye,' said Shirley, 'but we have the paint scrapings to go with it, and that definitely will narrow it down. If we find out the shade of green, then find out which manufacturers use that specific paint type, how many vehicles of that type, age and colour are registered in Scotland—'

'Okay. Excellent.'

They didn't all need to know the infinite detail. If they had leads, then they also had actions, and it was Alex's job to allocate and impel. Time was pressing; the first forty-eight hours of a murder investigation were crucial. That was bollocks actually, it was the first twenty-four that were truly imperative, but he was only expanding the parameters to fit his personal circumstances, the way that people played with ages. *Och aye. Forty's the new thirty you know.* If he told himself that two days on was still fresh and fertile ground, it kept the adrenalin sharp. It was adrenalin that was driving him, not panic. He was calm, he was flying his high, bright kites.

He turned to Shirley. 'You dealing with that then?'

'Well, maybe that's something Mandy could be working on, along with driving licences et al.'

'Sure.'

Mandy nodded. 'Thanks, sergeant.'

'I prefer blueberry muffins, by the way.' Shirley tilted her chin.

'I'll remember next time.'

Enough with the tea and chat. The car was a positive line of enquiry, the DCI was panting down his neck and Alex needed to get out of this room, with its insipid walls and lack of light and Francine's death mask staring down at him. He owed her nothing more than he owed any victim, but, with Francine, he could hear her actual voice; he could see her big sister, shambling, high on heroin, and Francine – live sparking Francine – holding her arm to keep her from falling. The monkey-god crept on to his back.

'Now, to go back to the dry-drowning.' He uncapped his nice blue pen. 'Are we happy to at least consider that this may indicate a degree of torture was used on Francine?'

A few mumbled 'ayes' and 'sures'.

'Good. Well, on that basis, let's also assume that the killer may well have been known to her, and that this is not just your random sadist. So Shirley, I need your guys to go back to Calder Riggs and interview all the staff there again. Find out if there were any fights, arguments, vendettas, innuendo to do with Francine, any suspicious characters, incidents, blah-de-blah-de-blah. And Ian, I'd like you to make contact with all of Francine's previous known associates if you can, and do the same thing. I'll draw you up a list of any of the girls I remember that she used to pally about with.

Oh, and do a trawl of any recent assaults on prostitutes too, just in case there's some connection.'

'Sure. But d'you want me to check assaults right back to when Francine was hooring it?'

Alex thought for a moment. 'Nah.' That would use up more time they didn't have. 'No, just stick to attacks in the last twelve months for the moment.'

'Will do, boss.'

Alex stood up. 'And we definitely need to trace that Mary Brown. It's a bloody big coincidence that she arrives without any history whatsoever, then disappears the exact same day Francine gets killed.'

'Right you are,' said Shirley. Ian was already calling three or four DCs around him, tasking them with various duties. He was certainly a grafter, when he had to be. You had to give him that.

'Oh, did you want a shufty at the body at all?' asked Shirley. 'Lynne Campbell's going back down to the mortuary to see that boy that got stabbed in the arse. Stupid bastard just sat in his motor and bled to death. Imagine that; draining to death out your arse.'

'Imagine.'

'So. You want another look at her? You could get a lift with Lynne?'

There was a simian chattering in his head, irritating hiccups of noise.

'No, you're alright. I'm away to work on my list.' He grinned at her. 'A Hoors' Who. *Boom-boom.*'

She tapped the side of her head. 'Boom, boom yourself.'

Chapter Twenty-One

There was a noise outside. Mary jumped up, pulling her top straight. Her head ached, mouth thick and dry, and there was one dull instant where she was unaware of anything. And then it hit, at the same moment the door swung open and Celine strolled in. Her cardboard Costa cup rocked in her gloved fist: 'Christ! You're in early!'

It was like Mary was watching herself from up above; this dishevelled girl saying, 'Yeah. I wanted to make a good impression, you know?' as a tight chain wrapped and pulled her back down, but past herself, down inside the ground until she was filled with mud and sickness.

Bernadette was dead. That man had killed her over paltry land. Perhaps Fiona was complicit; who knew? Mary doubted it, but who knew? And now he would come after her. Mary had seen his face. She began to shake.

'You okay?'

The involuntary spasms were in her teeth now. She had to seize some kind of control. She was safe in here, she was safe. Nobody knew she was here, it was a place with strong walls and security guards; she could hide until she had worked out what to do, but if she broke down and started screaming again someone would want to take her home. Or have her committed. So she cannot, she CANNOT. She wants to say *My best friend has been murdered. I am terrified.* She lets the heavy, deadening chains do their work, and they pull her into place.

'Yeah.' Buttoning up her jacket. 'Freezing in here, isn't it?'

Celine shrugged. 'It'll warm up soon enough. Once all the hot air starts churning. Jesus. Takes two caramel lattes before I'm fit for anything in this dump.' She swigged from her cup, scowled at Mary. 'Hot air, yeah? The bullshit people talk in here?'

Mary nodded. 'I get it. So. What do you want me to do first?'

Celine shook the pile of padded envelopes and slim white letters clutched in the hand not reserved for Costa's caramel latte. 'Well for a start, you're supposed to pick these up from the mail room, not me.'

'Sorry.'

'Did Cilla not tell the guys yesterday when she took you along? They're meant to hand the mail to you when you come in in the morning. Useless shower of shits they are too. I'll have a word—'

'No, it's fine. My fault. I didn't realise.'

'Right. Well, we're supposed to go through all the cuts and tick what we think are the most important stories to do with the council, who all should be alerted to any breaking news yaddah-yaddah, and also where the stories should be circulated and filed.' Celine put down her cup, then dropped her heavy, fur-trimmed coat on to her desk. 'Quite frankly, though, I can't be arsed, because no one reads them; no one listens to anything the Press Office says or recommends. They all think that just because they "communicate" with people every day, then there's no skill involved. But, by Christ they're quick enough to phone us in a panic when any shit hits the fan—'

'Would you like me to do the cuts then?' Mary wanted to sit somewhere quiet and focus on a task, any task.

Celine unfurled her mohair scarf. Held one end mid-air, as if she was considering its weight. 'Yeah. Why not? Good experience for you anyway. High time they were done electronically, but Margaret likes the "feel of paper in her hand". Not that she actually does much with them. Yes, I'll just . . .' She headed back towards the door. 'Yeah. I need to see someone anyway. Just leave them on my desk when you're done and I'll check them, okay?'

'Sure.'

'Mind and get them all done before Bill comes in at half past, right?'

'Will do.'

After Celine had gone, Mary checked the clock above the fireplace. It was eight a.m. She found the remote control for the TV screens lying beside the fax machine, switched the tellies on. Their background chatter was comforting, and the Scottish news would be on soon. There was a cluster of mugs round the kettle, a tin of shortbread biscuits, some loose teabags in a cup. Mary made herself a kind of breakfast; she'd not eaten since yesterday lunchtime. The shortbread made her cough, but she swilled a piece down with some milkless tea. Then she laid the cuts out across her desk. Swimming pool closures, a flower show in Royston. The Kingston Bridge roadworks. Christmas shopping down on last year, even though it was mid-November. There was a lot about the protests yesterday outside the City Chambers, complete with a photo of that eejit on the Cenotaph.

And there was this. The news for which she was – and was not – searching.

Police are appealing for information regarding the death of a woman in Maryhill. The female, a Francine Gallagher of Calder Riggs Farm, Maryhill, was last seen in Maryhill Road at approximately two thirty p.m. Monday 12 November. Her body was found in the Forth and Clyde canal later that evening, at around seven thirty p.m.

They were talking about some woman called Francine, but it was Bernie's picture staring at her. Of course it was what Mary had been looking for; but it didn't mean she wanted to see it. It was her Bernadette, thin-faced and wearing a challenging sneer. Head titled at an angle, up and to the left; a pose Mary was bitterly familiar with. It was a police mug-shot.

Detective Inspector Alex Patterson, who is leading the enquiry, has confirmed that police are treating the death as suspicious, and is appealing for witnesses to come forward. DI Patterson said: 'Francine may also be known to some people as Bernadette Murphy. Whatever name you knew her by, what's important is that this is a young woman whose last movements are at present unknown to us – and we really need the public's help. It's vital we speak to anyone who saw Francine between the hours of two thirty and seven thirty p.m. on Monday 12 November. Francine was of slight build, with long black hair, and we believe she was wearing a red sweatshirt at the time.'

No, thought Mary. I had it on, not her. Seizing on a futile detail, because to think of the sweatshirt was not to think of Bernie's drowned, wet body lying empty in the dark. Her shivering hand sought more shortbread, sweet, thick sawdust which she could cram into her mouth.

Police have been concentrating their search around the Stockingfield Junction area of the Forth and Clyde canal. DI Patterson continued: 'If you saw or heard anything suspicious at all, either on the canal towpath, on Lochburn Road, or anywhere in the vicinity, please contact the incident caravan we have stationed in Lochburn Road, call Crimestoppers on 0800 555 111 or speak to one of my team at Maryhill Police Office. We'd also like to talk to anyone who knew Francine, even if it was some years ago, when she used to stay in the Townhead area of the city. I can assure you that any information given to us will be treated in the strictest confidence.'

The man that had killed Bernadette would come after Mary. Except Bernadette had never existed; she had lied, the same as Fiona, same as everyone fucking did. Who was Francine Gallagher? Was that why Bernie had plucked Mary from the street? Because she'd been there too, when she was Francine bloody Gallagher? Mary looked again at the hard-faced portrait: a young girl old before her time, with the unfocused eyes of a junkie and the made-up face of a whore.

It had been a warm summer evening last year, five days since Mary had been released from prison, two nights since she'd walked from her mother's house for the last time. Walked was a misnomer. It was more like: prise open bedroom window and dreep from sill to kitchen window-ledge, then fall on to the ground, spraining her ankle and alerting the neighbour's cat in the process. For the first day she had managed, determined to show her mother that heroin was just a hobby; Mary could come off it any time. She didn't need her mother to imprison her like some middle-class Rapunzel. She'd gone to a pal's house, had a smoke, nothing more. See – smoking, not injecting. Only addicts injected. By the second day, her pal had got sick of her. Mary had no money, and her desperation was growing. Even locked up, her mum had fed her limited doses of methadone, which took off some of the edge but didn't quell the hunger. Alone and penniless in the arse-end of the city, she had resorted to shoplifting in a twenty-four-hour garage on the Broomielaw. But her reflexes were slow. She had fumbled, dropped. Was chased. Found herself, eventually, in Cadogan Street, a narrow, sunless stretch of glass-clad offices and cruising cars.

She had been desperate. Desperate, and at first she was only begging, then one of the girls had come across the road from the doorway she was standing in, had slapped her. Told her to *get tae fuck*, because this bit was for working girls, *no fucked-up wee dossers like her*. Of course, that had given her the idea.

The pain where the girl had thumped her was excruciating, Mary's nerve-endings shrieking without the balm of heroin. She had shambled further down the street, cramps in her gut, body aching worse than flu. Turned right and ended up on Argyle Street, beside a tawdry shop selling rubber items and red nylon lace panties. The window of it looked like Hallowe'en. Mary had shrugged off her cardigan so her upper arms were exposed, pivoted her waist so her tits stuck out from her frayed grey T-shirt, which may once have been white. And yes, she had seen her reflection in the shop window, but she hadn't cared. Being clutched by withdrawal and clawing want is indescribable; forces so potent that they crush your natural shame or sensibilities, because all you crave is that euphoric rush. Your body makes bliss from endorphins, when you run or laugh or love. But a junkie does none of these things. They vomit and shudder, they fart, go limp, are paranoid. Wraiths who rob and lurk in a half-life until they are filled up with heroin and are briefly whole. Like an evil impostor, the heroin locks on to the endorphin receptors in your brain, begins to flood between the nerve cells and for one, perhaps two minutes you are on the fastest, highest ride, opiates bathing your brain. Then they seep into your bloodstream and it all calms down. You are safe, beautiful. You are replete. If there was heroin in front of Mary right now, stashed in the shortbread tin beside the biscuits; she would take it all.

She sipped some more of her watery tea. That evening in Argyle Street, she had been prepared to sell her body for drugs. But an angel had rescued her. Much smaller than the gleaming ones on the lampposts in George Square, this little, jagged angel had come bearing a Thai carry-out.

'Alright?' she had asked Mary's recumbent, lolling head. 'You waiting for someone?'

Mary had registered the voice was female, and that it was soft, not shrieking like the female who'd hit her. Thrown that her first would be a woman, glad that it would soon be over, she had blurted, absurdly: 'D'you want sex?'

Bernie had laughed. 'Cheers, but I'm alright with my curry, thanks. Thai Royale. You know it? Just past the Hielanman's Umbrella?'

Mary had tried to shake her head.

'Best Thai restaurant in Glasgow. Been going there for yonks, so I have.'

Mary didn't reply, but the food had smelled delicious.

'When did you last have something to eat?' The angel's face was very close, scrutinising her.

'Dunno. D'you want sex?'

'You've no done this before, have you, hen?'

And only now does Mary realise the significance of what Bernie had said next:

'Listen. Naebody asks "do you want it?" That just gives them the chance to say no.'

Bernie had taken Mary home with her that night, and thus Mary's new life at Calder Riggs began. Food, bath and bed; it was all a bit hazy, but she clearly remembered Bernie coming into her room the next morning. She had sat on the bed, told Mary she would be eating cold turkey for a week. Then she had touched the back of Mary's hand. 'Best not to say how we met, okay? I'll tell them you're an old pal.' So how they met never did become nostalgic folklore, to be reminisced over during dinner. Mary had thought it was to protect her, and she had repaid Bernie with silence and devotion. But it had been all to do with protecting Bernadette bloody Francine Gallagher.

She re-read the newspaper report. No way could she go to the police, not if what wee Jess had said was true. The police thought *she* had done it?

But, if she didn't get help, then the man would come after her.

The edges of her knuckles grazed her teeth. She quite liked the sensation; the little darts of pain were stimulating. It felt right that she should be hurting herself. Maybe if she had returned home that night, she would have found Bernie, bumped into her like she hadn't on the bus. Together they would have walked to Calder Riggs and no bastard would have been able to touch them.

Mary switched on her PC, fired up the Internet. It took moments to find the address for Maryhill Police Office. She cut the address from the website, pasted it on to a new document and carefully typed *DI Alex Patterson* above the address. Then she printed it off, trimmed round the text so it was label size. Another Word document, another few lines.

Murder of Francine Gallagher: You need to check out Robert Crilley.

The planning papers were locked in her desk drawer. One day, and they had given her keys. Mary unlocked the drawer, checked the application form. Then she typed:

14 Dungavel Crescent, Barlanark, Glasgow.

They are builders and they are trying to steal Calder Riggs Farm. A fat middle-aged guy who works for them has already attacked—

She stopped. If she wrote 'attacked her', one of the kids at Calder Riggs might remember Mary had also been there, when the man had jumped out on them at the woods. She deleted 'has already attacked', inserted 'killed her'. The word bawled at her from the page, exploding fragments of ink. Her finger hung over the delete key for a while, then she printed it off as it was, deleted the file, and put the letter in a plain brown envelope. Before she even lifted it from the printer though, she pulled her sleeve down, so her fingers never touched the page. No handwriting, no fingerprints, no voice recordings from a phone call. This was as anonymous as it gets. There was a mail basket by the door of Bill's office. Mary slipped the envelope under some other stuff and returned to her seat just as Celine came in, munching on a bacon roll.

The man would always come after her. Unless she went after him.

Chapter Twenty-Two

'And finally, this Citicard thing.' Mrs Reekie held aloft what appeared to be a green and gold credit card. Anna was sitting at the far end of the conference table, her belly pushing her even further to the fringes, and the only bit she could read was the word 'specimen', stamped in red across a photograph of a young female.

'Is that you, mum?' asked Colin Potter. 'My, you were a looker in your day.'

'This is my day, right now, Colin. I am in my prime, little girls, my prime.'

They all laughed, Colin simpering and running one finger along his eyebrow.

'There's been protests all week outside the Chambers, ma'am,' said Stuart Barrowman. 'John Balfour down there has been keeping me updated.'

'I know. But it's all low-level stuff at the moment, which is fine. I'm happy just to give these people their space, so long as they're not being intimidatory or obstructive, okay? Just tell your troops to keep a watching brief.'

'What about Special Branch, mum?' asked Colin. 'Shouldn't they be prowling about with their secret cameras and stuff? Especially now Scotland's on the terrorist map.'

Did he have to keep saying mum like that? She wisny his bloody mother.

'Who's to say Special Branch are not there already, Colin? But of course, if I told you that, I'd have to kill you.'

He touched his forehead. 'Touché.'

'Anyway, in the absence of any breaches of the peace etc, etc, I want these folk treated with courtesy.'

'Ooh-er. That wouldn't wash in the Met, mum. Thought you Jocks was tough? We'd have had the water cannons out by now.'

'Thank you, Colin. These protesters are exercising their democratic rights, and, funnily enough, it's a democracy we police, way up here in Jockland. Otherwise I'd have you impaled on a stake and popped on top of the City Chambers by now.'

Colin allowed his back to slump while his eyes roamed the room for a straight man. *Feed me lines, feed me lines*, he blinked. Stuart smiled, Anna turned over her agenda. Mrs Reekie ignored him.

'I reckon everything'll bimble along fine until they've ironed out exactly who and what's going to be on these cards,' she said. 'And the cooncil tell me that they'll keep us informed regarding any further developments. I believe our Press Office is liaising with both theirs and Greater Glasgow Health Board's, just so we don't get any nasty surprises. So easy does it, aye? Oh, and the only other thing you need to be aware of is that there's a loosely related rally on in Edinburgh today. One of those generic climate change/anti-Big Brother state/we hate G8 fandangos, complete with samba bands. L & B arny expecting huge numbers to attend and, as far as I know, it's all focused round Holyrood, so it should have no bearing on us at all.' She riffed her fingers, hitting the tabletop in a little drum roll. 'Right, well, if that's us, have a good weekend folks. I need to shoot off early. Got a dinner date tonight.'

'Ooh-ooh!'

Colin, all fired up again. He was just skirting the right side of being funny, but Anna wondered if his constant need for witticism was pissing Mrs Reekie off as much as it was her. It wasn't quite innuendo, but there was an element that was unsavoury, or disrespectful. Would he talk to his divisional commander like that if she were a man? Still, Mrs Reekie was well able to put him in his place. And she was kind of smiling at him and shaking her head, so maybe the problem lay with Anna. Was she becoming one of these po-faced political-correctives who saw insult in the everyday? She was certainly becoming paranoid, that was for sure, driving a different route to work this morning because she'd glanced at her horoscope whilst eating Bran Flakes.

Routine may lead to mishap today.

'For your information,' Mrs Reekie was saying, 'my date is with the headmaster of St Saviour's School and the Steering Committee of the Commonwealth Bid. Which reminds me Anna – the first of no doubt gazillions of Games-related events will be coming up soon. I'll brief you early next week, okay?'

'Okay, ma'am.'

Without protest then, or any further consultation, Anna appeared to be destined for the Commonwealth Games team when she came back from maternity leave. There was little point in questioning it; that was the way of the police. There might be an illusion of choice the higher up the ranks you got, but the reality was the same. You're a cop, you're a number, and you'll bloody well do what you're telt. Which was as it should be, really. Though change would eventually filter through there as well, as it was in every other aspect of policing. It was like watching knitting unravel, first one stitch, then another, then before you could stop it, whole rows and shapes and seams had fallen. She was well-versed in the hassle many of her sergeants had with their newest recruits, kids reared on a culture of *I know ma rights*, but with no concept of their responsibilities. Obeying an order? *No way gaffer. Not until you explain it to me first, what your rationale is for making that decision, who did you consult, how will it impact on me? Is it dangerous? Oh. What do you mean, the bad man's just got away?*

It used to bother her, but now it was immaterial. Hour by hour, Anna found herself retreating from any real interest in the cut and thrust of A Division life. Whether it was caused by the growing, gnawing fear that was moving over her, or by her imminent confinement, she didn't know. She fanned her face with her agenda. It was roasting in here; she felt heat and cold, terror and joy far more acutely than before.

She rolled the word in her head. *Confinement.* There was the truth in three syllables. Daily, you withdrawing into your body, becoming limited and obese. Yet, as your physical world was curtailed, your horizons widened massively. Meditatively. You, your brain and your belly becoming separate entities; you were aware, as never before, of your own ticking mortality. In your quiet confinement, you listened to your belly with its independent life, all that glorious writhing and hummocking which you couldn't control. Your brain was roaming freely, much freer than it had ever been. Emotions strung, senses heightened. She could taste the very metal in her blood. She sat on. Wise, aware, and very, very fat.

She watched the men in the room get up, shuffle their papers, and was content to wait. She had cleared her in-tray before coming to Stewart Street, because Anna, too, was leaving early. Friday was swimming day, the one slim link that still entwined her with Laura. In the summer that Rob and Anna had first got together, Laura had been trying out for the local swimming team. Her speed, her strokes were good, but her diving was atrocious. She would stand at the pool edge, toes gripping on to rimmed blue tiles. Encouraged to *relax, lean forward,* she would only freeze until, at last, knees wide and bent, hands clawed, she would drop like a dying crab. Anna had said she would teach her to dive, and so began their weekly swim. Even when Laura decided that early morning training and Sunday swimming meets were not for her (thank God, thank God), they had kept it up, going after school every Friday to the local pool, racing each other in neat fast lines. Laura was still to properly master diving, but, she could easily beat Anna at swimming. If everything had been fine between them, Anna might have been able to say: *Actually, Laura, can we take a wee break until after the baby? I get so breathless now, and I'm frightened my pelvis will disjoint.* But there was an easy familiarity to their side-by-side swimming which Anna couldn't let go. Occasionally, she had felt Laura slowing down to pace her, and that was worth any amount of dismemberment.

Voices bounced from water-shadowed walls. Slowly, Anna lowered herself into the pool, one hand shielding her bump as the other clung to the ladder-rail. Next rung. *Oh, God, God it was cold.* Big stretch down: two rungs at the one time. *Ah-ah-ah.* The water lapped over her bum, sneaking into the space where her bathing costume was stretched so tight it created an open gap above her buttocks. One more step. *Fuckfuckfuck.* A big splashy wave rode up her breasts, as a boy plunged in about ten centimetres from where she was standing. Both feet on the bottom of the pool, Anna turned to draw him a specially sharpened *look*, but she couldn't work out which one the culprit was. The baths were much busier than usual, kids shrieking, queuing for their turn on the diving dale. It was due, no doubt, to the Commonwealth Games adverts starting to go up round the city. Very clever they were: line-ups of athletes and swimmers, each group with a kid in the middle, and the slogan: *He'll be ready. And so will we.* Thus, Glasgow's youth was currently gripped with sports-fever.

It would be a transient thing, it always was. Every summer, when Wimbledon was on, the tennis courts near Anna's old flat would swarm with youngsters in trainers and joggy-bottoms, doing actual running and jumping in their unaccustomed, slouch-cool shoes. A week or so after Wimbledon was over, the courts would revert to stony-red silence, and the weans to drinking and snogging.

When Anna had gone to pay for the two of them today, the woman had only charged for one adult. 'It's because of the Citicard,' she said. 'We're offering free swimming to all under-eighteens in the run-up to the launch.'

'Excellent idea,' said Anna, putting away her purse. Everyone liked a freebie, so maybe this enthusiasm would stick. Anna just wished they'd all pick some other pool in which to be enthusiastic.

She shook out her hair. It too was expanding, thicker and longer than before. When they watched TV together, Rob would run it through his fingers as if it were gold. Gentle, stroking pulls, Anna with her head tipped back, tingles all over her scalp. *God bless you, hormones.* Her, stretching like Alice, hands ready to knead the cushions beneath her. She'd have been happy to let her hair grow for that simple pleasure alone, but there was also the anticipation of the months to come, when she wouldn't have to cram it under a bowler hat.

Another kid dive-bombed into the water, almost striking Anna's shoulder. She looked for Laura, who'd jumped impatiently in at the deep end several rungs ago. There she was, on her second lap already, sleek head bobbing through the throng. It was a rule: no chatting while swimming, just a steady count of lengths until you reached fifty. Only then were you allowed to muck about. Anna wasn't sure who had initiated the rule, or indeed how she was going to catch up with Laura, or manage more than ten lengths in this melee, but she took a breath, then pushed out from the side.

Immediately, that sense of weightlessness; a great landlocked creature gone loose-limbed and free. Slicing through molten ice that embraced her, then went warm. Oh, she was so *light*. This was glorious. She always did proper swimming: head full under, great long sweeps along then up. Chemical ozone-buzz, the sting of chlorine in her eyes, her throat, a blur of bodies, back down for more. It was a beautiful feeling, she was swimming, she was flying. Rocking on the water to the echoes all around. Up and down, up and down, body lapping water lapping body lapping self. And her baby, swooshing to its own erratic rhythm.

She swam down, down as if to catch it, tracing the bottom of the pool. A forest of legs and feet, her halting, rising up. Angry at the three older women in front who were impeding her, necks arched and high so their hair wouldn't get wet. They should rope off a lane for proper swimmers. 'Excuse me,' she muttered, bucking past. Deliberately kicking water high behind her, gleeful when she heard the squeals. She was building up her speed now, swerving, gulping. Sly as a cat, except cats can't swim, but she was finding all the nooks and the channels between these stubborn forms, the plump white shapes that waded and stood. *Get out of the way! Get out of the way!* Why come to a pool if you didn't want to swim? There was a long, lovely space; she could discern tiled wall through body soup and she drove herself forward, gaining on them all, on Laura, she would catch her soon. So light, so free: what had she been scared of? This was Anna, she remained Anna who was powerful and strong and the past could not bite, not when she'd been right.

She *had* been right.

There was the wall, there was space enough to tumble-turn. She forced her head down, her bum up to the tipping point. Felt her legs flail, unbalanced in the shifting reflections of water. The long shrill slide inside; it wouldn't stop, she couldn't find the wall. Her toes were searching, were they in water or air? What was she thinking; she was a bloody Weeble, a pear-shaped disaster of a water-bomb; which way was up? Brightness above her, and legs and feet, she tried to flip back, forward, face down to grey, grey water, then a tug, a sharp fast tug and her head shot sideways. Bubbles from her nose, she could see bubbles and the wall and all these feet and hands. A quick deep fear, a hand pushing, pulling at her hair, her lungs were hurting. She could see the brightness up above, the filmy flick of limbs, but she couldn't reach them. Something was dragging her down. All the bubbles and her hair being pulled, it was caught, her lungs were hurting, full with the need to breathe.

I need to breathe.

A foot kicked her hard in the face. The water red. Red bubbles, red breath. No breath, her hair all caught. She clawed at water, felt it rush away. The chlorine was in her eyes and in her nose and in her throat. Her feet were writhing for some substance, she was screaming as she struggled, in between her lungs. The hand reached out. She felt it, touching. Heard the piercing of a whistle, her hair ripping, scalp ripping. Smooth tiles, her hand on tiles, she could feel the air above as her head jerked free.

'Mum!' a voice was screaming. 'Mum!' Laura, yanking on her hand.

'Careful, she's pregnant,' said another, arms supporting, pulling her up. All Anna could do was gulp and breathe, the air painful as it went in, her mouth thick and stinging with chlorine. They laid her in the recovery position, on grubby grouting and puddles. Anna had no energy to move, her outstretched fingers were inches from a dirty Elastoplast.

'Mum, Mum!'

She could see wet, dimpled knees, then Laura's screwed-up face was by her own. She was crying. 'Are you alright?'

Anna moved her head. The motion made her dizzy. She raised one hand to wipe Laura's cheek. 'Hey baby.' It came out in a cough. 'I'm okay.'

An attendant brought her a towel, they sat her up. Someone else wrapped the towel round her shoulders.

'Look at her nose. It's bleeding!' Circling of buzzards, half the pool had assembled to watch.

'What happened?' said a woman.

'She got her hair caught in the filter.'

'No.' Anna felt her head. There was blood and hair and water on her palm. 'No, I—'

Laura took her hand again. 'What is it?'

'Someone kicked me . . .'

The attendant squatted down. 'Look, the filter is perfectly safe. You should have been wearing a bathing cap. Health and Safety. We can't be held—'

'Mum, what do you mean? Who kicked you?'

'I don't . . .' Anna pushed on to her elbows, her legs slithering on the wet tiles.

'Woah, don't stand up yet.'

'No, it's alright. I need to get up.'

Between them, Laura and the attendant raised Anna to her feet. Folk were mumbling, shaking their heads. Christ, her belly felt like stone. She pushed at her navel, panicking. Nothing moved. Massaged her lower abdomen, deeper, prodding.

'Mum, *don't*. You'll hurt yourself.'

Anna looked at Laura's terrified face.

'*Who* kicked you? You mean on purpose?'

Carefully, Anna moved her neck to scan the bodies in the water. Some folk were staring still, most gone back to their chattering and splashing. Nowhere could she see . . . what? A smug face and a raised hand? *What about yi doll? It was me kicked your melt in. That's right, over here, pig. Me! I'm back.*

Oh Christ, oh Christ. She had to get Laura out of here.

Anna held on to her daughter's arm. 'No, nobody kicked me, pet. I'm sorry. I was confused. Can you just phone your dad please? Just tell him to come and take us home.'

Under the towel, as they helped her off to the changing rooms, Anna kept pressing on her tight, quiet belly.

Chapter Twenty-Three

There was a smudge of mud on his shoe. Joe rubbed the toecap on the back of his opposite trouser leg. All the senior school had been called to an assembly. Last thing on Friday, too, when all the state schools got away early – *Privilege brings responsibility* being one of the headmaster's many mantras. Rumours were rife: the assembly was another lecture on the holiness of chastity; it was about them dogging school and going to the protests at George Square; it was a dire warning about behaviour at the forthcoming Autumn Ball.

It was about finding out who had set fire to Joe.

Surprise us, Patrick had said. It had been Joe's idea to go to George Square, but Patrick had said: *Yeah, why not?* and *then* the others had agreed. Apart from Patrick performing like a monkey on that monument, it had been a bit of a damp squib. No promised riots or marches on the City Chambers, but it had, they all agreed, been a good laugh. Good idea that, Patrick, Doug had said, and Patrick had turned and winked at Joe.

He tried to keep his gait steady, curling up his toes so he wouldn't sway. Joe knew what awaited him if an investigation into the science lab was launched. It amazed him, really, how folk couldn't see the you inside which was always soft and desperate. A casual observer would see a tall, confident young man in the midst of friends he was comfortably at ease with. He must be so good at holding it in, so that not even an ounce of the inside him dribbled out. Of course, if you truly knew what you were looking for, if you cared long enough to stop and scrutinise, you might see it bursting out of a person's eyes. Not him though. Big, placid, daft-but-smart

Joe. He hadn't even told his mum about his burned blazer yet. It lay under his bed, darkly singed and ominous. He would wait until dustmen day, then chuck it in the wheelie-bin at the last minute. But what if she cleaned his room? She always cleaned at weekends. Joe gnawed on his lip. He was working tomorrow – he could just take it with him and stuff it in the lost property box there. Get rid of it before the school phoned.

The assembly, it transpired, was about none of the above.

'Gentlemen – and ladies – as you know, or should do, if any of you bother to take an interest in the world of current affairs, Glasgow was recently chosen to be host city for the Commonwealth Games in 2014.'

On occasions such as Mass and assembly, the head liked to wear his black graduation robes, no doubt evoking the spirit and gravity of the past when none but Jesuits ruled at the college. Did donning a floaty black cape make him think they would take him more seriously? wondered Joe. The head also enjoyed sweeping his arms when he had his cloak on, doing neat, brief turns and peevish marches to punctuate his points.

'Now, Scotland is famed for many things, but one thing we do better than most is, WE KNOW HOW TO PARTY!' He tried to effect a weak little punch in the air at this point, then obviously realised the cringe-factor had become so high it was now unsustainable.

Patrick was seated next to Joe. 'DJ Wanko, in da house,' he whispered.

Joe made a kind of 'hmph' noise, scared to risk actual speech, but equally scared that if he didn't respond at all it would piss Patrick off and he'd direct his next comment to Andy on the other side.

'Hogmanay is a time when people from all over the world make their way to Scotland, to celebrate the ringing out of the old year, and the ringing in of the new. And of course, Christmastide, the birth of Our Lord, is at the heart of our winter celebrations. So, our city fathers, in their wisdom—'

'Check out the teeth,' mumbled Patrick.

The headmaster was wont, in times of extreme stress or excitement, to lose his grip on his dentures. You'd often hear their cheerful clack as he stood in the dinner queue or surveyed a bustling corridor; he liked playing with them, in the way some men played with executive toys or stress balls. Or just their own balls. In the heidie's case, when he was getting himself in a palaver, the teeth took on a life of their own. Already loose from all the clicking, if he was shouting at some poor first year, or going all cheesy-grin hyper-guy like he was now, his upper dentures would simply drop from the roof of his mouth, presenting themselves in a skeletal grin. It was horrible and hysterical, particularly when he realised and began trying to slurp them back up and keep talking at the same time.

'... have ... excuse me – um, have decided that they should mark the occasion by inviting members of the Commonwealth Committee to share in "Glesca's" welcome to the Festive Season—'

Doug, standing behind Joe, sniffed. 'What, ten cans of Special Brew, a good-going rammy and a night in A & E?'

'Yes, indeed,' continued the heidie, 'I'm referring, of course, to the city's magnificent Christmas Lights switch-on.'

A collective apathy drifted over the assembled kids. The man had no idea how to work a crowd. He was an administrator, not an orator. 'But boys,' the heidie was droning on, 'and ladies too, of course – the real honour is that they have asked for some representatives from *this* college to take part, in what is sure to be a gala event.'

He paused, desperate for some oohs and ahs. Not even the teaching staff obliged.

'Um, now, last year, some of our current sixth year were heavily involved in the refurbishment of a local barge. Can anyone remind us of the name of the barge – or indeed of the trust that we were supporting?'

Joe put up his hand.

'*Fucking Slowjo.*'

He knew it must be Doug, and where before this would have been a fact that he simply blanked because it would make no difference whatever he did, now Joe hesitated. It was not cool to raise your hand, to offer knowledge freely and with enthusiasm, like it was not cool to wear your tie a certain way, with the knot pulled neat and all the buttons done. So many subtleties and codes, they hurt his brain.

Slowly, he lowered his hand.

'Yes Joseph. You had something to say?'

Shook his head. 'No sir.'

'Well, *you* should know.' A little hint of teeth. 'You were one of the leading lights of the whole operation.'

I know I was, I know I was. His heart all swollen-full. It would not be cool to give a response. He tried smiling with his eyes.

The headmaster sighed. 'The barge in question is the good ship *Firebird*. Out of the ashes comes new life – a sentiment that rings with the truth of the Gospel, does it not?'

He was looking straight at Joe.

'The Phoenix Trust is a charitable Glasgow enterprise which works with persons from disadvantaged backgrounds, whether it be through poverty, abuse or mental or physical health issues . . .'

Joe closed his eyes, imagined he was lying on the splintered deck again. Could almost smell hot tar and pungent water, hear the rub of rope, the sound of them all sneezing because of the sawdust up their noses. Him and Brillo, Patrick, Alan and Doug. That was how he'd got to the exalted position of being permitted access to their lunchtime clusters. He had loved helping on that barge. Over a hundred years old it was, and their job had been to revamp the wheelhouse, give it a gloss of white and red. All the heavy work had been done already – replating part of the hull, extending the bow and putting in a lift for wheelchair users. Joe had thought that's what he'd been signing up for, the welding and sparks and precision engineering, but it turned out that the gentle slap of paint was just as satisfying. That and meeting some of the locals, like Auld Tam who'd taken the boys out on one of the other barges, shown them the backwaters of Maryhill – the Big Man sculpture, the spooky everglades of The Stocks. And shown him how old double-decker windows could be remade into the windscreen of The Firebird's wheelhouse. After Joe had offered him two split-new, sealed units, courtesy of his uncle's coach-hire firm, Tam had even let him have a shot at steering, in that open splay of Stockingfield Junction.

'*The Firebird* has enjoyed several trips since our boys assisted in its refurbishment,' droned the heidie, 'but none will be as thrilling as the trip it will make a week on Sunday. Glasgow is a city of ships and industry as well as a city of God. Built at St Mungo's behest, on the banks of flowing water, what more fitting entrance to the city could there be for our Commonwealth guests than to arrive in Glasgow by boat – conveyed on *our* barge, *The Firebird*?'

The last four words came out in a oner as the head beamed his revelation, teeth flashing, flailing, then finally descending, coming to rest on his tongue. He coughed, made a play of hand at mouth, but you could see the frenetic workings of his jaw trying to re-anchor palate to denture. A thin plume of giggles rose, teachers began to shift, to stalk the edges of the rows of seats, biting their own lips and searching for miscreants.

'*Schonboard* … ahem, on board, there will also be musicians, dignitaries and celebrities, all heading to the Christmas celebrations in George Square. And, as a tribute to our college's strong links and ongoing support of the Phoenix Trust, four of our senior pupils have been invited to join the assorted VIPs, sailing down the Forth and Clyde canal and into Glasgow.'

'Haud me back,' muttered Doug.

Patrick shook his head. 'It'll be head boy, head girl—'

'*Kelly: shut it,*' rattled a patrolling teacher.

'Yes,' continued the head, 'details are being kept quiet for security purposes– far be it from me to say there may even be *royalty* present – but those confirmed to attend include panto stars Elaine C. Smith and Gerard Kelly, plus Glasgow's poet laureate, who will be delivering a poem written specially for the occasion, and … um, a popular girls' band who are in town for another concert—'

'Shit,' said Patrick, 'it'll be Notre Dame's choir again. Fuck, what a shite way to spend your weekend.'

'Um . . . called Girls Aloud . . .'

The long-delayed whoop did go up at this.

'A popular choice, I see. As I hope, are our delegates. This is a real honour for the school – and I'm delighted to tell you that our representatives for the evening will be our head boy and head girl Marcus and Claire—'

'Telt you,' came Doug's belligerent rasp behind him. 'Fucking fannies.'

'. . . Alan Blair, who designed *The Firebird*'s new logo—'

'Did he?' said Doug. 'I don't remember that. Cunt.'

'. . . And finally, an individual whom staff tell me threw himself wholeheartedly into the renovation project – congratulations, Joseph Grier.'

The mutters were crisply truncated, becoming that same long dull silence – as before, after Joe had shouted out in Chemistry, only this time the nothing was leavened with disgust. He was not imagining it, you could feel it rise in thick waves, like the blood that was rising on his face, a giddy rush of joy immediately extinguished.

'*Slowjo*,' whispered Doug. 'You fucking do it and you're dead. I swear to Christ, you little fuckwit. Even *I* did more on that barge than you.'

'Aye,' said Patrick, 'you didny bribe them with old windows, but.'

Joe was looking, just looking at his feet, and thinking he would kick, just kick and punch and put his hands round people's necks and why and why, what had he done to them, just standing and helping out and asking folk to his house and being their pal and not one person in this whole entire room was happy for him and the need to break this silence was overwhelming, it had lasted hours and seconds and for all his life. If he could make folk laugh, just *laugh* and like him and he was on his feet, so tall, the tallest in the year, his hand was up, he could feel his fingers rigid-straight.

'Joseph.' The heidie smiled. 'Did you want to say something?'

'Yes sir, I did. Are you wearing those teeth for a horse, sir?'

Chapter Twenty-Four

A big white page of nothing. How many fresh Word documents was he going to open today? Alex loosened the top button on his shirt. Guaranteed flu, going from the chill to a stuffy office. He had walked the canal towpath again at lunchtime. The beginnings of ice crystals on the leaves and grass, his breath constant round his mouth. Into this hazy speech bubble, he had strung out words – saying them softly, but aloud. It helped him think, all this. Being outside and alone, talking to himself – the one a prerequisite of the other. Punter or love triangle? A girl or a guy? Dead in the water or out? And where were her clothes, watch, mobile? He had broken a twig from an overhanging branch; the snapped smell clean and sparse. It was winter now, definitely. The damp spongy rot of autumn had been ousted.

It was also Friday 16 November, five days since Francine had been found. Was the car in Lochbroom Street a wild goose chase? He had Mandy and two other uniformed cops phoning every car dealer in the West of Scotland, trying to match up the paint, which had come back as: 'medium charcoal green metallic'. Most likely a Ford from '98 onwards. But what kind? He had swiped his stick at the sparkling reeds. Escort? Galaxy? Mondeo? With each strike, glitter-dust rose in bright, mineral drifts, joining the puffs of breath expelled as he recited names. Alex liked winter. Bleak could be good. Empty. It was a necessary hiatus, like sleep before waking, the cold shower after the sweaty game When he was a boy, Alex had a dog called Sandy. Walking him in all weathers, you got to realise how distinctive the seasons were. It wasn't simply temperature and colours, each had their own smell and taste too.

He adjusted his desk lamp, so the glare didn't hit the screen. People forgot about the seasons, sealed in their thermostatically controlled cubes.

'Alright there, Alex. How's it going?'

Behind him; the fragrant Hayley. Her perfume was distinctive, grapefruity, almost like aftershave. He swore he could feel a breast brush lightly on his back as her neat, pale hands appeared either side of his shoulders. 'How we getting on with the Gallagher murder then? Any movement – or am I going to have to come down hard on you?'

Yes, that was definitely soft tissue, pushed against the bones of his spine. Alex clicked on his screensaver, turned his head to face the superintendent, forcing her to step back a little.

'How you doing, ma'am?'

She smiled broadly at him. 'I'm doing good, Alex. You?'

'Can't complain. Averaging five hours' sleep a night, one meal a day – usually chips – and juggling many potentially alluring balls as we speak.'

Had he *really* just said that?

'I bet you are.' Hayley came round to perch on the edge of his desk. Tweaked the seam of her trousers. 'Care to share any of them with me?'

He had initiated a game of chicken. Time to sit up straight and deferential, or he might burn all his balls.

'Well ma'am, as you know—'

'Oh, Alex. That sounds like a preamble. I don't do preambles, you know that.' She held on to her kneecap, leaned towards him. 'What about the bus route? Any joy there?'

All the bus drivers for the Maryhill Road route had been interviewed, except one part-timer who had yet to come on shift. Francine had been a striking girl, but she'd toned it down since her days on the streets, and asking a driver to remember if he'd seen a wee skinny lassie with a black ponytail and no make-up, possibly wearing a red jumper, in amid the dozens of wee skinny lassies and old fat lassies and stout, stooped men, and whiny, white-clad youths who all trooped on, proffering their coins and shuffling to their seats, was a futile exercise. On-bus CCTV was little better. There were several images of dark-haired women boarding buses on Maryhill Road; one in particular, near to the lock-keeper's cottage, but in that one, the woman wasn't wearing anything red. Four other images had showed women in red tops getting on various buses between lunchtime and teatime, but none of the respective drivers could match any of those to Francine's photo. Poor sods probably just saw hands and cuffs all day. Avoiding eye contact meant avoiding hassle. There was one image left, for the part-time chappie who was in tomorrow, although Alex wasn't holding his breath. That passenger was definitely wearing a red top, but she also had a hooded gilet over it – with the hood up, which didn't really help.

'Still working on it, ma'am. Nothing as yet though.'

'Thought not. Or you'd have come and told me straight away, wouldn't you, my sweet?'

'You are number one on my list, ma'am.'

'Higher up than the area detective super?'

'Tut, tut Ms Whittaker. How can you even ask a question like that?'

She dimpled prettily. *Oh man, quit it.*

Alex cleared his throat. 'And we're also moving forwards regarding the motor vehicle in Lochbroom Street – I'm pretty confident we'll have a definite decision on the model in a day or so, then I can release that as part of an appeal to the press.'

'Good stuff. And is it likely that there'll be a link with any vehicles at the farm?'

'Nup. Nobody at Calder Riggs appears to have any connection with a green Ford – there's a horsebox for general use, Fiona Cairns drives a maroon Range Rover, Francine didn't drive, and neither, it seems, did Mary Brown. She's never held or applied for a provisional – well,' he rubbed the heel of his hand in his eye, 'Christ knows if that's true, actually. We've no d.o.b., and no previous address for her either.'

'Are you still thinking she's a suspect?'

'I honestly don't know. More and more I'm thinking it was a guy, even though there's no evidence of a sexual assault.'

'How so?' Hayley flicked a length of chestnut hair from her collar. Her hair was a particular bête noire of Shirley's. *It shouldny hing down like that. Fuck – she's a super, no a supermodel. If she's in uniform she should have it up in a bloody bun.* Then she would growl. *She is a frigging bun.*

'By all accounts,' said Alex, 'Mary Brown is a wee slip of a lassie, as was Francine. And I don't know Mary from Adam, but I *did* know Francine. Total wee bauchle – if she was in a shit mood, and didn't think it was her turn for the jail, she'd think nothing of giving you a square go. Hook your eyes out with her nails, rip the inside of your mouth soon as look at you—'

'Hey, don't go all misty eyed on me. You sound like you miss her.'

'I just know it would take someone a fair bit stronger, or meaner, than her to bring Francine down, that's all. And from what Fiona Cairns and all the stable lassies say, Mary Brown isny a tough cookie at all. If anything, she sounds like a bit of a creeping Jesus – according to Fiona, any road. You know the type – grafts away fine, but sneaks up on you when you're not expecting it, says inappropriate things in the workplace . . .'

Ach, Alex couldn't do this. He smiled at Hayley. 'I mean, imagine that.'

'Imagine.' A tiny flick of tongue, and then the door came slamming open.

'Ho boss, you seen—'

Shirley halted when she saw the superintendent lounging on Alex's desk. 'Oh dearie me. I didny realise you were entertaining.'

Hayley's chin tightened, her face scarlet.

'Jesus, it's hot in here.' Shirley bustled to open a window. 'You should maybe get yourself a wee glass of water, ma'am. The weather's all over the place, isn't it? I mean, we've had sun, rain and frost all in the one week. I blame global warming.'

Hayley slid to her feet. 'If you can give me a copy of that report when it's finalised then . . .'

Alex stood up also. 'Sure thing, ma'am. Will do.'

The wry, clever Shirley that Alex knew was turning rabid. She had become a malevolent dog with a bone. 'You sure you're okay, ma'am? You're awfy flushed looking. Could be the menopause, of course. Can strike any time from your thirties onwards, you know.'

Hayley tugged down the bottom of her T-shirt. 'DS Clark, I meant to say to you – your overtime sheets weren't signed off properly. I'm afraid I had to reject them. Please do them again – or get someone else to help you.'

She left the room, pausing for an instant directly in front of Shirley, forcing her to move. As soon as the door was closed again, Shirley exhaled – not quite fire, but something pungent. 'Fucking cow. That's no even her job to check the ovvies. Now the troops'll not get their money till next month.'

Alex regarded his venom-spitting sergeant. 'Shirley – you are a total lunatic. I wouldn't be surprised if you get punted for that.'

'Couldny give a fuck. And you're nothing but a man-whore anyway, boss. Take a seat.'

'Eh . . . thank you.' He obliged. 'Why do you hate her so much?'

'You know on her promotion panel?' Shirley pulled out the chair on the other side of Alex's desk. 'You know what she did? Started snivelling and greeting 'cause the questions were too hard, then asked for a ten-minute break. When she came back in they fucking apologised for giving her a hard time, then promptly promoted her. And I'm supposed to respect *that*?' Her disgust was palpable. And then, like sun through cloud, nice Shirley re-emerged and all was well.

'Now – have you seen this?' She held up an envelope. The top was jagged where it had been sliced open, and Alex could see a stripe of white paper inside.

'Depends what it is.'

'Anonymous letter, giving us a name for the Gallagher murder.'

'Piss off! You're joking!'

'Ha!' She offered up a massive, tooth-filled grin. 'Didny think you had. Aye, we've got a name, address, occupation. Not got his shoe size, but pretty much everything else.'

Alex reached out for the paper. 'Let me see.'

'No touchy touchy. Look.' Shirley opened out her hand, exposing pale rubbery webs between sheathed fingers. 'I'm all gloved up. Of course, it may well be a pile of conspiracy-theory shite, but better safe than sorry. I've got two boys away down to see him the now. Chap by the name of Robert Crilley. A builder.'

'On file for anything?'

She shook her head. 'Sadly, no. Not even an honourable mention for cruising the Drag. I've asked the A Division DIO if he'd any note of him, but *nada*. What is significant though is that our lovely Mr or Miss Anon also hints at a motive. Says the builder is trying to steal the land round the stables.'

Alex rolled his chair away from the desk, his legs beginning to cramp as they stretched properly. Apart from jumping up like a moron when Hayley left, he'd been hunched here for, what, near two hours, poring over the case files and the newest inputs from the incident room.

'So we need to—'

'Alex, Alex. While you were canoodling with the boss, I was already on the phone to the Planning department. And, get this – there *is* an application already submitted, for a massive big housing estate. And double get this – it transpires that Miss Fiona isny the owner of the property after all.'

'So who is?'

'Dunno yet – but I'm chasing that up too.'

'Will I just go home then?' He clasped his hands in front of him, but, under the desk, his leg was performing a wee, excited jig. With every sentence Shirley uttered, another small muscle twitched. *Breakthrough, breakthrough, breakthrough.*

'No. Just tell me you love me more than Hayley Hotpants.'

'Ach, Shirley. How could you even ask me that? You know what you are: you are a MA-GI-COP.' He said it frowning, ponderously, a proud mother to a child.

'Ha, ha. I know.'

All probationers learned the acronym by rote when they started in the job, dutifully chanting the seven stages of successful crime-fighting: *Motive, Alibi . . . something . . . Intent, Opportunity . . .*

Opportunity. 'Can I see the envelope a moment?'

Shirley held it out to him. 'Posted in Glasgow, Thursday morning.'

'Yup. But look here, at the franking mark. No, not the post office one, this one. Where the stamp should be.'

A circle. Some wavy lines.

Glasgow City Council
Press Office
First Class Mail

'Right, two things,' said Alex. 'I want someone to go back to Calder Riggs and interview Fiona Cairns again, establish exactly what the position is with the housing development, ownership of the land, consent, any coercion made, etc., etc., and I,' he looked at his watch, 'am going to head on down to the City Chambers pronto, and find out exactly who has access to their franking machine.'

'Why pronto?'

'Lazy buggers clock off at five to four on a Friday, and it's quarter past three now.'

He'd get a patrol car to take him down – the weekend rush hour would have started already, and it was much easier weaving in and out in a marked vehicle than in his own. Just go to the bar, snap his fingers, claim his chauffeur . . . he was a DI, he was a conjuror. The unblocked magic was flowing again, and he, Alex Patterson, was about to fly.

As long as Hayley remained happy with his progress. Maybe he should just shag her and be done with it.

Chapter Twenty-Five

Everything is fine.

The doctors had said it, Rob had said it, Elaine, when she arrived whey-faced at the Southern General, had said it too. Even the baby had told her so, firm-kicking its way back to reality. Anna imagined it hiding behind the placenta, keeking out, its fat baby tongue protruding. *I was joking, Mum! Look, I was having you on!* It was the oddest sensation; she understood now why her mum had slapped her backside when she was about five, seconds after Anna had run across the road in front of a car. Relief and fury, ignited by love.

Anna had done nothing, yet she felt inordinately proud of her body's ability to shield her child from harm. All those years blowing eggshells; her hobby was decorating eggshells. How could she have done that? It was an obscenity, and, as she thought that, the roar rose up again, everything compressed into a single, shining thought.

Francine had not lied. He was going to try and kill her. Today, the small neat foot that drove into her head; it had been there before. Imprinted in her brain. It was him. Had to be.

Enough. Anna pulled back the covers, began searching for her clothes. If everyone was so sure everything was fine, then they didn't need to keep her in for observation. Her movements were deliberate, keeping her mind clear of Rob's stricken, lovely face, his entreaties to *lie still and get some rest.* She got dressed, opened the door of her private room – being a doctor's wife had some benefits – and headed towards the lift. It took an age to appear, but nobody ran after her or called out

her name. She'd have just kept going anyway, straight outside
past the huddle of smokers who scowled as she went 'Excuse
me', and out into the cold. There were always taxis loitering in
the periphery of the hospital, and it was simple enough to hail
one. She would make one brief detour to Cranstonhill, then
get it to take her home.

'Cranstonhill Police Office, please. In the town, bottom end of
Argyle Street.'

'That you handing yourself in, hen?'

'Something like that.'

She swallowed, caught sight of herself in the glass panel
separating her from the driver. It was a gaunt half-face looking
back. It shocked her.

He knows, miss. You have to help me.

Anna would track Francine Gallagher down, listen to her
properly this time. She had been so quick to reject her, almost
throwing her from the office, refusing to take her mobile number
or give Francine hers. A desperate denial, which she would remedy
now.

Miss, please. He's getting out and he—

Will you shut the fuck up? He won't be out for years.

He is miss, he is. And look – he sent me this!

The girl had held up her package, trembling, and it had
dropped from her hands on to the floor, spilling out its barbed,
bright accusations.

How did you find me? How did you know where to come?

I seen you on the news, miss. You know, at the airport bomb thing.

Have you told anyone anything?

*Naw! Fucksake, no, of course I haven't. But I didny know what to
do.*

Neither had Anna.

'Right pal, here's fine,' she said to the taxi driver. 'Will you hang
fire? I'll only be a minute.'

'How do I know the busies'll no keep you in there?'

'Och, Jesus, just forget it. Here.' She handed him a tenner,
waited for her change.

Inside, the office was quiet, just a gentle swell of classical music, which was quickly switched off as Anna buzzed through the inner door.

'Evening, ma'am. Thought you were away for the night.'

She waved an airy hand at her station assistant. 'Forgot something. Pregnancy amnesia.'

She carried on past her own office, down towards a room marked *LIO*. It was locked, but unless the keycode had changed recently . . . no, it was still 521, in honour of Rangers' recent win over Celtic. Paul, her local intelligence officer, was a Blue-nosed creature of habit. She closed the door behind her, sat down at the computer console without taking off her coat. Fortunately, he was also complacent with his passwords, sticking them on a yellow Post-it inside his desk diary.

Anna's fingers stumbled as she typed Francine's name into the Criminal History System database. In amongst her chequered history, Francine's last known address would be listed here. With any luck, this would all be very discreet. Under no circumstances did Anna want anyone to associate her with Francine Gallagher. Hopefully her last known address would also be her current address. One quick visit and . . . what? Find out what Francine had said, because she had, clearly, said something that had led him to Anna Cameron. Find out what he said he was going to do to her . . . she felt suddenly sick . . . to her family? And what was Anna going to do then? Tell the police?

Pressing her knuckles deep into her eyes, the sockets filling with bone and pink-black swirls. Pressing, pressing. The swirls spread raggedly, became black holes, and it felt like the edge of drunkenness. She could see inside the sockets, far, far in to the cage in which she lived.

She does not like what she can see.

She sees a river and a splash. She sees a woman, driven by a sense of righteousness, which is partially revenge. She sees the river ripple out, become a surge, sees a wave rise up, and she is running, running and it is gaining, and her mouth and eyes are sealed, the same as in the swimming pool today.

He was coming for her, and even with Francine's help, what was Anna supposed to do? If she could not deal with this herself, if she had to ask for help, then she was lost. She would lose her job, her family. She would go to jail. Eight years ago, Anna condemned a man – not an innocent man, not an undeserving man, but a man nonetheless – to be incarcerated for a crime he did not commit. And if that man was now set free . . .

Anna is not good. She is not virtuous, although she is filled with guilt. You can pretend guilt is a reflex in recognition of your sins, but it's not empathy or atonement that brings that slow cold creep. It's fear of being caught. Being made to face those sins is like looking at the black bones of yourself. Despising what you see.

She opened her eyes, pressed the enter key. A picture of Francine appeared, a list of dates, convictions, associates and warning signals. And this stark marker:

Deceased.

Anna's hand recoiled from the keys. It hung in the air, directionless, then slammed back down to log out, like that would eradicate the truth. She wanted to run, but she made herself sit still, sat on her hands, in fact, until they were calm and she could make them work again. A vicious babble in her head, the quiet tapping of computer keys outwith.

This time, she keyed in a man's name. Up came the response.

Released on licence 12/11/2007.

It *was* him. He was out, he was here, and he had killed Francine. The babble grew louder, until the weight of the noise became an incantation, a clamour of hungry ghosts.

Anna laid her head on her arms, one fist in her mouth.

Everything is fine.

Chapter Twenty-Six

The City Chambers' Banqueting Hall was amazing – a symphony of gold baroque, of painted plaques and friezes. Mary could barely take her eyes from the vaulted roof, with its intricate, gold-leaf panels and embossed roses. But the walls were even more beguiling. All the murals told a story. See there, triangulated below the ceiling: Bishop Jocelyn bestowing burgh status on Glasgow. And there was Glasgow's river, the mighty Clyde, and there was shipbuilding, and there was legend. Look, over on that wall, St Mungo's little robin, and that big long painting by the stage; that was the contrite queen with St Mungo. Her face was serene, but Mary knew she was really full of joy: her lost, adulterous ring recovered from the fish which lay on the grass at her feet. It was one of Mungo's miracles, a hidden gem miraculously retrieved from the Clyde – a tale which fed into the city's coat of arms, and the rhyme that every Glaswegian schoolkid knew by heart:

> *Here is the tree that never grew*
> *Here is the bird that never flew*
> *Here is the fish that never swam*
> *And here is the bell that never rang*

Mary's heart was broken, sure, but she felt it stir all the same. A weak, thin flick like a dying fish's tail. She could almost be in a cathedral. Would they give Bernie a funeral, she wondered, or would they keep her in a cold tin fridge, quietly suspended until judgement day? What could Mary do to make that judgement come quicker?

Cocooned in her own stasis, all she knew was what she could glean from the newspapers. As far as she was aware, the police had done nothing, and she daren't make contact with them again. There had been no arrest of Robert Crilley, no 'Wanted' pictures of him plastered on the city's walls. Why weren't there posses out searching, folk with flaming torches and brands? Bernie was a human being, yet all the papers referred to her as 'former prostitute', subtly denoting her as a woman of limitations, one with lesser rights to justice, maybe lesser rights to life. And the picture, the picture – it was always that mug-shot one, defiant and arch. Where was Bernie with her wicked grin, or her head thrown back, giving it laldy at the karaoke? She barely recognised this Francine Gallagher.

The tempo of the music altered, more applause. Mary had to be quick. The organiser had told her the reception might be getting cut short. Something to do with all the ID people protesting outside. Their numbers had tripled since lunchtime, and there was an air of anticipation lifting from them like the sweat on a horse before it jumps. They were daft to think they could rail against the system and that anyone would actually listen. Plus, it was Friday: they should all just go to the pub.

'Excuse me dear. The Ladies?'

Mary smiled at a silver-coiffured lady. 'Just through there, and it's the other side of the stairs.'

An impossibly lean female took to the stage, twirling in some concoction of silk and . . . tin foil? The seated rows of ladies-who-lunch-and do-a-lot-for-charity clapped even louder. It was now or never. Behind those curtains, in the wings of the stage, were bundles and bundles of clothes. Mary's trousers were bogging. She'd been wearing them for nearly a week, and they could probably walk themselves into a washing machine, if only there was one around. She had picked up a couple of tops in a shop in Queen Street (literally picked them up – the girl at the door was too busy foisting catalogues on folk to notice), so at least she had varied her appearance slightly, and she'd washed and brushed her teeth each morning at the sink where they filled their kettle. But she had absolutely no money left. Calder Riggs provided her with bed and board, and a small amount of income which she'd never thought to save. The cash came in every two weeks, and went out just as regularly. If it wasn't in her purse, it wasn't there. She'd not had a proper meal for days, surviving on biscuits and Cup-a-Soups that someone had left beside the kettle.

'Any takers?' A waitress offered a salver of ochre titbits. Mary popped a deep-fried prawn in her mouth, took another two for later. Finger buffets like this one were a godsend. Over by the stage, Gordon Thomson gave a little wave. Then he pretended he was drawing a noose around his neck, mimed jerking it upwards. She grinned. If she was finding it hard to pay attention, what must it be like for a proper journalist? Mary was supposed to be writing a story for the council magazine. 'How Young Scots Designers Are Saving Lives in Malawi'. Not the snappiest title; she'd need to work on it. God, that prawn was good. She wrapped the remaining two in a paper napkin. Mmm, fishy breath . . . *nice.* Even the toothpaste she was using had been purloined from Kate's gym bag. She was pathetic, she knew that, sliding out of her own life and into this manufactured one. Mary wasn't stupid. It couldn't continue. Certainly not after this morning.

Celine had caught her lying on the floor beside her desk.

'What the hell are you doing down there?'

'Bad back,' Mary improvised. 'I slipped on the frost this morning. Think I've buggered it.'

Celine had puckered her already disdainful nose, said nothing. But Mary had seen her talking later, with Cilla, then they had both looked over, with that side-on sidle where no eyes are focused and the protagonists speak only from the corners of their mouths. Mary had kept herself busy, copying and filing, then volunteering to write this article. Anything to get away from all those meaningful glances. She had made a point of going straight to Celine. Smiling, open. *See, I have nothing to hide.* Though she added a tiny wince, cupping her hand round the base of her spine as she approached. 'Celine. You're the depute on the magazine, aren't you?'

Bill was the editor, but he'd been out all morning at meetings. Celine had instantly bridled at Mary's question. 'Yes. Why? Look, I've enough on my plate with press enquiries – it's Bill's baby really. I just help out—'

'No, no. I think it's really good. Colourful, simple . . . anyway. I was just wondering if you'd like me to cover the Malawi reception this afternoon? I mean, the council are hosting this big fashion show . . .'

Full of clothes. Nice, clean clothes and shoes and stuff.

'Yes. And, so?' Celine had folded her arms. 'The dailies are covering it anyway. The council magazine's not a history book, you know. By the time it goes to press, the show'll be about a month old.'

'Yes, I realise that. But surely it would be reinforcing all that good PR for the council – and the fashion students. Plus it would be a chance for us to highlight the charity, maybe get some more donations in. We could get some really nice glamorous shots of the clothes and the models, then juxtapose that with a picture of a village in Malawi. In fact, is the Lord Provost not due out there next month? So we could tie the piece in with that . . .'

And they've got a really nice buffet. Please Celine. I saw them wheeling it in.

Celine shrugged. 'I suppose. If you like. Though I can't promise Bill will use it.'

'Thanks, Celine. I won't let you down.' *Torn-faced besom that you are.* Just as Mary was leaving to go up to the Banqueting Suite, Bill returned. Celine had shot her another of those furtive looks, gone into his room and shut the door.

Keep the heid, Mary doll. She had carried on up the alabaster stairs to the Banqueting Hall, calm as you like. Under her quiet, douce skin, her belly churned its watery contents round and round, a weak spin-cycle of angst. But nobody had summoned her back down. Maybe she was just being paranoid. Having your best friend murdered entitled you to that. Again and again, her guts rose up, joining the thick sensation in her throat. She had to keep moving and thinking and doing. Fuck, do *something* girl.

But do not scream. She had been in the Banqueting Hall for over an hour now, scribbling on her notepad and watching the door, interspersed with drifts to the buffet and clocking where the models went when they went off-stage. The makeshift dressing room was in the wings. From where Mary was standing, you could see some of the discarded gear on the floor, the odd flash of pink, bent limb. Who would notice one more skinny girl wrestling with clothes? Okay, she was ready. Inhale, exhale, and in we go.

A voice came after her. 'Hoi. Charlie. Charlotte!'

It was Celine.

'You some kind of Peeping Tom?'

'What? No! I—'

Celine wore her usual droop of boredom. 'Save it. I'm so not interested. Just tell me how I get up on the stage. I've to announce to these old biddies that their show is *finito*, as of this moment.' She glanced heavenwards. 'Apparently we'll all be under siege from crazed Citicard protesters in a minute. Talk about overkill. Oh, and by the way. Margaret wants to see you. Now.'

This was it then. Mary didn't argue, simply took the prawns from their napkin and shoved one in either cheek.

'God, you're gross.'

Yeah well, in Mary's experience, questioning usually led to searching, and from thence to confiscation ... incarceration ... lots of stuff ending in 'shun'. But she still felt she could brass neck it. What exactly could Celine have said? That she came in this morning, and Mary was lying on the floor? Plenty of folk with bad backs lay on the floor. If she stuck to her story ... if she went back on the streets tonight, maybe tried a hostel ... God, if she went home to her mum: clean, alive, repentant, then perhaps she could still work here. Imagine that. Imagine her mum, running to the front door, seeing the one person she had given up all hope of seeing there. Imagine feeling soft sweet arms envelop you and the wash of all that boundless love. For one pure moment, there would be nothing but love.

Imagine that.

And then, of course, the recriminations would start.

Mary knocked at the door of Margaret's office.

'Come.'

Margaret's tongue was sticking out, she was endeavouring to fix a kirby grip in at the nape of her neck.

'Ah, it's you. Come in, in. Sit.' There was a twang, and the hairgrip fired from her fingers in a spidery little arc. 'Bugger.' Margaret gave up, let the tendril of hair fall down to cover her ear. Outside the window, gabbling voices and a steady chant displaced the usual pigeon noises.

No ID. No ID.

'Honestly, drive you mad, that lot. Been giving me a headache all afternoon. I wish someone would just turn a big hose on the lot of them. Sweetie?' She held out a tin of Roses.

'No thanks.'

Brave Mary transformed immediately to Wary Mary, surprised she'd not been bawled at. She shrank a little in her seat. Margaret clipped the lid back on to the tin. 'It's about this morning, Charlotte. Celine tells me she found you sleeping on the floor?'

Whaddawe want?

No ID cards!

'I wasn't sleeping, no. I was stretching. I've got a really bad back, you see—'

'Charlotte. Can I just stop you there please? The cleaner came to me yesterday morning, told me she thought someone had been camping in the Press Office. Claims she went into that wee scullery cupboard – the one across the corridor, found toothpaste in the sink and a pair of pants drying on the taps. Now, I'm no Inspector Clouseau, but I have to say; the coincidence is quite remarkable, don't you think?'

When do we want it?

The descant refrain whipcracked across George Square: *NOW!*

Brazening this out was not going to work. There came a point in any scam where you realised that the edifice was crumbling; it was going to go, irrespective of what you did next, so the only options left were to either try and manage the collapse, then run like buggery the first chance you got, or wait for the whole thing to fall on top of you.

Mary hung her head. 'Margaret. I'm so, so sorry. I just didn't know what to do.'

And then it all flowed out. How Mary had fought furiously with her boyfriend. How he had thrown her out without a penny, and she didn't get paid till next month . . . It was inspirational, a bravura performance. Without consciously choosing to, Mary's lies lapped into the sumps of loss and despair that were actually true; they lit her confession and gave her tears a veracity she'd not expected. At the end, she felt hollowed out, and small, her hands nursing her elbows. She no longer cared what was believed, only that she was scoured inside, and that her mouth tasted of salty fish.

Margaret came over to stand beside her. An awkward rub at Mary's upper arm. 'Men can be such bastards, can't they?' she said. Mary didn't look at her. She heard the smooth *shsh* of a drawer being opened, then a clicking.

'Look, I can't do much about shitty boyfriends, but I can give you a sub until pay day. Would that help?' Margaret unlocked the petty-cash box. 'The most I can authorise without it being officially endorsed is £100, for . . . let's just call it ancillary expenses, yeah?'

Her kindness came like a kick in the chest.

'No, please. It's fine . . .'

'Charlotte, it's only a sub, okay? You can pay me back when your wages come through.' She stuffed the notes into Mary's hand. 'Which reminds me. I don't actually think you've given us your bank details yet, have you?'

The City Chambers wants your soul
Ee-ie, ee-ie, oh
They're all Big Brothers and they want your soul
Ee-ie, ee-ie, oh

'I've a form . . .' Margaret leaned to reach her in-tray, which was moulting sheaves of paper from both sides. The pile of folders, files and newspapers next to the tray was just as high and precarious. 'Personnel were on about it this morning . . .'

Directly below the window, a set of bagpipes mewed their way into life. The singing increased in volume:

W-I-I-TH . . . A . . . snoop snoop here,
A pry-pry there—

'Oh shut the fuck up will you!' Margaret battered on the glass, her yelling impotent as the pipes droned on. Mary could feel the jagged pieces of her heart chiming; if she moved at all, they would stab her. All the noises: the screaming, the music, the pounding, razoring round her face, then another, more deferential knock, and Cilla's voice saying, 'Em . . . sorry to disturb you, but I've a gentleman here, wants to see you, Margaret. Says his name is Detective Inspector Alex Patterson.'

Chapter Twenty-Seven

Excellent. A mad-eyed screamer and a hysteric with her hands clamped over her face, bony shoulders shaking as though she'd just been stung. Alex wanted in and out of here as fast as he could, but it had been difficult enough fighting his way through the motley crew at the front door. He considered the tableau before him. Clearly, the woman by the window was the boss. Her open-shouldered posture, the way in which she possessed the air around her, her lack of apparent contrition – even though all four persons present had heard her screeching higher than the bagpipes – was evidence of that. Mad hair going off at tangents, a gritted, absent gaze; Glasgow's head of Corporate Communications did not look well. Neither did she look as if she adhered to Alex's laid-back style of management. That was a wumman from whom you would not wish to receive a bollocking. The lady who ushered him in seemed to agree, scarpering without completing the introductions.

Time for a little soothing oil. He opened the single button he'd fastened on his overcoat, let the reassuring smile ease out of him. 'Excuse me, ladies. I'm sorry if I've come at a bad time.'

'No, no it's fine.' Scary boss-lady smoothed her hair. 'Detective Inspector?'

'That's right . . . Ms?'

'Oh, Margaret. Just call me Maggie. *Mags*. I mean *Mags*. Not Maggie-mags.' She giggled, a high, girlish shriek that did not fit with her tweedy blazer and ill-fitting slacks. 'Gosh, what am I like? Sounds like a pussy cat or something, doesn't it? How can I help, detective?'

Alex looked pointedly at the weeping allegory in the corner. Margaret followed his gaze. 'Och, leave her, she's fine.' *Boyfriend trouble*, she mouthed in moist, exaggerated vowel-shapes. The girl did not look fine, she seemed frozen in her pose.

'All the same, I'd rather we spoke in private.' He laid his hand on the back of an empty, padded chair. 'May I?' When Alex wanted, he could turn off the charm, make very small, still gestures. You would think it would mark you down as a soft touch, but he'd worked out that conserving his energy, talking more softly, had the effect of augmenting his authority. People would stop shouting to listen, or would come closer to be contained within the thin, tight circle of contemplation he had drawn. If you seemed ill at ease, it didn't work. There had to be steel beneath the softness, and precision too. No waste to your actions. You know, if you stood for long enough, silently watching the sky, a crowd would eventually form.

'Of course,' she said. 'Charlotte . . .'

Charlotte had already bolted, head tucked into her chest. The only impression Alex formed was a pair of swollen eyes muffled with a tissue, and sheathed by lank, dark hair. An emo, most likely. They always took things hard. He sat down, opened up the little wallet to reveal his warrant card.

'Ms . . . sorry, Margaret. I'm Alex, by the way.'

'Oh,' she said. 'Alex.'

'I work out at Maryhill, Margaret, and I'm currently investigating the murder of a young woman there. Now,' he nodded in the direction of the window. The pipes had tailed off, but the shouting was growing even louder, more unruly. 'I can see you're a woman who deals with crises on a daily basis—'

A long blink from Margaret. He'd gone too far; she thought he was taking the piss.

'That lot been at it all day?'

Another blink, more of a painful squeeze this time. 'All week, more like.'

'Nightmare. So, look, Mags, what I don't want you to do is get alarmed, but we recently received an anonymous letter regarding this murder – and I'm pretty sure it came from here.'

Her phone chose that moment to start ringing, just when he'd delivered his killer line. Margaret snatched up the receiver, tugging furiously at her ear. Was she angry? Glad of the distraction? Simply unhinged? It was hard to tell.

'Cilla, do not put any calls through here until I tell you. I don't care if the Queen is trying to storm the building, alright? Yes, we do have a comment on—' She paused, her face ashen. 'The Health Board too? Fuck. Right . . . look, I can't deal with this right now. Just pass all press enquiries on to Bill until otherwise instructed.' She hung up, but her hand remained on top of the phone. Alex could see the tension in the knuckles, the hard press of fingertips whitening the nails.

'Sorry, you were saying. It was sent from here? You mean the City Chambers.'

'No, *here* here. I mean your Press Office, Margaret. Look, is everything okay? Is there something else you need to be dealing with?'

'No, no. It's fine. Please carry on.'

'Okay. So, all your mail gets franked, doesn't it? With a Press Office stamp.'

She frowned. 'Eh, I'm not sure. Yes, it must do, I guess, when Cilla puts it through the machine-thingy.'

'And where's that machine kept?'

A limp gesture. 'Over there.'

'There? He pointed at a console table, with what looked like a grey and white set of digital scales on top.

'Hmm. We weigh it and frank it once, then they stamp it again in the Mail Room.'

'Well, what I need to know is: who would be able to send such a letter? Who has access to the franking machine, is that access regulated – you know, do you need a pin code like on a photocopier or whatever—'

'Gosh.' She seemed distracted still, her eyes kept turning to the window. The mood in the office had shifted, from one of tension to anticipation.

That was it. All the shouting had stopped.

'You'd need to ask Cilla. I'm not really sure . . .' Margaret's phone rang again. 'I'm sorry . . . I think I'm going to have to get this.'

He felt suddenly sorry for her. She looked like a woman entirely out of her depth, defeated and frightened, but with a stoicism that moved him. It was how those boys he was reading about would have regarded one another in the trenches, he thought, just before they went over the top.

'Yes?' Her fingers, working through her hair, kneading the already random hanks and ribbons of it. 'Okay, and they've called the police? Fine. Look, I'll have to go up and see the Chief Exec. The BBC can use the . . . yeah. Two minutes – oh, Cilla. Wait. Tell me, is it just you that works the franking machine?'

Margaret nodded a couple of times as she listened to the response. Her elbow was on her desk, her hand now cupping the side of her face. 'Okay, thanks Cilla. Yes, two minutes, I promise. Just stall them till then.' Alex's sister used to play with her hair when she was upset. Margaret put the receiver down with both hands, again, pressing like she was trying to flatten the thing out of existence.

'Sorry . . . I . . . there's a bit of a crisis going on out there.'

'I noticed when I came in. Had to beat them off with a stick.'

'Yes, well it's going to get worse. You know how there's a train through from Edinburgh every fifteen minutes? It seems that the last three trainloads have been full of more protesters, coming from that march in Edinburgh – and they're all converging on George Square.'

'Shit. That's going to be fun, trying to get home through that.' Alex hadn't brought anything with him except his mobile, otherwise he could have switched to the A Division frequency and heard what was happening outside. 'Look, I hate to press you . . .'

'Oh, sorry. Yes.' Margaret stood up. 'I have to . . . Well, not sure how much help this is. Cilla says that only her and one other person – a girl called Lisa Grant, tend to use the franking machine. And there is a code, so it's unlikely anyone else would know it – Cilla's pretty efficient, you know. Been here for years.' The mobile on Margaret's desk began to vibrate. Her hand crept back to her hair. 'Bad news is, all the letters are sealed when the girls receive them, so technically, *anyone* could have put a letter in the mail tray, at any point during the day, and we wouldn't know who it was.'

'Anyone in the building, or just the Press Office? Sorry – do you want to get that?'

She put her mobile in her pocket. 'No. We-ell, anyone in the building I suppose, although it's very unlikely. We keep the mail tray in the main Press Office – in the senior media officer's wee sub-office actually. So someone would have to walk across the main office, let themselves into Bill's room and walk back out without being challenged. Our office is staffed from 8 a.m. to 6 p.m. – even at lunchtime, we always have someone manning the phones. Then it's locked up for the night. Only Press Office staff have the access code.'

'Okay. So we're pretty sure it would need to be a member of your team. How many folk work in the Press Office then?'

'Um . . . we're talking about twenty, twenty-two maybe?'

'Right, what I'm going to need from you, Mags, is a list of all your staff: names, addresses, dates of birth. Here's my card. If you can get that to me as soon as possible – email will be fine. Meanwhile, we'll be checking out the information contained within the letter, and we'll also check for any discernible prints.'

'Prints?'

'Fingerprints on the paper and the envelope. Ideally the notepaper – less folk will have touched that. So we might have to come back and take some fingerprints from your staff too.'

'Oh.'

'Don't worry – it doesn't hurt.' He allowed himself a wee joke. 'Not unless you struggle.'

Margaret tried to make a smile. She was softer this way, nicer without all the flashy brashness. Alex stood up too. Time-to-go time; that mob was large and grumbling enough when he came in. 'And the only other thing is: I'd very much appreciate it if you kept all this to yourself at the moment.'

'Of course.'

He buttoned up his coat. It wasn't his place to say it, but he would say it anyway, so she'd know that he cared . . . did he care?

No, not especially, but he still felt that nag of sympathy, a collusion maybe that said: *Trust me, I know about pressure.*

'Look, don't worry about what's going on outside either. George Square's no stranger to revolting citizens. It'll die down soon - maybe they'll send in the tanks,' he added cheerfully. Margaret didn't respond. Once more, the desk phone began to shrill.

'I'll just away.' Alex raised a hand, left her to her troubles.

By her accent, he guessed she wasn't originally from the city. But his patter was crap anyway; few born-and-bred Glaswegians knew about the tanks either. And they should have known. It was their history, their truth. They should have known how, on the last day of January 1919, the Red Flag was raised in George Square, flying above the thousands of workers, police and soldiers that clashed in bloody confrontation. Bloody Friday, they called it. Workers assembling in support of striking shipbuilders and engineers. The miners, too, were clamouring for more pay, there had been furious, female-led rent strikes in the preceding years; ordinary folk, questioning the existing order.

Where would the world be without questions? Alex had just amassed twenty more people to question, and probably all a waste of time. Ach, bring it on. He could handle it. He did a nifty wee shuffle as he passed through the corridor. *Monkey Ma-gic* – that song was dancing in his head again. How did it start? *In the world before Monkey, primal chaos reigned.*

Oh Francine, pet. Your whole life was chaos. And so's your death.

He made his way into the Chambers' foyer. Tons of Italian marble dripping down the walls; all that opulence. For the people, by the people. Which people though? The city fathers would have sheltered in here during Bloody Friday – right here, while the Riot Act was being read, while their citizens were being charged and trampled over by their constabulary. And it had got worse – they'd locked the Glaswegian soldiers in the Maryhill barracks, feart the Scots would join the mob, revolt like they had in Russia. Ten thousand soldiers were shipped up from England to keep the peace. For days, the city had bristled with tanks and machine guns and occupying troops.

Alex approached the huddle at the revolving door. Aye, folk should know that, as they strolled through George Square's flower beds, taking in the view.

'Jesus!' He took an involuntary step backwards. A sparse laugh from one of the concierges. 'Aye. You'll no be going out that way the night, pal.'

The front entrance to the City Chambers was entirely blocked, great reams and folds of bodies milling outside, pressing on hastily erected barriers, the wire mesh only waist high. Only a symbol. If you'd wanted, you could have hurdled them, or given them a dunt at the slotted-in base, and they'd tumble like a house of cards. But the barriers gave an illusion of control, a firm line drawn in the sand which relied solely on the British love of queuing to be in any way effective. And there they were, in their thousands: the Great British public, come to confront democracy in the raw, or as raw as the horse-trading, parochial campaigning of the local government office bearers of a let's-call-it-devolved-not-neutered-pretendy-parliament could be, he thought. Still, besieging the City Chambers was a sight more relevant than smashing shop windows.

Alex peered through the iron-worked glass panels at the side of the rotating door, all thoughts of Francine tumbling away. A skinny kid in a skinny suit was cooried by the pillar next to the door, also transfixed. The square was utterly seething, full and spilling with hundreds of urgent forms. With banners, placards, samba drums and dubious knitted hats. Stewards in yellow with megaphones were being ignored – they reminded him of the tour guides you see in Venice, each marshalling their own wee army behind a brolly or flag. There were angry women with pushchairs, whistling men with kids upon their shoulders, daft boys with Rangers jerseys and Celtic stripes and the odd confused jakey or wide-eyed school kid who'd been swept up in the maelstrom. Girls in tutus and painted clown faces leered and jeered, and, yes – there was that twat on stilts again. What was it with that guy?

Did he no have a home to go to? It must have been the sheer
force of the crowd keeping him upright; no way could you balance
between those swirling, wheeling waves of folk that surged in all
directions, all directions leading them here.

The thin lad beside him was on his mobile. 'I'm telling you. You
need to get some cameras down here now.'

At the front of the crowd was a group of nurses in uniform.
There was a lady in a wheelchair, too, mouth set, dignified hands
clasped. Her shoulders were hunched, protecting her ears against
the clamour of the human sea behind. And there was the piper.
Of course there was a piper, heading up the charge. This was
Scotland, for God's sake, all its microcosm represented here.
Someone would toss a caber in a minute. And there were bound
to be several choruses of *Flo-ora Scotland* before the day was
done. Whoever had stage-set the front few rows was a clever guy.
A photographer maybe; an artist at any rate.

Two clerics with their dog collars stood directly in front of
Alex's line of sight. One wore the thick white band of the Kirk, the
other, smaller man sported the white dash on Nehru neckline of a
Catholic priest. They chatted affably with the poor shift inspector
who'd had the misfortune to be on duty this afternoon – at least
it seemed affable from here. Alex craned to see if it was someone
he recognised from his time at A Division, but he could see only
the clerics' faces: drawn but animated. Articulating their protest;
a benedictive arm raised in offering: fat sheaves of papers which
could only be a petition. The inspector, whose back was still to
Alex, nodded, his right hand touching the upper arm of the priest.
The see-what-I-can-do exchange of reasonable men.

One face Alex did recognise was that of the cop standing just
to the right of the inspector – the legendary John Balfour. John
had two hundred years' service at least, and it was to him that
every A Division probationer was dispatched early in their career.
Based now at the City Chambers, for many years John had driven
the divisional car, which was ostensibly at the service of the
senior management team, but was really John's personal office.
Probationers were taught to 'wash its wee face' with vinegar, to

fetch the boss's newspapers, to listen quietly to the indiscreet chat from the back seat, to shine their shoes and smile smartly. They learned how to put a line on at the bookies, where to acquire the best discounts or the most roadworthy used cars. But from John they also learned to know every inch and crevice and nerve and nuance of the division's geography and soul, its miscreants and its saviours. Where to get a cup of tea, and who needed one the most.

John shifted slightly, obscuring Alex's view. John was posed on the topmost step of his beloved Chambers, a Marshal Pétain ready to declaim the immortal words '*Ils ne passeront pas*' should the great unwashed decide to mount an assault. Only in John's case it would more likely be: *Get tae fuck away fae here*, delivered sideways from an immobile mouth, arms folded, feet askance. And it would work too. Nae cunt messed with John. Just say the word, and John would get them all hunted – and be home in time for tea.

Someone blew a whistle, three sharp parps like the old polis distress call, and the front of the crowd parted to reveal a purple-haired clown, wearing a plastic police helmet and riding on a bike. He saluted the inspector, who merely shook his head. Alex caught the guy's profile, didn't recognise him. The clown then mimed a sad face, twittering fingers tracing tears, and the inspector laughed. Soft grey pigeons shook themselves on the Cenotaph as some boys scrambled on to the plinth and Alex felt a jolt of inexplicable pride. Not just with the uniforms. It welled for all these folk, his own thrawn, mongrel folk who represented everything and nothing all at once: the establishment and anticapitalism, the law and the lawless, democracy and anarchy, gallus Glasgow and a furious, heartsore world. Where else would you get a bunch of Buckfast-drinking neds dancing with the Militant Barmy Army, the scholars from the Mosque linking arms with the Christian Church in all its schizophrenic schisms? Students, trade unionists and farmers aligning with the Greens and the climate protesters and the hunt saboteurs while po-faced cops winked at young lassies doing the conga?

Above all, these people stood for powerful outrage, and for impotent despair.

Yes, Alex felt a wee bit of pride. A mawkish, transitory pride right enough, the kind you got when you watched that daft film *Independence Day* and the world put aside its differences to defeat the slimy scaly things in spaceships. But, still. These folk bobbing and chanting and living in front of him were soft-fleshed testaments to all that was right and was wrong with the human race. Few of them would think that polis who ringed them might ever share their views. But Alex didn't want a world where his kids couldn't breathe either. He didn't want a world where the council could tap your phone, or ten different databases could share your supermarket preferences, your bank balance, your shoe size. Where you were wary of every dark-skinned backpacker and where the map of every holiday you'd ever taken was given swift passage through silent, fibrous, filtered channels, to end up Godknew where.

'Aye. Aye,' said John, stepping back inside. 'It's yourself, Alex. Think you'll need to go out the Gatehouse, son. Either that, or hunker down for the duration.'

He should have said 'boss', or 'sir' or something. Not son.

'Right you are,' said Alex.

Nae cunt messed with John.

'And you. Ho – Thomson, I can see you skulking there.'

The skinny boy came out from the shadows. 'Evening all.'

'Away through the back with Ricky here. He'll hide yous under a blanket, won't you, Rickster?'

The green-blazered curator at the reception desk smiled. 'Should we no send a decoy out first?'

'Oh for fucksake,' said Alex. 'It's no that bad. I'll just nip out the front.'

'No you'll no. *Sir*. How you gonny get through they crowds? I don't want a riot on my steps. For all they know you're the chair of the bloody committee that's sanctioning these cards. No, Cochrane Street's still open at the moment – you can nick out there.'

'Naw, wait the now,' said the curator, glancing at the CCTV screen trained on the gatehouse door. 'There's your chief inspector coming, John.'

A single, corrosive thrill. Anna Cameron was an A Division chief inspector. Alex's spine snapped straight as his eyes stayed focused on the square outside. What if it were her? His mouth ran dry.

'Aye, the Web,' continued Ricky. 'You can maybe get a lift back up the road with him.'

John strolled over, clocked the screen, scowled. 'Oh fuck, aye. Right you, paper boy. Out the back now. I'll no tell you again.'

'But I'm press,' said the lad. 'I'm entitled to report to the people of Glasgow—'

'Aye, and you can do it where you'll no get crushed to death. Ricky, show Mr Thomson out please.'

'Don't touch the suit. I'm telling you – I'll bloody sue.' The journalist was still wittering threats as he was ushered through the rear of the building.

'Web?' asked Alex.

'Aye. Potter. The Wee English Bastard. Watch him – thinks he's a right funny cunt. But,' John sorted his hat in the reflection of the glass door, 'he's no.' He turned, a military spin. 'Afternoon there, sir.'

'Afternoon, John.' A large, ebullient figure swept from the panelled door the journalist had just been marshalled through. Alex didn't know about the rest of his nickname, but the 'wee' part was definitely erroneous. The chief inspector was not a particularly tall man, granted, but he was as stout as he was tall. His cheeks shone roundly in pale electric light.

'How goes it at Mafeking?'

'What?' said John.

'Natives getting restless, are they? Well, we'll soon put a stop to that, eh lads?' The Web pinched his trouser waistband, shoogled about a bit until everything settled under his girth. He came over to peer out the front door.

'Jesus. Would you look at the state of them lot? Right: Inspector Kelly out front is he?'

'Aye. I think they're giving him a petition.'

'So where's the Lord Provost then? Can't he take it off 'em? Or the Chief Exec, or the Leader of the Council, or whoever the hell else it is they're wanting to see.'

'I don't know that they're wanting to "see" anyone in particular, sir,' said John. 'I've told the cooncillors just to keep their heids down until we decide what we're gonny do. The whole thing's been spontaneous – like a flood, know? They started arriving in dribs and drabs once the rally in Edinburgh was over. Then they showed that footage on the lunchtime news when it said the Health Board were definitely committing to Citicards, and the place just went mental. Hunners of folk all pouring in – most of them coming from Queen Street.'

'They must have come from the march at Edinburgh.'

'That's what I just said. Sir. You'd think BTP might of telt us.'

'No their problem once they get off the trains, I guess,' said Alex.

The Web beamed pinkly at him. The contrast of wet gums and lush-haired moustache was disconcerting. And somehow lewd.

'And what are you, young man? A refugee councillor is it? I'd stay well away from the line of fire if I were you.'

Alex extended a hand. 'DI Patterson, sir. Maryhill.'

'A dick, eh?' His fleshy shoulder buffeted Alex's. 'I mean 'tec, of course I do. Course I do, mate. It's only the Traffic that're dicks, yeah?'

Alex allowed him a wan smile. *Turn it down, pal, for fucksake.* He was uncomfortable with folk who didn't give you the chance to absorb them slowly, insisting on full-frontal exposure from the word go. Especially guys like this, all bluster and so much front it made you wonder what they were suppressing. Should the man not be out there, dealing, rather than in here bantering and peeking through net curtains?

John opened the door. The rush of babble and whoop poured in like the tide. 'I think Inspector Kelly wants to speak to you, sir.'

'Well he can come in then, can't he?'

'Aye, but I think he's wanting you to have a word with the protesters.'

'I said, tell 'im to come in.'

John shrugged, signalled to the inspector to come inside.

'Alright, sir.' Inspector Kelly entered the foyer, followed by a couple more uniforms.

"Ello, 'ello; it's Kelly's 'eroes. This it then? You, me and Laurel'n'Ardy. No offence, lads.'

'My entire shift's out there, boss, bar one single-manned car for calls, and we've got some mutual aid coming from E and Q Divisions.' The inspector's face was flushed; he sounded out of breath. 'We've recalled the men who were out for the Townhead drugs raids, and British Transport Police have five cops available. They've also got all entrances to the station secured. I've suggested we simply close Queen Street at the moment, have all trains stop at the station before, but they're none too happy about that.'

'I'll bet they're not. D'you know – I've never noticed that before.' The Web seemed transfixed by his feet.

'Noticed what, sir?'

'All them teensy-little mosaics on the floor. Heh – that's amazing. Like a Roman villa or something.'

John, Alex and Kelly shared a three-way glance.

'Right sir,' said Kelly eventually. 'I reckon if say you and the Lord Provost accept their petition, promise to get it off to Holyrood or Westminster or wherever, then they'll start dispersing. Most of them have been through in Edinburgh already, been on their feet all day. They just want someone to acknowledge them. They're pretty knackered really. Like overtired weans.'

'Bullshit.'

The Web leaned forward to open the door again. A speaker had climbed on to the Cenotaph, was addressing the crowd through a megaphone. The words '*demand the right to be heard*' echoed through tin.

'Listen to that. They don't sound knackered to me.' He let the door swing shut. 'You've got some heavy-duty professional agitators out there, mate. We can't negotiate with those types. No, standard operating procedures here, I'm afraid. It's kettle time.'

'Pardon?'

The Web's mojo was evident again, in the bounce and swing of his step. Pacing as he spoke, arms wide and expressive. 'What we'll do is corral them. Just circle 'em and let 'em sweat it out. I've got the Support Unit en route too, fucking horses, the lot, so we can get them to wade in, split them down the middle, get them pushed up tight as they can go, either end of the Square. Squeeze the fight out of 'em till they're begging to go home.'

Kelly tipped his hat back, his full expression clear. Teeth and gums evident but not smiling. 'Sorry, sir, but I absolutely don't agree. There may well be a minority of troublemakers out there, but you've got folk with weans, you've got wee shopgirls out for a nosey—'

'Well hell-bloody-mend them then. If you sup with the devil—'

'Sir,' said Alex, 'I agree with Inspector Kelly here. You only have to look at the front few rows to see they're mostly decent folk, not rioters.'

'And that's how they work, *mate*. Fuck me, I thought you Jocks knew the score. Put all your limp, sad misguided gimps at the front, they're the sheep. Draw us in, get our guard down – then bring in the fucking wolves.' He shoved a stumpy finger up against the glass. 'See those clown girls there, *mate*. Well, I've had my balls fucking twisted damn near off by one of 'em. Standing in a picket line – a fucking picket line, where these people have no business to be because they've never worked a day in their lives, yet there they are. Smiling for the cameras and spitting in your face. Kneeing your groin, razoring your body armour. I've seen one put nails in an apple, then chuck it at a police horse. Oh, they're fucking sly, these bastards.'

He blinked, twice, then recovered his beat. Eyes flashing round the foyer like a weathered whip.

'Chop, chop then, mateys.' Nodded at the screen. 'That's them Unit vans coming in the back now.'

Kelly's hands formed a triangle round his nose and mouth. It looked like he was praying. 'Sir, can we at least give them a warning to disperse?'

'Give them a heads-up to run amok you mean? Not bloody likely. You tell your men to stand by until the horses get here. I'll get on to BTP, tell them the fucking train station has to close, whether they like it or not. Bugger me, they're only jumped-up stationmasters.'

A roar outside, the shattering tinkle of flying glass. It was a bottle, that was all, just a stupid bottle, jettisoned at the orator who swung on his plinth. The world slowed down; Alex could have left, then. Slipped out the back door with his hands and conscience clean but something held him, a kind of fascinated shrinking where he drew so far inside himself that he was there, but not there and if he was not there, was not culpable. And so he watched Inspector Kelly close his eyes and press his palm against the door. Watched it hang there for an instant, as if mustering the strength to tilt that stern, glazed door, before he vanished outside and the Support Unit troops appeared behind him, in front of him, arriving from all sides and the Web rubbed his hands.

'You comin', sunshine?'

Thereafter, Alex found it difficult to remember exactly who said what to whom. Or how it happened that he was out there, in George Square, in his suit and overcoat and split-new shoes. It was not in the initial wave, which slid blade-straight through the heart of the crowd, shields up and fixed like their faces. Not even when the realisation dawned, and folk began to struggle, to force their weight against the bulk and rub of centurions marching, reaching hands out for balance or to catch on to a friend as the swelling of high-visibility vests spread like a virus. Nor was it when the outer flanks of police squeezed from north south east and west, their breadth augmented by the impenetrable flanks of the horses, who flicked and whinnied, rolled wild eyes. No, Alex was still invisible then. He thought, possibly, it was at the point when he saw the wheelchair buck, saw the lady's face, a moment of uncomprehending shock before the chair stuttered, reared and was lost in feet and flailing. Him leaping down the littered steps; the barrier was toppled by this time, he could smell the animal fear of the people trapped beneath. Sweat rising, the fumble of his hands as he tugged and exhorted others to stay and do the same, and some did, God bless them and they got the lady out but then it was too late to detach and he was in it, he *was* the crowd as it spun and lashed out. A thousand flashes of mobile phones held high, the weapon of the crowd against batons and shields, which were not raised in anger, but defence: Alex could see that, but it felt so different when you weren't behind the shield. You could not see the faces of the men and women who were equally panicked, who were sheepdogs herding sheep.

They did not mean to bite.

It begins as arms held out, a defensive gesture, then someone stumbles and the cops can't breathe and so they shove, right arm up, cudgel high, the left arm extending to form a gap through the crowd which does not recognise this gap, but surges, sea on rock and you are drowning and you cannot breathe and get *back, get back* becomes a push, a rush and shields are wielded, *not my face, not my face* and before you know it your shield has become a baton and the sea has many faces but they all make up the sea. It is dragging you under, you see a guy protecting his girlfriend from the onslaught and you try to give them passage then the guy tries to speak to the visored form who manhandles him on and away from his girlfriend he will not listen, *he will not listen none of them will fucking listen,* Alex touches the shoulder of the cop, who swings, arm up and fisted, it should be open, his palm should be open but the commas of yellow are few and desperate compared to the vast mass of the crowd with their flashing, flashing phones which are photographing and recording so that this can be validated – same as everything bloody else – through the medium of television. As if anyone will forget.

Jesus, it's not like your holiday snaps, this is fucking mental he's lost a shoe one hundred quid's worth of leather is being mangled underfoot in fact; he doesn't think he can touch the ground, thinks he is being carried without anchor the cycling clown is lying on the ground, Alex treads on soft flesh looks down and sees the purple wig can feel another's blood soak through his tattered sock as a teenage girl bawls: 'Just who the fuck are you protecting?' A cop lifts his stick to the girl and Alex seizes his arm: 'I'm a cop I'm a fucking cop!'

The cop is young, has lost his hat. His eyes are black with adrenalin. Alex shakes him a little, willing him to focus.

'There's a man under here. Get him out. Help me get him out.'

The cop nods, goes under like a diver in for pearls. He does not hesitate, does not dispute the veracity of what Alex says, his bare fingers fumbling, Alex fishing, heels stamping someone kicks his jaw and together they pull the clown up. A shoulder and a leg first, tugging, then the rest pops free. The wig remains on the ground, a dirty mauve against the rose-pink of the Square; she is a girl, she's just a little girl. Alex hoists her in his arms, the cop battering a path for him. Bodies bump and grind, men are crying, women thumping with the strength of ten. He skids on oily moistness, the cop senses it and looks back. Takes his elbow, pulls him safe. Eventually, they reach more cops, bodies take the weight, an opening is torn, ragged as the breath in Alex's lungs and they are out. Out into another world of sense and order can she feel it too? Is she breathing? They take her towards Queen Street station.

Ambulance? ETA 30 seconds, and the cop, the girl are gone.

Alex curls to the ground, his back held by firm stone. He is in George Street, on the far side of the City Chambers. The street is entirely empty, barricades and cops and horses sealing it from the rudderless mob; from the world rushing by without him.

'You okay, son?' John Balfour comes from a shadowed alcove. He squeezes Alex's shoulder. He too has lost his hat. Collar torn, lip bloody. Alex can feel the tremor of his hand.

'Don't know yet.'

Sliding down the wall to join him. 'Fag?'

'No ta.'

Both of them, staring at the Parish Halls, at the long dark street of nothingness and the crowded tumult beyond. Occasionally, cops would pass by them, some hauling a prisoner, others nursing heads and arms. One rested a jaunty stick over his shoulder like a job well done. Or like he was leaving home.

'You're too young to remember the miners' strike.'

'Aye.'

'I'd no long joined myself, but they never sent me. My dad went though.'

John took a long draw of his fag. 'Bought a fucking conservatory with the overtime. Not that we got to enjoy it, mind.'

'No?'

Alex embraced his knees. He didn't know where this was going, but there was a soporific quality to John's voice. He liked listening to it, found he could switch off from the bawling and screeching down the street. Which was fading anyway; the good guys always won.

'Naw. We lived near Ravenscraig – you know they had secondary picketing there? Steelworkers and that?'

'Aye, I'd heard.'

'Aye.' John blew a steady plume of smoke. 'Boys I went to school with, men my da drank with. It was fucking horrible. My mum got spat at in the street.' He shook his head, a vapoury depth to his eyes. 'No, we had to leave. Couldny look our neighbours in the face again.' He stood up, stiffly. Brushed the fag stour from his knees.

Alex didn't move, all the hardness in him spent and curved. He just wanted to go home. Francine could wait till the morning, she was safe enough where she was. That war book he was reading, the cover of it. It's the picture you always see. The exhausted soldier, cowed in on himself like a nautilus.

Chapter Twenty-Eight

MONDAY 19 NOVEMBER

Anna couldn't shake it, this deadness she was carrying. All weekend, wrapped in the house, insisting they got take-aways, a DVD, that Laura should miss the sleepover at her friend's. Anna had traded on her fragility: *don't you know I nearly drowned?*, and her darling, good Rob and Laura whom she didn't deserve had complied. All weekend, intentionally whitening out the threat. And then, just at that point where the blankness was winning, the thrash of it engulfing her. Mark John Galletly was coming for her. Francine's terror had been extinguished, and, as it thinly fled, it had passed like a homeless ghost: straight to Anna. She was the sole recipient now, the only target of Galletly's wrath. Every part of Anna's body hurt, her nerves calling out to the backs of her eyes which throbbed in her fingers as her life shrunk back. Could feel her skin, her gums receding, leaving only blank white.

She had to get back to her office. She'd get her head straight there.

What she needed to do was find Galletly, before he rediscovered her. There must be some trade she could offer him, or better still . . . Meet fire with fire. Galletly was only out on licence. She couldn't risk associating him with Francine's death, but – and here her mind was rushing away with her, sure and amoral as an evil genius, it whirred though a clinical analysis, Anna to one side of herself, looking on, appalled, but listening, nodding, lapping it up. Her disadvantage was also her advantage. She was a police officer. She had access to all manner of databases and criminal intelligence, to information on planned raids and unsolved crimes. If she could implicate Galletly in some other offence, something that had no connection with Francine or her, then it would be straight back to jail, do not pass go.

Okay, that was a plan. A shitey, desperate one at that, two wrongs adding up to one huge mess, but it was a plan. Being inside the dark, sharp uniform of a police officer was giving her a plan. Kill or be killed – it was no better than the bastard deserved.

For the first time since Friday, Anna calmed. All this heaving panic could not be good for the baby; it would come out as an adrenalin junkie with a revenge complex. She became a little more focused, listening to what was going on around her. She was at the Monday meeting. They may have been in Stewart Street, but it felt like being back at school. The George Square riot was sod-all to do with anyone but Colin, yet Mrs Reekie had decided to give her entire senior management team a bollocking. Anna could hear her bawling at Colin:

'But it wasn't your bloody decision to make! And then you fuck off down to England for the weekend and leave me to pick up the pieces—'

Anna had never noticed Mrs Reekie swear like that before. Her oaths clanged and clattered round the room, biting in tiny darts and the shame that you were all complicit somehow, that you had made this fine, good woman curse and be hurt. Heads were lowered, eyes averted. Colin's plaintive defiance was no match.

'Look, ma'am, I acted as I saw fit. There was a dangerous protest mounting – a real and genuine risk to life and limb, to the safety of Glasgow's streets – and I got it sorted.'

'And now there's a young woman on a life-support machine at the GRI—'

'Yes, and there could have been a lot more like that if I hadn't acted when I did—'

'Colin, your confidence is astounding. I only hope it's no misplaced. I'm going directly from here to see the Deputy Chief Constable, where we'll be spending the remainder of the morning studying TV footage of the whole bloody thing.'

Anna sensed her boss's eyes were roaming, no longer forensically pinned to Colin's face. She stopped picking at her nails, turned her attention fully on Mrs Reekie.

'Well? Is it misplaced? I sense a definite air of reticence about the room. If any single one of you has anything to add about Friday's debacle, I want to hear it. Now.'

No response. What, was Mrs Reekie going to give them all detention? It had been Colin's shout entirely – he'd not even contacted the superintendent before launching his grand battle plan. So hell bloody mend him.

Mrs Reekie took a brief sip of water, pitched the next bit of her tirade lower; which was good, because she'd been in danger of shrieking, and then Colin would think he had won in some small way.

'Now, you know that I would back each and every one of you and your decision-making processes to the hilt, as long as you're straight with me.'

Again, only silence.

'There will be a full enquiry into this, so I hope all the witnesses agree with your recollection of events, Colin – all these fucking witnesses, hundreds of fucking witnesses . . .'

Swear-and-stab, swear-and-stab, Mrs Reekie letting a litter of press cuts drop on the boardroom table. All front-page headlines, all damning of Strathclyde Police.

SCENES OF MAYHEM
SQUARE GO IN THE SQUARE
SQUARE BASHING FROM CITY POLICE

Lots of cudgel-raising type pictures, too. No wonder Mrs Reekie was so angry, it looked like Armageddon. And that poor clown-girl had still to regain consciousness. She was only . . . twenty . . . shit. Were they supposed to be reading these cuttings? Anna looked up. Mrs Reekie's cheeks were trembling. Behind rage you could see the shock in her, puckered lines of regret for all the shoving and the sticks, for the girl, of course, and for the bitter recriminations that would stick and grind their way further between public and police. A vague notion of giving her a hug drifted up, but it was distant, and it passed. This, all of this, felt distant, a squall that had no business with Anna. Stuart Barrowman was shuffling half-heartedly through the pile of news cuts as well, everyone else had their heads down; she supposed it was okay to continue. One letter caught her attention, less angry and more erudite than the articles.

This unwarranted and ill-planned assault on the citizens of Glasgow seems to me endemic of a wider malaise within our police force. Almost half of all complaints against the police now relate to incivility and oppressive conduct. As a former police officer myself, I firmly believe that a lack of experienced officers is affecting the on-street training that recruits receive. This – along with the ongoing transfers of police powers to bodies such as local councils – is eroding the consent on which policing has traditionally been built. We no longer know who is responsible for what. Marry this with increased state surveillance – typified in such initiatives as the 'Citicard' – and it's no wonder that public confidence and indeed tolerance of interventions by authority is severely diminished. I despair for the future.

You and me both, pal.

A slow gulf of silence. Anna pushing the paper away. The metallic, tense charge of the room had fractured, fizzled out into hesitant throat-clearings, then shuffles. One brave soul got to his feet, followed by another, and another, momentum building into escape as they finally realised Mrs Reekie was done. Anna waited until everyone had left the room, initially to avoid being bumped by subdued men jostling for freedom, and then, because she saw that Mrs Reekie also remained. She sat, glasses in hand, at the head of the table. Her shoulders down. Going to see the Depute was shorthand for going to hell. Marion Hamilton was now the force's Deputy Chief Constable. A woman more malevolent or less empathetic would be hard to find. Like wary animals, Anna and Hamilton had maintained a circling distance over the last couple of years, aware that each had the ability to damage the other but neither willing to test it, just yet.

Anna collected her things, stood up slowly to prevent the dizziness she'd been getting. A sympathetic smile on the way out, that should do it, but her feet were not listening, carrying her off at a tangent until she was there, right beside Mrs Reekie's sloping profile.

'Ma'am, I'm sorry.'

'For what?'

'All this . . . shit. It's not fair. It's not your fault.'

Mrs Reekie breathed on her glasses, polished them on the edge of her untucked T-shirt. 'Ah well, that's not the way Mrs Hamilton sees it, I'm afraid.'

'Is there anything I can do?'

A weak grin. 'Any good at lion-taming?'

'I think you should know – one tiny wee sniff of me and a certain person goes apeshit.'

'Dinny take it personally. She's like that with everyone. Oof.' Knuckles on the arm of her chair, Mrs Reekie pushed herself up. 'I'm no getting any younger, that's my problem.' She put her glasses on, drew the scattered press cuts towards her.

'Here.' Anna scooped up bits of paper that had landed further down the table.

'You know actually, yes, Anna. You could help me.'

'Really?'

Her boss was grinning, strangely. No. *Anything but that. Don't make me go up to see Mrs Hamilton.*

'Yeah. The Central Crime Prevention Panel have asked me to judge a poetry competition.'

They both paused in their paper-chasing, Mrs Reekie's grin becoming laughter. 'Your face! But you're a clever lassie with the words – could you do it? It's called "What Glasgow means to me" and it's open to all the schools in the city. There's about a hundred entries, and I'm supposed to . . .' Her glasses shook a little as she sniffed. 'Ach, I'm sorry. That's probably no what you meant.'

'No, no. I'll do it.'

'Och, that would be wonderful. It's just one more thing I've to . . . I'm not saying you dinny have enough to do, mind—'

'Where are the poems and when do you need it done?'

'Here.' A bulging envelope was fished from her briefcase, 'I keep carrying the damn things around, meaning to get started on them, and – ' she checked her calendar – 'oh dear. Due end of this month, I'm afraid. Oh, and while we're on about schools, that meeting I had on Friday night? Cut short of course, thanks to bloody Colin playing cowboys and Indians, but the gist of it is that there's going to be a barge piled with schoolkids and Commonwealth dignitaries next Sunday, sailing down the Forth and Clyde canal. Now, the route goes through both B and A divisions, but I volunteered us – you, really – to co-ordinate the policing of the route. Good way to start getting into this whole Commonwealth palaver, don't you think?'

Anna said nothing.

'I know it's a big ask, and I realise this is a duty normally overseen by Force Operations. I had to fight for it, promised them you were shit-hot. Even so, they dinny trust us. They've made up a kind of pro forma for you to fill in and send back to them, just to check we've done it right – and you'll need to liaise with the search adviser folk in the Unit too.'

'Seems like a lot of effort for a few folk in a boat.' Anna picked at the corner of the poem-stuffed envelope.

'Bear in mind, Anna, the Commonwealth role will be a force appointment, not a divisional one.' A brittle glittering in Mrs Reekie's voice. Now was probably not the time to wind her up. 'So I can recommend and push as hard as I can for you to get it, but I canny guarantee it.'

Anna didn't even want the bloody job in the first place, and now she was being given extra work to facilitate her application for it. She was seven months pregnant, working in the busiest division she'd ever experienced, had wall-to-wall teenage angst necessitating some nifty eggshell-walking at home, some jailbird fuckwit was sharpening a knife with her name on it and, oh, now she was judging a poetry competition too.

The world gone mad indeed.

Chapter Twenty-Nine

Mary stared at the sky. Grey, dragging clouds; a bland smugness about them. Monday. The day the world wakes up, washes the glitter from its hair and goes to work. The day, last week, when Bernie died. When you thought about it, Monday is the last day Bernie ever lived. And this was the last place Mary had ever seen her. She drew the blanket tighter round her shoulders, ensuring one hand was always free and uplifted to catch the pennies from heaven. (Although they rarely fell. This, she decided, looking up again at the blank apartment blocks and wide, quiet street, was not the best of pitches.)

How was it to be endured? She had spent an entire weekend sleeping on the streets of Glasgow, and it was worse, so much worse than before. It wasn't just the ache of Bernie grinding through her. Although her death was raw, unbearable, for the first time Mary seemed able to regulate it a little, like she was sieving it through in manageable doses, whereas at first it had been a constant, waking shroud. Same as when you were really hungry, so starving that your belly yawned and hurt, your brain light with all that thinking about it – indeed it was all you thought about, constantly – until one unspecific moment when the feeling sheared away. You stopped struggling, went flat and numb. Oh, you still knew you were hungry all right, you just no longer felt it.

Mary had tasted no food since soup and sell-by sandwiches from a van on Saturday night. The queuing folk had been rough, jostling her to get to the front, and, in the rain and confusion, a man had swiped half her cheese and ham. Instantly, Mary had found herself yearning for the nice dull life of the nine-to-five, with a sturdy office and your own safe drawer within your desk. Where there was a rhythm to the day not born of night or drugs or weather, and it was always warm and dry.

'Spare ten pee for a cup of tea? Her hand raised higher, an automatic response to the feet edging by. They kept walking. Busy, busy feet with places to go.

'Watch out you don't slip!' she shouted after them. *Oh, bad Mary.* That was against the rules. You didn't answer back. No, you shrivelled up quiet and kept your place. Arse on cold stone, close to dogshit. That's all it took though. A wee slip, a tilt to the surface of your world and . . . whoosh. That's you away. Sliding off the edge of society, folk – nice folk, decent folk – contorting their feet to keep from getting tangled in your flailing wake.

She had even tried to get back to her mum's house. Yesterday morning; had got as far as the end of the cul-de-sac, where she had stood, letting the cold air run across her palate. She could almost taste the quietness of the kitchen. Feel her mum's little sighs as she fussed for some lost thing in the cupboard, her mum's hands, with their smoothness and soft round nails. Her hands, touching your face . . . Then she had seen a police car parked outside.

So, that was that. Now they all knew, and there was another door slammed shut. The police, aware of who she really was, and her mum knowing that, yet again, Mary McLennan was in trouble. Ach, but she'd gone for the gold medal this time. Stuff shoplifting, Mum – how about suspected murder? Will you still love me when they tell you that? Her mum had been very clear. *This is your last chance, Mary. Your very last chance.* If she had got there before the police. If she had showed her mum she was clean. If she had had time to sip tea, quiet and side-by-side, then begin to explain the mess she was in, and how it wasn't true and she had loved Bernie, would never hurt her. But the police car glowered on there, a squatting silver bird of prey, and it was shitting all over her nest and she just could not bear all that she had brought to her mother's door.

Lost, tired and hungry, Mary had come to sit here instead. In the absence of a ceremony or grave, here, the last spot she'd ever glimpsed Bernie, would suffice for some kind of elegy. And for begging too. Hey, if nothing else, Mary was a multi-tasker. She had tucked herself between a baker's and an off-licence, to maximise local passing traffic. This was Anderston, a place where there was only a very thin net separating the hardly-have-anythings from the have-fuck-all-at-alls. It was a fallacy that you only made money in the swanky bits of town. Okay, footfall might be slow, but this morning had seen her make two quid and half a can of Tango – which kept repeating on her in rich empty burps.

A lady came out from the baker's shop. She was frowning. Mary began to gather herself up, ready to move on. She had no desire for confrontation. Sitting so close to the police station, which was just across the road and along one block, she had expected to get moved on long before now. For a flickering instant, as she'd chosen her step and sat on it, Mary wondered if it was a death-wish that had brought her here. If you are trying to avoid the polis, sitting directly across from a police station might be considered a somewhat cavalier approach to take. Equally, it was probably the last place anyone would look. Who would have the effrontery? Plus Maryhill was miles away, that's where that inspector had been from – and what a fine-looking big shag he had been, by the way. Male, female, it didn't matter. Sometimes you just saw one of those people who made your jaw drop. But that was by the by, because he was the enemy. The cops here, they wouldn't know Mary from all the shit that was scuffed in the margins beside her. And yes, maybe a tiny, weak bit of her did just want to give up and say, aye, alright you've caught me. *The game's a bogey.* She was so, so tired. So, if they came to get her, maybe that's just what she'd say. Yes, that is what she is doing. She is saying farewell to Bernie and she is tempting fucking fate.

'Here, hen.' The woman bent down, still scowling. Mary watched her feet, waiting. 'You look frozen. You want a wee bridie?' She passed her a greasy bag, smelling of spicy meat and buttery flakes of pastry. Mary's stomach rushed into her chest, with the smell and the kindness and the biting, biting hunger which was rushing in as well.

'Yes please.' She spoke hoarsely, her voice unused and small.
The woman's hand sandwiched the paper bag and Mary's own
hand. 'Nae bother.' Still holding on, but crouching a little lower,
until she was almost at Mary's level and you could see the soft grey
sparks in her eyes. 'But listen, hen, the boss-man comes in around
twelve to cash up – we're only open mornings on a Monday. And
he's a total bastard, so mind and be away by then, yes? Or I'll
get my guts for garters!' She gave a wheezy, smoker's laugh, then
hoisted herself back to standing. 'There's a wee Paris bun in there
too, for afters.'

Mary waited until the lady had returned to the shop before she
opened the bag. It seemed more civilised, that and the pleasure
of anticipating the first, deep bite. When she tore open the bag,
there was the bridie, there was the Paris bun, its currants gloss-
plump and perfect. And there was a five-pound note folded neatly
in between. A tight pressure in her throat, then she was gorging,
gorging on thick, delicious food. For two, possibly three minutes,
nothing existed except the warmth and the weight. A texture of
filling up, the flavour coming after, like it wasn't all that important.

She made herself pause between the bridie and the bun, using
her tongue to sluice out crumbs. A bath of grease on her chin.
Occasionally a policeman would go in or come out of the station,
but none ever looked her way. Back of the hand wiping over the
mouth. Mary was hardly a catch. Too much paperwork, probably,
and for what? To shift some grubby nobody from street to cell to
street?

Once more, she wondered what had driven Bernie to go in to
a police station. Especially now she knew about Bernie's past,
a life she'd worked hard to eradicate. Bernie had gone there for
help, she must have done, but she had ended up dead. A horrible,
quick itching – could the police be involved? Mary's mouth was
on her knees, the breath keeping them warm through the thin
wool trousers, which looked more like bin liners now than part of
a designer suit. When she was younger, she used to love those little
style snippets you got in magazines, where they stop folk on the
street and they list the source of all their trendy gear.

*Well, I like to be quite individual. Eclectic, you know? I'm wearing
a lovely two-piece from Whistles, but it's been customised. See all the
staining and the pulls, yeah? Did that masel'. On my back is a stinking
blanket, liberated from a tramp sleeping in Anchor Lane. Oh, and
under my nails, I am wearing essence of horseshit.*

Her mind was playing in stereo, the light, stupid side narrating
her silly fashion show while the faster, deeper rushing bit was
battering down through the archives, trying to think if Bernie
had ever mentioned anything at all about the police; there was
something, *something* sleeping there but she couldn't nudge
it awake and why would Bernie take that package into a police
station? What was in it? Mary had squeezed and shaken, but she
hadn't opened it. Was Bernie blackmailing a cop, a former client
maybe? And was this nothing to do with Calder Riggs at all?

Mouth working on her knee, the damp patch spreading out,
and hot. Slowly, a rolling-out secret was sleeping and stretching,
it was real and moving, just one bit of it moving up and down as
it drew on a cigarette and she was aware that it was an arm, and
that she had been aware of it for some time now, this arm and the
motion, but like a wild animal that you want to catch, you dare
not look at it direct. Just let it be, stay quiet and wee because it has
not noticed you, why would it, it is too busy, too intent on looking
casual as it smokes its cigarette and watches the door of the police
station, the same door you are watching, for the same unknown
person, then it drags on a last breath of nicotine, tosses the filter
to the ground.

The arm is part of a man. *The* man. It is the fat man. He
stands in the same bus shelter through which you viewed your
Bernadette. The poster of the bra-woman is still there, except a
penis has been drawn at the side of her mouth. It's a crude cock-
and-balls, and the man is leaning next to it, almost on the graffiti,
and you wonder if it is fresh, and if the black marker will rub off
and he'll have a penis on his back.

He clears his throat. You are so fucking close you can hear
his throat, and your own throat is closing. You notice a silver car
turn into the car park at the side of the police station. The man is

watching it and you are watching him. He stands looking at the car park for another few seconds. Then he coughs again, begins to move away from the bus shelter, and you don't hesitate. You get up and follow him quietly, so quietly because it's easy to move quietly when you are invisible. Already, you have looked at people today, have met them dirt-streaked face to face, and you have seen yourself disappearing; a pinprick in their eyes.

She hopes he doesn't have a car. He walks slowly up the street, in the direction of Charing Cross, and then turns, sharp, into Elderslie Street. He is following the path of their recent chase, does he know she is behind him? Is he playing with her? In the Mitchell, he'd been talking to someone else on the phone. Might that have been a policeman? It was not long after Bernie had gone into the police station; it would fit. Mary tries to fix on what the man had said, but the words won't come. Was that who he had been watching for just now? His accomplice, coming out of the police station?

And then she remembers. The man had called Bernadette a whore.

He *had* known her from before.

When they get to Sauchiehall Street, the route alters, and he crosses over. Mary waits for a minute; she can see him make his way up the slope towards Woodside Terrace, then she follows at a distance. It is him, there's no mistaking it, and her daft split-brain is coursing on its two levels, the high-up part tiptoeing and afraid, the deep bit just a crush of rage. It's chilly; she realises she's left her blanket by the baker's – no matter, it was never hers to keep. Same as the money Margaret in the Press Office gave her, which remains on Margaret's desk. Margaret will have noticed that by now – shit, she better have noticed it on Friday, otherwise some other bugger will have taken it. From Woodside, the man cuts across Lynedoch Terrace, which is just a little street. It is here that he stops, and Mary freezes, exposed. She crams into an office doorway, one of the many elegant sandstone terraces that line these streets, and is petrified he will hear her heart.

But he's only lighting another cigarette. Puff, puff, cough and then he begins to walk down Lynedoch Street, and over Woodlands

Road. There are lots of 'eclectic' folk here, Mary blends in again, feels safe. Feels hate. She is close enough to kill him; if she picked up a big jaggy piece of wood, or had a knife, she could run and plunge it in his back. She could scream *this is for Bernie* as she stabs and stabs into the ugly roll of fat that is his neck. She feels so cold, and it's a cold that runs entirely through her. She has dark, numb water instead of blood; it is the swagger of the man, the fact of him enjoying his walk and all this air and the promise of sunshine to come. From Woodlands, down to West Princes Street, which is long and dark, and to an ugly grubby hostel at the end. The man tosses his still-lit cigarette aside and removes a key from his jacket pocket. Mary sees the dull flash of bronze. He unlocks the door and enters.

She checks the number on the front. 4 West Princes Street.

Now I can find you any time.

Chapter Thirty

Back at Cranstonhill, Anna sought out the Local Intelligence Officer. His map-bedecked office was the usual clutter of mess and random objects: one Toby jug of a florid, waistcoated man, a large box of Bonio biscuits, the usual copse-worth of papers and files and, a new one this, a sports sock hung over the unlocked Nobo board. The board was locked up at night; Anna wondered if Paul stored all his dirty washing behind its shutters, or was this a random act? The grubby grey wool was part-concealing the family tree of local criminals written on the board, their connections not genealogy, but association and crime. Viewed from here it would appear that Grunt McGibbon was currently residing with *Adidas* Forsythe. It could happen.

'Alright Paul. How's things?'

'Fhn shanks.' Munching on an apple, a *Daily Record* open across his computer keyboard.

'Busy?'

'Crazy busy, ma'am. Want a coffee? Kettle's just boiled.'

'No, you're alright.' She nodded at the in-tray on top of the filing cabinet. 'Mind if I have a wee nosey?'

'Help yourself, ma'am. Not enough gen for you at the morning meeting then?'

'Let's just say we had other things to discuss.'

'Oh, aye. Heh! We heard the shouting from here.' Paul lobbed his apple core at the bin. Missed. '*Any-hoo* . . . there's quite a few juicy bits and bobs come in the day. But you'll get them all in the intelligence update tomorrow. I've just finished typing it.'

'Och I know – but I like to be ahead of the game, me.'

He scratched his belly. 'Well, ma'am, my top tip for this week would be housebreaking. Got a wee team spent the weekend working their way – quite systematically – through a variety of student flats: iPods, laptops, mostly small, portable gear of high value. Beginning to wonder if they've a wean working for them; they're getting in through some gey tight spaces. Oh, and we've also been given intelligence that there's a factory operating round about Sandyford, Newton Place, that neck of the woods.'

'Drugs factory?

'Naw, wee twist there, ma'am. *Music*. Music and films – illegal CDs, pirate DVDs. The copyright folk want us to do a raid once they've taken some observations. Still big money in pirating, even with everyone and their auntie downloading.'

'Hmm, I'll take your word for it.' Flicking through the sheets of intelligence, rolling over the words Paul was offering. Housebreaking was a possibility – Galletly was wee and wiry, she remembered, had pre cons for dishonesty as well as violence. She placed the papers back in the basket. Here, in the reality of holding on to actual facts that she might use to do this wrong thing, the certainty fell from her. This was absurd.

'What about new prison releases?' she asked. 'Any local bad boys come back to haunt—?' Clipping her question short, because she could hear, then, Galletly's flinted tones. *Pig burds smell different.* Galletly wasn't local, he was from Northern Ireland. He'd only ever been here on 'business'.

'Nothing I can think of ma'am, no. Why, were you expecting someone?'

'No.' Said too swiftly. Not seeing the words, staring and re-reading at a scramble of printed text. Just the hum of the computer and a gentle slurp as Paul started on his coffee.

'Oh, and I hear we're steering this Commonwealth Barge thingie. Ho, *steering*, ma'am, geddit?'

'How did you know that? Mrs Reekie's only just told me.'

Paul tapped the side of his nose. 'That's my job, ma'am. Want me to start doing a risk assessment – you know, a wee rundown of any potential troublemakers we have in our midst. I'm talking embryonic terrorists, political protesters, rampant racists, nationalists, fascists, hunt sabs, professional anti-sporting event agitators—'

Anna raised an eyebrow.

'Joke, ma'am – and, well, just your general fist-shaking heidbangers too, I suppose.'

'Sure. Go for it.'

She gave the in-tray another desultory poke. Didn't know what she was looking for. A secret tunnel she could dig? Dig and keep moving and hide until the world had gone away.

'Suppose I'd better start checking out the route too,' she said.

This should have felt like a privilege, she knew that. She should appreciate what Mrs Reekie was doing for her, but the hope of a bright long career had receded. It was a mirage shimmering from a story book. There, the idea of it visible in your imagination, but you'd never really reach it.

'Och, you don't need to tramp the streets, ma'am. There's a map up there, look. Shows the whole of the Forth and Clyde canal.'

'Paul, that's hardly the right attitude now is it?'

He shrugged. 'Virtual policing – it's all the rage. Could do you a digital one, too. Google Maps, the works. Looks realer than the real thing. Better actually. No litter, dugs or unidentified pongs.'

Anna slid the folder containing details of the spate of housebreakings out from the rest of the pile. 'I'm sure you're far too busy to be wasting time on that, Paul. And I don't intend to walk; I'll get someone to drive me.'

Waddle four miles without wetting herself? No chance.

'But thank you for the offer.' Speaking nice and steady, and transferring the folder into a larger file relating to outstanding warrants. 'Um . . . I'm just going to take this away. Think we're due a wee warrant harvest before Christmas, eh?'

'Sure.'

She held the weight of the file, felt the point at the corner, the squared-off nub which caught and caught as she smoothed it with her thumb.

If you do this thing, you cannot, in all conscience, remain a police officer.

Yes, you've done it before. You've enhanced and omitted, you've lied, Godknows you have, but you could convince yourself, always, that it was for the greater good. Before. But life has made you soft. Life has smoothed your sharpnesses, you hold love where you used to be empty. There's a sweet, live ache in your belly. And fear at your throat.

If you *cannot* do this thing, you will go to prison. In all probability, you will die.

Anna has seen what Galletly did to those women, how he opened their faces with knives. In the mist and veils she remembers his feet, how hard they kicked, kept kicking. Did he kick Francine, did he scar her first too? Galletly is bad, and Anna is good. Bad is insidious, it's a parasite feeding on the healthy. Her job is to cut away the badness. Her job is to protect.

That is solid, it runs through your spine. You are full of right and it gives you carte blanche. Another picture now. A cell corridor, Anna crouched by an open hatch. She is a probationer.

'Put your arm back through.'

'No darlin'. I got to breathe.'

Thin-haired arm, persistent in its defiance.

'You have to do what I say. You have to obey me.'

'I don' want it shut, man.'

You draw your stick, bang it hard against the door. 'I'm in charge. Put your arm back through.'

'But baby, I got to breathe.'

And it won't go back, this wizened spider limb that can't reach you. So you hit it and you hit it to protect yourself.

I don't want to be that person again.

She takes the folder and goes through to her room.

Chapter Thirty-One

Some weekend for unravelling strings. First it was the bus boy, clear as his West End accent that he had seen Francine, that she was definitely on his bus. Oddest bus driver Alex had ever met, which lent his statement credence. A posh kid, who in the course of a half-hour interview flashed between egghead professor and lost wee boy. It made Alex think of traffic lights – the smart bit of the boy was alertly green, adamant, eloquent to the point of showing off, while the childish side of him turned red and silent at Shirley's suggestion that the girl was pretty, and did he like girls? Was that why he remembered Francine? Did *he* have a girlfriend?

Alex had paused, thought about getting a parent or a social worker in, but the lad was eighteen, he was a working man as well as a wean. And he glowed amber too at times, a sly hesitancy which made Alex wonder if he knew much more than he said. One to watch. For the moment, though, the position was that the bus driver had picked up Francine, alone, last Monday, around 3 p.m. She had got on at the stop nearest Calder Riggs and been deposited just past St George's Cross some twenty minutes later. They had sourced the on-bus footage, which confirmed two people got off at that stop, a stout middle-aged woman laden with shopping bags and a small, thin lassie with a black ponytail. No red tops though; this girl was wearing a khaki hooded jacket and leggings. Side on, the sharp nose, tight chin with its defiant lift could be any lippy Glasgow girl. The image enlarged, there was no doubt it was Francine. Ian and Mandy were currently pulling together data and footage from every CCTV camera Citywatch had sited round St George's Cross, to see if they could track Francine's movements thereafter.

The second thing had been Shirley yesterday, God bless her, doing a bit of lateral thinking. She had come back from Calder Riggs, bursting in on the team's Sunday morning meeting. He'd not see her since Friday, when she'd been tasked with interviewing Fiona Cairns regarding the land ownership. This transpired to be another layer of lies and wrong-footing, right enough. Fiona had lived there all her life, even after her father went into a nursing home, getting up at dawn to tend the animals, trying desperate marketing schemes to attract new custom. Imagine her shock when her father died and she discovered the farm was no longer theirs. Her dad had lost it, years before; it had been taken in payment of gambling debts and unpaid loans by his pal Bob Crilley. Crilley was not a bad man, was content for Fiona to stay on as a tenant these last few years. However, Crilley had recently retired – off to Portugal, no less – and his son Darren was of a different mindset. 'And I'm telling you this from the horse's mouth,' said Shirley, 'because I went over to see him too. Nice-looking boy, but hard as nails when it comes to business. He goes to me: *That Cairns family have being paying my dad a peppercorn rent for years. Plus it's a dump. Have you any idea how much I could make flattening the place and putting up houses?*'

'Is he hard enough to be violent?' asked Alex.

'He's no need; Miss Fiona agreed to the development weeks ago – she just hadny let on to Francine yet. Feart that Francine loved the farm more than her, I think.'

'So this anonymous letter then?'

'Waste of time, in my opinion. Either someone's deliberately winding us up, or they've just got the wrong end of the stick. Came from the cooncil, didn't it? Maybe someone no happy about the planning application?'

'Maybe.'

'Trust me, boss, that Darren Crilley is a smart lad – uni degree, good business, nice car, nice hoose. Even Miss Fiona says he's always been very reasonable with her, for all he takes no nonsense.

So I canny see what possible motivation he'd have for hurting Francine. And, before you ask: no, he disny have a green Ford. He's the registered keeper of a Mini Cooper, a grey BMW estate and a silver Merc, all less than a year old. *Bastard.*'

They now knew they were looking for a 2001 green Ford Escort. The age and composition of the paint and some mathematical genius work from the Traffic relating to depth of tread, dimensions and chassis weight had narrowed it down significantly. Ian had been entirely wrong about tyre treads. You might not be able to match them up like fingerprints, but tiny nuances, the waves, curves and blocks embedded in each design, helped to distil it further. From a tyre imprint, it was possible to ascertain who the tyre manufacturer was, when the tyre had been on sale – even which vehicles and rims it could be mounted on. Plus, a minute trace of extracted rubber residue had been stored in the lab, waiting to be compared with the suspect vehicle's tyres – if it was ever found.

Shirley, still grinning and breathless, had bitten into a bacon roll.

'Is there more?' Alex asked.

'Aye! Mind you wanted to know about any disturbances at the Riggs? Well, one of the stable lassies tells me someone tried to mug Francine, week past on Saturday. So that would be, what: eight, nine days before she died? Big fat man bowfed out of the woods and tried to yank the reins out her hands.'

'Now we're talking. How come Fiona didn't tell us this last week?'

'Says she forgot. And I believe her – you've got to remember the woman's grieving. Francine didny even tell her when it happened, and she really downplayed it, so I'm told; said it was nothing when one of the kids did tell Fiona later on.'

'What did Francine tell Fiona at the time then?'

'Well, this is maybe where all the "get off my land" confusion arises. Fiona says, when challenged about it, Francine insisted it was someone from the builder's, trying to scare them. But it clearly wasn't, seeing as Fiona had already agreed to all Crilley's terms. Methinks that Francine was blustering eh? Trying to cover up the real reason?'

'Which would lend credence to the theory that she knew her attacker.' Alex drummed a happy wee tattoo on the desk. 'So, have we got a proper description of this "big fat man"? Could the stable girl identify him again?'

'There's a camera rigged up when you come into the riding school,' piped Mandy. 'That big field. Would that have picked up anything?'

'I thought of that, but they've no film in it. Just keep it there for show. And the lassie didny see him, unfortunately. It was only a bunch of weans riding with Francine at the time. I'm getting all their names and addresses, but what the stable lassie did tell me was that she heard Mary Brown was there too. One of the weans seen her hiding in the same woods.'

'Fuck – so you think she *is* involved then?'

Alex felt he was running up and down a maze. High, thick green, all narrow tunnels, then a blast of light, then another dead end. It was beginning to feel claustrophobic. He needed a big wide sky, needed to be up high to look down on all this and see it clearly.

'Either that,' said Shirley, chewing, 'or she was scared 'cause he's after her too. But it did get me thinking. She keeps cropping up, that lassie, and I just canny shake the feeling that she's no . . . *right*, you know? I went up to her room again, turned the place, but it's empty – I mean empty, empty, like devoid of personality, nae sense of who she is. She left in one hell of a hurry, hasny even taken her clothes, but everything's . . . insipid. Nae posters on the wall, nae books . . .'

When she got excited, Shirley talked really fast, but it was always best to let her flow, get it off her – most awesome – chest, then go back and sift out what was necessary.

'So, I thinks: this Mary Brown lassie – crucially important or a nobody? Demented killer on the run or no-good drifter who wandered in to Calder Riggs then fucked off into the ether just because that's what she does, that's her nomadic wee pattern, you know? Either way, seems hell of a strange we can find no trace of her at all, no photie, no background, no national insurance, bank accounts, blah, blah, blah. I mean, *everyone*'s got records nowadays: a wean taking out a library book's got a record. So then I thought – duh – Mary Brown: could you get a blander name? I bet that's no her real name at all, and it's not, of course it's not.' A pause for breath, her fingers nudging a piece of flimsy paper towards Alex. It was an CHS printout.

'*Et voilà!* This is your woman here. Mary McLennan. Aged twenty-two. Last known address: Twelve Burntbroom Vale, Mount Vernon.'

'Shirley, Ah luv you. Ah've always luvved you.'

Alex had felt instantly light, high enough to put on silly voices. He had no reason to doubt what she was about to elaborate on. Bouncing in the slipstream of her logic, Alex knew Shirley's delivery of old. Stun you first, give an excited wee wriggle, or pat herself down, then wait for you to ask.

'How?'

Aaa . . . nd she's off. Again. Gleeful, the shine of her cleverness enlightening them all. She was generous with it, keen that it be shared round and welcomed into the mix.

He did love her.

'DNA. Well, we had the samples already, didn't we? Francine's underwear, Mary's towel, her toothbrush, the inside of her work gloves. Now, the DNA taken from Francine's fingernails at the post mortem was compared and crossmatched with the DNA taken from all the clothing samples at Calder Riggs. We were ascertaining who the victim was at that point, not the killer. That's how we got the instant response, based on the limited samples they were working with. But, at that point, the DNA samples taken from Calder Riggs still hadn't been compared against all those banks of DNA samples we have on file.'

She had broken off here, turning directly to Mandy. 'See, it can take two or three weeks for an extensive search of the database. But I spoke very nicely to those lovely people at SPSA, explained how this was an absolute priority, how we didn't know if Mary was a vulnerable missing person or a violent killer and, lo and behold

– the DNA under Francine's nails, the DNA on Mary Brown's towel, becomes the DNA of one Mary Alison McLennan, known to us for various crimes of dishonesty. She's a fraudster, mostly, and an intravenous drug user. Did her last stint in Corton Vale a year and a half ago, and was released—'

'About the same time Mary Brown turned up at Calder Riggs?' said Mandy.

'Good girl – you've been paying attention. Maybe she and Francine met in jail, or through associates, I dunno. But that lassie is definitely your Mary Brown – and now we have a picture and an address.' Shirley clapped her hands twice. 'So who wants a wee trip to Mount Vernon?'

Of course, Shirley wanted to go herself, and she had taken Mandy with her, the two of them chatting quite affably as they left. Alex liked seeing them together, Mandy less waxen, Shirley less stiff, as if they were rubbing the false edges from one another as they walked. No Mary to be found in Mount Vernon sadly, just an anguished mum and a bedroom like a shrine, but Alex had arranged for the most recent photo her parents could provide to be circulated. Just internally, at present; he'd need to get the Fiscal's permission to put it out to the press and nationwide if she'd not been found by the end of the week, say. He pressed down hard on his forehead. If he kept the pressure firm, the pain behind his eye would move to the back of his scalp. It was less intense there, more room for it to spread out. His front brain was too cluttered with crap. Sandra had spent last night nagging him about missing Sunday lunch with her parents, on and on until he thought he would have to pierce his eyeballs, to release the tension in his head. And then there was this morning.

It had just been a name. The sight of a beautiful name, that shocked him when he saw it. A name he'd not thought of for months, and here it was, tugging twice at him in almost as many days. But he had shrugged it away and after that came Hayley, enquiring about his progress and did he need a one-to-one meeting with her? Maybe grab a bite to eat after work? He found himself grinning. Maybe a quick burst of sexual activity would just rinse out his brain, relieve all that pressure.

Man.You do realise you're being sexually harassed?

'Afternoon, boss.'

Was it? Afternoon already? Shit, he'd not even had lunch.

'Ian. How's it going?'

His DS plumped a huge concertina of papers in front of Alex, helped himself to a chair. 'That's stills from all the CCTV footage . . .'

'Christ, Ian, I was hoping you might have gone through it – no just gathered it into a massive pile.'

Crumple of Ian's sullen mouth. 'I bloody have. Just wanted to gie you an idea of how much crap we'd to wade through, before you start bending my ear about how long it's taken. You any idea how many cameras there are in the city centre? Fuck me, I had to—'

'Whoa. Calm down, pal. I'm sorry, okay? I wasn't meaning anything . . .'

Ian sniffed. 'Right. Well, the position is, we've went through the lot, and I think we've got a trace. See here,' he pointed at a grainy image of a stick figure, rustled through the sheaves until he came to a set of enlarged pictures and the stick figure became . . . her. It was Francine. Beneath the desk, Alex's fist contracted.

'I'm getting it all on disk, but I thought this was quicker. Now, look . . .' Ian flicked through page after page of enlarged images. It was like watching the making of a strip cartoon. 'We've got her coming down here, see, then turning into Argyle Street, yeah?'

'Yup, got it.'

'Then we see her coming all the way down Argyle, past the Anderston flats and – check it out!'

Alex scrutinised the photographs. Francine's hand on the door. Next one, pushing it open, her body half inside.

Francine going into Cranstonhill Police Office.

'Fuck me.' Swooping fast, falling from the clouds he'd been bestriding. A cold, queer knot pulling him down.

'Exactly. Now, do you no think some cunt at Cranstonhill might have mentioned it before? Her details have been circulated all round the houses. Plus, the time lapse between her going in and out is over an hour, right? I mean, she's definitely in to see someone. No just asking for directions. And then we have her exiting the building, going back up Argyle Street the way she came, turning right into North Street, all the way down here, see, and then passing under the motorway. And that, unfortunately, is the point that we lose her.'

'How do you mean lose?' Alex blinked. His eyes were hurting, and his head. The whole damn lot, in fact; that whole hard curve of temple and brow, squeezing on his eyeballs. 'Does she no come out the other side?'

'Nope. She could have got in a motor, or kept walking down towards the Broomielaw. It's a blind spot there until you get to the walkway on the river.'

'Bollocks.' He could hear Ian tutting. Trepanning, that's what he needed. Alex, not Ian. Big drill in his heid and a nice calm hand, sliding across to take all these pictures away from Ian. Calmly, slowly.

'But great work Ian, thanks. That's given us a real boost. Leave it with me—'

'I was gonny head down to Cranstonhill—'

'Actually, I'll do it. Thanks. I'm going down there anyway.'

Ian shrugged. 'Suit yourself. So what are my instructions for this afternoon then, sir?'

'Ach, Ian, don't be like that, eh? Ma heid's nipping, I need some fresh air, alright?'

'Aye fair enough.' Ian took out a fag. 'But so do we all, boss. Tell you what, how about you give me your list and I can start—'

'My list?'

'Aye. Your who's who of hooring.'

Shit. He'd completely forgotten he was meant to be collating details of Francine's former co-workers. *Shit, shit Alex – that's no good enough son. You're the man. You're supposed to be on top of everything – and no just the ladies ha-ha, you're no even funny, ignore that wee chittering sound, just think you stupid bastard, think. Stop thinking about her and think . . . yes. Her.*

'I . . . that's why I'm heading over to the Central, pal. Need to chat to a few former colleagues about that very list, so I do. I'll give you it tomorrow, but. Promise.'

Ian sighed, fag shoved back in the packet.

'Look Ian, why don't you take a wee flyer? You're knackered, you've been on all weekend.'

'You sure boss?' He pretended to be reluctant, but you could see the gleam in his wee piggy self, all the feigned exhaustion sloughing from his skin. 'It's no really very fair—'

'Positive. You head off early the day, and I'll let Shirley do the same tomorrow, yeah?'

'Fair dos. You're the boss.'

Ian gone, the office returned to Alex and just this one thing. This name, which would merely have been a small thing, probably an inconsequential thing if Ian had not descended. This strange, strange knot, which he wasn't sure how to untie, or even if he wanted to. Wasn't technology wonderful? You could spy on your fellow cops now, only they didn't call it that. When conducting an investigation, it was possible to request a 'Police Info' tag be placed on a criminal record. This meant any time that record is called up, Intelligence are made aware, and can contact the cop in question to ask why they're checking out that offender. This had been done with Francine Gallagher's file, and on the Friday after her murder, Alex had been advised that her file had been accessed by the LIO at Cranstonhill Police Office, guy called Paul Norris. He had been contacted, and had given this response:

On annual leave that day. Only other authorised person with access at this time would be SDO/ Dep SDO. SDO currently sickness absence (stress!). Dep SDO: CI Anna Cameron. Do you want me to enquire with her?

Anna Cameron. Beautiful, chiselled, fingers-through-your heart Anna Cameron. Who knew Francine as well as Alex did. Better, maybe.

Alex keyed in 'No'. Pressed *Send* before he could change his mind.

Chapter Thirty-Two

So. Where does Galletly live? The terms of his licence will say to which address he's been released. When Paul goes out – and he will, regular as the ticking of Anna's watch, go out for an *Evening Times* at four o'clock because Monday is his five-a-sides night, and he has his tea and reads his paper in the office before he goes – she'll nip in quick and check SID again. Last time, she'd only seen Galletly's name on the database, didn't want to see anything further that would bring him closer to home; but, seeing as it appears he is, very close, to be forewarned is to be forearmed. Find out where he stays, find a way inside, then plank a load of gear that fits the description of stolen items from elsewhere. Then . . . appear as if by magic and arrest him? Say a little birdie told you, tell a little birdie, who'll tell another little birdie . . . leave an anonymous tip-off, whatever way you do it, it will all fall into place because of course Galletly will have been in Glasgow at the material times, and of course he will have no alibi and of course that alone will be sufficient to convict him, and of course he will never, ever, get out and of course that will be the end of it all and, even if it isn't, hey, he'll bear no further grudges. *Good call, pig burd! I like your style. Hats off to ye, it's a fair cop, cop.*

Her pen, tapping on her teeth, not in contemplation but because her hand is trembling. Her other hand cups her belly, holds the bobbing orb of her baby's skull. She is a wee mouse in a trap, one of those 'humane' ones, where you don't die at first but are allowed to contemplate your own demise for hours, sometimes days, until, when they come to get you, you're so weakened and shit-scared that you've no choice but to accept your fate. Galletly wasn't going to do that to her, he was a fucking murderer, a piece of shitty scummy shit oh God she wanted somebody to talk to. Download all the several conversations she was having in her head – there was pious Anna, clad in sackcloth and ash, mouth open as her palms stretch out in appeal: *Admit your sins and be saved*, while aggressive Anna goes 'No fucking way', gives her a Glasgow kiss, vaults over a wall and away. Logical Anna is writing long strings of lists; the more she procrastinates, the more the words coil and stick round her ankles, twisting and tripping and pulling her into a web. Pregnant Anna – well, all she can do is wobble plaintively, shouting 'wait for me!' every five minutes, but no one else is really listening, apart from exhausted Anna, who is fading like a ghost.

Jesus – what then? What can she do to get rid of him? Kill him? Lure him to a meeting, then say he attacked her? Get some wee guy – there's always some wee guy, who'll oblige for a couple of grand and a ticket down south – and then Galletly reappears eight years down the line and she cannot believe she is even considering the efficacy of this option. She is insane.

She puts her hand in front of her face. Surprisingly, real Anna's fingers are still visible, full and swollen larger than life thanks to a build up of oedema. They say honesty is the best policy. How honest, then, can she be? Could she actually fire Galletly in for Francine's murder? Simple as that, just leave an anonymous message on Crimestoppers. They'd have to check it out; interview him; he has no alibi. Hopefully his DNA will be on the body . . . and if he starts bleating about being fitted up all those years ago for Ezra's murder, if he points his stubby little finger at Anna, it's only his words, the words of a convicted killer, against hers. As long as there is nothing whatsoever to link Francine to Anna, apart from their long-past association with the Drag, then Anna is safe. Francine swore she told no living soul that it was her, not Galletly, who killed Ezra Wajerski, and Francine is dead. If Anna has the balls to ride this out . . . yeah, mud sticks, but her career is over anyway. There is more, much more she wants to do with her life – with these lives. She has an almost-husband and Laura and this belly which is a wriggling, pulsating fact, and it still gives her a thrill every time she realises this, that people want her.

Anna could do this. She can do it. Anna can be brave, resourceful. When something is worth dying for, it's worth lying for too. And she can lie and feign outrage without one single crack of her façade.

For a glorious instant, positive Anna returns. A frenzied energy suffuses her, a dam has burst and she is beautifully full. She empties out her in-tray, ticking and binning, allocating and opening. It's the pregnant-polis version of nesting. Shame on her – there are unopened letters from more than a week ago in here, oops, and there's that bloody pro forma about the procession through Maryhill. She suspects it has mythic proportions, it is an air-sucking cloud, yet as she actually scrutinises the form for the first time, she sees it's all about required road closures and cops on points to direct the traffic. What a lot of nonsense. It's a bloody canal they'll be on, and she can picture the route: through Maryhill, along into Speir's Wharf and Dobbie's Loan. Ach, bugger it – a scatter of cops strategically placed along the canal banks, a few extra . . . here, she scribbled and . . . here, where you could reasonably expect missiles to be lobbed by local kids, and that's it done and dusted. A flourish of signature at the bottom and lo, direct from the in-tray to the out. Lovely.

What else has been chewing at her? Spinning in her wheely-seat, she pulls the pile of poems from the unit behind her, picks one. It's pish. Yeah, yeah it's for secondary school kids, but even so. Rhyming Glasgow with 'here we go' and 'lots on show'. Hmm. Relax Edwin Morgan. She picks another . . . another *hmm*. Bit schmaltzy, but it'll do. Picks a third for luck, and it's perfect. She rereads the title: *Flourish*.

> *The thrill of the new*
> *Of the new, of the*
> *New*
> *New shops and pubs and clubs and flats*
> *All glass and steel and twinkly*
> *And old*

Old new
Façades and malls and skinny walls
Propped with girders like wir ither national drink
Turning bank to bar and banning cars
For courtyards
and cafés
and places to be happy
and more stores than before
and so we grow and grow
and flourish as we nourish
all that old and all that new
And is it true
that St. Thenew
Was the patron saint of shopping?

The poem makes her laugh – St Enoch's is one of Glasgow's famed shopping malls, but St Enoch's real name was Thenew. Anna takes it as an omen – anything that makes her laugh at this juncture is good. She puts the poem in an internal envelope and marks it FAO Mrs Reekie. Two things now that she's going to make: first a coffee, then a phone call. They never trace the calls, but regardless, she'll go out, use a payphone. Hell, she might even get Paul along the road now she no longer has to sulk and skulk until he vacates his office . . .

And then she remembers the camera at the desk. How it picked up Francine's face and shone it back at her.

And then there is a knock at her door and a man walks in.

'Anna?' His smile is tentative. Her stomach lurches. 'How you doing?'

He's filled out from the skinny boy you shagged, fits his suit in that so-sharp, overtly sexual way you always knew he would. Shadows under his eyes, but they only add to the appeal. You return his smile, though your head is in the foyer thinking how long do we keep the bloody tapes? Then he draws out a chair and sits down, eyes huge at the girth of your belly.

'I guess congratulations are in order?'

'What? For eating loads of pies?'

You both laugh, and then he says:

'Look, I don't know if you're aware, Anna, but I'm the SIO on the Francine Gallagher murder. You remember Francine, yeah?'

And then you swallow. Try to dampen papery lips.

Chapter Thirty-Three

He watched Anna raise her chin. 'Who?' she said, cool as you like.

'Mind, Angela's wee sister? They lived up the Townhead? I'm trying to build a picture on what may have become of her after we all left the Flexi.'

Man, she's pregnant. Mega-pregnant. Swept way off course, for a flicker, Alex didn't know where he was going with this. The whole journey here, just the name of her; at night, for months after they slept together, he would masturbate to the rhythm of her name. Hating himself, and hating her more. Now here she was, pregnant and beautiful with it. Chips of glitter in her eyes, her hair. The moon beneath her skin, smoothing it milk-silver perfect; he had licked that skin, licked all around and in it, had felt the give of her under his hands. She was looking at him funny. He must be staring.

'Alex, I didn't even know she'd been murdered.' She met his gaze, so much calmer than him. Her lips half parted.

'I-I . . .' Stuttering, because either she was lying, or he was thinking that she *could* lie. Had he got it wrong? He wanted to have got it wrong, to believe in this version of Madonna with child.

'Oh sorry, I'd assumed you would . . . well, you know how she was found?'

'No.'

'Drowned in the Forth and Clyde canal.'

A twist in her mouth. 'Nae luck.'

'Yeah, I mean, Francine's been off the game for years – living under an assumed name, in fact – and then, whump, some bastard grabs her off the street and ends her in a canal. Totally random, or motivated by her past? That's what I'm trying to find out.'

'So why are you asking me? Christ, I know we were all girls together, Alex, but d'you think I keep in touch with hoors?'

Her glitter turned to granite; she was angry, furious with him, but it was an innocuous enough question.

His head went down, the doubt swinging back, biting. But he persevered, giving her numerous chances to explain it all away. 'No, of course I don't think that. Basically what I'm wondering is, can you think of any reason? I mean, why would she have hidden herself away for years—'

'For a fresh start? It's quite hard to get a job when you've got pages of pre cons.'

'Yes, yes I realise that, but . . . ach.' He sighed into his hands. 'Look Anna, obviously this goes no further—'

'Look, *DS* Patterson, I'm a bloody chief inspector. I don't need lessons in discretion from you.'

His heart lurching as Anna stressed the *DS*. Meaning it to wind him up, but what it meant, what it really *meant* was that she'd been following his career. She *knew* him. He tucked the thought inside, drilled on.

'As I was saying, ma'am, this is confidential information, but Francine Gallagher was tortured before she was killed. With almost military precision. I believe that her assailant was trying to extract some kind of information from her before she died. Here, look.'

From his briefcase he extracted the sheaf of photos that he'd picked up and put back twice, before finally deciding to bring them. Until they were neatly bound and en route as a production, the pictures should never be taken out of the incident room. He shuffled through a couple, searching for the best one of Francine's face.

'See, the bruising round her neck and temple – that didn't show up at first. And the PM states . . . well, I won't go into gory details—'

'Please don't.'

'But she was submerged several times before she died. You know, up and down like a ducking stool, held under for just long enough not to die before being brought back to the surface, and then down again. Five, six, seven times maybe, until she drowned in her own lung-fluids. And she's naked too, you'll note.'

'Yup.'

'But no evidence of sexual assault. Anyway – the details are all there. I'll leave them with you if you like. Not the photies, obviously, but I've done you a wee synopsis.'

'Why?'

'For old times' sake – so long as you swear it didn't come from me. As you so kindly pointed out, I'm only an acting DI.' He folded the sheet of A4 twice, passed it like a love note. 'I just think it's really important that you realise the severity of this attack. Given that in her past life Francine was a prostitute and in her current life – well, you know what I mean – most recently, she was an instructor at a riding school, my money's on the information her killer worked so hard to extract being related to prostitution. Not ponies. Now, seeing as you were the OIC of the Flexi Unit at the time we both worked there, I don't think it's unreasonable to ask if you might have any prior knowledge that could be considered useful in this case. Do you? Ma'am?'

She graced him with a smile, cheekbones rising in soft arches until the gleam of them reached her eyes. 'Cool it tiger. Okay, I take your point. I apologise. Hormones. What can I say?'

How could you be mad at that?

'So who's the lucky man then?' he said.

'And is this part of your investigation too?'

'Nope.'

It was like observing a piece of art. His hand on his chin, just lapping her in. She was like an archetype of motherhood, one of those austere, noble poster-girls with Slavic profiles and a Cyrillic exhortation to breed painted beneath.

'Nobody you know. God, you're a nosy bugger, aren't you?'

'So, who then? Husband?'

'Not quite. We, um, we live together.'

'Cop?'

She laughed. 'No way! Nah, he's a doctor, a consultant at the Vicky. And he runs an old folks—'

'Oh yeah – that guy from the place in Mearns. Him?'

'You know him? Rob?'

'Nah, but I read my newspapers. Tut tut, madam, I'd forgotten about that. Illicit affairs, granny farms, counterfeit money. All that intrigue, and you up to your old tricks: chucking old ladies out of windaes when they piss you off.'

'Fuck off.' But she was still laughing, they were passing the laughter between them and he didn't want it to stop. 'And what about you?' she said. 'Still shagging for Scotland?'

'Ooh. That's a bit harsh, isn't it? I'm a married man, don't you know?'

'Really?'

'Yeah. Don't sound so surprised. Married to Sandra – she's a nurse. So, yeah,' he stretched his knuckles out, enjoying the crick-crick and the face that Anna pulled. 'That's me. Retired as a sex god now. I like to think I peaked about two or three years ago.' He lowered his hands down, stared straight at Anna. 'No, two years. Definitely.'

It was a quip too far. A wash of scarlet, turning her cheekbones to round fat suns.

'Look Alex, it's been really nice catching up with you, but I've got a ton of work to get through. Plus, if I don't pee every twenty minutes, my eyes fill up and I—'

'Point taken. Just give me five more minutes.'

'That's usually enough for you, I've heard.'

She was like the weather; she had always been that way. Capricious, random seasons passing through her. In a single exchange, you could experience ice-wind then a flash of sun. And, like the weather, it was an independent force that drove her, one Alex couldn't influence. He doubted anyone could. He could only wait with his metaphorical brolly, enjoying the light breeze while it lasted. Maybe this Rob person had it sussed. *Good luck to you pal, if you can manage Anna Cameron.*

'Anna. Look, can you think of *anything* Francine got tangled up in down at the Drag? Who she pallied about with, even? Did she ever get any bad beatings, weird clients, whatever? I've racked my brains, but I can't think of anything. I mean, she wisny one of the ones that got slashed by that loan-shark nutter was she—'

'What? Fuck, no way.' And she was angry again. Angry with him, or with poor dead Francine? He wondered how much of Anna's anger was real. When he'd first met her, he'd thought it was an act, a bluster to cover up her insecurities, or imbue her with something she thought was missing. Now, he wondered if she'd been relying on it for too long.

'No.' She shook her head – as *if* Alex was going to argue with her. 'No chance. No, Francine was a right smart lassie, far too clever to get tied up in anything like that. Alex – listen to yourself. Where are you getting all this torture spy stuff from? I bet you're still reading those war books, aren't you?'

She had remembered what he read. He felt unaccountably glad, and then an immediate plummet of sickness. It was like being on board a bloody boat, straining to see the horizon.

'Couldn't it just be the case that Francine's attacker was a boyfriend with a really nasty edge?' she said.

'I guess. Except she was a lesbian.'

'Away!'

'No joke. She's been living with a woman for the last three years.'

Anna thought about this for a minute. 'Well, you can't really blame her, can you? Based on her experience of men.'

He could no longer dance round it. She was never going to open up to him. She couldn't even do that when they were lying in bed together. The closest they had ever got was when she'd sunk her teeth into his thigh. Alex clicked the top of his pen. Nib down, head up so he could see her. Pretended he was writing the date at the top of the page.

'And has Francine ever got in touch with you? I mean recently.'

Look at me. Look up at me.

There was still the hope that he'd got it all wrong.

Anna glanced down at her cup, then lifted her chin. Cat-slit eyes, colours like heavy skies. But steady. 'Like I said. Nope. Why would she?'

Oh, man. I canny deal with this.

'It's just, we have CCTV evidence that Francine attended at Cranstonhill, the afternoon of the day she died. She was here for a good hour, so she must have been speaking to someone—'

'And why would you assume that was me, Alex? Oh that's right. I forgot. I run the Prostitute Pals section of Friends Reunited, don't I?'

'No Anna. I'm assuming it because of this.'

He had printed out the email, brought it with him as well as the pictures. Had underlined *C I Cameron* both to elucidate the point and keep himself free from the eye of the storm.

It's nothing personal . . . I'm just the messenger.

Without fear or favour, I am only doing my job.

He waited for a reaction. Apart from the briefest of shrugs, there was none.

'So Paul was off that day. Big deal. It's like open-house in his office. The eejit leaves his passwords all over the place.'

'So you're his boss. Discipline him then.'

'Aww, Alex. You wee pet. Did someone give you a pair of fake balls to go with your fake promotion?'

He ignored her, pretended he was reading a bit in his notebook. 'What about you, Anna? Can you remember what you were doing between – ' he checked the details – 'Three thirty and five p.m. on the twelfth? Can you confirm if you were present in the office then?'

'Jesus Christ. So I'm supposed to be the Amazing Memory Woman now, am I? I run a busy subdivision, I've a—'

'Aye, Selective Memory Woman anyway.' Rolling straight from his mouth. It was an accident.

'What's that supposed to mean?'

'You tell me. You fuck me – several times as I remember – then make out you can barely remember my name. What was that all about then, Anna?'

'Och Alex, grow up. You still bothered about that? You were trying to chat me up in front of my men – put your fucking mark on me so they'd all know; start winking at me behind my back.'

'Jesus, Anna. I was saying hello. That was it. I was saying bloody hello. What the hell is up with you? Why d'you always think folk are out to get you? D'you ever think that maybe it's you, projecting your own issues on to other people? I mind Jamie saying—'

'Right, that's it. Get the fuck out my office now. How dare you discuss me with Jamie Worth?'

He stood up. 'Gladly.' Then promptly sat down. 'Naw. No, wait a minute. I want to see all your front office CCTV footage for the last two weeks. See exactly who Francine Gallagher was talking to when she came here. Then I want to interview whichever of your station assistants was on duty that day. Plus . . .' He was aware he was shouting at her. It was really quite loud, and kind of slevery, like he wasn't fully in control of his tongue or his teeth. '. . . Either you ascertain who it was that accessed your DIO's computer or I'll do him – AND YOU – with neglect of fucking duty. How's that for starters, Chief Inspector Cameron?'

Anna began to cry. Soundless tears, welling and falling, and her face like a sheet which had been roughly tugged aside.

'Oh Anna, don't. Please, don't. I'm sorry.'

Quick with the need to hold her, notebook falling to the floor, his feet making too much clumping noise as he got himself round the desk; he was not moving smoothly. Alex should always be smooth. But it didn't matter. She sat on like sculpture, rigid, immobile, just the tears running, and he found he couldn't touch her at all. Frightened she would shatter, he stood there, useless. Eventually saying, 'Is there anything you need to tell me?'

'No.'

'Anna, we used to be friends, remember?' He couldn't help it, his hand went to her face, palm cupping the heart-shape. Thumb close to her mouth. 'I'm still your friend.'

Feeling her lips graze the edge of his thumb.

'I know.' She closed her eyes on him, on everything, and it was only then that she seemed able to speak.

'I . . . I'm finding it really difficult, being taken seriously at the moment. This . . .' She flapped her hands over her belly, 'This, you know. It doesn't make things easy. Mrs Reekie can't wait for an excuse to pap me out of her division. And I know I've allowed Paul to let things slide and, the truth is – the CCTV's buggered and I was supposed to authorise a repair . . . but I didn't,' she was sobbing again, 'and two of my station assistants have been totally taking the piss – they keep swapping their shifts without running it by me and . . . I just can't cope any more.' She literally threw herself on Alex's mercy – or as near as dammit, considering the press of her belly between them. He shifted to the side, so she could nestle in. Hot breath on his chest, tears through his shirt. Her hair in his hands, thick-smelling of flowers and him, up above the clouds. Cruising at that slow-fast velocity that feels like you're dreaming but is really fast enough to kill and he doesn't care. He is holding Anna and she needs him. That's all.

That is all.

'Alex.' She lifted her face from him. Eyes wet and wide. 'Let me sort it, please. I'll speak to the station assistants myself, and I'll drag Paul in here too – kick his arse about security. But please don't you take over and do it. It'll look really bad for me. *Please.*'

His heart was clunking too fast. Too low down as well, it was scraping through the barrel and the tightness in his head was twisting, knotting like thorny scrub. And that fucking chittering like laughter.

'Sure.'

He heard himself colluding with her. Because it suited him better that way. To tell them both that everything would be okay.

Chapter Thirty-Four

After Alex had left, Anna couldn't move. Even though the warm rasp of heartburn was threatening to overspill and she desperately needed a drink, she stayed hidden behind her desk, holding the smooth rim of wood and simply breathing. Her phone rang a couple of times, the muscles in her throat numbed as saliva pooled and she kept breathing. All those hundreds of interviews she'd sat through; some she'd led, in others the silent partner, but she must have absorbed it by osmosis; how to make yourself sealed-off and small. Snatching answers from empty air, trying to weave a coherent, convincing structure while leaving yourself big enough gaps to step through. And the one thing, above all, that Anna had definitely learned in all those years: Never admit a thing. Oh, they can build a dazzling tower of circumstantial crap, pile it all around you so you think that they're shutting out the light – but without the foundation of corroborated fact, it is thin, baseless.

And what's the one thing they want to corroborate it? You. You and your confession.

Well, that was never going to happen. Deny all knowledge, keep moving forward.

Mind Robert the Bruce and that stubborn wee spider?

She had bought herself a little time, that was all. Her throat was burning, her bladder nipping. Alex's card stared back at her, with its urgent black type and the wee cell-phone logo by the mobile number. It wasn't an official card, he must have got them made up himself. *Big wean.* His aftershave still clung about her. She refused to believe he'd meant those soft words. Alex was Alex: superficial, slick Alex. He was feigning hurt from two years ago, not meaning it at all. How could Anna have wounded him like that? Nah, he was at it, and he'd come back soon enough, he'd want answers. If he didn't get them from Anna, he'd start asking elsewhere.

Mind that stubborn wee spider and its tangled web?

There was no way now that she could bring Galletly to the enquiry's attention. Alex wasn't stupid, he *knew* Francine had been here, he just couldn't prove it. By now he'd be taking a walk down memory lane, and he'd be thinking about when they'd all been together down the Drag, and had anything happened between Francine and Anna? No, but there was that time Anna got a doing – remember? Guy kicked her head in, she was off for weeks. What was his name again? Oh, yes, Galletly. Oh, and that's right, he was the one who ended up being done for all those slashings we were just talking about – and the old Polish boy's murder. Which Anna was really cut up about, if you'll excuse the pun. Thinking it out the way Alex would, joining the neat triangular dots between Francine and Anna and Anna and Galletly and Galletly and . . . so *did* Galletly know Francine after all? Alex would check, would wonder about it more and more because he was an excellent cop and Galletly was out of jail and it would all nudge back to Anna.

She felt thoroughly ill. One thing at a time. Chip away at what you can in the interim, keep moving forward. She picked up the phone and dialled the internal code for Mrs Reekie.

'Ma'am, I've a wee favour I wondered if you could help me with.'

'Hmm?'

'One of my station assistants – Jean Williams. Any chance you could give her a transfer to another office?'

'Why?'

'Let's just say we've not been hitting it off recently. I don't want to make it official or anything, I'm just thinking a change of scene might be better for us both.'

'Anna, I canny just move someone because they're annoying you—'

'It's no different from you moving Colin.'

'Eh? Who said I was moving Colin anywhere?'

'Oh, yeah. Sorry. It's just that . . . well, it's what I would do if I were you. Punt him to Drumchapel and let him stew.'

'You're not by any chance psychic, Anna?'

'Don't think so. Psy*cho* maybe.'

'We're not having this conversation, okay?'

'Look, I'll even take Whisky Mac. I don't mind.'

Whisky Mac was the station assistant at Drumchapel Police Office. A retired soldier and recovering alcoholic, so fully soused was he in liquor that, when he sweated or belched, soft waves of the angel's share would rise in their fumey glory. A very useful person to stand beside if you had the cold though: cleared your chest in no time. Whisky – Christopher McAuley to his mum – had had his long military service book-ended with tours of both Northern Ireland and Afghanistan. He deserved a peaceful life. Now single, teetotal and taciturn in the extreme, some folk found him hard to deal with. Anna would be doing Drumchapel a favour really.

'Anna. Unless you've some specific reason, I canny—'

'Ma'am. I think she's having an affair with one of my cops.'

'*Ah.*'

'Look, I don't want to name names, but he's married. Got two wee kids . . .'

She heard her boss sigh.

'I think it's just a bit of fun at the moment, but if we can try to defuse it quietly, without either if them knowing that we know . . .'

'Fine. You're taking Whisky Mac though.'

'Done.'

Inside Anna, the baby wheeled round. An elbow, arrow-sharp, pushed at her tummy-button. She sat for a while, just watching the undulations of her belly, trying to picture the little person within. Then she called up the duty rosters on her PC, and deleted Jean Williams's name from the rota last Monday afternoon. In its place she typed: *emergency cover – shift to man.*

Of course, nobody would have done, because nobody had been asked. But she'd say she'd checked with the entire office. Francine's appearance, or otherwise, at Cranstonhill would just have to remain a mystery. Poor Jean didn't deserve to get shafted, but what else could she do? The overtime for this month had not yet gone in. She'd bump up Jean's hours, give her a few quid extra. *Classy Anna, classy.*

She switched off her PC, shoved herself out of the chair. The room shimmered. Momentarily, she thought she was going to hit the deck, but she found the chair's headrest, clutched it grimly until the sensation passed. Her jacket was hanging on the back of the locker door. It was too hot to wear it. She slung it over her arm, locked the office door behind her.

On the way out, Anna stopped at the front bar. The probationer who had been plonked there nodded gravely. 'Afternoon ma'am.'

She nodded back, reached into a low cupboard under the printer.

'Oh, can I help, ma'am? Do you want me to get you something?'

'Yeah. Could you maybe nip to the refreshment room and get me a wee cup of water?'

'Oh. But I'm not supposed to leave . . .'

She smiled at the lad and his serious, unformed face. 'Don't worry. I won't tell your sergeant, I promise.'

Soon as the boy hurried off, Anna pulled out the box of tapes, neatly filed in date order. She took the one for Monday the twelfth, and one from the day either side, just for good measure. Panting with the effort of bending, she slipped the tapes into her bag, kicked the cupboard shut.

'Here you go ma'am. Your water.'

'Oh cheers. Thanks, you're a pal.' Just a small sip. It felt dusty in her mouth. 'Right, that's me away. Anyone needs me, I'm on my mobile.'

'Right you are, ma'am.'

'And I'll be in a bit later tomorrow, okay?'

'Yes ma'am.' He took up position, elbows by the phone, pen at the ready.

'You still enjoying the job?' Anna could not for the life of her remember the boy's name.

'Oh, I love it ma'am. Absolutely love it.'

'Good. Great stuff.' She felt a terrible stab of nostalgia . 'See you tomorrow then.'

'Yes ma'am.'

It was time to go home. She opened the back door into the yard. As she was taking out her car keys, the probationer ran out.

'Excuse me, ma'am – there's someone on the phone for you.'

'Is it my husband?'

'Eh, don't think so. Is he called Maddie?'

'*What?* No, of course his name's not Maddie. Och, look just tell whoever it is I'm not here.'

'I tried to, but he says it's vital that he speaks to you. Wants to know if you've a mobile. I . . . didn't think I should give him that, but I said I'd try and catch you.' The lad dropped his voice. 'He sounded like he was nearly crying.'

She sighed, clicked the central locking shut. 'I've no idea who Maddie is. Right, put him through to my office. But next time, when I've said I've gone, I've gone. Alright?'

'Yes ma'am. Sorry.'

She stomped back into her office, snatched up the ringing phone. 'Yes?'

'Oh Maddie. Maddie doll, thank fuck Ah've got you.'

Nasal, lilting; a pure-Glesca assault. Anna dropped into her chair. 'Shelly – is that you?'

'Wheesht honey. Is your phones bugged in there?'

'Eh? No. Well, yes, they're all recorded.' The thought, and his voice, kindling fire. It was bringing all sorts of ashy, bad tastes to her mouth.

'Aye, I bet they listen in an' all. Gie me your mobile, doll, and I'll phone you right back on that.'

'Shelly. What the fuck is this about?'

'See you, ya wee midden.' She heard his breath quicken, then he went quiet.

The last time she had spoken to Shelly, he had accused her of abandonment, had wept on her shoulder as he related the indignities of jail. And he had been Michael then: withdrawn bitter Michael. Now the lilt had returned, and so, it seemed, had glorious, garrulous Shelly: brother of Andrew Semple, Galletly's co-accused. Shelly, who was Anna's friend.

But she didn't know how much he knew. She had to stay speculative when what she really wanted to do was run into his open, frill-swathed arms. Use his shoulder this time, not hers.

There was a click, then the sound of puffing.

'You started smoking? That'll stunt your—'

'Maddie, I think you know what it's about. Now, do you want tae get us both—'

'Okay, okay.'

She recited her mobile number, Shelly carefully repeating it back to her. Two-thirds of the way through, he chuckled. 'Well, seen you're no a phone-floozie, eh? This is the same number you've had since nineteen canteen, isn't it? I could of just called you direct.'

'Well just phone me now and let's get this over with.'

'Ooh, you're a touchy besom, so you are. Right. Hang up then and quit yakking.'

A second later, her mobile rang. She looked at it tremble, its little dance for attention threatening to send it skiting off the desk and into her bin. Perhaps that's where it should stay. Her fingernails going at a hundred miles an hour, jagging into her thigh. What did he want what did he want what did he know?

'S'me.'

'I know it's you. What's up?'

'What's up? What's up? Maddie – you in danja, girl, that's what's up.'

'Shelly, I'm either Madonna in her Eva Perón phase, or I'm Demi Moore in *Ghost*. But I canny be both at the one time.'

'Says who? It's ma game, so it is. Ma rules. But oh fuck, baby, you've nae idea how much trouble you're in, I'm telling you.'

'How d'you mean?'

A quick, angry sook on his cigarette. 'Right, you're clearly mair stupit that you ever were.' *And ... blow ...* 'D'you no read your papers, doll? D'you no still play at being a polis?'

'Do you want a thick ear?'

'Christ, Anna, be serious, will you? And before I say anything, anything a-fucking-tall, you've no heard a dicky bird fae me, understand?'

'Understood.'

'Okay. Well, you mind wee Francine? Angela's sister, thon big hoor with the scabby feet?'

It was the worst thing she had thought it could be.

'See you've still got a way with words. Yes, I remember her.'

'And you know that she's dead, do you?'

'Yes.'

'And you know how you ended up in hospital on Friday night?'

No it wasn't. This was.

'Pardon?' Her fingernails slicing deeper into her leg.

'Don't you come the haughty-snotty cow with me, doll. You heard me.'

'But how do you know that?'

''Cause I know who put you there, that's how. Or at least who engineered it. You're the talk of the steamie, you know.'

'Oh God. I thought . . . I thought maybe it was an accident.'

She had still clung limply to that hope. But the steady wrecking of her kept coming, a huge black-iron ball that just bashed and bashed. The baby felt it too; she was kicking at the thin skin that separated them, she could feel all the lies her mother was telling and, with each untruth, Galletly grew stronger. He was poisoning her baby. Making her swim in acid.

'Aye sure,' sniffed Shelly. 'Get real, doll. Someone boots you in the face, then stuffs they lovely locks doon the drain for good measure? I mean, I heard you caught it like a fucking football. And you in your nice swimming cozzie too.' He assumed a pseudo-gumshoe drawl. 'Word is, sweetcheeks; that was just a wee warning to get your juices running.'

'Oh fuck. Oh Shelly. But why?'

'Ah hoped you could tell *me* that precious. All I know is that a mutual friend of ours is out of jail, and he's gunning for you.'

Stick to the lies Anna. Deny, deny and lie, no matter how much you're begging to give in.

'*Who*? Shelly, who is it you're talking about?'

'Are you being deliberately stupid? Fucking Galletly, that's who.'

His name out loud; it made the shape of a claw, a boathook.

'Shelly, I don't understand what's going on here. What exactly do you know?'

'Look.' The *p-phph* of his inhalation. 'I've tried to keep away fae all of this awful fucking mess – you know I have. It's no ma fault Drew got in tow wi that vicious wee Irish dwarf. From the hour and minute I went intae jail, I have kept my retroussé nose clean. I fucking killed aff Shelly Semple before some other cunt got there first. Took ma maw's name, "Meek", and that's how I played it: meek and mild. Nothing to do with ma brother or Galletly or any of that shite. Because Galletly works for some utter nasty bastards, you know? And they hate grasses mair than anything. I just kept ma heid down and ma mouth shut until I got back out. And it was fucking hard. I mean, you seen me after I got out. I, eh . . .'

Another sniff. A big back-of-your-throat grog it up one this time. 'I wisny doing so well that last time we met—'

'Shelly, I know. I came back to the hostel, looking for you. I left a letter – did you get it?'

'Naw.'

'And I'd sorted out for you to see Julie Andrews as well.'

'Did you doll?' His voice broke. 'Oh, man. How is ma wee puss-tat?'

'Oh honey, I'm sorry. She died last year. Jenny sent me an email. She was an old cat, you know?'

'I know, I know. Fuck, she'd be . . .' Anna could hear him struggling not to cry. 'What happened tae her? Did she suffer?'

'No. Jenny looked after her really well. Wee soul just went to sleep one night, and didn't wake up . . . but daughter-of-Julie is doing great.'

'Yeah?'

'Yeah. Gallus Alice totally rules our house. She's seen off my husband's scabby old dog—'

'Fuck-a-doodle-dandy. You've got a dug? You've got a *husband*, ya total housewife?'

'I do. And a teenage stepdaughter.'

'Away. Hey! Your man's no—'

'No. It's *not* Jamie. It's Robert. And, well, he's an almost-husband . . .'

'Ooh – are you living in sin, ya big slapper?'

'Yup. Shagging like crazy every single night.'

'Yeeha! Ride him, cowgirl.'

Even in the midst of this, he was giggling like a daft wee lassie. It was a Shelly-perspective on life, pasting all the cracks with liberal dauds of glitter.

'Shit, Shelly. I've missed you.'

'I've missed you too, Maddie.' He sniffed again. Third time lucky: this time he spat something out.

'You are *bog*ging, by the way. You kiss your boyfriend with that mouth?'

'Aye, chance would be a fine thing. So. What are we gonny do?'

'Dating agency?'

Give him more banter Anna. Make this go away.

'About Galletly, ya dizzy bitch.'

'You tell me.'

'Right, I'll tell you exactly what I've heard, okay? And then you tell me what you want to do. Now, this is only third hand, mind?'

'Go for it.'

A fine, bright phrase, ringing with insincerity. The thing about a mobile was that you could move with it. Anna could get up and leave the office, step into her car and drive away, except she was rooted to her chair. Held steady by some dreadful inertia, and the weak hope that Shelly was going to lighten her load, not keep adding to it.

'Well, when Galletly was in prison, he shared a cell with a boy called Donaldson. Nasty wee drug dealer, but his bidie-in was a hoor called Molly.'

'Molly Laurence?' Anna remembered her from the drop-in centre down the Drag. A soft, fat girl who painted red spots on her cheeks, teased her hair into an unbecoming beehive. 'Molly the Dolly', they called her.

'Aye, I think so. So, at some point this Molly tells her man that all the lassies down the Drag were feart fae Galletly, because, as well as killing that old Polish man, he'd murdered a hoor as well. That Tamburrini girl. She tells Donaldson that one of her pals – the lovely Francine tae you and me – had had a lucky escape from Galletly herself. Apparently she'd been up at the old boy's house the same night Galletly had come and stoved his head in. Must have only missed him by minutes. The old Pole – hee-hee: *Old Pole*. You like what I've done there?'

'Poetry.'

'Well, he was a regular of Francine's, all the lassies knew that, and Molly aye wondered if Francine must of actually been there when it happened, because she wouldny talk about it at all. When they heard the old boy had been killed, all the girls were asking Francine about it and she just pure clammed up and said she'd never been near the place – which they *knew* was a blatant lie. So, this daft bitch Molly asks Donaldson to ask Galletly if Francine really had been there.' Pause for a big long suck. '*Just* because her fucking big nose was bothering her. And at this, of course, Galletly goes mental. Just about throttles Donaldson and gets him to tell him everything he knows about Francine – which wisny much. But it was enough for Galletly to latch on tae. Because he always said he never done it. Killed the old man, I mean. Even tae me and my brother, he swore blind he hadny done it, know? So anyway, Galletly gets out of jail and, next thing, Francine ends up deid.'

Yes, but he tortured her first, Shelly. Did you know that? He tortured her so that she would tell Galletly all about me, this poliswumman who took an incriminating war medal from her, knowing it was Ezra Wajerski's. Who told her to fuck off, then let her go. Who went to the witness box and lied by omission after omission. Who dropped the fucking medal in the Clyde, so how come Francine was holding it when she came to Cranstonhill? And did she have it with her when she died?

'Are you going to go to the police about this, Shelly?'

'So what are you then? A stripogram?'

'No, but—'

'Look – this has nothing to do with me, petal. See Shelly, she just keeps on keeping on. I'm getting involved in burlesque you know.'

'Really?'

'Aye. Cabaret nights are fair picking up in the toon. I mean, I'm too old for all they nipple tassels, but I can still high-kick with the best of them. But, I digress. Like I say, I hardly knew Francine, so it's no skin off my nose if G wants tae end her. But then I hears that he's after you and all – and that, my darling, isny on.'

'But *who* did you hear it from?'

'Ask me no questions and I'll tell you no lies. I may be reformed, but it disny mean I'm in purdah, know? I have many intermediaries – the ghost of Liberace for one.'

'You're no funny, Shelly. This is my life we're talking about.'

'I fucking know that, Anna. And I'll tell you this: when someone's planning tae end a cop, the whole fucking underworld bubbles with it. All he's doing is playing games with you at the moment. Because, I'll tell you this for nothing. If Gilly had wanted you deid in that pool, you can rest assured you would be. Bottom line is, you need to get some mega-protection – and *très, très* quick.'

The baldness of his statement shocked her. She wasn't stupid; she'd already filled in most of the subtext. Hearing another person spell it out to her though, someone whom she trusted, who had risked his life – no, who had *given* several years of his life, given up his home and family to help her, meant the truth hung there in all its starkness. Shelly stating the obvious made it immutable fact.

'You hear me, doll? You need tae get your polis buddies mobilised and get this fucker jailed.'

'Shelly – I can't.'

'How no?'

'I just can't.'

'Anna. What is it you're no telling me, hen?'

'I . . .'

And they were there, all those fat, golden words like fish scales, shimmering and swimming upwards, desperate to be caught. The relief of spilling up her twisting guts, laying them out for someone else to inspect and sort. It would be unimaginable, like giving birth.

And change her life just as hugely.

'Nothing. Oh, fuck, you need to help me Shelly.'

'What do you think I'm doing, doll? Do you have any idea what would happen if Galletly found out I was communing with the enemy?'

'I know, I know – but please. There's no one else I can turn to.'

'That's very flattering, seen as I'm such a butch big bastard. You gonny be straight with me, Anna? What did Francine say tae Galletly that made him come after you?'

'I . . . I can't tell you, Shelly. I . . . don't know. Maybe he's on a quest to clear up unfinished business.' Getting faster as she chased some plausible explanation. 'Yeah. He probably blames me for getting him arrested in the first place. It was after he gave me a doing that we stepped up patrols in the area and caught him in the first place, remember?'

'Okay, okay. Save me the fairy tale, yeah?' His voice faded a little, she could hear him take a deep, deep draw of his cigarette. 'Look. I'm only doing this cause it's you, and I love you, right? Do you want me to try and make contact with him? See if we can negotiate some kind of a deal?'

'What do you mean, a deal?'

'Well, everything has a price, Anna.'

'A price?' Seizing it like a little clump of grass appearing in the quicksand. 'Like a ransom? You mean, buy him off?'

'Look gorgeous, I don't know. I don't even know what he's ransoming, do I? Cause I don't fucking think you're telling me. But it's worth a shot, I suppose.'

'Tell me where he's staying, and I'll bloody negotiate myself.' A horrible thought came to her. 'Shelly – is he staying with your brother? Are they still working together?'

An uneven quality to the silence; Anna dragging breath in, Shelly pressing it out. Eventually he went, 'Like I said, I don't see ma big brother any more, Anna. Meek and mild, that's me. But I *very* much doubt they're together.'

'So how're you going to get in touch with Galletly if you don't know where he is?'

'I telt you. Through the medium of Liberace. Fuck lassie, stop asking so many questions, right? Do you want me to do this for you, or no?'

'I don't know . . . I . . . yes. Okay, yes. Just find out what it would take to make him go away.'

'You sure?'

'I'm not sure of anything any more. What about you, though? Will you be okay? He knows you gave evidence against him. What if you're on his list too?'

'Don't you worry about me, Maddie. I've got ma fireproof knickers on.'

'That part of your burlesque act as well?'

'Sure is, doll. Because I . . . have the hottest cock in Glesga.' He wheezed. It sounded like he was lighting another fag. 'Anna, gonny do me a favour.'

'Of course I will.'

'See when this is all over – can I come and see Alice?'

'Och Shelly. Don't be daft. Come today if you want.'

'Naw, no way. What if Galletly seen me?'

'C'mon. You're making it sound like he's got spies all over the place. Christ. Has he?'

'Fuck knows. He kent you were at the baths that day, didn't he? You go there regular?'

'Every Friday.'

'Well, he's no even been out a week. Unless he's had folk watching you for ages . . .'

'Oh don't say that, Shelly. Please.'

'Well, is the swimming near where you stay? Maybe he's been watching your hoose; waiting for a chance tae say hello. Sees you come out, follows you down. Slips a twenty tae a kid in the queue, then disappears. I mean, there's weans in Glasgow would drown a pregnant polis just for fun, but if they got a bung for their trouble . . .'

'Christ, now you're just being ridiculous.'

'Well, maybe he *has* had folk watching you then. Fuck, I'm daeing ma best here, doll. It's no like I'm privy tae his every movement—'

'Shelly, that's crap. I mean, I went straight from work. I *drove*. And I'd have noticed if someone was following me. I'm a cop, for God's . . .' She stopped. Remembering the guy in the café, the car she thought she'd seen and seen again. Her conviction that she was not going mad.

'Do you really think he knows where I live?'

'Ach, I don't know. You still in the sooth-side?'

'Yes, but I'm not in the flat any more. We're in Newlands now. Monreith Road.'

'Ooh. The big hooses. Very swanky.'

'It's not mine – it's Rob's really. He was married before . . .'

'Listen doll, I'm no dissing you. You sound like you've got a nice life. I'm glad for you.'

'Shelly,' she whispered. 'Please help me keep it.'

'I'll see what I can do, pet.' He blew her a kiss down the phone. 'Feel that?'

'Aye.'

Chapter Thirty-Five

The heating was stuck on full. Alex's shirt was stuck on him. Through the window he'd forced open, he could hear birdsong, the wee buggers getting excited about the coming warm breath of spring. Except it was the end of November.

'Sorry, sir,' said the maintenance guy he'd phoned, 'but it's on a central timer. It's set by date, you see.'

'Date? Not temperature?'

'Aye. Date. Heating's on till March, then aff till September. I mean, how are we meant tae keep up? It was freezing last week, now it's warm. Nothing I can do if the world's gone haywire.'

'Okay, okay. Thanks anyway.'

Alex hung up. He needed a drink. Cold water, not more coffee. Yes, some crystal clear water to wash out his brain. He knew hormones made women go all psycho-hosebeast, and no doubt pregnancy made it worse. But even so, for Anna Cameron to greet like a baby, that was unprecedented. Maybe it was all the emotion of seeing him. *Not.* Man, he'd had some bizarre dreams last night – and the best sex he and Sandra had enjoyed in months. Which was really not healthy, whichever way you looked at it.

Anna's outrage, the alacrity with which she had brushed away any interest in Francine's death – he couldn't let that go. Any cop would want the juicy details of a murder, especially if it was someone that they knew, and those details were being offered up on a plate. Professionally and personally, Anna Cameron was the kind of woman who always '*had to know*'.

Okay, so he'd still no evidence to prove Francine had gone specifically to see Anna, but he now felt even surer that she had. He could use that knowledge to narrow down his search. He'd have to scrutinise each case Anna had ever put in regarding Francine – Case Management at Stewart Street kept these things for years. He didn't need to say what he was looking for: the fact they were all cases relating to a murder victim would be reason enough for his request. Hey, there should only be about a million of them. Nae probs for the Lord of Chaos-Ordering, who had nothing else to do anyway.

For all he thought Anna was lying, he trusted her. No, trust was a perverse choice of word for what he felt. Understood her? She would be protecting someone. There was an integrity harrowed through Anna, a strongly linear sense of righteousness that ran untrammelled in her veins. It was what gave her that glow, long before she was pregnant. Alex often did the wrong thing because it was the quickest, the path of least resistance. Or the most enjoyable. But whenever he'd known Anna do something wrong, it was for a right reason. Even the way she'd treated him two years ago; it would have been to send him back to Sandra. And it had done, and they were fine.

See, he had convinced himself already. It was wrong to try and fight a force of nature. He loosened his tie. Shirley was right about global warming. All just evidence of the world biting back. Served us right, too. If we kept bending nature to meet our demands, whose fault was it when it sprang back and slapped us in the face? Experience was teaching him that the world was best enjoyed when you stopped trying to control it. Take last night, him and Sandra. Her veins all silted up with disappointments and disdain that he'd tried so many times to unblock with fights and questions and half-meant hints. Then he came home angry and needing her and he'd just kissed her, hard, and she'd moulded into his shape like that's all that he'd ever had to do.

If he let her be, Anna would end up helping him. He just had to trust her.

Ian Morrison lumbered into the room. A wee scratch at his balls then a shake of his arms.

Alright pal. I get it. You've been working really hard and now you need a break.

'No joy at Crannyhill yesterday, boss?'

Alex kept staring at his screen. 'Eh – they only keep live feed from the cameras for a week, so it had already gone. But they're interviewing all the station assistants to see if any of them remembers Francine.'

'Well, she bloody went there to see someone, boss.'

'Aye, I realise that. But can we focus on where she went afterwards, too? After all, she wisny killed in the polis station, was she?'

'No, but—'

'And yes, I have done a list of her former associates – here. Take a look at them and see if you can make any further links or connections with Francine.'

'Like what?'

Maybe Ian could do all the legwork for him. 'How the fuck would I know? Check if all her old pals are alive or dead. Look through all the cases that have ever been submitted against Francine, check out any co-accuseds, read the reporting officer's comments. You're a detective. Detect. Oh, and have we traced that Mary bloody McLennan yet?'

'Eh, naw. But that jumper you found – her DNA is on it as well as the victim's. And a ton of horsehair to boot. Not a great help really; they stable lassies seem to wear whatever's lying about, so all the sweatshirt's telling us is that either Mary, or Francine, were on the towpath at some point.'

'Or a big horse wearing a sweatshirt was.'

'What?'

'Never mind. So, apart from the tights, we've still not traced any of Francine's clothes.'

'Nope. *Nada.* The boys in rubber have trawled every inch of that canal, I reckon.'

'Well, they have to be somewhere. Do you reckon the Tube's right, then?'

'Galls me to say so,' said Ian, 'but I think he is. Naebody at Calder Riggs has ever seen Francine sporting sussies – she's hardly going to advertise her former career, is she? – and our man has taken great pains to remove and dispose of all her clothing. Apart from a pair of fishnets.'

'So what are we saying? That he knew her as a prostitute; wants to tell the world that's what she was?'

'I think so.'

Alex sighed. 'What about the green motor?'

'There's around a hundred and twenty vehicles in the greater Glasgow area that meet the age and type. We're working our way through the list, visiting registered keepers, checking for recent accident damage. Mandy and the Tube have also been checking with garages, repair shops—'

'Fine, fine. Well don't let me keep you then.'

The vastness of this enquiry was scaring him. That and the way it was yawning ever outwards, like the loose-flowing water at Stockingfield Junction. Slow, slack water, forever inching downstream.

Chapter Thirty-Six

At last! Some action. No wonder the lazy bastard was so fat. Mary rose stiffly, the cartilage grinding in her knees. Then she realised the man was only putting out his rubbish. What day was this? Tuesday, she thought. Possibly. She had slept quite well under cardboard covers in an alley, and brunched on a delicious lemon pancake from the *Crêpe et Croissant* van in Ashley Street (well, this *was* the West End). Of course, you never slept properly on the street, it was more a series of power naps, which was what made you so disorientated the next day. Many nights seemed to have come and gone, yet no time at all because you were still in the same place, still cold and hungry. Last night had been quite mild for November, mild today too, but she didn't know how she'd managed it before, in the depths of winter. Probably because she'd either been comatose, or so fraught in her quest for heroin that the cold had ceased to exist. It was funny, but she still didn't feel that aching need to score. She'd thought she would have done by now, but dealing with Bernie's killer seemed to matter a whole lot more.

The lemon juice stung her lips. She swallowed, holding in the coughing fit that threatened as she watched Fat Bastard turn towards the busy St George's Road. He was still lugging his bin bag. Weirdo. She waited until he passed out of sight. Only then was it safe to move. She was beginning to get a sore throat, could feel catarrh running down the back of it, as well as down her nostrils. Rubbing it away, knowing a streak would gleam across her dirty face. Sticky on her hand, too: grey-smudged grime and crystals of sugar. Mary was not yet properly feral, but growing more animal by the hour. She quite liked it, it was liberating, just you and your wits and your unsuspecting quarry. But what to do with him when he was properly caught? It would have to be somewhere dark and disorientating, a place from which he couldn't run. And then what? There was nothing really, beyond the blank, compelling desire to see him dead like Bernie. After that – who cared?

Towards the end of West Princes Street, a little lane ran parallel with the main road. There was nothing in it but a few lock-ups, and Mary could hear the scraping sound of an overhead door being cranked up. It was just a narrow strip of land, and she was worried that he'd see her. But her curiosity was stronger – plus there was something baldly fearless about her today. She'd pretty much fallen as far as she could go; there wasn't much left of her to protect. Slowly, skliffing her feet right to the sharp ridge-end of the lane's wall, she could see the man's big arse poking out of a lock-up, his head inside the opened boot of a car. Into it, he was stuffing a black, crumpled mass – his bin bag. Definitely a weirdo. She jumped back as he clanged the boot shut, made herself invisible against the wall. But he didn't look in her direction, just carried on towards the main road.

St George's Road skirted the motorway, there was plenty of passing traffic to screen her progress as Mary continued in her stalking. She watched him go into a café, come out a few minutes later with an oversized paper cup. Envied him his slurping – she'd had insufficient begging money left to buy both crêpe and coffee. From St George's Road, the man waddled across the tangle of roads and bridges that made up Charing Cross, and carried on into Sauchiehall Street. She hoped he wasn't going too far; her feet were wet and blistered, each step carving a little more skin from her heels.

A stunning Art Deco building rose up to the left of them, and he hesitated at the entrance. Mary hung back, sheltering in the lee of another building. She knew the Art Deco place as Baird Hall, though it had been built as the Beresford Hotel. Glasgow's very first skyscraper, its thrusting curves the tallest affirmation of post-first-war hope and pre-second-war ignorance that the city had seen. Her mum had lived there when it was a student hostel, when she'd come up from the Borders to the city. American servicemen had stayed there during the forties, and Mum said that you could hear the ghosts of them, singing at night. The uni must have sold it, though, because the frontage was newly painted, and back to being 'The Beresford'. Apartments this time, not a hotel.

Moving a little closer. The man was preoccupied, squinting for a while, and then pressing on the bell panel. Neat rows of them, each with a little illuminated square of white. An echoing click, the man going, 'That's him been tae see her now . . .' then a squawk of noise, but she couldn't make out what the noise said. But the fat man jumped back, you could almost say recoiled, stood slumped by the bell panel. After a couple of minutes, another man appeared inside the foyer, hurried out, pulling the door behind him.

'I fucking told you not to come here!' A furious wee Irishman, he bristled like an irate bug, jabbing at the air and shoving the fat man further up the street. All at once, Fat Bastard became a joke, a dumpy balloon who was quivering in this smaller man's shadow. They marched across the road and into a side street. She didn't know if she should go after them, but if this was a chain of some sort, then she had to follow it to the end. Maybe there was another, even smaller man, lurking in the side street, who was the boss of them all. A set of rabid Russian dolls come to life.

When she reached the street, there was no trace of the men, just a bobbing mass of flat caps and pastel perms. Several big coaches were pulling up on both sides of the road, dropping off theatre-goers for the matinee at the King's. 'Sing Yer Way Doon the Watter!' whooped the billboards, and the chattering old folk looked set to oblige, arms linked, cheeks sweetie-packed. For a brief moment, Mary wanted to join them, get rushed up in their exuberance and spend the afternoon singing songs. Then she saw them, saw Fat Bastard's close-cropped head and its stubbly neck-folds, disappearing into a lane beside a pub. She waited one beat, two beats, then ambled by the lane mouth, looking in as she passed. Her view was partially obscured by the wheelie-bins docked like ships at the various back doors, but she clocked a staccato movement. They were about a third of the way up, had stopped walking, and she could see a bit of gesticulating coming from the fat one. It was still the back of his neck visible; they were both facing the other way. Was there enough wheelie-bin cover to risk entering the lane?

The secret agent rolled on to her belly, her elbows scraping through the swampy ground as she made for the trees. The enemy was up ahead and consisted of . . . two real men, one of whom had killed her friend. Would there always be a loop in her head that did this, made a game when it was all too fucking real?

She got down on her hunkers behind the first row of bins. No closer. Ugh, it stank worse than sewage here. Must be bad if she could smell the bins over the unsweet hum of herself. She was still too far away to pick up more than snatches, the low murmur of the Irish one, a 'but it wisny her' from Fat Bastard, another growly jab from short-arse, and then this plaintive, rising rant.

'I telt you,' whined the fat one, 'I've done ma bit. I'm no getting ma hands any more dirty than they are, Gilly. Alright? I'm no, I'm no, and that's a fucking end tae it, right?'

The Irishman didn't even look at him. Just raised up his hand, a sense of his whole body swelling, and battered him full across the cheek. Mary could see a glint of keys or rings at his knuckles. Fat Bastard clashed against the wall behind him, his skull smacking brick as cleanly as it was intended to. Blood melting from the new gash on his face – Mary couldn't help feeling slightly awestruck by the little guy.

'You will do as you are fucking told, boy.'

Chapter Thirty-Seven

Alex switched off his desk lamp. There were a pile of Post-its stuck by the phone, people waiting for him to ring them back. He'd asked the support staff to try and filter his calls: one pile for urgent, one for enquiry, one for whenever, but if there had been a trio of yellow clusters at one point, they were now a single sticky heap.

It was four o'clock. Alex had been summoned to a meeting with the area detective super at five, and then he was heading off to stage a reconstruction of Francine's bus journey for the press. The getting-on the bus bit, at least. If he left the office now, he could get a kebab at the place beside Sandra's work. It wasn't a date, more of a waving from two passing ships, but that was one thing they had agreed on last night: carving out more time.

'Boss, sorry to bother you.' Mandy's cute face took away the sting of interruption. 'But I've the lady on from the council again. Margaret Riley, head of Communications?'

'Oh yeah, her.'

She'd been one of the call-backs he was planning on doing tomorrow. He'd never gone back to get her list of staff, nor to interview them, but it all seemed a bit superfluous since they'd spoken to the Crilley chap. Whoever had a bee in their bonnet about Calder Riggs was simply being malicious, and he'd no room for time-wasters at the moment. Days of producing no real results kept ticking by, and Alex could feel the reality of a substantive rank ticking away with them.

'She really wants to talk to you,' said Mandy.

'Fine. I'm all hers. Put her through.' He stuck his feet up on the desk, bade farewell to his kebab.

'Hello, Mr Patterson?'

'Margaret. Sorry I've not been back down.'

'No, no, it's just that I thought you'd want to know. One of our girls, Charlotte – an agency temp – well, she went off home early last Friday and we've not seen her since. I tried to phone her house today to find out what was happening, I mean, she's a really good worker. Sparky wee soul, you know? But the girl that answered said she didn't work for us, never had.'

'Who didn't work for you?'

'This Charlotte. But that's who was answering the phone. The same girl – well, the same name. She said she was Charlotte Deans and that she *had* had an interview with us, but she'd never made it.'

'I'm sorry, Margaret, I'm getting a bit confused. Are you saying that you're reporting someone missing?'

'Well . . . kind of, I guess. What I'm saying is that the person working for us who we thought was Charlotte Deans *isn't*, and now she's gone. It's just with you looking into this murder . . . and I wondered if it might be something . . . you know. Plus it was directly after you'd been here that she disappeared.'

His feet, swinging to the floor. 'I'll be right with you, Mags. Give me ten minutes.'

Alex drove his car into the City Chambers quadrangle off Cochrane Street, parking in a councillor's bay. Well, they should all be using sustainable transport anyway. Practise what they preach in this grid-city of frequent buses. Aye, but nobody liked getting the bus, did they? It was the democratic cramming-in of the germs and steamy windows, the foul-mouthed neds and the wifies with their messages, the lolling drunk girl sleeping past her stop, the businessman trying desperately not to touch the seats or his fellow passengers, and the old boy who would not take a seat when it was offered, though his legs had rickets and his spine was done. That and the fact buses never quite took you door to door. And Alex needed to be door to door, he needed speed and cutting the crap and a sense of his own importance reinstated – before the area super kicked it all out of him again.

Margaret was waiting for him in her office. 'Thanks for coming so quickly. I did phone earlier—'

'It's been pandemonium up the road, I'm afraid.'

'Oh. Would you like a coffee maybe? Some tea?'

'You know, a cup of tea would be lovely.'

She beamed at him. Inside Margaret Riley was a desperate housewife bursting to get out. A kind one. He watched her bustle with the kettle.

'So. This girl?'

'Yes. The one I spoke to this morning, Charlotte, says she's registered with the agency we use, all the details we have are hers, but it wasn't her that came last Monday. Her boyfriend had whisked her away the weekend before her interview, and it had clean gone out of her mind. Do you take milk?'

'Please.'

'Sugar?'

'Sweet enough.'

A wee giggle frothed up, as she stirred vigorously. 'So, as I said, this girl Charlotte never gave the job another thought until I called her today.'

'And did she tell other folk about this interview? Cheers.'

He took the mug from her, a chunky green and gold one that declared: '*Get on, Get in, Get access. Citicard's for You!*'

'Could it be a pal of hers maybe, that came and took her place?'

'Well, I don't think so. She said the request had come in an email from her agency, and she'd ticked the box to say she'd do it, then pretty much forgot. I'd only contacted the agency the week before . . .'

'So what you're saying is some total stranger just turned up and you assumed it was Charlotte? I mean, did she identify herself as Charlotte?'

'Eh . . . you know, I'm not actually sure she did. The place was jumping that morning. Oh, the other thing you should know is, just before the fake Charlotte—'

'We'll call her stunt Charlotte, will we?'

She grinned. 'I like that. Okay, just before stunt Charlotte disappeared, I'd challenged her about, well, staying here overnight. There had been . . . evidence that someone was actually sleeping in the Press Office at night.'

Someone quick on their wits, and their heels. Who had nowhere to go. Who was probably hiding, from either threats or guilt. Alex still wasn't clear yet which it was. He brought out the photocopy of Mary McLennan's CHS picture.

'It's not a great photo, Mags, but is this the girl who said she was Charlotte?'

Margaret held it close to her face. Moved it back down, tilting it appraisingly. 'Possibly,' she said slowly. 'Ooh, it could be, although her hair was different. Dyed I'd say. Tel you what though. She got her photo taken for her security pass. Personnel will still have a copy, I'm sure.'

'Excellent.'

If he got an up-to-date picture, he could put that out to the press at the same time as they did the reconstruction. A picture was worth a thousand lumpen footsteps from an embarrassed, black-haired policewoman. He was yet to be convinced if reconstructions were worth all the hassle. Other than providing a spectator sport for nosey locals, and giving a nice visual to go with your three-minute slot on the news, how many genuinely new leads did they establish? *Oh, you mean that lassie that was dragged aff the towpath and drowned in the canal? Oh, aye, I mind her now. See, until I seen it, I thought yous were all talking about some other lassie. Aye, och aye I'd seen some big bloke pure bundle this girl up and fling her in his motor – but until I seen thon wee bit on the news, well, I never thought anything of it.*

'Shall we go up and see Personnel?' said Margaret. 'It's a bit of a labyrinth, they're away through the Link Corridor and up the stairs, so I'd probably best come with you.'

'Mags, it would be a pleasure. Although you've been very helpful already.'

'Ooh. Have I?' She blushed a little. 'You know, I think you're a bit of a smooth-talker actually, DI Patterson.'

'Och me? Away.' He crooked his elbow. 'Shall we?'

Chapter Thirty-Eight

Joe rubbed the inside of the windscreen. It was misty, the heater wasn't working right, and it was hard to see in the smudged evening light. He'd never driven down such narrow roads before, not in something this size. He couldn't turn up late, or with dents and scratches in the pristine red paint. No, this had to be perfect. Joe's stock had being falling gradually since the assembly. Yesterday, folk had still been talking about it; by today, it had been worthy of a few more jokes, but acknowledgement was definitely growing less frequent. As if he had lied about himself, like that wasn't the true Joe. People couldn't call him a liar, those men at the weekend had insinuated it too. He was *not*. Joe was brittle with brains and knowledge. It was bursting out of him in crystal spikes. People didn't realise: if they touched him, he'd explode.

Surprise us Joe!

Joe cranked the radio louder. This was going to be superb! He could not stop fidgeting in his seat. The leather creaked beneath him, his legs moist inside wool trousers, hands damp on the wheel. Two minutes and he'd be there. They'd all be waiting. It was the annual Autumn Ball, to which Joe never went, like he never went to the Summer Fling, or the Christmas Party. Yes, occasionally he got a grudging invite to come to the pub, but that was only because Joe was head and shoulders above the rest of them, and would easily get served. That was a given, that was the deal, and he accepted it.

Throughout all the years, though, he had never attended a single social event at school, citing (granted, to his mother only) the noise and the crowds, the lack of order, all the furious flux and boom that troubled his equilibrium. But Patrick had said 'surprise us', and, in doing so, Joe was even surprising himself. He'd thought about it, a lot. There would be no mystique whatsoever in chucking school – who would remember Joe for doing that? And yes, him turning up at the ball would, in itself, cause tongues to whisper. Appearing as the driver of the coach that would transport the sixth years to the country-house venue would, however, be bloody amazing!

Nobody outside his immediate family had a clue that he'd held his PCV licence for months now. Or that, since they'd dropped the age limit from 21 to 18, Joe had been driving proper buses as well as coaches, actually driving buses for a living, through the city streets. A furious, secret life raged inside Joe, and it was going to manifest itself in one minute thirty seconds, right in front of his classmates. He hadn't decided yet if he would put his hat on, concealing himself until everyone was aboard. They wouldn't believe it, they'd be shouting *Yo! Joe*, not *Slowjo*.

He'd told the lads before that his Uncle Euan owned the Silver Chassis luxury coach hire in East Kilbride; no one had responded. But then he had offered to get the organising committee a discount for the ball, and immediately Doug had kidded on they were pals and gone: 'Mates rates, eh? Cool Joe, you do that.' So they all knew Joe was connected with the glorious world of passenger service vehicles, but what they did not know was that Joe had been driving vehicles of one sort or another ever since he could see above their various steering wheels.

Coaches were alright, but the public buses were more liberating; you didn't get trapped with the same people for the whole journey. Plus, you got paid more. He'd been loving it, couldn't believe how proud it made him feel – far more than getting six As did. Weeks of summer shifts through town, just the short routes, because his age prohibited him from driving longer ones. Back to school, got some evening shifts, which were troublesome. People grew steadily meaner as the light faded; they spat more and slurred their words and made him stiffen behind the boyish joy of driving his bus. So he'd asked for some day shifts again, working round the gaps in his timetable – getting all As at first sitting allowed for gaps. Joe was only doing three Advanced Highers: Chemistry, Maths and History, which left two whole afternoons free a week.

When they'd given him the Maryhill Road route, Joe had thrilled at the thought of discovery. Several of the lads used that route to get to rugby: Brillo and Doug and Andy. Each shift he took the helm, waiting to be revealed, but it was all old women and sour-faced men. You got a few pretty girls too, but mostly the thin, cheap kind who scared him. Sniffing out your virginity, and chewing it up.

Speaking of which . . . Joe could see a bevy of breasts and thighs. He turned the radio off. Long legs, short skirts and shivering bodies, all waiting outside the school. Pagan Hallowe'en was long past; they were not permitted a Hallowe'en Dance, and Christmas was for ball gowns and punch, for prayers and festive heavy petting. Thus, in-between autumn became the all-encompassing framework in which the senior school lived out its fantasies. This year, it looked like there was an abundance of fishnet, and tutus on several fairies. Lorna Ramsay was a witch, it would seem, but one who wore only the skimpiest of rags. Behind them clustered the boys, their exposed skin glowing in the cold. Probably already pished. There was a pumpkin-clad Brillo (you could not disguise that hair), a Gorilla, two clashing, padded superheroes.

Apart from donning his driver's hat, Joe hadn't put on a costume. As usual, he'd been dressed by his dear old maw.

'I've ironed your shirt, Joseph, that nice cream one.' She hadn't knocked, simply waltzed in, the shirt on a coat hanger before her, like a flag, and Joe standing in his boxers.

'*Mum.*'

'Och Joseph,' she'd bustled. She always bustled when she was pleased about something, frothing with negative energy being carefully held in check. In their kitchen was an old World War Two poster that summed up his mother perfectly, the framed words exhorting all who passed before it to *Keep calm and carry on.*

'Now, look, will I hang it up here, look? On the outside of your wardrobe. And I've pressed your jeans too.'

A sharp neat seam where none should be.

'I don't want them pressed.'

'Well, thank *you*.'

From bustle to huff; it was a quick and frequent reaction – but one that Joe was always perturbed to witness.

'Thank you very much,' she repeated. 'It took me ages, that. Two refills of water to get enough steam up.'

'Well, thank you, Mum, but I didn't *ask* you to—'

Not for the first time, he was aware that both her bustles and her huffs were virtually identical. They were both about repression – the one of joy, the other anger. If you'd been watching her with the sound turned down, only the tightness of her lips ('pursed' for huff, 'set straight' for bustle) would give an indication of which was which. She did have a beautiful face, though.

'Where is it again, this disco?'

'It's a ball, Mum. Near Loch Lomond.'

'Yes, but you said something about a party after? On a school night? And what about the coach? You can't just hare all over the city in it . . .'

'I *told* you, Mum – it's because the Prelims are finished. We've got tomorrow off, and Thursday and Friday are in-service days. And I've arranged it with Uncle Euan already. I take everyone to the party, then I bring the bus back here. Uncle Euan will send someone round for it tomorrow.'

'So where is it, this party? Who's having it?'

'Oh, yeah. Some girl's house. It's only round the corner.'

He knew exactly where it was, but was determined to remain vague. Could you imagine the red-neck if your mum turned up to take you home? He wouldn't put it past her, either.

'Is this a girl from your school?'

'No. Her cousin's at St Sav's, not her.'

'You mean you don't even know the girl?'

'No, but I know her cousin. For God's sake, Mum.'

'Look, I just don't want you be getting into any trouble tonight, Joseph. I mean it. You're being very difficult at the moment, you know you are. Honestly, I don't think I've ever been so embarrassed at having to face your headmaster . . .'

Joe shook his shirt from the hanger. It was warm, smelled of washing powder and the thin spritz of steam. It had been entirely worth it. Yes, he had lost his place on the barge to bloody Doug – had almost lost his place at the school, but for the pained intercession of his mother and a generous donation from Uncle Euan – but it had provided him with the most wonderful epiphany too.

After eighteen years of confused acceptance, Joe had realised that the strange vagaries of human behaviour were actually quite simple probabilities. He'd spent far too long analysing the responses of others to him, when what he needed to analyse, only, was *his* response to them. In maths, proofs came from deductive reasoning, not from empirical arguments. You could predict the outcomes, as long as you knew your xs from your ys. He didn't know why he hadn't seen it before. If he offered his flat observations on the world, without mediating them, he was laughed at, was seen as pointless. If Joe suppressed the real him, offered instead a stylised, deliberate parody of himself, who said daft but pointed, not point*less* things, then he was laughed with.

His mother had sat on the bed, patted the quilt. 'Please, love. Sit down a wee minute.'

The boys were counting on him to buy their carry-outs. That was the deal.

'Please, Joseph. Sit.'

He sat.

'Remember, Joe. Remember when you were in first year at that other school, and the lady came to talk to you.'

'Yes.' He was looking, just looking at the buttons in his shirt and his thick, tight fingers trying to do them up.

'Remember what she said? "Sook it all in" – that's what she told you, isn't it? And you've been doing really well. We all have lots of thoughts in our head, all the time, but it's not always good to say them out loud.'

'Like if I said to stop treating me like an idiot, Mum, because it's really, really annoying? Like that kind of thought, do you mean?'

It was exactly what was inside his head; same nippy words that his brain was letting slide and rise across the lobes to see if they would fit. *Fit for purpose* – he liked that one. That was a buzz-phrase you heard constantly, ever since some hard-jawed politician had levelled it at the Home Office, or the Prison Service, or some other behemoth that had nothing to do with Joe. He had all these words, these facts, these luscious phrases folded like linen in drawer after drawer. He saw them all stretching back in his head, a mighty, dark subdural filing room that reached into infinity, just waiting for a light to be switched on. That woman his mum was going on about, Ms Schumman, she had been mightily impressed with Joe's vocabulary, with his huge and random outpourings of knowledge and phrasing and syntax that he had snipped and cultivated and kept warm. Joe was delighted that another human had asked – no, wanted – to get inside his mind. *I am like an incubator,* he had told the woman.

'You certainly sook things up, don't you?' she had smiled, using the vernacular to ingratiate herself, Joe presumed. And then the killer blow. *But maybe you need to sook some of it in?*

His mother had apparently finished giving him his row, because she was stroking his forehead instead. Her hand felt lovely, perfumed with the steam of his shirt.

'I'm sorry, Mum.'

'Och, darling. You can't help . . . you've no need to be sorry. No need at all. Now just you go and have a lovely time tonight, okay?' She had stood up, ruffled his carefully gelled hair. 'No chasing the girls, mind.'

Joe put on the brakes, depressed the lever that whumped air-propelled doors apart. The girls clattered on first, giggling, forever giggling; it couldn't always be at him.

'Alright, mate.'

Doug clapped Joe's back as he weaved past.

'Alright, Doug.'

Doug faltered, thinned his eyes. 'Do I – FUCK ME! Ho, look guys, look. It's fucking Slowjo driving us!'

'No way!

'Way, man. Way!'

Joe felt like a star. Patrick, Doug and all the lads crowded round, asking him how come he was driving, for how long, but how *come*? what did it feel like, then? Folk bantering with him, their animated speech wholly different from the low, dismissive monotone that was standard-when-you-talked-to-Joe. It continued all the way to the hotel, jokes being made about his parking, about how he handled his big machine. A few of the girls spent the journey standing behind him, hands on his neck. 'Ooh. I like your hat, Joe. Can I get a shot of your gearstick?' Lorna Ramsay continually asking: 'So can I get a *ride* home?'

It was the same at the ball. Word spread to the fifth years, who had arrived in the immaturity of hired limos and daddies' cars. Person after person, coming up, grinning. Shaking their heads, offering to buy him a beer. Joe wasn't drinking, he was driving, but that didn't matter. If he never did anything else of note in his life, he had done this.

'Jojo – d'yoowannadance?'

Lorna again, barely able to bite her fist. Amy and Allison were holding her up, one at either elbow. Joe went to shake his head, found himself taking to his feet, his hand in Lorna's, the slumping weight of her being passed on to him as they shuffled round the dance floor and he felt the warmth of female breasts.

'That you getting your hole the night?' Alan jigged past, the matted fur of his gorilla suit steaming lightly in the bright heat. Joe had no sense of anything other than Lorna's breasts, heavy and hot against him, and the flash of flesh through fishnet tights. The way Lorna was draped over him made her bum stick out, their groins tipped wide and apart from one other, and he couldn't begin to imagine how that might feel, to touch a live, moist space, to have a person want him that much that they would open their actual body to him. Would let him in.

'Lorna,' he whispered. 'Lorna.'

Her mouth was slack, he could feel wetness on his shoulder. 'Fuck . . . afeel . . . sick.'

After the record ended, he lugged her back to her friends.

'I don't think she's feeling too well.'

He waited for the joke about Joe aye making folk feel sick, but Amy nodded, took some tissues from her bag.

'Thanks Joe.'

Two round syllables of equal weight, said without inflection or impatience. Just a simple exchange, and the wideness of Joe's mouth, splitting in a smile. He would have to start expanding his frames of reference. Driving felt like driving, but this was like . . . shit, like bungee-jumping or something.

At the end of the ball came the fireworks.

'Quick, c'mon yous lot!' Patrick was tugging on the patio doors, his schoolmates spilling after him. Clad in stained, bedraggled costumes, they returned to what they were, little kids chittering in the cold as fingers of light burst into open, outstretched palms, scattering gold coins and silver rain. Infants who gasped and shouted as threads of electric pink, of twisting, spinning blue pulsed and fell, pulsed and fell. A manic whizz of waving white squibbed across dark outlines, painting faces with childish light, plumes of colour and thin grey wisps arranged like ghosts before them, behind. Joe at the edges, believing in magic. Wanting to make his own bright light.

He wanted to punch a hole in the sky and yell: 'I was here!'

Chapter Thirty-Nine

Anna was sleeping really badly now. Two days since Shelly had been in touch, and she'd heard nothing since. The weight of the baby pressed constantly, crushing organs as she tried lying on her back, dragging her belly askew if she lay on her side. The recovery position was easiest, legs angled like a running man, one arm curled over her head as if averting a blow, but it was only ever a temporary respite.

Rob slept on beside her, oblivious to all the shuffles and hot-flushed heaves. His peaceable stillness made her angry, made her wonder if he'd sleep through the baby crying too. She was going to give breastfeeding a try. She'd watched a woman do it once; it had looked, well, beautiful. A perfect circle of give and take. It had made her greedy, wanting to become that bountiful herself. That vital. What must it be like to feel the food your body has made, pulsing out of you? Already warm, filtered through your skin. It would feel strange, she guessed, but no more strange than having a wee person swimming in your belly. That was strange too. It was mind-blowing, actually: nature's way of totally screwing with your head so that all your prior frames of reference just dissolved, and you were born anew. Ready to take on anything. Yeah, she wouldn't mind these long watches of the night at all, if she was sharing it, feeding her baby. She'd prod Rob awake for nappy-changing though. Good for bonding.

In the long dark, Anna would pretend it was pregnancy keeping her awake, that strange amalgam of Christmas Eve excitement mixed with the anticipation of a looming exam. Occasionally, her eyelids would droop, warm, drowsy, a head full of imminence for the birth and beyond, but then they would slam back open and Galletly would be there, or sometimes it was Francine. Sometimes just the darkest haze, a shadow so intense you couldn't see its shape. When she woke suddenly like that, she always needed to pee. Like a wee scared child, Anna would hold it in, wriggling in her bed, scared to put her foot on the floor in case the monsters got her.

It hadn't helped this evening, Elaine phoning her, all agog.

'Oh, oh! You'll never guess who I saw today.'

'Who?'

'Alex Patterson, that's who. And my God is he looking fine. Still got that swagger, like he's got a two-foot willy crammed down his trousers – which, *by* the way, I've heard he has – but he looks more . . . I dunno. Sophisticated maybe? Like he's wearing himself better. He's no just a gorgeous big puppy any more; you can imagine he *really* knows what to do with that—'

'Elaine, is there a point to this?'

'Duh. I just had to gloat to someone, and I thought you'd be interested . . . I mean it's not every day that a bona fide sex god comes into Personnel—'

'At your work? What was he doing at the council?'

'Oh yeah, well, that was quite interesting too, actually. It seems that our security's been breached.'

'Those Citicard folk again?'

'No, no – by a, well, I don't know what you'd call her actually. An interloper? We'd a girl who turned up at the Press Office last week, said she was from an agency. Only it turns out she wasn't. She'd been bloody working there for five days, kidding on she was someone else, when in actual fact she's on the run for murder!'

'What murder?'

'Some woman in Maryhill. It's all very exciting.'

'Whoa, wait – back up a wee minute. Did Alex actually tell you this lassie was wanted for murder?'

'Eh . . . oh, I'm not sure. Was too busy dribbling at him really to pay that much attention. I know she worked with the dead girl, and then she did a runner the night she was killed – at least, I think that's what Alex said, but you only need to put two and two together, don't you? And then she ends up here. How very bizarre, eh? Who'd think of lying low in the City Chambers?'

'And did Alex tell you her name?'

'Mary something, but we all knew her as Charlie. Hey – d'you think I'll get called as a witness?'

'No, Elaine. I do not think you'll get called as a witness. Did Alex say anything else about this girl? Where she stayed, where they were going to look next?'

'Um, nope, don't think so. Why d'you ask?'

'Well . . . because the city centre is A Division. And we should know if there's . . . we should just be kept updated, that's all.'

'Oh Anna – you take your work *far* too seriously you know. Anyway – gotta go. Ralphie's wanting his mammy – can you hear him singing? I'm sure it's the *EastEnders* tune – boy's a total genius.'

'Bye Lainey.'

All night, she had been fretting, turning it over and over in her mind. She still didn't understand. Galletly had killed Francine, Shelly had confirmed this, yet the police were looking for someone else. And a woman too. Why hadn't Alex said any of this to her? Was it Shelly's information that was wrong then? Maybe Galletly wasn't after her at all – maybe this was all a mistake; a big fucking mistake.

She drew the duvet up nearer to her chin. Watching Rob breathe, wishing that she could wake him. Even Alice was out for the count, sprawled at the foot of the bed with her belly upwards. She had no shame, that cat. If Anna could talk to Rob now, what would she say? What bit of her badness would she reveal first and would he stand by her, no matter what? Again, her eyes were growing heavy. She could feel them roll of their own accord, another, weaker part of herself trying to fight it, forcing all the huge depth of her eyelids open, fixing on a faraway point to keep her anchored. To the pale shaft of light that washed the carpet, to the window above, its draped curtains open and the cream blind down.

The room pitching hellwards.

On the blind, through the blind, in the blind, the black outline of a man was crouching. Clamped like a spider, watching her. Anna trying to scream and scream and scream. Brain acute, body dead.

'Rob,' she whispered. 'Rob! ROBERT!'

It was out now, her voice was screeching it out and she was yelling, 'ROBERT! Robert!' his arms about her, holding her even as his sleepy face opened out.

'It's okay, sweetie. It's okay, I'm here. Just go back to sleep.'

'Rob – there's a man. Look there at the window.'

He followed her quivering hand, searching into the darkness, but of course there was nothing there.

'It's just a dream, baby. Go back to sleep.'

'No, I saw him, I saw him. He was just there.'

'Mmhm.'

'Rob, please.'

Rob hauled the covers from her, turned over on his side. She couldn't stop shaking, he had to feel her shaking, surely? Was she dreaming this? She made herself get out of bed, the carpet clawing at her bare feet, telling her not to look. Her hand on the blind cord, waiting for her heart to settle, before she yanked it up and the room filled with yellow glare.

'Anna!' Rob sat up in bed. 'What the hell are you doing?'

'I saw him,' she wailed into a window smug with fuzzy streetlight and no trace of any intruder.

'Anna, for goodness' sake – will you come back to bed.' Rob punched his pillow into a nice, comfy dent. 'You been eating too much cheese? How on earth could someone get up to our window?'

'Next door's scaffolding?' *Knowing* that's how he must have done it. The thought made her sick.

'Come back to bed, you big daftie.'

'In a minute. I need to get a drink.'

She went first to Laura's room, checking for her curls and the steady breath of sleep. Arms flung above her head, Laura looked like she was sky-diving. Her quilt was thrown back, exposing her shoulders, the loose neckline of her nightshirt. What if he had been watching her too? Anna checked that Laura's window was locked. She pulled the curtains viciously shut, then bent down to kiss her.

Next, she went downstairs. Felt a creeping at her neck as the darkness folded round her. Checked the doors, both satisfyingly solid and locked. Felt Alice pass like water through her legs, fat tail waving hopefully at the back door.

'No chance lady.'

What if he came after Alice, tried to hurt her? Sick bastards did things like that. Maybe Elaine could take her for a while, or even Elizabeth. God, things had reached the utter depths of despair if Elizabeth was the best hope left.

The fridge hummed on, the leaky tap kept dripping. This was their home. She poured herself a glass of water, approaching the sink side-on, keeping as far from the kitchen window as she could. She should check the garden next, all the curtilage of the house, but it could wait until morning. Everything was secure. Unless he was planning to firebomb them, they were as safe in here as anywhere.

She returned to a snoring Rob. Piling the pillows up behind her back, her heartburn too acute to allow her to lie flat. For the remainder of the night, she kept vigil, getting up at regular intervals to check the windows, check on Laura, check the cat. When she heard the rattle of milk bottles on the step, she let herself relax. Daytime had arrived.

Up so early that she had time to make pancakes.

'What's this for?' asked Laura, taking one pancake for each fist and another for her mouth. Rob reached over Anna's spatula-wielding arm to help himself.

'It's all part of the nesting experience. Your mum's been sleep-baking – it's like sleep-walking, only more constructive.'

Laura didn't flinch when Rob said 'your mum', just nodded. 'They're good. Any jam going?'

Over her head, Rob and Anna gleamed. She turned off the frying pan.

'You not having any?' said Rob.

Anna patted her stomach. 'Watching my weight.'

The bin under the sink was overflowing. She pulled the bag out, a steady drip of teabag-juice following her progress. Still in her dressing gown, Anna shuffled to open the back door. It was another mild day, she could see flecks of green shoots peppering the mud. Those poor wee snowdrops would get a shock when the cold returned. Alice ran gleefully on to the grass, making straight for the bird table in the centre.

Chipped stones on the path digging into Anna's slippers. Reality biting. She'd do one circuit of the house – well, a half-circuit: they were only semi-detached. Check for graffiti on the walls or a banner hanging from the scaffolding. *Lying bitch lives here.* Perhaps a dead raven would be pinned to the door. She crunched round the side of the house, where their bins were – a black one for household waste and a green one for garden rubbish. Then a blue box for glass, a nylon sack for newspapers and another bag for plastic. At the top of the bin bag she was holding lay a box of broken eggshells and some soggy kitchen roll. Could you recycle that? Probably not, and she wasn't delving through to rescue anything else. Household waste it was, then. She opened the black bin, expecting it to be empty because the dustmen had only been the day before. But there was already a large black plastic bag taking up the bottom third of the bin. And it was open, neatly opened out like its contents should be on display.

Which they were.

She noticed the stain first, the one like old rust which blossomed across the khaki, hooded jacket. Dark tights, leggings possibly, all askew and crumpled up; it made Anna think of broken legs. There was a lilac bra and a pair of grey-striped pants, folded, not dumped. Automatically, she didn't touch. Got a garden cane and moved the jacket over. Could see shoes below. Shoes and a mobile phone and a purse. And in the purse would be a bus pass maybe, or just a snap from a photo booth and it would show a black-haired girl who did not deserve this. She did not merit her life played out as a game, and put in a fucking dustbin.

Anna dropped the lid down. Left her bin bag where it lay, went back into the kitchen.

'That's me away.' Warm Rob-breath on her cheek. 'You okay to give Laura a lift to school? I'm running a bit late.'

'Yeah, sure.'

'No, it's fine. I'll walk,' said Laura.

'No, I'll take you—'

'I'll *walk*,' she reiterated. 'Um, a couple of friends said they're probably walking too.'

'Wouldn't be a boy, would it?' said Rob.

'*No.*' Laura reddened, buttered another pancake. '*And* I'm walking home.'

'Well, you better leave now then, or you'll be late.'

'Al-*right* Dad. I'm going.'

Anna waved them both off, a paragon of domestic virtue. Then she ran to the toilet to be sick.

When the street and house were fully empty, and she was sure no one would come back for lunch money or a briefcase, Anna put on the freshly rinsed rubber gloves she had used to clean the toilet – a task not long completed once the retch-reflex had abated – retied the belt on her dressing gown and went back outside to the bins.

This was just another stage in the clean-up process.

She raised the lid, praying that she'd imagined it, that it was a lack-of–sleep–fuelled hallucination and the bag would be gone.

It wasn't. This side of the house was hardly overlooked at all. But the weight of silent watching was immense.

'Come on then!' she yelled. 'Come on, you wee fucker. Come and get me then. Just come and fucking get me!'

A flurry of barking from across the way. Her shouts ringing off the sandstone wall, which glittered blankly. Anna scoured the garden, daring its shapes to morph into her stalker. She could see next door's potting shed was open; fuck, why couldn't the bloody man take up golf? The two bare rowan trees which grew beside the boundary fence nodded; they were supposed to ward off witches.

Ashamed, she bent to lift the bin bag out. It looked like Francine was lying there, like she'd been broken up and her insides drained.

She couldn't pick it up.

She crept back to the house and lay with Alice. Curtains half drawn, fire on full. Just lying, just still with her knees in against her tummy as far as they could go. Staring at the empty, fathomless sky. So much for Shelly intervening. Nothing was going to stop Galletly from destroying her. She had to get proper help, go to Alex.

She couldn't go to Alex.

There is nothing.

There is no one.

Only Anna and the despair skewered in her belly. Her heart beats faster, and she's fighting for breath, for some respite from the dull rise of bile. All the world is rippled squint, that safe little dent marked 'Anna' has snapped straight and gone, as if shaking out the sheets. Lying here with her heart on fire. It doesn't matter how sorry she is, or how scared. She can pray and pray until she's shriven clean away, until she's only bones and sinew, fat and skin. But her soul will be flayed and gone. And she never wanted this to happen; she thought there was always hope. Crushed hard up against the back of the box, hidden behind need and fear, there was hope. How do you live without hope?

Hours passed, drifting in and out of sleep and nightmares. Inside and outside her body at the same time; she was trying to climb up glass, sliding, forever sliding, and people were laughing. A bell kept clanging. *Drung-drung*, a steady, doleful ring. Eventually, the noise clarified itself as real, as her mobile ringing. Alice jumped down from the couch, stretched. Anna ignored it. It would stop eventually, and it did, but whoever it was kept ringing back. She checked her watch; too early for Laura to be wanting a lift home. Unless she was sick, maybe she was sick and Anna was lolling here like the Lady of Shalott. She snatched up the phone.

'Yes?'

'Hoo-fucking-ray. Are you corned beef or something, Maddie?'

'Shelly! I thought I wasn't going to hear from you again.'

'And why would you think that? You think I'm at it or something?'

'No ...' There was a fuzziness packed inside her mouth. 'But he was here, Shelly, he was bloody well here and you couldn't stop him, could you?'

'Who? Gilly?'

'*Yes.* He was peering in my windows, and he ... he, oh fuck – what if he comes back? He's just playing with me, like a bloody cat.'

'No way!' Shelly, all squeaky when he got outraged. 'Fucking cunt that he is. Fucking duplicitous fucking cunt.' His string of shrill invective was comforting. 'Maddie, I don't believe ... well, naw, I fucking do actually. That's totally his style. He's pure ramping up the pressure, precious, so's you'll agree.'

'Agree to what?'

'One hundred thousand pounds. That's what he says he's wanting.'

'A hundred ... Shelly, I don't have money like that.'

'It's non-negotiable I'm afraid, doll. According to my sources, he sees it as a fair price.'

'Shelly, I can't find money like that, I just can't.'

'How no? There must be pure hunnersa money kicking round a polis station. Drugs money, stuff fae housebreakings – how no just wheech some of that?'

'Don't be so bloody stupid. I'm a police officer—'

'Listen, doll, fae where I'm standing you'll be a fucking deid police officer if you don't get your act together rapido. He sees this as compensation due, you naughty, naughty girl.'

'What?'

'Aye, I fucking *dae* know now. What the fuck did you expect, Maddie, if you fit a man up? How could you no be straight wi me?'

He must have heard her sob.

'Look doll, I canny do any mair for you. I've pleaded and begged and this is the best we're ever gonny get.'

Galletly made her raw. He had won, no matter what she did.

'How long have I got?'

'He didny say.'

Chapter Forty

So. Nothing but the truth. Mary picked up a stick from the ground, poked it about her toes like a witch stirring spells. What could she do with all these facts she had?

There was the Fat Man, she now knew where he lived, and that he had a car. There was the other guy, the Irish one, who she knew was staying in The Beresford flats. Then there was the name of the builder, Crilley, that she'd already given to the police. God, she'd given them his bloody address, but still nothing had been done. Well, that wasn't necessarily true. She was a bag lady now; when was the last time she had looked at a telly or a newspaper? Let alone a mirror. And let's not forget that maybe the police were part of it, a massive conspiracy that had seen Bernie end up dead.

Who else could she turn to then, if this was bigger, so much bigger? If the police were in on it, then what could Mary do with all this information she possessed, rich and heavy as the coins in her pocket – it had been a reasonable day's begging, actually. She was finding that the grubbier she became, the keener folk were not to look, but they would assuage their guilt by flinging ten pees at her as they passed. Here, by the subway station at Kelvinbridge, was the best place, down in the shady hollow of the riverbed. It was nice and secluded and had the added subtle threat of mugging, which made commuters hurry their step and dig deep in their psyches (if not their purses) chucking their change at the ferryman to let them cross. Plenty of tourists tripped by too, going up to see the Art Galleries or the Hunterian at the university. They were good as well, because they were never quite sure about the currency. If she smiled from beneath tired eyelids (which wasn't bloody hard, because she was bone-weary), they tended to overcompensate. Mary rarely had to say a word, just hang about between the entrance and the river, poised in a Charonian skulk.

She drew a circle in the dust. Water and death. That bit in *Harry Potter*, where he's trying to get across a lake full of dead spectres – what was that if it wasn't a version of the Styx legends? Tolkien too, there was a marsh full of the floating dead in that, and in *Pirates of the Caribbean*, when the murdered dad bobs by in a boat – she remembered taking wee Jess and some of the other kids to the pictures to see that one.

Harry Potter.

That man, the skinny correspondent guy she had met in the Press Office. She had completely forgotten about him. She guddled for his name. Gordon something. Could remember his greasy enthusiasm more easily than his face. Why not him? He'd said he was desperate for stories. Maybe he could work his magic. Yes. She stabbed her stick into the red blaes of the cinder path. She would just phone him, why not? She would brush down her PR suit (jacket with one arm coming away at seams, trousers shiny, torn at right knee and adorned with stains of dubious provenance), ring the number on the card he'd given her – the one that lay in her desk drawer at work – and call him on her out-of-charge mobile that, even if she did have a charger, she wouldn't dare use in case the police could trace her on it.

Phones, clean water. Credibility. Four walls to hide behind. When you're stripped of them, these basics become fairy dust, like fantastic animals from one of her stupid stories. She watched a mother struggle with her buggy up the Victorian stairs which led from the station to street level. People like Mary couldn't go home and shut it all out and draw the curtains when it started to rain. She got up anyway, because the ground was damp and her bum was getting corners. Beside the stairs, at the top so he could catch folk coming from the station, a vendor started cawing.

'Eee'ning Tiii-s. *Gerya* Eeen'ing Tiii-s. *Free mini Mars bar with your* EEE'ning Tiimes.'

She checked her takings: £8.22 and a drumstick lolly. That was alright. She could get a drink and burger and chips at the community café in Elmbank Street; it wasn't that far if you walked along Woodlands Road. *The Times* was, what, 40p or thereabouts, and was it still 10p for the phone? It had been 10p for the phone when she was at Brownies, so maybe not. The clock over the station said it was five to three. Well, if she went to get something to eat now, then she could be back to resume trade before rush hour began. There. It had all the makings of a wee routine. This was her office and she was on her break.

Mary made her way along the pathway by the river, then up the staircase, a beautiful construct of wrought-iron curlicues squashed in against the rising stone parapets of the road-bridge above. What a lot of effort for a utilitarian structure that rarely saw the light of day. There had been a cotton mill here once too, where the car park was now. You could still see the weir-rubble beneath the arch of Kelvin Bridge.

She climbed up until she was on the pavement at Woodlands Road, and the fat sky finally opened. Mary held her face towards the clouds, drops of water washing her, her trying to catch them on her tongue.

'You'll get acid rain,' said the vendor.

'How much is it?' she asked, before he launched into his 'come-and-get-it' roar again.

'Forty-five pee, hen. And you get a Mars—'

'Yup, I know. Here you go.' She handed him a fifty-pence piece, lifted one of the newspapers from the top of his stand.

'Many thanks. There's five p to you, and there's your Mars Bar.'

She looked down. He'd given her two. 'Ach, they're awfy wee hen. Wouldny fill your back tooth.'

'Thanks.'

He nodded. Took a big breath. 'Eee'ning Tiii-s. *Gerya* Eeen'ing Tiii-s.'

There was a phone box further along Woodlands Road and, amazingly, it was working. Best thing was not to think about it, just do it. She crammed both mini Marses into her mouth. The chocolate caramel clagged round her tonsils as she gulped, making her throat sorer, but it was worth it. Swallowed. One final, rinsing rummage of her tongue to scour out all that sugary goodness. What she needed first was to find the right number, and his name. She glanced at the masthead. *Wednesday 21 November.* Wednesday. It really was Wednesday. There was a switchboard number at the front of the paper. She'd heard Celine ask for the newsdesk before, but this had to sound professional; she couldn't just go on and witter, 'Eh, can I speak to Gordon, please?' Inside the phone box, surrounded by *eau de pis*, she searched through the newspaper for a byline she recognised . . . here it was. Gordon Thomson, boy wizard and local government correspondent. Right next to a reproduction of Mary's council security pass and the heading: *Call Girl Suspect Goes to Ground.*

Hot, burny paper dropping to the concrete floor. All the windows of the phone box lighting up. Neon flashes, her naked and on show, everyone looking at her, that's what it feels like that's what it feels like.

Calm down, she had to calm down. Nobody was staring at her, if she kept her head down, kept well out the road of the world, then this too would pass. It would be tomorrow's chip papers and Mary would remain just another faceless down and out. She had acquired an old duffel coat which she wore over her battered rucksack. From the back she must look eighty-odd. Team that with a woolly bunnet and she'd be fine. So long as she avoided the Community Café and the hostels and all the places where she might get warm and fed. Fuck. She retrieved the newspaper from the floor. She had to do this. Carefully dialling the number, a twenty pence at the ready.

'Good afternoon. *Herald* and *Evening*—'

'Can I have the *Evening Times* newsdesk, please?'

'Putting you through now.'

It buzzed, then a beep instead of a ring.

'Newsyeah?'

'Hi. Can I speak to Gordon Thomson please?'

'He's out.'

'Oh. Um . . . can I leave a message?'

'Hmm. Name?'

'No, I mean, does he have an answering machine?'

A tut. 'You should phone his direct line then.'

'I'm sorry, but I don't—'

Another buzz, then Thomson's drawl. 'Not here right now, but you can get me on my mobile or leave a message after the tone.'

Mary had no pen to write down the mobile number, no option but to wait and leave her voice behind. She tried to disguise it, chin down, puffing air like she was starting a bagpipe.

'Eh, hullo.' She paused to resettle the pitch, it was sounding constipated. 'You don't know me, but I have information regarding the Be-Francine Gallagher murder in Maryhill. It was carried out on behalf of a builder called Robert Crilley. He has an application in to build on the land at Calder Riggs – you can check with the council, and I think Francine was standing up to him . . . eh – she found out he was planning an incinerator . . . and a huge dump on the site. The guy that did it lives in West Princes Street and he has a green car. He's really fat and he stays at . . .' she could not remember the bloody number . . . 'it's near the top . . .' The silence changed to a squeak and then a dialling tone. She'd run out of tape. But it was all there, all the salient points that any decent journalist would need, plus a few elaborations for good measure. Job done. She would get another paper tomorrow, see what Mr Thomson had to say to his public then.

Black smudges of newsprint on her fingers. The girl in that picture seemed quite happy, as if she had something to look forward to. Yeah, well what did she know, silly cow? Reluctantly, Mary read the whole article. They had given her full name, and background – charming. Convicted fraudster . . . had the whole City Chambers convinced while she was on the run, yeah, yeah. Bullshit: no way was she a drug addict. Saying that Calder Riggs was a rundown riding school, too – that was crap – and that they were selling off the horses already. *No way*. Fiona couldn't do that. How could the bitch do that when Bernie loved them so much? And the headline was crap as well. Nowhere in the entire article did it say that Mary was a suspect in Francine's murder, just that the police wanted to question her. In *relation* to Bernie's disappearance.

Tomorrow, Mary would also get a haircut.

Chapter Forty-One

It was after midnight. The streets had taken on a monochrome sleepiness, holding the same thick quiet you get after snow. Anna was in a Black Hack and it was taking her to Maryhill. She'd hailed it at Sauchiehall Street, near to where she'd parked her car. Which was hidden up a side street that she knew had no CCTV coverage. Cloak and dagger indeed, but it helped to have a polis mind, because then you worked back in logical links from the point of discovery to the point of execution – of the subterfuge, obviously, not an actual beheading.

Anna had the same light, giddy resolution she'd felt the day Mrs Hamilton had shafted her, had threatened her with discipline, dismissal and quite possibly death. It was a panic-high. She was frozen through, even though she was wearing a horrible duvet coat, fat and pillowy enough to draw a padded shroud over whether the thing inside was animal, vegetable or pregnant. But they'd still guess she was a female of the species, owing to the carrycot she balanced on her lap.

'The wean still sleeping?' said the driver.

'Aye.'

'Mine's were like that, the pair of them. Screamed the hoose down all night, but stick them in the motor, and they'd drop off good as gold. Now, how far along Maryhill Road is it you are?'

'Och, just here'll be fine. Cheers, driver.'

He leaned over, handed her the folded metal wheels she'd stowed in the space beside him. 'You take care, hen.'

She rested the carrycot on her hip, pretended to be fumbling for a door key. Where he had dropped her had a row of tenements and some darkened shops, but this wasn't the place. There were several blocks of flats about half a mile along the road that she remembered, each with three or four storeys of homes, and it was close to the canal as well. By the time they'd interviewed everyone there . . . well, that could take days.

She clicked the carrycot into the pram frame and began walking. It was unlucky to bring the pram home before the baby's born, that's what Elaine had told her – but as far as Anna was concerned, it was bloody lucky indeed. Rob didn't know it had gone from the spare room; she had hoisted it downstairs before he or Laura had got home, stuffed it in the boot alongside her baby.

Her 'baby' bobbed companionably beneath the waffle-weave. Ugly wee soul, if anyone saw it in the daylight, with its shiny-shrivelled lumps. Pray God there would not be an old wumman up at this hour, who would see the pram and follow the time-honoured tradition of slipping a wee minding under the pillow for luck. *Omagod hen. Yir wean's a poly bag!*

Francine's clothing was still in the bin bag, which was safely in the carrycot, and wrapped in a brand-new shawl that her mum's friend Joan had knitted. Spanish wool and beautiful crocheted fringing. It was a one-off from La Manga, nothing you'd find in any shop. Not even if you were the police.

Anna's first instinct had been to burn the clothes. But it was proof of what Galletly had done, and no matter how clever he thought he was, there would be traces of him on those garments. There were always traces. She'd lost the ability to think beyond the next thing she had to do; it hurt her head too much to consider all the permutations of presenting this evidence, and could it possibly lead back to her? If she concealed her own actions well enough, why would it? She just knew she had to get rid of them. Anna did not want this on her conscience; she was still a cop. She did not want it at all. But she knew a man who did.

The one thing she had removed from the bag had been the photograph. Anna had been wrong, there were no snaps inside the purse, but there was one slipped between the layers of clothing. It had been placed carefully, face-up on a bed of pale lilac knickers. She had worn gloves to go through the entire bag, used a garden cane, touched nothing. She was not stupid.

Galletly had chosen well, because a picture says a thousand words and this one said it all. There was Francine and her sister, and in the middle was Molly the Dolly with her rouged-up cheeks and silly hair. They were all laughing hugely, a moment of drunken joy; you could see Francine's shoulders raised, her arms reaching over the shoulders of the women either side of her, the pose pushing up her jacket and accentuating the brooch pinned to her lapel. A pretty little enamelled star.

It was a six-pointed Polish medal.

Anna had burned the photograph, simply held it against the gas-fire flame and watched it shiver and shrink. She had burned her thumb as well, holding on too long until she dropped the picture into the grate. There was a blister now, on her thumb-tip.

She loosened her grip on the pram handle. It was smooth on top, then ridged below where your fingers curled. Felt a bit like a steering wheel, that same cool-sliding satisfaction of grip and give. Anna had never pushed a pram before. Never. Here was something else that Galletly had poisoned. But she liked the feel of it, it made you stand upright and proud, gave you bounce in your step as you matched the wheel-springs. What if Galletly cheated her of this for real? You didn't get many prams in Corton Vale prison – where would you push them to? Or what if they took your baby away – they did that, didn't they? After a year or something. That was barbaric; she must be mistaken. What civilised society would take a child from a government-controlled institution that contained its mother, and put it in one that did not?

That was not going to happen to them. Tomorrow she would make an appointment at the bank. Most of the money from her flat sale had gone into propping up The Meadows, the nursing home Rob ran. Now that it was on an even keel again, and their house was no longer collateral, then maybe they could take out a second mortgage. Anna had no idea if she could do this alone, on the strength of her salary. Plus the house was in both their names . . . oh shit, there was a man with his dog. She was desperate to cross the road, did not want him to see her face, but the other side was very dark, there were no houses there. Just the black-lapping canal.

How stupid is she, how vulnerable can she make herself other than walking naked? No, it's okay. He's crossing.

The man was crossing, his dog yapping with excitement as he smelled the otherness the canal brought down from the hills.

Maryhill Road was wide and quiet again. Only the rustle of the pram wheels and the clopping of her clogs and the dog barking down by the water. Anna's feet were too swollen to fit in proper shoes, the fluid was building up more each day. Rob hadn't noticed, but when he did he'd want to take her blood pressure. How would Mrs Reekie feel about her turning up for work in flip-flops?

'Hey you.' She glanced down. Sometimes she talked out loud, other times you just did it in your head, so the invisible string running from you to your baby would let the words slide down without having to leave your body. Folk would think it was the baby in the pram she was talking to, but it was her real one, coiling and kicking as she tried to swim. There wasn't much room left, she hung like a sling in Anna's lower belly. Rob said the head was engaged, which meant that it was lodged in her pelvis. Ready for lift-off, no going back.

'We're stuck, kiddo. You and me both.' We are merely bodies under the action of given forces. This bit she said in her head, and the baby kicked a little more. 'Hey, you're not happy about that, are you Mini-Me? D'you want to be your own boss or something? It disny work that way, you know.'

No matter how relentlessly you forged your own path, and willed – no, *demanded* – that the fates give you what you thought you were due, it seemed they had other plans. Or maybe no plans at all and it was just you, drifting in the wind, pushing and flailing, but utterly impactless against the drift. Should she give up trying to make it stop? Was this her reaping her just deserts? A memory stirred in Anna, came rushing through like a gasp. Shaking itself of dust and time, just a single breath away. And her heart tore after it.

Those folk that said you forgot it, what did they know? And what was fitting up a murderer, compared to what she had done?

The pram creaked beneath her, it juddered on the cracked and pitted flags. Anna was almost at the flats. She thought if there was a communal midden, then she could chuck the bag in there, but this was better. A skip, stuffed with planks of wood, plasterboard and the ubiquitous mattress stood unlit and filthy by the kerb. She could just stroll on by and lob the bag in, not breaking step, and all anyone would see was a woman, with the same pram, coming out the other side.

Rob thought she was working tonight. He was furious with her, threatening to phone Mrs Reekie and complain. He didn't know that Mrs Reekie had taken her off the on-call rota two weeks ago. But the freedom suited her.

The freedom to lie. *And now, for my next trick, I will phone the police. And then, I will rob a bank.*

The street watched her, with greasy yellow eyes. She pulled her duvet-coat as tight round her as it would go. She couldn't use this pram again.

Chapter Forty-Two

Anyone who'd ever worked a nightshift without sleeping in advance, or who'd spent a watch-night vigil at a bedside or had a teething vampire baby that came alive at night, would know the feeling of torpor that dogs you in the day. You are part of the living dead as you zombie your way through the morning, only coffee and the exaggerated kick of your heart triggering responses, and you will continue to droop steadily Lethe-wards as you roll into afternoon. That was where Alex currently was, the desk beckoning his head to land on it, just for a wee minute. *Go on, son. I'm softer than I look.*

He'd been woken up at three a.m., in the worst and deepest part of sleep, the first full night he thought he'd been heading for in almost two weeks.

'Boss, sorry to call so late – or early, I guess, but we've had a wee development.'

It had been Shirley, her voice too loud and rapid, Alex's ears still fogged with dream-shapes and an Ikea pillow.

'Mmh?'

Sandra had shifted; he moved the phone to the other side.

'Anon female reporting Francine's Gallagher's clothes had been dumped in a skip in Maryhill—'

'Have they?'

'Yes. Mobile too. I've no looked at it yet.'

All neatly packed in a bin bag inside a skip, every cubic centimetre of which was in the process of being examined, as was the clothing, purse and phone. Hayley had made some calls on his behalf, she was presenting herself as the loyal shield behind which he could hide his inadequacies, but he no longer cared. If it got things moving, she could intercede until she was purple. She would be keeping all favours owed in a ledger anyway. Thank fuck she didn't know he'd virtually shared a cup of tea with Mary McLennan, down at the City Chambers. Not a fact he was planning to mention, and there was no need anyway, not with things moving nicely forwards. Preliminary forensic results had identified fragments of animal skin on the recovered underwear, which got all the boys very excited, and a book was opened on what animal it might be, and where, exactly, he had put it, until Shirley pointed out it was most likely from leather gloves.

They'd got a couple of beat cops to help Mandy and two DCs begin the door-to-doors. The team was all invigorated; it was a great wee boost. Worth the wake. Plus Ian had just informed him there were only twenty green Fords outstanding. He was confident he'd have every registered keeper interviewed by the weekend. Bright sunshine outside too, forceful enough to penetrate the grubby window of his office. In fact, bugger it. Alex was going to go for a little walk. Five minutes round the block, to ease off his neck and shoulders.

He made it as far as the foyer.

'Excuse me! Excuse me!' Alex recognised the face, but had not a scooby who it belonged to. A youngish man, mid-thirties, in a camel overcoat. Wearing an unpleasant, meat-coloured tie.

'Mr Patterson?'

'Yes?'

'It's Darren Crilley. I've been waiting ages to see someone, but they said you were all too busy. Well, we're all busy—'

Alex took the man's arm, guided him towards a little interview room that was also used to store the local lollipop lady's stick between her shifts. From Crilley's charged demeanour, the waiting hadn't chilled him out in any way.

'What can I do for you, Mr Crilley?'

'You can stop putting out all these disgusting bloody rumours about me for a start. I've spoken to my lawyer, and he says it's totally malicious, bordering on harassment.'

Oh man. I just wanted five minutes on my own and a breath of bloody air. You could suffocate in here. Drown in it. He gestured to the one chair in the room. Folk were forever 'borrowing' stuff from this forlorn space, then never bringing it back.

'Sit down sir.'

'No thank you.'

'Fine, well, we'll stand. Right.' He held the bridge of his nose a second. 'Okay. Can you tell me what exactly these allegations might be, and why you think they're emanating from here?'

'*Duh*. I get interviewed by two of your "finest" regarding totally scurrilous rumours that I'm involved in a plot to murder the occupants of Calder Riggs Farm and steal their land – which I already bloody own, might I remind you—'

'Sir, it was explained to you at the time. That was just one of many lines of enquiry we were following—'

'Yes, and I was also advised that the interview was in total confidence and would be taken no further. So how come, then, I get a phone call from a journalist yesterday, asking me if it was true that the police had been to see me and was I involved in Francine Gallagher's murder? And then, when I tell them to piss off, they start calling all my other clients, asking them if I'm trustworthy, can they say what problems they've encountered with me in the past—'

'Sir, I have no idea why—'

'And the upshot is, today, my biggest backer pulls out of the scheme for Calder Riggs. So I'm left with my professional reputation in tatters and a fucking huge tract of land I canny afford to develop. I mean, who's going to compensate me for that, eh? And all because one of your lads canny keep his big mouth shut.'

The door swung open.

'Everything okay in here?' smiled Hayley. Give her her due, she was smooth. Slinked over to Crilley, hand outstretched like she was welcoming him into her garden party. 'I'm Superintendent Whittaker. I understand from your solicitor that you're upset about a journalist? Harassing you, is he?' She took Crilley's hand, shook it whether he liked it or not. 'Scum of the earth, aren't they?

So, what can we do to help you, Mr Crilley? Though, I warn you, it's never easy. They're unscrupulous these people, listen in to private messages, pretend they're relatives of the deceased – oh, you've no idea.' Gently enfolding his elbow, leading him closer to the door. 'I have all the details from your solicitor, Mr Crilley, and rest assured, I'll be contacting the editor of the newspaper as soon as we've finished our conversation. I will tell him in no uncertain terms that this is unacceptable, that you are in no way connected with the Gallagher enquiry and that I will consider it an attempt to pervert the course of justice if he suggests that you are. How's that for starters?'

'Um. Yes,' he said quietly. 'Great.'

'My pleasure. Perhaps I can give you a call later on today, let you know what's happening?'

Bending in towards his face. *Man.* Both he and Crilley were thinking it, any man would think it, those sulky lips just floating by, catching it like perfume. But she was merely opening the door.

'Please don't let us keep you any longer, Mr Crilley. You can rest assured I'll deal with this. Personally.' She followed him into the foyer, practically waved him off, then hooked Alex's arm in a much less tender way than she had Crilley's.

'Right you. His solicitor is Garfield McBain.'

'Crap.'

'Mmhm. Now, this is a lot of pish, but knowing that obnoxious little man, he'll milk and distort it for all it's worth. The journalist's name is Gordon Thomson, and he works at the *Evening Times*. Get on to him, find out where the fuck he got this information from, explain to him it's a load of slanderous shite and tell him in no uncertain terms what you're going to do with him if he prints it.'

'Is it no libel, ma'am, if it's written? Anyhow, do we not call it defamation here?'

She glowered. Magnificently, of course. 'Do you want me to punish you too, Detective Inspector Patterson?'

There was no one else in the foyer. He glowered back. 'You tell me, ma'am. You're the boss.'

Chapter Forty-Three

The sleeve of Mary's jacket had finally parted company with the torso. She'd been engaged in a lunchtime struggle with a woman over who had squatting rights at Kelvinbridge subway, and the bitch had got her in a drunken headlock. Big heifer of a lassie she was too – looked like a sumo with very bad teeth, so it was just as well that the seam had given up the ghost, allowing Mary to slip away and leave the heifer wrestling with an empty arm. The girl was as slow as she was big, giving Mary plenty of time to make her retreat. On any other day she would have stood her ground, but the last thing she wanted was to draw attention to herself. Not with her being famous and all. She thought about tearing the other arm off, so it became a gilet, but one arm was better than none. That was quite a good wee adage when you thought about it.

She laughed out loud, a double *hee* that drew suspicious glances and doubtless confirmed her full induction into the status of gibbering outcast. If you had no one else to talk to you but yourself, what were you meant to do? Go mad? No, it really was a good saying – a bit quirky, but with an air of positivity. And it was inclusive too, ticked the disability box and everything. Henceforth, it would be the expression Mary would use instead of 'a bird in the hand' – how relevant was that to modern day society, really? Who caught birds nowadays apart from rich, chinless yahs?

With her begging curtailed, Mary had only amassed £3.74, but that would still get her lunch and a copy of today's *Evening Times*. A spangle of excitement flickered, that perhaps she was making progress. Gordon Thomson was a good choice; he would be tenacious, she'd no doubt of that. Much as she would love to see the Fat Man dead, had actually considered picking up a smooth, flat stone and lying in wait for him and his little friend, Mary was not a murderer. She would only go back to jail – but for years this time, not months. Years and years of her life unrealised, after Bernie had given her a chance. Of all the people in the world, it had been Bernie. The best way to honour that was for Mary to do something with her life, not destroy it. These days on the streets were sweeping Mary further from humanity, she realised that. The less you had, the less you mattered. And you would think, the less you cared. But even sumo-bitch who could barely run the length of her self and had no choices left in life but where she sat to beg, she was human too.

All Mary wanted was to live quietly. She wanted to see the men who killed Bernie being called to account for what they had done, she wanted to stop them building on Calder Riggs's scrubby fields and she wanted to live quietly, somewhere good. Maybe with a horse.

Mary had a new haircut too. That always lifted a girl's spirits. Granted, it had been facilitated by a pair of display wallpaper scissors she'd knocked from the front of a shop in Park Road, and been styled in the wing mirror of a car in the subway car park, but it was bang on trend. An elfin crop she believed the fashionistas called it. It felt better, anyway, her neck longer and lighter, and it made her feel less exposed. Mary's wee news vendor was waiting for her at the top of the stairs on Woodlands Road. She hoped he didn't read his own paper too closely. He shook his head. 'You could of taken her doll.'

'I'm sorry?'

'Aye, I seen you. You should of kneed her in the balls, that one. Then just dropped her. Once she was on her back, she'd never have got up. Like a turtle, know?'

'Any Mars bars left?' she asked hopefully.

'No the day. Today we have a free Santa sack.'

'But it's November.'

'Aye, and they're pish and all.' He waggled his fingers in a red and green plastic bag. 'Paper-thin, look. *They'll* no last till Christmas. *Times* is it?'

'Yes please. But no sack.'

'There you go. Nice hair by the way.'

'Thanks. It's . . . eh, it's easier to look after this way.'

'Suits you. Och, naw, naw.' He brushed away her money. 'You're fine the day, hen. I'd pay far more for that on the telly, tae see two lassies wrestling.'

Just as well her pitch had been stolen. Forming personal attachments to genial old pervs was not a wise move. She walked across Woodlands and into the park, searching through the newspaper, rifling the pages initially, then slowing, methodically re-reading all the little columns, but there was still nothing there. A squall of helmeted kids swept past her, their spinning wheels en route to the skate rink. Kelvingrove was Scotland's very first park; how would the Victorians have felt about vagabonds flying on concrete slopes? She carried on, enjoying the sun on her face, the sense of small anonymity that walking on grass could bring. The skaters were whooping, little wheely-monkeys greeting other monkeys who were already executing lithe helixes on the ramps. They *owned* this park, owned their world. That was cool. Mary didn't even own a toothbrush.

How come Thomson could write a load of shite about her yesterday, and then, when he's given the real killer, gift-wrapped and hand-delivered, he writes nothing at all? She crunched over crisp orange leaves. Time for another phone call. She was in the middle of the park now, close to the Stewart fountain. A Gothic celebration of the provost who brought clean water to Glasgow. It was a curly explosion of grotesque beasts and zodiac signs, topped by the Lady of the Lake, forever straining to hear her lover. Forever being vandalised and refurbished and vandalised and refurbished, the fountain was once again switched off and, once again, there were plans to renovate it. She'd heard Celine talking about it in the Press Office, on the phone to some journalist. Grafting hard, she was comparing Glasgow's sculptural heritage to that of Paris, which was a pretty big 'bigging-up'. They might insouciantly pee into the fountains of Paris, but Mary didn't think they actively spray-painted them or snapped the beaks off gryphons whilst going: *Haw, beaky. How you gonny pick yir nose now?*

It would be lovely to hear the tinkling water, to rinse your face beneath its spray. Maybe this time they'd come up with a plan to guard the fountain better, have parkies working undercover shifts, complete with scuba gear and a nice sharp trident.

Mary carried on to the gate that led to Kelvingrove Street, the other side of the park from where she'd come in. There was a phone box outside the shops in Argyle Street, it wasn't far. She would go there. Near to that excellent baker's too, where she could buy more bridies.

This time, Mr Thomson himself answered his phone. Out with it, she thought. Time is money, and you've only got 50p in change.

'Why haven't you followed up the lead I gave you about the Francine Gallagher murder?'

'Fucksake. Who *is* this?'

'Doesn't matter. All you need to know is it was me left that message yesterday. And you shouldn't swear at a benefactor.'

'A benefactor? Do you have any idea of the bollocking I've taken because of you? I did follow up your message, and all I've got to show for it is a big bite out my arse where my editor chewed it, plus a thinly veiled threat that the polis might throw me in jail.'

'Ah, but that's because they're in on it.'

'Who? The police? Je-*sus*.'

'I think so. You see, I've been following the two guys—'

'Two guys?'

'Yeah, there's two now, and they keep, well, no, it's only one of them actually, but he keeps hanging about outside a police station, like he's waiting for someone. I think it's connected with when Francine was a prostitute, you know, that she was sleeping with one of the cops and there's blackmail now or something so maybe if you checked her clients—'

'Whoa, whoa, mad lady. Please. Can I just stop you there. I'll be doing no more checking of anything, thank you very much. I'd quite like to keep my job.'

'But you *said* you wanted to be an investigative journalist—'

A plash of stone falling into silence. Mary biting on her lip, salt stinging.

'Is this who I think it is?'

'No.'

'Where are you? Why are you doing this?'

'Because I know the truth. And Bernie was my friend.'

'Is that right? Well how come your theory about Calder Riggs is a load of bullshit then? Nobody at Crilley's engineered the death of your friend, because they own the bloody land anyway.'

Ah. So he had followed it up, right enough. She doubled back on herself, ad libbing with increased vigour.

'Yeah, I know that. And . . . okay, yeah . . . but I still know who killed her, and right, maybe they're not working for Crilley then, maybe they *are* working for the police, eh? Have you thought about that? What if this is a big fucking conspiracy, with sex and murder and corruption, Glasgow's scandal of the decade and you're going to let it slip through your fingers because you're too bloody feart to ever be anything other than a local government correspondent covering fucking fashion shows and – oh, my money's running out.' She slotted in her last twenty pence.

'Okay, here's the deal,' said Thomson. 'You prove it. You bring me all the bucket-loads of proof that you have, and I'll—'

'I saw it,' she yelled in desperation. 'I bloody saw him kill her, alright? Will that do you?'

She heard him breathe. It reminded her of how horses snorted when you offered them hay.

'Yeah? So how come you've not gone to the police?'

'They think I did it, don't they? What about all that pish you wrote yesterday – you think I did it too, but I didn't. I didn't,' she cried. 'I loved her.'

'Hey, hey. Calm down, Mary. Can I call you Mary, is that cool?'

'I don't care. Call me anything you like.'

'You've got to understand, Mary, I need proof before I can take this any further. Major proof. Especially if you think the police are involved.'

Patronising arse.

'What kind of proof?'

'Well . . .'

You could tell the guy was thinking on his feet. He'd never done anything like this before either. 'Okay. I'd need you to describe to me exactly what you saw, see if it marries up with the police report. I'd need to know *why* these guys were after your friend – I mean genuine reasons, proven links, not just wild guesses. Ideally, we . . . yeah, we get him on tape . . . incriminating himself, I suppose. Yeah, that would do it. That's the gold standard, really. If we could set that up, we'd be laughing.'

'*Piss* off. You want me to do all the work for you, so you can take all the glory?'

'Mary, what I'm asking you to do wouldn't even be making a dent in it. You clearly don't have a clue how hard it would be to get any paper to print a story about cops and extortion and prostitution, let alone murder. It needs to be absolutely watertight. Look, why don't we meet up?'

'No chance.'

'Well, in that case, I really can't help you. Unless you come back to me with names, dates, descriptions—'

'Fine. But it'll cost you.' She just blurted it out, thinking of the horses, and that soft snicker Gerry made when you took off his bridle.

'Pardon?'

'You want me to do all this, it'll cost you.'

'Get stuffed.' He hung up the phone.

Shite. You took that too far, Mary doll. Far too far, with dreams of lavish reward money and buying up Calder Riggs for your own. You stupid, foolish, hopeless little girl. But she had got Thomson interested, she knew that. And she had found out loads of stuff already, it was like a jigsaw, she had the edges, had the bone-coloured sky and bits of water and some feet, but the rest was still in bits. So, how is it you build your jigsaw? You start with the pieces that you know, and look for other pieces that might fit. You look. You think. You crouch behind a bin in a smelly lane and you look . . . at feet and hands. At furious fists.

She was still holding the receiver. It whined gently until she put it in its cradle. Mary had been looking at the wrong piece. It was not the Fat Man who would shape this picture. It was the wire-thin Irishman she had to watch.

As she opened the door, she saw a woman come out of the police station across the road. Even through sticky glass, you could tell she was beautiful, a glacial blonde with a self-assured luminosity about her and geometric features that made you instantly want to retreat. Even the bump which preceded her was high and pointed, a baby-prow swinging through her open coat. It was a fawn trenchcoat, but the woman looked like a cop. There was the vaguest memory of having seen her elsewhere. Not here, a busier place. A club, a department store? Quite possibly she had arrested Mary at one time or another – a lot of that period was fuzzy. She'd a black smock on anyway, and those dull black brogues that you'd have to be paid – or made – to wear. Could you get pregnant policewomen? Mary had never see one before. Were they allowed out?

This one darted over the road, taking it diagonally so she crossed Elderslie Street too, but there was a bus coming down the main road; it seemed to be going too fast, and, for a second, Mary thought it would clip the woman's shoulder. She saw her turn, shout 'Ho!' at the receding driver, who gazed back as if he was powerless to stop the vehicle he was on. A lost round mouth, which echoed the policewoman's chiding one. Then the woman shook her head, and carried on over to the bank at the next block down. Mary headed in the same direction. She was going to set up camp near The Beresford.

When she first got there, she wandered up and down the high, thin streets at the side of the apartments, into pends and through back lanes. Even considered a perch on a fire escape until an Indian man shouted at her, waving a dishcloth from the back door of his restaurant. Then it dawned on her. Fat Bastard had seen her, but the Irish man didn't have a clue. She didn't need to hide, could sit in Sauchiehall Street all day, all night if necessary. Just pick her doorway, cross her legs, and stick out one hand as usual.

It was the perfect reconnaissance disguise; she was a natural. And if she made a few quid while she was waiting for Paddy Pintsize to hove into view again, well, bonus all round. Of course, if the Fat Man waddled up the road, she might have to rethink her grand scheme.

She smoothed out her new blanket on her chosen step, across the road and slightly to the right of The Beresford. It was a nightclub, so there'd be no one wanting past to get up the stairs. Even Glaswegians didn't go boogieing at three o'clock in the afternoon. This part of Sauchiehall Street still had traffic in it. Further up, at the junction with Rose Street where the old cinema was, the street became pedestrianised, but the steady flow of buses and taxis here was good, acting as her own wee screen. Mary arranged her feet in two neat lines, and sat back. Blanket off at the moment, so she'd appreciate the warmth later on. Didn't matter how bright the sun was; sandwiched between the chill of concrete steps and the long song of wind that channelled up Sauchiehall Street, you got very, very cold. She would have to get a new jacket. Quickly, before she became known as the One-Armed Bandit.

Her ever-present rucksack cushioned her from the knubbly door; one of those pressed metal ones, embossed to look like pewter or an old dungeon. She sniffed the air. Upwind of Bradford's Bakers, another Glasgow institution. Bradford's was slightly more upmarket than Greggs, but then the sausage rolls were skinnier. She'd forgotten to go into the baker's by the police station, and the smell was delicious. But she'd only just sat down. Swithering, could she just leave her blanket, like a towel on a sunlounger, nip in; she'd only be a minute? She'd have to eat it quickly though, cram it all in before she took up position. Nobody liked a beggar who was stuffing their face. Oh, but she was starving . . . and then the dilemma was settled, quite abruptly, by the Irish guy emerging from his apartment block.

Serendipitous indeed.

The Lady Serendipitous sprang to her feet, silver heels sparking on the delicate cobbles. Her quarry was making great haste, but she matched him step for step, her woven cloak flapping over the saddle-

bag she was forced to carry. As they neared the brow of the Alley of
Willows, she hung back, conscious that the two paths they were on
would merge here. Once the renegade dwarf had scaled the summit,
and was descending the other side of the hill, she scurried after him
again. And, in this stop-start fashion, she pursued him all the way to
the centre of the ancient city, unto the place of the Iron Horses.

At Central Station, the concourse smelled unpleasantly of fried
fat, and was seething with baby Goths and confused backpackers
(who should really have been at Queen Street, because that's
where you got the trains that went north, to scenic places like
Perth and Aberdeen and Inverness). She watched the Irish man
scan the electronic board, then make his way to Platform Eight.

It seemed they were going on a journey.

Mary followed him. She only had £3. *Thus it was that the*
Lady Serendipitous and the man who checked the tickets must forever
remain strangers. She read the front of the train. Or would that be
the back? *Neilston?* Where the hell was Neilston? She shrugged
and climbed aboard.

Chapter Forty-Four

Bloody bank managers. A handsome old gent, one who clung grimly to his leather chair in an office full of plate glass and bright, abstract posters, he would not entertain the idea of a heavily pregnant woman borrowing *what is not an unsubstantial sum, Miss Cameron* against a home she only jointly owned, without the consent of the other party and without a clear explanation for what the money was for. *It is rather a lot for home improvements, wouldn't you say? Why don't you discuss it with your, ah . . . boyfriend?*

Anna couldn't blame him. *I am not a safe bet.* His character assessment was spot on. But it didn't help her any as she stalked and stalked, joining the four corners of her office. She shouldn't be at work at all, she was incapable of making any decision, was simply hiding in this room under the pretext that she was busy. She had become the worst kind of boss: distracted, weary, unfocused, uncommitted, walking in circles of nervous energy. Everything was contaminated, and it was worse at home; here it was impersonal, these people relied on her, but they did not love her, did not mind or notice this circling to the point of exhaustion, this soothing of herself with the steady plat of foot on floor, with her crushed-in arms and her belly jogging.

Her maternity leave wasn't due to start for another four weeks. She should be thinking of layettes, and soft-flailing fists; she should be pressing and flexing her pelvic floor, massaging oil into her heavy breasts, and yet she was considering . . . theft, or was it fraud? There was money in the safe at Stewart Street. Money from a major drugs haul, it was a production and she had a key. Fifty-five thousand pounds in all and it wouldn't be moved until

Monday and it was in the safe and she had a key. Her phone was ringing, always bloody ringing, and she walked out and into the car. If they asked when she got to Stewart Street, she was looking for Mrs Reekie. If they asked when her hand was unlocking the squat grey door of the safe, she was checking on something else. If they asked when it was in her hands, in her pockets, out the door . . . she was desperate.

Sky high and blue. The familiar bright blue panelling was reflecting the light, illuminating the dull streets that surrounded it. Stewart Street was like a giant Tardis. She thought of all the people that had ever walked inside there, generations of cops in their tunics, raincoats neatly sliced over one arm, doing drill in the yard; old Sam and his van that was secured by tying a dog-lead round the door; wee China, who was dead, and Francine, also dead, and her sister Angela and nippy Jenny who was not dead, but would stick by you like grim death, and Alex and Jamie, and how much she had loved him. How Rob was a kinder version of Jamie. Although he was a man who'd known real hurt in the past, he had the grace to carry it lightly. Being a widower didn't define him, it didn't make him scared to pour love on to Anna, love which she'd lapped up greedily. He'd made her understand why people needed to replicate and splice their genes. Creating a baby was a visceral thing, she couldn't *not* have a child with Rob, and she'd never felt that with anyone else. Not even Jamie. Not enough to see it through.

She looked again at the door to her divisional headquarters, with the crest above the door and the Saltire-polis-blue. She would not see this through either. Anna depressed the clutch and moved into first, leaving Stewart Street behind. Drove past the fire station, turned left for the motorway and home. When she got there, safe in her own place, she was going to prepare two letters. One would be for Alex; she would tell him the truth about Francine, then throw herself on his mercy. The other would be to Mrs Reekie, and it would be her letter of resignation. And then she and Rob would talk.

It always made her happy, seeing their house come into view. Her mum would have loved it too. A solid, pale sandstone, it was the epitome of a douce Glaswegian middle-class whose children went to tennis club and played at least one, if not two musical instruments. Galletly had infected all of this as well. She drew into their gravel drive. Even the crunching glide of this gave her pleasure. She wished her mum had met Rob before she died. There was a movement inside the dining-room window, a mottled brown shadow jumping down. Alice.

Anna took out her door keys, heard her mobile play a rap tune. Laura had preset it with different rings for different callers, and she didn't know how to change it back. She glanced at her watch. Three thirty. A mercy call for a lift home from school. Lazy wee besom that she was, it was a lovely day – cold and clear.

'Right, Lady Laura. It's not even raining—'

'Mum?' High and shrill, Laura sounded terrified.

'What's up?'

'Mum, I think someone's following me.'

A sick sweat, pleating her. 'What's happened? Has he hurt you?'

'I'm at the shops on the main road, I'm in the newsagent. No, he's not touched me. It's just this man—'

'What does he look like?'

'He's quite wee, I don't know, I was just walking and I could tell someone was behind me, but he wouldn't go past.'

It was hard to make out what she was saying, she was starting to cry, and there was the noise of machinery or cars in the background.

'Laura. Calm down. Tell me exactly what's happened. Is he there now?'

'No,' she wailed. 'He just kept slowing down when I did, so I crossed the road like you told me to, and then he crossed after me, so I crossed again and then I speeded up and he speeded up too—'

'Okay. It's okay darling. Where is he now? Is he in the shop? Let me speak to the shopkeeper.'

'No, no he's not here. I think he's waiting . . .'

'Right, stay there, you here me? Do *not* go back outside, I'm coming to get you, okay? I'm coming for you right now.'

'What?' she heard Laura say. 'No, I don't want to buy anything. My mum says I've to—'

'Laura! Laura – you stay in the shop, you hear?'

The line went dead. Straight to answerphone when she redialled.

Anna clambered back into the car, stalled it. Fingers numb, stalled it again. Gripped the wheel, forcing blood back into her hands, and started the engine on the third attempt. Galletly wouldn't attack a child in broad daylight, he was goading her, that was all, showing her the awful power of what he might do if she didn't stop him. Was that what he wanted? Did he want her to confront him, was that where all this was heading? At this moment, she could kill him. Could hold his neck in her hands, pressing, pressing until the Adam's apple popped beneath her thumbs and his eyes were bulging, bloodshot. No matter how he begged, she would be deaf, consumed with nothing but the strength and necessity of her hands round his neck. Just like a real killer. Like him.

She couldn't see the road properly, there was a sticky gauze on it, on her windscreen, her hands. Her mobile again, urging her to *showmewhatyagot*.

'Laura! I couldn't get through—'

'Where are you Mum?' Her breath was ragged.

'I'm just at the lights.'

'Go back, go back. I'm nearly home.'

'Where's the man?'

'I don't know, he came into the shop and I ran away—'

'What road are you on?'

'Bottom of our street, I'm okay, I'm—'

Then there was an intake. A scream, kind of polite, stilted scream you would expect from a well-brought-up girl. Anna mounted the pavement as she wheeled the car round, blasting her horn at a gaggle of school kids, could see green leaves, a privet hedge, the car tearing a chunk from it and she had a vibrant image of spinach in your teeth, that is how the front grille would be. She maintained her speed, kept going. Could see the square church tower of this street, and the houses of the next, speeding into the next again, which was theirs.

Could see her Laura running.

She could see Laura running and a man running, close behind. Gaining on her, this whippet-man.

Galletly.

She tried to block him with her car, up on the kerb, but he'd already gone past, Anna screeching at someone to phone the police, to stop him as she struck the low wall of her neighbour's front garden, the impetus of the vehicle lifting her up, the whole front end of the car up, so it was resting and rocking, just the tip of it, on the wall. She got out, the seatbelt tangling with the stupid clip that held it down round her pregnant belly and she tried to run, she really did but it was like being paralysed. Her legs did not know what to do, and it was Laura coming back for her, holding her, weeping as their neighbour came running out and then another girl was helping Anna, holding her up. The girl smelled sour, her jacket half off. She was talking to Laura. 'He didn't hurt you?' Over and over, repeated like a charm. 'I was watching, you were okay. He didn't hurt you.'

The girl turned, and Anna realised her jacket only had one arm. She tugged Laura away. This was not a schoolfriend.

'Who are you? Do you know the man who was chasing her?'

Galletly had vanished, as had Anna's neighbour. Anna couldn't let go of Laura, must be crushing her head, she was holding her so tight. The girl opened her mouth, then blinked. Her pupils swelled; it was as if she'd recognised Anna. 'No,' she mumbled.

'Who are you? Why were you watching my daughter?'

Laura pushed her face deeper into Anna's shoulder. 'Mum, just leave it, please. Can we just go into the house? I just want to go into the house.'

'Okay. Come on now. Let's get you inside.'

The girl started to walk away. Anna could feel Laura shuddering, she was in shock. Skin bleached in the bright, pale sun. She stroked her daughter's back, led her towards the house and the steaming, rocking car.

'*Mum*. Did you crash the car?'

'Och, it's just a wee scratch. What about you, did that man touch you?'

'No, well, yes. He jagged me.'

'Jagged you?' Immediately, Anna thought of needles and infections. 'Where? Let me see?'

'On my chest, I think.'

'That's him away!' Anna's neighbour hailed them from the end of the street. The poor soul was bent forward, hands on his retired accountant's knees. Wheezing. Anna waited for him to catch them up. 'He's gone. Jumped in the . . . back of a car. I tried to get the number, but . . . the plate was filthy.'

'Oh, thanks Roger. Thank you so much for coming out—'

'And I called the police.'

'You did? Oh, there's no need. Really. I mean, the guy will be long gone.'

'Mum, he was horrible. He had these horrible mad eyes. What if he goes after someone else – oh!' Laura yelped, moved the lapel of her blazer. 'Look. That's how he jagged me.'

Pinned to her chest was a small metal star. Six points of gold hanging from a blue-striped ribbon.

Chapter Forty-Five

Back on the train and into the city. The carriage smelled of damp fur, which was interesting as there were neither dogs nor rain in the vicinity. Then Mary wondered if it might be her. She had a wee sniff, but it was hard to tell. Your smells were like your breath, just part of the general miasma that you walked through every day. Like your aura, she supposed, or your personality even; it was unrecognisable to you, but immediately quantifiable to others – *she smells of dead sheep, he is a grumpy bastard, she's definitely purple.* If Mary could properly read auras, which she couldn't really do, but, like spotting ghosts, it appealed to her sense of the dramatic – but, if her instincts were right, then that policewoman would be red.

At one of the drugs dosses she had hung about in, another squatter called Saira had told her the basic colours to look out for (Mary, nodding earnestly as the room turned violent bursting orange, had managed to retain the information; it had infiltrated her consciousness precisely because she was having a colour-rush at the time, and had stayed with her). It had become a synaesthetic first-impression game she played. Often, when you got to know the person, it turned out you had been right. Yellow was inspiration, intelligence and the spleen (Mary wasn't very sure what a spleen was); green was growth and change and lungs, blue was calm and throats, while red was the densest colour of all. Saira said it created the most friction, attracting worry and obsessions. Unforgiveness too. In a good, bright state, red energy could serve as a healthy ego, but this woman's colours were all churned. She made Mary feel really sad. There might have been a touch of black in there as well. Black consumed light; Saira said it indicated past life hurts. It was odd that Mary thought of this when the policewoman was such a pale, glimmering creature, but she had.

It had taken her a while to assemble all the pieces, but she thought she had it now. It was the policewoman's face that framed everything, her wide arched brows and her stern milk-skin. Seeing her in two sharp slaps like that – first coming out of the police station and then chasing after the Irish guy, had lured Mary to the edge of her memory again, the way it had when she was outside the police station before, and thinking about how there was a recent something Bernie had said or done. Only this time it had taken her further, because she could quite clearly recall Bernie, all of them, watching the telly. Calling Fiona and Jess in from the fields to *come and see* because someone had blown up Glasgow Airport. You couldn't believe it, it was so alien, the thought of terrorism, of true, pure murderous intent in with the Sock Shop and the queues and the overpriced coffees, so you'd be looking for something familiar, to make you feel better. Bernie must have found it, because she'd shouted out: *Oh! I know her!* when this policewoman had appeared on screen, telling the reporters that there was nothing to tell. Fiona had asked *how do you know her?* in a slightly jealous way – and Mary had noticed that the policewoman was blonde and sharp and striking, in the way that you would admire anything beautiful – and Bernie had reddened, which only made things worse.

It was the same woman Mary had seen today. A fatter version, but it was her.

She had to be the person Bernie went to see before she died. Why else would the Irish man be snooping round; why else would Fat Bastard be watching the police station? Between the two of them, they had sussed out where the policewoman lived, and were evidently not about to send her flowers. Mary had been careful to keep her distance as she followed the Irish one out of the station – they'd never made it to Neilston, alighting instead at Langside – but, even viewed from across the street, there had been a shine on him as bright as a warning beacon, a greasy shine of anger that permeated his stomping walk, the way in which he wrenched open the door of the newsagent's, the leering as he lunged at that young girl. His aura was haywire, dense greys and blacks galore. He scared the shit out of Mary, far more than the fat one did. And *he* had been bad enough, all that sweaty panting in the library. She tried to imagine how Bernie must have felt, seeing the Irish man's face, maybe both of them, as they had leered over her, stripped her of her clothes.

The paper said she'd been found naked. Mary's eyes had attempted to skirt over that, before it fully registered in her brain, but the dark imprint had already slipped in, and there it remained. Pulsing.

Mary had never seen Bernie naked, but she'd seen her breasts once, purely by accident. Bernie had been washing at the pump in the stableyard, just wheeched off her top so she could scrub right up past her elbows. She must have thought she was alone, but Mary had been in her room, up at the window. Bernie didn't wear a bra, her breasts were small and pointed like the rest of her. It hadn't been sexy at all. Jolly was the word that came to mind. Bernie had been jolly, whistling and scrubbing while her tits bobbled freely in the air, nips like wee pom-poms. A small, power-packed woman who was laughing as the drops of water struck her breasts.

All that life, just taken.

Maybe that policewoman could have helped her. That's what they tell you, when you're wee. A bad man's chasing you? Go straight and tell the police. Mary was sure now, that's what Bernie had been doing; not blackmailing at all, but looking for help, and she'd gone to someone that she'd known from before. Someone she'd trusted? But that policewoman was scared too. Mary could taste fear. It visited her frequently; she knew all its different flavours. And this woman's fear of the Irish man was even stronger than Mary's. Which gave Mary an advantage.

The wires in her brain began to sparkle, ignited by how smart she was – she may look scabby, but she was *really* smart – and the rush of possibilities felt like drugs. Oh. Oh. For a long lovely moment she was high on life, until she asked the lady opposite her if she possibly had a pen Mary could borrow, and the lady got up and moved away.

Ha. But the silly bitch had left her raincoat behind on the seat. Mary hooked the belt with her toecap and drew it under the table towards her. *Cheers for the coat dear,* she didn't say. She would find a pen somewhere else.

Chapter Forty-Six

A gentle puckering of rain on the windscreen. Soft Highland rain, the type that kept the midgies away and made the earth smell sweet. Rob insisted on having a window slightly open, and what could Anna say, since she'd dragged him up here in the first place? In the distance, all you could make out was the low wide sky, then a loch, then the supple arc of a bridge reflected, then the bridge itself, three graceful arches leading to a jumble of four-square towers and tiny turrets.

'It's like Disney,' said Laura from the back.

'No. Disney's like it,' said Anna.

'Whatever. Oh – hey! Wait! Is that the castle from *Highlander*?'

Rob turned down the radio. 'Think so. Eilean Donan. It's beautiful, isn't it? Wasn't this a good idea of your mum's, to get away?'

'No.'

'But you're missing a day of school.'

'So?'

Anna laid her hand on Rob's knee, squeezed it. He'd been gamely chipping away since Crianlarich. There was a party on back home tonight, and it was all Laura cared about, so she said. Being attacked, being followed by a stranger and interviewed by the police, she had apparently shaken it off the way Donna used to dry her fur. That was yesterday. Today was today and the party was all. She had begged and fought to be allowed to go.

'No,' Anna had insisted. 'Your dad and I've talked about it. We really think after what happened yesterday, we all need a little break—'

Just give me one day, two at best. A place apart where we can be a family in a bubble. It'll be our calm before the storm. Breathing you both in, taking you somewhere safe and painting it in my head.

If this were a thriller, Anna would be upping the ante about now. These quick, vicious twists would have corkscrewed her hard, the rubber-band momentum sending her snapping after Galletly with the fiery sword of truth and a Magnum .45. Instead, she was running away. Anna's pace, her tone, it was all wrong. Everything was wrong. She felt dull and lumpen and dead.

Laura was unconvinced by Anna's logic. 'Why? D'you think that man is going to come back? You told the police you didn't know him.'

'I *don't* know him. I just think that in the circumstances, I . . . well, we all got a bit of a fright, and it would be good to just have a couple of days up north, that's all. Away from everything.'

'Up north?' she'd shouted. 'What the hell does up north mean? You mean sheep and cowpats and rain? Dawn's got her big cousin DJ'ing for her and—'

'Is Ross going?'

Rob had smiled it out, in his steady, calm way. Fondly mocking like he did with Anna when she was being silly or secretive. Rather, like he used to, before she closed off to him and pretended she couldn't see the unsure hurt, and how he was trying too hard all the time. Anyway, it had got worse. At Ross's name, Laura had erupted, calling Anna for everything – a betrayer, a wrecker of homes. The three of them had had a huge row, which ended with Rob threatening to cancel Laura's school trip to France if Laura did not SHUT UP, apologise and get in the bloody car right now.

Two out of three wasn't bad.

Anna suspected Laura's party offered the same kind of escape as this fleeing up north did for Anna. She closed her eyes, drifting with the folksy music Rob was humming to. He'd had to arrange cover at work, so they hadn't left Glasgow until the foggy afternoon,

Anna staring into the mist, arms wide as a mother hen's as she clucked them all into the car. Then checking and rechecking in the mirror as if the act in itself was talismanic. But they had gone nearly two hundred miles now, for Godsake.

She had called Mrs Reekie last night, after the police had gone, and she'd been given assurances that they'd speak to Corporate Communications, to ensure nothing would be reported.

'Just with me being a cop and all, guys. Don't want the neds to know my business – might give them all ideas!' Assuming they were all pals thegither, not pulling rank at all. 'You know how it is.'

'Sure, ma'am. No problems. But do you think it might have been someone you've jailed or had dealings with?'

'No idea. Certainly never seen the face before. Plus he was following my daughter, not me. Who knows. Only sorry I didn't get a closer look.'

Initially, she had phoned Mrs Reekie to apprise her, give her the Anna version before she read the cop's report that would surely wing its way to her by morning. But the soft sympathy, the cradling voice had made all her pain suddenly unbearable. Anna knew she couldn't go on.

'Ma'am. I really feel we need to get away for a couple of days. Would that be okay? If I took tomorrow off, maybe Monday too, that would give us a long weekend.'

'Of course. Anna, I've telt you before that you should be easing up. Maybe thinking about starting your maternity leave sooner rather than later?'

'Yeah, maybe.'

Just two days of nothing first. Enough to fill herself up again, so she was strong enough to write her resignation, to plan out exactly what she would say to Alex, and Rob. To think how she could protect her family from the aftermath of shame and loss and jail. Christ, she remembered visiting Jamie Worth in prison, the horrible, damp feel of pity then relief as the door clanged shut and she savoured the walking out to unbounded air.

Galletly had won.

'Oh here, just the one thing,' Mrs Reekie was saying. 'Did you get all that Commonwealth canal stuff sorted? You know, the route assessment? Mind the thing's on Sunday night.'

'Yeah, yeah. That's all away. Sorry – did you not get a copy?'

'Aye, I got a copy of the pro forma you sent to Force Operations, but I'm assuming there's a fuller brief somewhere too?'

'Oh yes, of course. It's all with Force Ops, don't worry.'

'Good lass. And I got the poem too. Is it meant to be funny, d'you think?'

'The one about shopping? Yes, I definitely think it's meant to be funny. How? Did you not like it?'

'Och, poetry's no my cup of tea, dear, specially the stuff that disny rhyme. But I'm sure it's fine. Now you take care of yourself, you hear? Total relaxation for a couple of days, because once that bairn arrives, you'll no know your days fae night, and that's the truth.'

'Thanks ma'am. I'll see you Tuesday, okay?'

'Fine. You take it easy, lass.'

After speaking to Mrs Reekie, Anna had pressed the 'off' button on her mobile, had pressed it firmly because she did not plan to turn it on again until after the weekend. She had intended leaving it behind in Glasgow. Shoved it in the drawer in the hall table, slammed the front door shut and got into the car. Alice was yowling, ears down and fangs bared. One incisor could be seen protruding through the gap in her travel basket. It was a wicker one, and they'd had to use fusewire to repair the damage her teeth had made the last time she'd been in it. Happy Alice was off to her Auntie Elaine's, Auntie Liz being unavailable.

I mean, a walking holiday in Portugal? In November?

'It's southern Portugal,' Rob had said. 'And who knows – she might make some new friends.' 'Or walk off a cliff,' said Anna. Then Laura had shouted 'Ugh! Oh God, Alice is peeing! Oh God, it stinks!', so they'd all to get out again, Anna going back to the house to get some baby wipes and a clean blanket. 'And the Febreze!' bawled Laura. In the hall, by the door, as Anna was returning to the car, a shadow passed through her. It came from nowhere, left just as quickly, but she had taken the phone back out of the drawer. It was in her pocket now, but it was still off – unlike Laura's which seemed to be twinging and trilling every few minutes.

'Laura – are you glued to that thing?'

'For God's sake. Can we put on Jay-Z or something?' said the moaner in the back.

'No,' said Rob. 'This is nice.' His left hand reached out, trailed through Anna's hair. 'This is nice, isn't it?'

'Yes.'

'Yay! More sheep. God this is *so* boring. Are we nearly there yet?'

'Nearly.'

'I'm hungry.'

Chapter Forty-Seven

'Fish supper, boss?'

Alex looked up. Doodling on his notes; it was meant to be a cormorant, but had turned into a man-o'-war, with big guns pointing at him. Or possibly a sunset, dangling from a coat hanger? The draw of vinegar tugged him from his masterpiece.

'Mandy, you are a star.'

'I know.'

He fumbled for his wallet. 'How much do I owe you?'

'My treat.'

Hot paper curling, sweet and savoury mingling. 'Och away. Can't have you fetching and paying for it.' The smell was distracting.

'Amount of ovvies I'm raking in, I think I can afford a fish supper, sir.' Her bangles jangled as she put the parcel in front of him. 'Your wife will have forgotten what you look like. I don't think you've made it home once for dinner this week.'

'Ach, no difference from any of the rest of yous.'

'Yeah, but you're the one holding it all together, eh? That must be a strain.'

What exactly was he holding, though? A few tattered strings and a sense of impending doom.

She pulled out a chair. 'I mean, I know on paper we're kind of—'

'Up shit creek?'

'No! No way. We've got the clothing now, we should get the results back from that any time, we've got a witness seeing the green Ford—'

'Aye, a witness who also sees little green men and pink elephants—'

'DS Morrison is out doing the last of the registered keepers as we speak.'

'But what then, Mandy?' His chin in his fists, knuckles rubbing on his lips. 'When they all come back negative, and we find out there are no definitive traces of DNA on Francine's clothing and we accept that we have no further witnesses coming forward – despite that bloody re-enactment—'

'Look, I'm really sorry about that, sir.'

Mandy, posing as Francine, had picked her way along Maryhill Road and on to a number forty bus, pursued by a film crew and several reporters. Sitting primly in her seat on the upper deck, camera rolling over the dark ponytail and khaki jacket, a brace of neds up the back had begun to catcall.

'Ho doll – you a film star?'

'Can I get your autograph, gorgeous?'

Ignored, they had come closer and closer down the aisle until one was almost sitting in Mandy's lap. The other had bent over and in a swift move that belied his shambolic languor, had dropped his kegs, mooning full view into the camera. Whereupon Mandy had dived in front of her PR minder and promptly arrested him for indecent exposure.

'No, no you did the right thing, Mandy. Really. It's my fault, I didny think. We should have hired a bus, not just jumped on an in-service one.'

'Well, it *did* probably get it bumped further up the news . . .'

'Yeah. And we'll probably get to appear on one of those "Cops do the Silliest Things" shows . . .'

'That's the spirit.'

Unbidden, Mandy stole a chip from his dinner. Which, as she'd paid for it, seemed only fair. 'Here,' she said, tossing him a newspaper. 'Brought you an *Evening Times* too. Now, is it okay if I head off home?'

'I *knew* there was an ulterior motive for being nice to me.'

'Really?' She blinked baby-doll lashes. 'You think?'

He was too tired to flirt. 'Ach, away and bugger off. Leave me to my chips. I'm going to wait till Ian gets back anyway.'

'Night then, boss.'

'Night, Mandy.'

Alex bent his elbows, pushed his chair away from the desk so he could stretch out his legs. Stuff it, so he could sling them up on the desk. Nobody else was here. He balanced the open fish supper on his chest, but it was roasting. He lifted it up again, opened out the *Evening Times* to lie on him like a bib, then put the food on top. Reclined once more. Six thirty, Friday night. Mind when Friday night was your going-out night? No matter what, even if you were early shift the next day, Friday was your safety valve, your get-pished, get-laid guarantee. Alex tugged the ringpull on a can of Coke, the angry little *phzzt* coming out like a last breath. He probably could go home, it didny look like Forensics would be coming across now. That bastard Ian had probably sloped off home and all.

He pressed a chip into the roof of his mouth, the warm burst of it bland and filling. Idly flicked through the *Times* as he ate, one greasy hand turning the page as the other raised and lowered the packet of food. An excellent system, until your phone rings and you have no third hand.

He wiped his right hand on his trousers. They were due a wash.

'Y'ello.'

'You sound chirpy.'

'Alright Shirlster? Nah, think I may be in the early stages of mania. What's up?'

'Well, as you know, Pitt Street is on my way home.'

'No it's not.'

'Don't interrupt. And there's a lovely wee forensic scientist called Gilbert who's aye telling me I should just pop in . . .'

Alex recognised the trill in her voice. He sat forwards. 'And?'

'And they were just finishing off the report on Francine Gallagher's clothing. Gilbert tells me it would get typed up on Monday, probably come to us on Tuesday . . .'

'And, and, and?'

'Don't you just love deoxyribonucleic acid?'

'Shirley. For fucksake, stop arsing about.'

Deoxyribonucleic acid was the Sunday name for DNA, the genetic material found in the nucleus of every living cell, and the magic bullet that the world thought meant the good guys always win. But use of DNA evidence relies, firstly on having two distinct samples to compare – the reference (or known suspect's) sample and the crime scene sample – and secondly, on the principle that, if there is a match between these two, then the probability of these samples *not* coming from the same individual is more than one billion to one. Until now, Alex had neither sample nor suspect, just a bundle of dirty clothes.

He could hear Shirley snort. Was she laughing at him, or doing something unmentionable with poor Gilbert? 'We have ourselves a reference sample!' she said. 'A human one this time – not bloody animal skin. We've got a shred of fingernail inside the pants, and some hairs that aren't Francine's. These samples also correlate to material taken from under her fingernails—'

'Fuck me. Mary McLennan right enough?'

'No. They've analysed this material again – it's showing two separate DNA strands – the one from Mary which we know about already; the other is the same as what's on Francine's clothing.'

Alex tried to stay calm, but the adrenalin was demanding that his heart speed up, that the muscles in his forearms flex until the blood was effervescent. Up and down like a hoor's bloody drawers – this job was not good for your health. Exhilarating, but insane. 'Okay, I need that sample checked against the DNA database. Now! I don't care how long it takes – all weekend if necessary. And I want both databases done simultaneously; here and down south. Christ, I thought Hayley had asked for this all to be hurried up?'

'She had – *boot* that she is – and they already did. They've done five repeats actually, and we have a match on all STRs. Our man is one Mark John Galletly.'

Galletly. Where had Alex heard that name before?

'On file for what?'

'Serious assault, usury, extortion, firearms offences – and murder. Released from jail same day Francine was killed.'

Gah. It was a curved, harsh sound. It said *getaway, get off;* the whole name had a sneer to it, he could hear it, sharp and rapid rat-a-tat, coming from a machine-gun mouth. Fish eyes and stars on his fingers.

'Irish? FTP tatts on his fingers? And wee stars, like asterisks?'

'Oh, *now* you know him. Well you bloody well should, because he was very active in A Division at one time—'

'He's the guy that killed old Ezra Wajerski.'

'Um . . . wait a minute and I'll check the name.'

'No need. He's also the guy we jailed for slashing hoors.'

'Yes! That's what's so perfect about this – it holds out your theory about someone from Francine's past. She must have been involved in the loan-sharking. Maybe helped herself to some of the proceeds?'

'Who knows. What address was Galletly released to?'

'He's a sister in Carlisle. I'll text you the address.'

'Find out if he's had any social work supervision there since his release.'

'Oh, Alex. Now?'

'Yes, now. Is there a problem?'

'Mmhm.' She was whispering, mouthpiece so close to her face that the words rumbled. 'I'm going for a drink with Gilbert.'

'You dirty wee besom.'

God love her. Shirley deserved a break. And for someone to lie on those big floury breasts. Alex scratched the back of his neck. Was Gilbert the one with the splay of grey hair or the skinny bald one? Christ, she'd smother him.

'Okay then, in the circumstances, I think I can allow it. You just leave it with your Uncle Alex. And don't you be going all the way on a first date, you hear?'

'What. Like you, you mean?'

'*Love* you.'

'Love you more.'

Alex tossed a handful of chips into his mouth, raised his Coke can to the sky.

'I thank you.'

The chips were minging, gone cold and coated with lard. He bundled them up for the bin, the newspaper with it. No time for the Quickie Crossword now. Shook his Coke can; only a mouthful left. He bent it in half. A blurry headline caught his attention, or maybe it was the notion first, the notion and the slicing motion of his hand above the headline and then the headline, because as he was bundling he was thinking *where is Anna in all of this*, and of course, she was slap-fucking-bang in the middle, the way she always was.

Pregnant Cop attacked at Home
Exclusive, by Lucy Manning

Police are searching for a man who attacked a pregnant policewoman and her daughter in broad daylight in a quiet Glasgow suburb yesterday afternoon. Residents of Monreith Road in Newlands were shocked to witness what appeared to be a car crash and then a scuffle between the females and a male, who is described as being forty to forty-five years old, small, of slim build and wearing a dark-coloured jacket. It's believed the male fled the scene in a green-coloured motor car, driven by an accomplice. Police are refusing to comment on the incident, or name the forty-two-year-old woman involved, but it's understood that she's a senior officer, based in Glasgow City Centre.

A green-coloured car. A small, thin man. The blood in his veins stretched thin and furious. Aye, Alex's instincts were as true and trusting as ever. Anna Cameron had been protecting someone. Herself. It was no more than he'd expected, really. Had known, in the centre of him. He flung his Coke can at the bin, and missed. Spilling brown arcs, the tin folded like a muzzle, chattering mirthlessly on uncarpeted floor.

Chapter Forty-Eight

Plockton was the quiet lap of water, the bright tang of kelp. And, in this warm northwest pocket of Scotland, it was real palm trees, susurrating their foliage in the Gulf Stream breeze while raucous gulls berated the sea. Anna could taste the ozone; salt sloughing off the coating on her tongue.

'Good choice then?' Rob took her hand.

'Rob, it's beautiful.'

Rob used to come here as a child; his gran was from Kyle of Lochalsh – five minutes away, but not so pretty. Plockton's main street was an ellipse of white cottages curved round a sea loch, which was peaty brown and heather-coloured and deepest teal, depending on which way the wind was blowing, or how the angle of lambent light flashed colours in with the bobbing otter heads and the fat wash of seals. She breathed in again. This place was perfect. With the water and the hills sheltering the village, it felt safe as well as beautiful.

'Anyone hungry yet?' asked Rob.

They'd already earmarked three different seafood places for lunch. Last night it had been dark when they arrived, and Anna was too knackered to do anything but flop on the bed with a bag of chips Rob had brought in, and the 'wee cup of tea' their landlady, Mrs Anderson, had made for her.

'I'm still stuffed after breakfast.'

'Oh, look, Dad! Look at the wee baby coo!' Even Laura was thawing to the charms of Plockton, albeit she'd checked her phone ten times already for an update on last night's party.

Highland cows wandered freely through the village, grazing on the wide expanse of tussocked shore when the tide went out. Up close, they were big-horned beasts, but amiable ones, content to let the world pass them by as they chewed and blinked and rubbed their tangled orange backs against things – mostly walls, although one had tried to get up close and personal with Anna's midriff. *It's the hormones*, Rob had said. Mine or hers? thought Anna.

'Well, why don't we skip lunch and go for a nice walk instead? I mean, it's really mild,' said Rob.

'A nice walk? To where?'

'I dunno – the hills?'

Laura's mouth fell open. '*Hills*? And what's gonny be up the hills exactly?'

'It's "going to", not gonny.'

'Hi Laura.'

'Hi Laura.' A cluster of youngsters went by, one girl about Laura's age; the other two girls and a little boy much younger.

'Hiya.'

'Who's that? asked Anna as they trailed into the café-cum-sweetshop on the harbour.

'Just some kids. The one in the blue jumper's Rhona. Mrs Anderson's her gran. I was talking to her last night in the residents' lounge, after you two went to bed. At bloody eight o'clock.'

'It was *not* eight o'clock, you.'

Laura waggled loose fingers at the side of her mouth. 'Talk to the hand, Mother dearest. So how far will we get on this walk then, d'you reckon Dad? With superfast pumpkin lady here?'

'Quit it. Your mum can walk for miles, can't you?'

Anna eyed up the hill he'd been staring at. 'On a straight road, maybe. To be honest, I'm not too sure about hills. Especially when they're really mountains.'

'Okay. Well, what about a nice drive—'

'Oh God,' said Laura. 'We *drove* all day yesterday.'

'Yeah, but we could go to Applecross. The road there's amazing – you've got to zigzag up over mountains, it's really steep.'

'Like a country-bumpkin rollercoaster?'

'Kind of,' Rob said, excited that he'd captured her imagination. Laura examined a strand of her hair. 'Nah. You're alright.'

'I quite fancy that, Laura,' said Anna. 'And there's a really good pub at Applecross, I was reading the wee tourist brochure in the room. We could make a day of it, have our tea there.'

'Are your stomachs all you two think about?'

Anna glanced down ruefully. 'Canny really think about much else at the moment.'

'You're fun-nee. And it's cannot, not *canny*.'

'Hi Laura.' The posse of kids traipsed past again, most of them munching on crisps or chocolate. The older one, Rhona, held back. She smiled shyly at Laura. 'Thanks for that download, it was really good.'

'Cool.'

'You can come round to mine some time if you like, and I'll show you that book I was talking about.'

'Excellent.'

'Well . . . do you want to come today? You could come to the ceilidh with us after? Not with that lot,' Rhona indicated the chomping children, one of whom – the little boy – was swinging a tin bucket at his companions, globs of wet brown sand flying everywhere. 'I mean with me and my mates.'

'Yeah! I'd – oh, no I can't. I'm being kidnapped and taken to Apple Crumble.'

'It's Applecross, Laura.' Anna smiled at the girl. 'Hiya. I'm Anna. This is Laura's dad . . .'

Rhona wrinkled her nose. 'Why? There's nothing to do in Applecross.'

'Exactly.'

'Well, why don't you come rock-pooling with us.' Rhona gestured again to her entourage. The taller of the two girls broke away from the group and came over.

'Rhona, gonny hurry up?' She had a very earnest face, it scowled at Anna from under dark curls.

'They're just kids really,' said Rhona, 'but sometimes Michael—'

'Fisherboy Michael?' said Laura.

'Yeah.' They both giggled.

The younger girl elbowed her way in between them. 'Hey, don't say I'm a kid, Rhona Anderson. I'm not a kid. I'm nearly the same age as you.'

'Eilidh, you're *nine.*'

'Yeah, well I'm nearly as big as you.'

'Oh, *you're* Eilidh,' said Laura. 'Rhona says you're the smartest girl in Plockton.'

The child turned her scowl on Laura. 'You at the wind up?'

It was a singularly Glaswegian thing to say. Anna bit on her tongue; it wouldn't do to laugh at such a serious little girl. Who knew where she might deposit her bucket and spade? Who were all these people Laura had insinuated herself with, in less than twenty-four hours? At her age, Anna had been a timid wisp, blending as hard as she could into thin air, keeping speech to the bare minimum. Rhona ignored the younger girl, turned to Anna. 'Laura could have her tea with us after – my gran wouldn't mind.'

'*Please,* Mum. Go on. I'll be fine. You and Dad can go Applesauce and snog all afternoon if you like—'

'Laura!'

The three girls burst out laughing.

'Och, why not Anna?' Rob put his arm round her. 'Get some peace from moaning Minnie here.'

'I don't know – where is the ceilidh? When does it finish?'

'It's in the Plockton Inn, just there, see.' Rhona pointed at a whitewashed building with black paintwork and baskets full of small bright chrysanthemums. 'See. Two minutes from the house. You could come in when you get back – it's on till midnight.'

'Oh, we won't be that late, don't worry. There's only so much snogging I can do in one day.'

'*Mum!*'

She touched Laura's hair. 'As long as Mrs Anderson doesn't mind – and I'll check with her before we go, right?'

'Okay.' Laura reached up, gave her an unexpected kiss. 'Thank you.'

By the time they'd found Mrs Anderson – *oh, it would be a pleasure. She's a bonny lass. A bonny lass. I'll keep an eye on her, never you worry*, picked up the guidebook – *a wee flask of tea for the journey, dear?* – the walking boots – *fruit cake? I've wrapped it up in tinfoil, so it should stay warm for a bitty yet* – met Rhona's mum – *oh you're from Glasgow? I was a student in Glasgow* – approved the outfit Laura was planning to wear, gone back for a blanket to sit on at the beach, it was another hour at least before they finally set off; Laura and her new best friend waving them a vigorous goodbye.

As soon as they left the gentle bowl of Plockton, Anna began to feel uneasy. 'Are you sure she'll be okay?'

'Relax Anna, she'll be fine. It'll be good for her to have a break from us – we've been virtually sitting on top of her since yesterday.'

'You mean *I* have.'

'Well . . .' He grinned at her. 'Actually, you do seem a lot happier since we came away. More relaxed.'

'I am.'

'Good.'

Anna settled into the padding of her seat, pressing against it like the cows and their walls. The flute of her shoulder blades was an impossible place to reach. She was so taut and tingling now, everywhere: her hands and feet, her thighs and spine, the stretch marks at her groin a literal depiction of how her skin was splitting from the inside out.

'You okay?'

'Uh huh.'

'You need the loo?'

'*No.*'

'Good, because once we're on this road I'm not turning back. We're talking two thousand feet above sea level you know, and the Bealach just gets steeper and narrower and twistier all the way. I don't actually think you can turn back.'

'I don't need the toilet.'

Of course, now that he'd mentioned it, she did. They began to climb higher and higher, the earth spinning dizzily in whorls of green and brown. The car, a Mercedes, was too genteel for this terrain – she grumbled and wheezed her way onwards, the ground gritting through her elegant tyres. Anna began to feel sick. She kicked off her mules, closed her eyes. With the rocking of the car, and perhaps the vast light freedom of being so far from home, she must have dozed off.

A serrated drilling noise woke her. Rob was navigating a cattle-grid, the shudder of it juddering bone no matter how slow or fast you went over.

'Sorry. Alright you two? Did I wake you?'

'Mmhm. Wasn't asleep.'

'Oh really? So you snore when you're wide awake then?'

'I do not snore!'

'Yes you do. Like a big pink pig. No wonder that poor baby's always awake. Every time you drop off, the wee yin must think there's an avalanche coming.'

'You're not funny.'

Anna shook the hair from her face, straightened herself up. She could see a vista of blue water to her right, rolling grass and stone dykes to her left. Below them, the road swept downwards. It was an incline, yes, but a long swift ribbon, not the hairpin bends she'd been expecting. 'I thought this was a massive mountain pass?'

'It was. But you missed it.'

'You're joking.' She looked at her watch. She'd been asleep for nearly an hour. 'Shit.'

'Don't worry – you'll see it all again on the way home.'

'Sorry.'

She'd left him to navigate the treachery on his own. He'd been driving and swinging, cursing maybe, swallowing hard and keeping her safe while she'd not even bothered watching him do it. He'd wanted to show off to her this mountain road, to tell her why it was called the pass of the cows or the hill of the ospreys or whatever – and the difference between them was, Anna would have woken him up. She would have felt baleful and cheated and insisted that he share.

'Sorry? What for? For sleeping? Anna, you've not slept that well in weeks.'

'I know. I feel great actually.' She loosened her neck, easing it from left to right. Kept the stretch, staring at Rob's profile, at his nose, which was perfectly fine and straight. She looked at his chin and the darkness of his skin, how it was pale, then ran dark underneath the way peaty water is light and deep. And she loved him for it.

'How do you know I've not been sleeping?'

'Because I lie beside you every night?'

They drove on. In the distance, across the bay, the dark mass of the Cullins glittered. Someone, the laird or clan chief or whatever had tried to sell them not so long ago. *Come and purchase your ain wee bit of Scotland. Buy two hills – get one free!* It was absurd to think of owning a mountain; it was like people who bought and sold stars or chunks of the moon. And it was worse still to talk about transferring that ownership; a mountain range wasn't like London Bridge that you could dismantle and rebuild piece by piece in America. A clan chieftain was supposed to be a guardian of his land and of his people, not a shopkeeper. Although it wasn't a modern phenomenon – you only had to count the number of sheep versus people for evidence of the original big clearance sale, a legacy that lived on in the empty stretches and rubble cairns littering the land. Imagine being made to leave this place for the cramped squalor of Glasgow, where they spoke foreign words at you, made you swap your hard-digging, plain-fed tiredness for lice and emphysema.

Rob rested his hand on Anna's belly. Casual, proprietorial.

'So. Are you ready to talk to me about it yet?'

The swell of her heart matching her shape. Physically, the distance of a splinter – the thickness of her duvet coat – was all that separated them, but it was a splinter nonetheless, and it had worked its way so far in that it had swelled to an angry sore ridge. It was damaging them apart, Anna knew that. She looked out of the window again, straight into the disc of the sun.

'About what?'

'About why you don't sleep, why you're chasing shadows and look like death?'

'Cheers. I'm meant to be blooming.'

'Anna. Stop it. Please stop pretending, and tell me what's wrong. I'm not an idiot.'

A long funnel of air, compressed through her teeth and tongue. It was the breathing she'd been practising for months, and strangely it did work a bit, the light ripple of it deflating her.

'Okay,' she said eventually.

'Yeah?' His shoulders tensed, like he was steadying himself.

'Once we get there, okay?'

'Okay.'

They continued down the slope, neither speaking, Rob fixed on the road, which was broadening out, wider and flatter as they wound into Applecross, the very road breathing out in an echo of every driver's relief as they made it over the pass.

'How did folk get here before the road was built?'

'Boat.'

Rob manoeuvred the car between a parked camper van on the shore side and a wooden picnic bench and trestle on the grass outside the pub. The road was surprisingly busy with parked cars, but the single street – if you could call it that, when it was really a beach, then a track, then a short row of cottages and the pub – had only three other people in it: hillwalkers with their muted, earthy fleeces, their gaiters and their poles.

'Anna?' He ratcheted the handbrake.

'Mm?'

One of the walkers was trying to retie his boots, but, rather than bend down, he had raised his leg up, stork-like, to rest boot on opposing knee. It looked uncomfortable, he was beginning to sway.

'There isn't someone else, is there?'

The walker was overbalancing, his female companion hurrying over to offer a guiding elbow. Her hat was mauve, and massively bobbled. If it hadn't been for the held-in hurt turning Rob's voice raw, she would have laughed.

'Of course there isn't! Och Rob, don't be so daft!' She made her face go serious. 'I think you've well and truly claimed me.'

'I'm not sure anyone could do that, Anna.'

She tapped her stomach, like a satisfied diner. 'Well you certainly have.'

Ignition off, and with it went the CD player, so that the lovely, lilting music vanished and the beige interior of the Mercedes was full of the dull gleam of him, hurting and being angry, so you couldn't escape it even if you concentrated really hard on the two wobbling walkers and their impatient companion who had stalked on up the path without them. Rob was usually quiet when he was angry, conveniently so if you wanted to pretend you hadn't seen it coming. This was quiet. Just.

'No I haven't, Anna. I only know what you let me know. I don't have a clue what you're thinking most of the time – or even what you're doing.'

'Rob, that's not fair.'

'Yeah?' His voice growing louder. 'Mrs Reekie phoned for you late on Thursday. I sounded like a right tit when I said you were on call. She says you've not been on call for weeks. So what am I meant to think?'

He was hunched in his seat, staring straight ahead, not at her at all. Anna took his hand. 'Let's go for a walk.'

'No.' His mouth was shirred at the edges, like an uneven seam.

'Rob, I promise you; this is all about work, not us. You are the only thing keeping me afloat – you and my unnaturally buoyant belly of course. Come on, please. We've driven all this way. Let's walk.'

His hand withdrawn. A shrug. Anna took that as yes and heaved herself out of the car.

She opened the boot, took out both sets of walking boots, but hers wouldn't go near her swollen feet.

'What was your blood pressure last time?' asked Rob.

'Oh, it was fine. Honestly, it's just because I was sitting all day yesterday.'

'You can't walk in those clogs.'

'Yes I can. They're dead comfy.'

She took his hand again, insisted on it. His fingers cool and steady. Wrapping one by one until they held hers completely.

They were healing hands: Rob's hands would measure the beats of a pulse, or administer a pain-relieving syringe, whilst hers specialised in wielding a great big stick. Yet they both did the same thing. They helped people. Saved them, she supposed. At least, that was the idea.

On to the beach they crunched, a hundred tiny shells shattered and shifting with every step. From the sea, a warm salt breeze reached out to stroke their faces. She let her breath sigh out. It felt good, like she was clearing out her lungs.

'D'you ever think about what you'd do if you had the choice – to be anything at all?'

Rob held her hand up to his lips. 'I'd still choose this.'

'Me too – of course this bit – you and Laura and the bump. But not the rest.'

'You mean your job?' Rob was still doing this eyes-fixed-on-the-horizon thing. 'I've been thinking about that too.'

'You have?'

'Aye, well, it was when I was talking to Mrs Reekie actually.'

'Talking? I thought she was phoning for me.'

'Yes, talking. She suggested that there might be an option for you to go part-time.'

'Bloody hell, Rob, don't mind me. Just you and Auld Reekie sort out my life and let me know when you're done, why don't you?'

'She's a nice woman, Anna. She means well. She also suggested training.'

'What, as in remedial? Thinks I'm that useless, does she? Well, you both do apparently.'

'No,' he said patiently. 'She thinks that you'd be good in training. An excellent role model. Suggested you apply for the super's post at Tulliallan. She said she'd support you all the way.'

'And how would that work, when I had a baby?'

'She reckoned you could commute most days – it's only forty minutes up the road, and you'd be guaranteed regular hours.'

The appeal was instant. Anna would love to go back to training. Books and drill; pure law, unadulterated by the twisting urgency of real life – and all doled out from a genuine castle, too. All those fresh minds to mould. Traditions to implant, standards to sustain. It appealed to the egotistical monster in her. Maybe she could reintroduce crisp white shirts instead of those horrible T-shirts . . . What did not appeal was the sense that she was being worked from behind. All the same, it was nice that she was being looked after. And then a sting as if an elastic band had snapped: Galletly. None of this was going to happen, not with Galletly waiting.

'Christ, can she not make her mind up? I thought the woman wanted me working for the bloody Commonwealth Games?'

'I think she just wants you to be in a place you're happy.'

'Aye, well that wouldn't be the polis at all then, would it?'

'You mean leave altogether? Ach away. Anna, you were born a cop. I bet you came out shouting at the midwife to move things along and reported your mum for a breach because she was swearing. What would you do if you weren't in the police?'

Apart from being in jail? Anna knew exactly what she would do. 'I'd run a craft shop.'

'You would, would you?' he laughed. 'Can't see it myself.'

She let herself enjoy the fantasy. 'Yes I would. I'd be really good at it too. I've thought about it loads. There's an old pub in Eaglesham; it's been lying empty for ages. Well, it wouldn't just be a shop, it would be a kind of arts hub, you know? I'd have a drama workshop, and they could put on wee plays, and we'd have a bookshop, and a café. Not burgers or anything, nice healthy stuff like falafels and smoothies. And there'd be artist studios and exhibitions, poetry readings—'

'And you'd be running all this all by yourself?'

'Oh no, it'd be a collective. We'd have a farmers' market once a month in the beer garden, and wee handicraft stalls, and I could make mosaics. Maybe have local bands playing there at the weekends – I've thought of a name for it too.'

'What?'

'The Craftworks.'

'Like those German electrodudes?'

'Mine would be spelled properly.'

Rob shook his head. 'Do you really want to leave the police that much that you've actually thought of a name for your shop?'

'Yes.'

Oh Rob, she had thought of everything. Two weeks of dark nights and her lying watchful as she travelled every possible exit in her head. 'But it doesn't need to be in Eaglesham. Could we not just leave everything: job, city, the works? I mean, what if we sold the house, came to live in a wee remote place like this? You could be a country doctor – the place is full of old people—'

'Anna, are you serious? What about Laura? What about the Meadows? I can't run it by remote control.'

'Sell that too!'

Was her grin manic or simply fixed? If she hadn't been so cumbersome, she might have skipped at that point. She was growing shrill, like a Noël Coward heroine being terribly, screamingly gay.

'You're just feeling unsettled because you're pregnant. When Amy was . . .' He stopped. 'Sorry.'

'Rob, it's not like I'm jealous of her. You're allowed to talk about Amy.'

'No, I was just going to say that she didn't want to go back to work at all. After Laura was born, I mean. She was a teacher, and she didn't want to spend time with other people's kids at the expense of her own. But after a couple of months, she changed her mind. Wanted to go back. Be a grown-up again, was how she put it. I bet you'll be the same.'

'Why? Are we alike?'

He let go of her hand. 'Wow. That's a question.'

Anna folded her arms around herself; it was windy on the beach. She steeled her body against the incoming breeze, the pushing pull of the water that glazed sand like icing sugar, then rushed away just at the moment you thought it would reach you.

'No,' he said, after two more waves had surged in and out. 'You're not. I love you more.'

Fine salt spray, soaking them both. His arms going round her. She could feel his blood in her breast as he kissed her. Warm lips, cold sea, and the bright sky high and huge.

They walked for ages, quietly on the beach, tracing sand-trails with their toes, him skimming flat stones, then they walked back through the village. He helped her over a stile and they tramped through wire-grass fields, the tight little pellets of rabbit droppings everywhere and he was Rob and he was patient, waiting for her when she fell behind, holding her arm, her elbow, the sore concave of her back. At the top of the hill they had climbed, he put his jacket on the ground; it was a nice one, a kind of taupy-green wool, but they'd forgotten the blanket. Anna lay on her side, in the recovery position. She was knackered. He lay behind her, stomach warming her aching back. Slipped one arm under her, the other on top.

Up here, with the sky only inches from your head, the blue was startling. The tepid wind slapped at them, air like lukewarm soup. She looked down at the bay, to where a heart-shaped mountain became a butterfly, its perfect replication apparently solid in the lightly-frilled, luminous sea.

'You warm enough?' Rob held her belly at the top, where their baby's bum was. The bump was still, tightly packed. Exhausted by all that floating about while her mother was hauling herself up cliffs.

'Mmhm.' Anna snuggled in. 'You should move your arm though. You'll cut off your circulation.'

'Ach, you're worth it.'

She liked that she was facing away from him, it made it easier. She let the wind fill her lungs. A seagull surfed on a downdraught, its perfect grey shadow following it to the water's edge.

'Have you ever done something that you thought was the right thing, but it wasn't? Or, at least, it wasn't your right to do it?'

His breath against her hair. 'I'm a doctor. Of course I have.'

'Okay, so you know what it feels like. You make this decision, you do it quickly, and you do the thing. Then you think, that's that. I stand by my decision, it was made in good faith. Only it isn't.'

His upper hand moved to her breast, fiddling with the toggles on her coat. 'Anna. Quit talking in riddles.'

'Right, stop distracting me then.' She smacked at his hand. 'Just hold me.'

He did as he was told, and she tried to relax into him again. But the fit felt wrong.

'About eight years ago, I was involved in a murder investigation. It was an old man I knew – vaguely, and we thought we'd got the right person for it. An evil little shit, a moneylender who'd been hurting women – I mean carving IOU slips on their faces. But, after he'd been arrested for this murder – and that bit was all kosher, he wasn't fitted up or anything, but afterwards I discovered that someone else might have done it.'

Anna. She closed her eyes, obliterating the sun and the view. It was too stunning to take in for the moment.

'That's shite, actually. I *knew* someone else had done it, a right poor wee soul, who'd had a crap life. But she said it was an accident, and I believed her.' She felt Rob's grip about her slacken. 'I never told anyone, just made her go away. I destroyed the evidence that would link her to the murder, and let the guy we'd charged with it go to court. Then I let him go to jail.'

His hands unlocked. Still hanging there, round her but not clasped, like his body was pausing. When he finally spoke, he didn't sound any different from before; she'd been expecting disgust at least.

'So you decided you were judge and jury?'

'Pretty much.'

'Why?'

'I've just told you why.'

'No, you've told me how it happened. Tell me *why* it did.'

'Because I believed he *would* have killed the old man, it was just that someone else had got there first. I also believed he had, or would kill someone soon, that he was dangerous. And because I hated him.'

She opened her eyes, because if she hadn't she would have been lying not on moss and rabbit droppings, but on the floor of a dank basement, a foot beating through her kidneys.

'He'd attacked me before – kicked the shit out of me, put me in hospital and I still don't know if it was revenge or . . .'

Without sitting up first, Anna tried to turn herself over to face

Rob. Made it as far as getting on to her back. The weight of the baby came after, two maybe three seconds later, suffocating her lungs. If you could imagine a ton of wet sand, dumped on you like a punch, then spreading out across your abdomen, crushing into the gaps between your ribs, holding you fast to the ground. That is what it feels like. That is why a very pregnant woman should never lie flat on her back.

'I'm stuck.'

'Hey, don't cry.' Rob took her shoulder, steered her towards him. The ground held her left side, Rob the right; her legs bent for ballast. She pushed her forehead into the hardness of his chest. Carried on speaking.

'Maybe it was, I don't know . . . but the girl that really did do it – all she did was push the old man away from her, he'd fallen, banged his head. He was a sweet old man, and I didn't want people knowing . . . and she wasn't a bad person, Francine. She deserved a break . . . But it wasn't for me to decide, it was for the courts . . .'

'And who says you *can't* be judge and jury?' Rob lifted her chin up, made her look at him. 'Anna, people like us are expected to make life and death decisions every day; we're supposed to deal with all the broken pieces that everyone else ignores. Why is a judge any more qualified than you, someone who deals with the reality of crime and poverty and perversion every bloody day, to decide what punishment fits what crime?'

'But the man didn't do it, Rob. He didn't. And it's not my job – my job is to report the facts, not make them up. I can't be objective – I wasn't objective.'

'Okay.' He kissed the top of her head. 'But he was a bad bastard, anyway, and you've lived with the guilt all this time. Is this all coming to a head because you're pregnant?'

'No, you don't understand.' She wriggled on to her elbow, higher than him, and it was like she was making herself bigger all round, bigger and braver, all camouflage and inflated girth. But the words, when they came, were tiny.

'He's out of prison.'

'Away. How do you—'

'Robert, I'm telling you. He's been released and he killed that woman they found in Maryhill – that was Francine. And he knows, he fucking knows what I did. The man that was chasing Laura – that was him.'

'Oh Christ.'

Rob sat up. Dropped her like she was toxic. Like the skin of her was burning through him.

'That's why we had to get away.'

'And we've left Laura down there. Alone?'

'Rob – don't be ridiculous. He's not going to follow us all the way up to bloody Plockton, is he?'

'How do you know?' Rob scrabbled to his feet, waving his mobile at the sky. 'Fuck – there's no bloody reception up here. Right, come on.' A rough hand, hauling her up.

'Rob, please. I would never put Laura in any danger. I love her.'

He wasn't listening, driving them on, down the pitfall-strewn slope.

'Rob please. Don't go so fast.'

'And that furore at the swimming baths – was that him too?'

She nodded tearfully. 'I don't know. I think he got someone else to—'

'Jesus Christ, Anna. You, Laura, the baby. What the hell were you thinking?'

'I don't know. I thought it would all just go away.'

'For fucksake woman. I've already lost one wife.'

'Don't swear at me, Rob,' she pleaded. 'You don't swear!'

Half dragged, half walking, she made it down the hill, the scree bouncing up and hitting her knees, pebbles biting inside her clogs. Rob charged on ahead to the stile. He didn't wait for her, just vaulted over and ran towards the car. She held on to the powdery wood of the stile and hoisted her body up. Dust motes in the sunshine, swimming at her, rearing in loops that distorted her vision and made her see black circles where there were none. A trailing fence-wire caught on her foot, threatened to upend her, but she managed to get over, get back on to the ground.

Rob had started the engine, reversed the car in an angry squeal, and she grabbed on to the door handle, part-thinking he would screech off without her. He didn't. Sat there, fingers drumming as she got herself inside.

'Rob please stop it. Please.' Anna began to hiccup. The lurches were in a different place than usual, below her diaphragm. They felt like gentle contractions.

'Put your bloody seatbelt on. And keep phoning Laura.'

She didn't know where her phone was. It had been off since Friday; it was probably still in their room.

'Can I use yours?'

He didn't answer, his hands tight on the wheel, wrist coming at an angle to slam and grind the gearstick. Anna took his phone from the little indent by the handbrake. A resolute, thin bar on the screen, no matter how she shook or positioned it.

'Still no signal.'

'Where were you when you said you were on call then?'

Anna shook her head. 'Don't ask.'

'Don't ask? You mean there's even more shite you haven't told me?'

'Please stop swearing.'

So they didn't speak at all.

The higher up the hill they climbed, the road began to twist more sharply, biting back on itself like the ugliest of serpents. The car clung to narrow, blasted ledges; it was a dragon's back, coarse diamonds of rock and grey-green moss, ascending to the clouds and then dropping, raging, down. Anna bracing herself, left hand splayed against the padded rim where the window met the door.

The interior of the Mercedes was not beige. It was flesh-coloured, the inside of a gloved fist. Anna scared, Rob's face clenched-white, and she wanted him to open up to her, shout at her again. If he clenched himself any tighter, his bones would crack. She could chart the progress of his blood, it was flashing through his temple, the vein up and pumping like a boxer, ticking at the comma-edge of his mouth, the corner where his lips joined in a perfect rising 'c'. It was the shape Anna repeated again and again when she was on the phone or thinking about what to say or bored at a meeting, ccccc all joined in cursive, rolling waves. She had to break the waves.

'Don't you understand, Rob? If what I did comes out, I'll go to jail.'

'Of course I understand. What I don't understand is how you couldn't involve me, couldn't tell me anything. Do you not think I could have helped? Exactly what compartment of your life do Laura and I fit into?'

'You *are* my life—'

'Bullshit. How do you think I feel, Anna, waving you off to work each day, knowing you're carrying our baby and that you could be a walking punchbag for any ned or nutter—'

'I'm behind a desk most of the day.'

'You're not when you're on late turns, or running the city centre plan on a Saturday night or checking the cells . . .' A slash of sun cut through the window. Little flicks of spittle gleamed on his chin. His eyelids glossy. He parted his lips, closed them, keeping whatever he was going to say at bay. Then, finally, he spoke. 'I let you go—'

'You *let* me go?'

'Yes, I let you go, because I assume that you're being careful and keeping your head down and doing everything in your power to keep yourself safe. So how do you think it feels to find out that your whole family's been put at risk, that you've been cheated and lied to—'

'Rob,' she screamed. 'Watch out!'

There is a car on the other side of the road. It has been zigzagging their way for ages; she has seen it vaguely in chinks of rapid light below, and now it is upon them, on the full width of the narrow road. A sudden glimpse of green. Ticker-tape flashing, the green of the speeding car, the dullish, beaten silver of the low crash barrier that is at the side of them, then not. It is below them, or they are above it, in perfect slow movement they are touching the sky she thought they'd left behind. For the vaguest second, it feels like flying, that joyful lurch when your dad goes too fast over the brow of a hill and you leave your tummy at the top, and then . . . it is cold and cracking down your back. An angry dreadful rush, with the sky on the ground and the ground breaking sky. Just breaking and rolling and the green flashing red.

How then, does it feel?

It feels like pushing out your soul, and seeing it face to face.

It begins, for you, in darkness. Then there is pink-orange light and searing pain; it comes on you, unexpected, because you've not been there. You've been walking in the hills, white hills, bleached out like an overexposed photograph, moss springing beneath your feet and your hand in his. Your hand is still in his, that's the second thing you feel, after the pain. The pain is everything, it leaps at you, consumes like fire; it is a slow stretching burn. And the pain is earth, it is fire splitting earth and rock, whole and deep and purposeful. It's in your bowels, an ancient pain, it is air and movement, bubbles of pressure you breathe in and you bear down. The air is blunt, your head is light. Dull drums and roaring, you are swimming somersaults in fluid but the pain never leaves you, and neither does his hand. Your body is a meaty valve, with pistons and bellows, it is *you* that bellows. The breathing and the lowing is primitive.

You feel a hand holding your arm as you try to push up. The pain is opening you and you need to be tall, it's a wave of golden air-filled sand, banking on you, making you rise to meet it. For a moment, his hand loses yours and you're bereft. You sink into the pain, thrashing until his hand finds you again and you're safe. You focus on the air and earth and fire, you ride it; they are letting you move with your body, now your arms drape over scaffold, the springy moss is under your knees and your aching-full pelvis yawns, it cracks and heals. It cracks and heals, cracks and heals and every inch of pain is focused there: it is a driving arrow, it is pincers, it is a deep round scoop.

The pain is breathing you out it is ripping it is stopping and you know, you just know to surrender your autonomy and let your body go. You block out the instructions someone is shouting like a cheerleader and you breathe and let your body push. Your whole body rippling fire. Water bursts, runs down your thighs, you are shitting earth and the air comes in. You ride the air, great weight cracks away as you coil and swoop, warm liver on your legs. You sag. Surprised. Hands guide you and your belly, your dripping stinging self until you can see that you are a domed arch. The urgency abates. As the contractions lose their brutishness, you do what you are told. This is precision engineering. So you wait and pant and open all your muscles up like beautiful bright paint on water, and the pain slithers clean away.

Wet warmth on your breast, a separate song. She's here. Her damp black head is moving blindly as she nuzzles, and you help her on.

You help her on.

Then the too-late drugs that they have given you take you back to dark.

Chapter Forty-Nine

SUNDAY 25 NOVEMBER

Galletly had never reported to his supervision officer in Carlisle, had never in fact arrived at his sister's at all, *who wasn't bloody surprised because she hated his fecking guts.* A warrant had already been craved. You didn't argue with DNA evidence, plus old Reggie McPhee had identified Galletly from an electronic montage of twelve different men. It was a total long shot; Alex had confidently expected him to shut his eyes and bring his grubby finger down at random. Clearly and deliberately, Reggie had studied the screen, had run his hand along the short rows of faces and had twice, with increasing conviction, indicated Galletly as the man he had seen in the car in Lochburn Avenue on the twelfth. Not a star witness by any means, but their only one, and the firmest corroboration that they had.

With the warrant would come a warrant enquiry form, on which you had to list evidence of all the 'due diligence' you were using to track him down. Not so easy when you had a subject of no fixed abode, with no active bank account or mobile phone, no interactions or claims with the state, the Department for Work and Pensions, all the usual ways you would locate and trace a wanted individual. But they would find him. Galletly's name and image had been circulated nationwide, with all the relevant markers put on the PNC. The team was delighted that the end was nigh – Hayley too, who had insisted on taking them all for a celebratory drink. Alex persuaded her to wait until they had a body. Once he'd laid hands on Galletly, maybe, at that point, he would feel the satisfaction of closure that was refusing to come. That ordered sense of evidence accumulated, of strings unravelled and running in a single thickened rope. On paper, it was there: Francine was drowned. Francine was naked. Francine's clothes and person were found to contain the DNA of Mark John Galletly. An eyewitness placed Galletly close to the scene at the material time. Galletly was a former associate of several of Francine's friends. Doubtless, when they found Galletly, found the vehicle he used, then more forensic evidence would arise to bind him even tighter to Francine's final hours. There might be skin or fibres inside, the paint scrapings would match with those found at the scene. They could test his alibis, check his movements. Interview him, of course.

Yet there was an emptiness around it all, a dull and scientific progression that didn't do justice to the passion, blood and struggle of a murder. None of this told Alex why. From what he could remember of Galletly, he considered himself a 'soldier'. Name, rank and number, that was it. Not for him the blessed relief of the confessional. They didn't need that, anyway; the Fiscal reckoned they had enough as it was. Motivation gave the lawyers more to get emotional about in court, but it wasn't essential. To Alex, though, to this case, it was. And not just because it was Francine.

Alex had been ringing Anna's mobile all weekend, but wherever she was, her phone wasn't on. It was now Sunday morning, the archetypal time to catch folk in, and Alex was standing outside her house, glaring at the upper windows as if the very force of his stare would make her materialise. A fine, big house, but it had the air of being shut up, the vertical line of curtains half-pulled, horizontal blinds frowning down at you and one car conspicuously angled in a driveway built for two. It had to be Anna's car – she'd favoured Audis since she was a sergeant, and the front undercarriage was accident-damaged, tying in with the newspaper report.

He rattled the letterbox, just in case there was a stray remnant of the Macklin family lurking in the sleeping house. The expensive, heavy brass fall was slow and padded, making hardly any noise, and he couldn't see a bell. Too posh to knock? Did folk in Newlands have a 24/7 butler on standby at the window?

He scooched down to look through the letterbox. Fancy wooden hallstand, nice paintings. Two newspapers lying on the mat. So. He could either contact Anna's work and find out where she was, or phone the *Evening Times,* who seemed to know more about this entire case than he did. Whatever he did would flag up that the SIO in the Francine Gallagher case was desperately seeking Anna. He was still furious with her, of course he was, but it was Anna. Once his Coke-chucking rage had abated, and he'd wiped the wall down, phoned Carlisle, and called up every shred of intelligence he could about Galletly, Alex had regarded his anger a little more objectively. It ceased to be a jammed, black mess and took on a clearer outline. He was angry for Anna, not at her. Yes, she was lying. Some might argue she had shafted him (again); she was certainly taking the piss; but it was the *why* that dragged at him. Alex was all about the motivation. It was the fact of Anna maybe being at risk, or being blackmailed. Being on some suicide mission, on her own.

He owed her the chance of a fair hearing at least.

Anna's involvement would make no difference to the forensic evidence. But he needed to get to her before they found Galletly, so he at least knew what he was dealing with. Did he still want to keep her out of this, entirely? That depended. He had a horrible, heaving suspicion that it had gone too far. And that it had gone too far years ago too.

'Excuse me, can I help you?'

An elderly man was on the doorstep next door, leaning over the hedge that separated them.

'Oh hello.' Alex flashed his warrant card. It worked just like Doctor Who's psychic paper, imprinting a person-specific message on to each recipient. Old ladies would insist on holding it, and scowl thoughtfully. Polite, middle-class folk like this would semi-swallow, nodding as if they saw them all the time.

'I'm a colleague of Anna's. I was just wondering if you knew where she was.'

'Oh, they've gone away for the weekend. You know.' He teetered a little closer. 'After all that business last week.'

'Of course.'

'Is that what you're here about? Because I saw everything that happened.'

'It's just a routine enquiry, sir.'

'Oh.' For a second, his head disappeared, then Alex could see it bobbing above the hedge, moving down his garden and to the gate of Anna's. He let himself in, closing the gate carefully behind him.

'Roger Blake,' he said, holding out his hand.

'Pleased to meet you.' Alex didn't offer his own name in return. He'd been wanting another wee rummage in the letterbox, a sortie round the back perhaps, and now this old codger was in his space. Damn you, Neighbourhood Watch.

Mr Blake cleared his throat. They looked at one another. Alex was buggered if he was moving before this old boy did.

'Do you mind me asking – is everything all right?'

'Yes sir, don't worry. Like I say, this is just routine.'

'It's just, your colleague – Anna. She was very shaken after chasing that man. I told her she should have gone for a check-up. If that other girl hadn't been holding her up, I think she would have fainted.'

'You mean her daughter?'

Alex had read the incident report of the events on Friday afternoon. Only three people were mentioned – Anna, her stepdaughter and a – presumably *this* – neighbour.

'No, there was an older girl too, a rather scruffy-looking young lady. Looked a bit of a tramp, actually. Certainly not from round here. I've no idea where she appeared from, or where she went afterwards.' He sniffed. 'But that's not the point. I really am rather worried about Anna. My wife and I were just saying the other day, we thought having a police officer move into the street would make us feel safer in our beds at night. But you do wonder if it perhaps attracts the wrong sort—'

'Sir, I've known Anna Cameron for years. I can assure you she's one of our most respected officers.'

'Oh, no, please excuse me. I don't mean *she's* the wrong sort. It's just . . .' The old boy rubbed his moustache. It was a fine specimen, darker than the hair on his head, and with a tinge of smoked yellow on the inner tufts. 'Look, can I cut to the chase?'

'Certainly.'

'Are you an actual friend of Anna's?'

'Yes, I am. We go back several years.'

'Well, I didn't say this to the other chap, but she's been acting rather strangely – before this thing with the car crash happened, I mean. Just the other day – Wednesday it would have been, because I was doing my seedlings – I heard her out in the garden. She was shouting away to herself, something like: *come ahead, come and effing get me.* But there was absolutely nobody there. I checked. And later that night, I saw her put a bag of rubbish into a carrycot, and then put it in the boot of her car. I mean, that's not normal behaviour is it? Do you think she's heading for some kind of a breakdown?'

Alex fixed an insipid smile over his desire to shove Mr Blake in his becardiganed, barrel chest and scream at the monkey-god who was currently pissing himself with laughter. *Wednesday? Ooh! Bin bag? Ooh! Anonymous female?* He was squatting on his cloud and directing a fine stream of monkey-pish all over Alex's parade. Alex stuffed his hands into the pockets of his coat, pressing hard on the car keys.

'Not at all sir,' he said. 'It's really nothing for you to worry about. And it's probably for the best that they're having a wee break. It must have been a terrible shock. For you too. I understand you saw the chap off yourself.' He was deliberately echoing Mr Blake's turns of phrase, nudging the old boy's thoughts in a far different direction from where Alex's own fears were straying. Fuck, they were donning their own confirmation dresses.

'Oh, it was nothing. Only did what any decent fellow would have done.'

'Just one other thing, sir. You wouldn't know where Anna and her husband have gone, would you?'

The old gent laughed. 'Do you lot never speak to each other? Like I told the last lad. Way up north. Plockton.'

'Right. No, sorry, nobody told me.'

'You not from Mount Florida as well then?'

'Mount Florida? No.'

'That's the police station the other chap was from. Chubby lad? Very close-cropped hair.'

Alex shook his head.

'Between you and me, I was a bit surprised when he said he was a detective. When I say chubby, I mean . . .' The man puffed out his cheeks and widened his arms. 'Wouldn't fancy his chances of catching the bad lads at all!'

'You didn't catch his name did you?'

'No. But he definitely said he was from Mount Florida office.'

There was no Mount Florida police station.

Chapter Fifty

When Anna woke again, it was daylight. She was tight-tucked in a narrow bed, the sheet folded over her belly in a broad white ribbon. Between her legs was bulky, she was packaged in rustling, padded paper and every part of her ached. She sensed something close to pain in her memory too, a fog that swept in at her the way the wind had, up on the hill. And then it parted, so she could see everything. Pixellated at first, then needlepoint sharp. She remembered the car flying at the edge of the road, the layers of road and sky twining and the pain and pushing. A deep tightening in her breasts and then, of their own accord, her nipples started gushing milk. It soaked through the thin nightgown she was in, spreading in wide, weird stains and she searched the room for her baby. She had a baby! Anna struggled to sit up, the bed was like a winding sheet. She could see no sign of a crib, or Rob or Laura, but she was definitely in a hospital, there was a telly on the wall and a wee wheeled table at the end of her bed. And a shadow by the window, which turned and smiled.

Cath Worth.

Anna thought she must be dreaming, it was one of those dreams that was scarier than monsters, because it seemed so nearly true, and you thought you were awake, but you weren't. Maybe if she lay back down, tried to insinuate herself into the dream, then it would pass.

'Hi Anna. How you doing?'

The shadow moved across the room, until it was dominating the whole space where the wheeled table and the telly had been. Cath took her hand. 'You need a drink?'

'No. Where's Rob? Where's my baby?'

Cath smiled again, positioned herself on the bed. She'd lost a ton of weight, looked younger than before. When had Anna last seen her? In the prison, when they'd both gone to see Jamie. Cath's husband Jamie, who had never really belonged to Anna. Anna had her own person to love, she had him here and she wanted him now.

'Why are you here? Where's Rob?'

'We live up here, Anna. Jamie's with the Mountain Rescue. They got called out when you had your accident. Do you remember?'

'Of course I remember it.' Evidently, Cath was still a stupid besom. You didn't forget flying at two thousand feet without a parachute. Although she didn't have any idea how they landed. 'Well, I remember bits of it.'

'You were incredibly lucky – the car only fell to the next level of road. I think the crash barrier must have slowed it or caught it. You could have gone all the way to the bottom. The fact you weren't wearing your seatbelt either – it meant you were thrown clear.'

Anna wrenched the rigid sheets from their moorings, swung her legs past Cath and towards the floor.

'Hey – where are you going?'

'Nae offence, Cath. There's three people I want to see, and you're not one of them. So if you're not going to tell me where they are—'

'Okay, okay. Laura's fine – she's with Rhona and her mum and my kids. Remember Eilidh? She says – Anna, will you sit there? At least wait till I get your slippers. You never know what's been spilled on these floors.'

Cath slid a pair of towelling aeroplane-freebie slippers across the linoleum. They were grey and grubby beside Anna's feet. She'd never seen her feet look so white before. Bones like a skate's wing and rich blue veins powering every inch. The swelling in her ankles had all but disappeared. Everything was separate and moving again, everything except her. She was making this pretence of rushing to get up when in reality she was terrified. The longer her breasts wept and Cath kept stalling she was terrified.

'Where's my baby?'

'Anna, she's fine.'

'She?'

Playing with the softness of the syllable, with its wonderful, gentle shush and her breasts pumped harder and her sounds dissolved in tears. 'I had a wee girl?'

'Oh Anna. Come here, you.'

'I knew she was a girl.' Anna's words fell wetly into Cath's jumper. 'I knew it.'

Cath drew her in, patting her back and stroking her hair. 'Anna, she's absolutely beautiful. I promise you. It's just that she's a wee bit early, so they've put her in the Special Baby Unit. But she's perfect. Totally perfect. I've checked all her fingers and toes, everything.'

'Can I see her?'

'Of course you can. Wait and I'll ring for the nurse to take us through.'

Anna held on to Cath's arm. 'Wait. What about Rob? Where's Rob?'

Cath took her hands again. Held the pulses of her wrists and was honest enough to look directly at her. 'He's in Intensive Care.'

'Why? But I don't have a scratch hardly—'

'I . . . I'm not sure, Anna. He's still asleep.'

'Asleep?' It was another woman talking. A slow, stupid woman who chewed her syllables thickly. 'You mean unconscious? In a *coma*?' She shook herself free of Cath's grip. ' Fucksake Cath, tell me the truth.'

'I'm sorry Anna. They don't know when he'll wake up.'

It was still this absurdist dream, melting in Picasso-shapes of things that were and almost were, things you could make out the real truth of, in with all the squiggles and elongations, one of which was this unfamiliar voice. Kind of yawning now, very slow and strained. Cath would think she'd had a stroke. 'But he can't be. He was with me. All through my labour – I felt him. He was holding on to my hand.'

'That was me, Anna. I stayed with you. That was me.'

And then your mind delves into a place it's never gone before because you know you're awake and it's always been about you, and even now a tiny piece of you is thinking *I can't be a widow I can't be on my own,* because the 'when' meant 'if' – Cath's eyes had shied away as she said that bit – and then you think of Laura and your nameless babe and you think of the speeding green car and the wicked balance of give and take and your breasts stop weeping. Just like that, they stop.

They went first to see her baby, Anna shuffling, Cath supporting. It was a lilac room, hushed, efficient, with four or five fish-tanks and lots of bleeps and hums. 'Baby Cameron? Follow me,' said the nurse, but Anna was already there. She didn't need to be told which one her baby was, she could smell her, had known her every unfurling for eight months. She was lying in an incubator, rosebud fists above her face and her thin legs kicking. Her eyes were closed, then they opened. Huge dark infinities, contained in her puckered face with the tube that lipped both her nostrils and ran behind her ear. The tiniest of sticking plasters was holding it in place, yet it took up half her cheek. Her bottom lip sucked in and she kept on staring at Anna as Anna stared at her. Her eyebrows were arched. Appraising. They couldn't focus more than twelve inches, that's what the baby books said, but she was entirely focused. Her head never moved, even while her arms and legs railed at the sky.

'She's a right wee wriggler that one,' said the nurse. They had placed a little crocheted cap on her head, but you could still see the hair. Spiky, almost jet black, but each exquisite strand was tipped with gold.

'Like tiger stripes.' Anna put her hand through one of the holes in the tank.

'Would you like to hold her?' said the nurse.

'Is it okay?'

'Absolutely.' The nurse unclicked the top of the incubator. 'Just watch you don't pull out any of the tubes.'

Far too slowly, the nurse picked up Anna's daughter, presented her to this snatching fiend whose leaky body was trembling, the way greyhounds do before a race. Anna's baby, with Rob's mouth, a glimpse of Laura in those supercilious brows. Anna held the gentle weight of her, built to fit this curve, this crook of arm and swell of breast, a tiny hand clapping at her naked collarbone, a head strained in vain for something more than skin.

And it flowed again, of course it did. Without thinking, Anna opened the vent on her nightgown. No, that's not true, she didn't think exactly, but there was a decision; it was like an urge, a basic compulsion to feel her flesh imprint on her baby's flesh. The searching pout clamped on to her breast.

'You're not really meant . . .' said the nurse. 'We could express some of your milk maybe—'

It was quite easy to ignore her, amazed as Anna was to see what her body would do. A building pressure, her whole breast engorged, nipple browner and bigger than it had ever been. How was she supposed to get all that in her mouth? But it went, as it was meant to. It folded and blossomed and it hurt, Jesus, it was bloody sore, her soft, huge nipple and the baby's hard greedy gums. Then there was a downward tugging flow and they were making each other complete. And it was perfect and lovely, and so so lonely. She wanted to share this, have him laugh and say how clever they both are. As the baby drank, Anna's womb contracted. The sharpness of the pain surprised her, and she had to find a chair.

'Do you have a name for her?' asked the nurse.

She didn't, until now.

'Grace. My husband's mum was called Grace.'

'That's lovely.'

'And Caroline too,' she added. 'Her name is Grace Caroline Macklin. Not Cameron.'

After she had fed her, when Grace was tucked up safe in her see-through box, she cried for Anna. Cath waited while they lifted her out again and Anna kissed her, sealing it all in that fine soft promise. Tasting her newness and warmth, her sweet milk breath. Then Cath took her through to Rob. She didn't know why Cath Worth, of all people, had granted herself the status of unofficial guide, but she was glad that she had. If it had been her, if Cath had stolen Rob, Anna would not be so gracious. She didn't dare ask where Jamie was and, honestly, she didn't care.

Rob was there. Black head on white pillows, propping him up so he looked alert. If you painted eyeballs on his inert eyelids, he would definitely look alert. He had tubes like the daughter he hadn't seen, many of them, running from his face and his bare, strong chest. Anna asked to see a doctor, and they talked of swelling and time and the miracle of the human brain, which they attested to as both profoundly fragile and robustly, mysteriously a mind unto itself. She didn't know which to believe, so she asked them to go away. She positioned herself as she had done with her mother and watched him breathe.

Cath remained. Hovering.

'Did they find the other car?' said Anna eventually.

'No.'

'It was a green one.'

'No trace, I'm afraid. Did he definitely see you?'

'Do you think you could bring me my mobile phone, Cath? It's at the B and B. In our room.'

'Sure. I'll give Jamie a bell. He was going to bring Laura in later anyway. If that's okay?'

Anna wasn't sure what the question meant.

'Could you ask him to bring her in now, please? I really need to see her.'

'Of course.'

Cath went towards the door. Stopped. 'There's a buzzer there, that wee orange button, if you need a nurse. But they're in every five seconds anyway.'

'Thanks. Look, I should've said before now, but thank you for everything you've done. I can't believe you stayed with me . . .'

Cath shrugged. 'We tried to get hold of Laura's auntie, but she's abroad somewhere?'

'Portugal. Best place for her.'

'Yeah, well . . . I could hardly leave you on your own, could I?'

'Plenty people would have done.'

'I decided not to. It was me, my choice, Anna. My power to do it or not. That's how I've got through a lot of things – I take back the power.' She stood in the open door, one hand ready to close it as she left. 'Don't worry. I don't owe you anything, and you don't owe me.'

When the door clicked shut, Anna lay her forehead on Rob's bedguard, so her hand could reach his hair.

'Love you.'

She drew a picture of their baby's face, so he would feel it through his skin. She drew the huge wide eyes and the dimple that hadn't yet arrived, but would. She drew their baby taller, holding Laura's hand. She drew a heart on his smooth, unresponsive brow. She stroked him and she sang to him and her heart stiffened with every beat. They were drawings traced in dust. This had been done to him. To her. Deliberate as if Galletly had held her down, smiled into her eyes, and pared back her throat with a blunt, dark knife.

Within half an hour, Cath had returned, this time with Laura. Behind her, Anna could see Jamie. He stood awkwardly, hands in a choirboy clasp as Laura ran to Anna. She barely registered him, only that he was stouter, and his dark hair was tinged with grey. Her arms were too full of Laura to care.

'Oh, Mum. I thought you were dead.'

'Hey now Laura-lee. Come on you. I'm here. Look – nip me if you want.'

Laura relaxed into Anna's lap, and it felt just the same as holding the baby, only heavier.

'I know, but I thought you were dead.'

'Darling, darling. I don't have hardly a scratch. And look at all the weight I've lost as well. Have you seen your wee sister yet?'

'Just through the window.'

'Well that's no use. How're you going to learn to change her nappy if you can't pick her up, eh?'

'How's Dad?' Laura stared at her feet, ignoring Rob's immobile form.

'He's doing good. He's still sleeping at the moment, but the doctor says that's the best thing, so that his brain will heal.'

'Are you sure?'

'Well, the doctor's hardly going to lie to me, is he? What is it that Dad always says?'

They recited it in unison. 'Trust me, I'm a doctor.'

'Exactly. So. Will we go and see your wee sister now?'

They stood up, Laura's gangly legs sliding to the floor.

'What are we calling her?'

'How about Grace?'

'After my granny?'

'Yeah. Why not?'

She was getting so tall, up to Anna's shoulder. Anna felt a wild terrible pang for Amy who had missed so much of this new life springing up, crazy-growing the way lush grass did. It was Amy who'd held Laura at the start, and she would have known then that life was an utter miracle. But she'd never got to *see* it. Cath strode on at the head of their entourage, pointing out the pastel-hued mural that marked the entrance to SBU to Laura. 'You'll need to put some of that gel stuff on your hands, mind.'

'Here's your mobile.' Jamie touched Anna's arm. 'Cath said you wanted it.'

'Cheers.'

She switched it on immediately.

'I don't think you can use that in Intensive Care.'

She held up a hand to make him shut up.

You have five new messages.

They could wait. Anna scrolled down the list of numbers, not sure if she'd saved Shelly's or not. There was one here with M beside it. That must be it: Michael.

'Excuse me. I need to phone someone.'

But he stayed right by her side. She dialled the number anyway, walking away from Jamie and into a beige room scattered with potted plants and squeaky blue vinyl chairs. A gold-framed poster on the wall invited visitors to *find a moment's rest in the contemplation suite.*

'Hullo?' A disembodied, reedy voice answered.

'Where the fuck is he?'

'Oh Anna, baby.' Shelly was crying. 'Are you okay? Did you get ma message, doll? I've been totally frantic so I have.'

'You better not be fucking me about. Just tell me where he is.'

'He's here. That's what I telt you. Came back down the road this morning, high as a bloody kite. Says he ended the both of yous – they're having a fucking party.'

'If you tell him you've spoken to me I'll fucking kill you, Shelly. Do you understand that? Keep your phone with you at all times. When I get back I want you to arrange a meet. But only then – only when I know we're both in the same place and he can't come back here, right?'

'Anything you say, doll. Is that you gonny pay up then? What about your man – is he alright?'

She hung up, just as Jamie came in.

'Everything okay?'

'Fine.'

She walked past him and into the corridor.

'Anna, I'm so sorry about your husband.'

A hard, grim smile. 'He's not my husband. We didn't make it that far. My fault, of course.'

'Well, I'm sorry anyway. It's this way, dummy.' His hand was heavy on the curve of her spine, where her muscles hurt. 'You always did have a crap sense of direction.'

No she didn't. She was acutely certain of where she would go now.

'I need you to do something for me, Jamie. Will you do it please? Without asking why?'

'I guess.'

'Is your car fast?'

'It's a Beamer.'

'Can I borrow it? I have to go back to Glasgow.'

'Well, I think the plan is to move Rob down when he's stabilised. But Mrs Anderson says you can stay on at the B and B as long as you like. No charge. And the baby looks like she's doing well—'

'No, I mean now. I need to go back to Glasgow right now and I need you and Cath to look after the kids for a couple of days.'

'Don't be so bloody daft.'

'Jamie. This wasn't an accident.'

There was a secure door buzzer at the entrance to the unit. Cath and Laura had already gone inside. They'd have to buzz again. Cath had better not show off Grace to Laura before Anna got there.

'I know who did this. I thought it was just me he was after, but he's trying to kill my whole family. I have to stop him.'

Jamie was shaking his head. She hated how he did that, how disappointment and scorn could be wrapped in a simple tilt. He used to do it a lot, she remembered. At her. 'Jesus, Anna. What have you got yourself embroiled with now? Just tell the local plods, they can deal with it. Christ, do you never stop with the dramatics? You had a baby less than twenty-four hours ago – she needs you.'

'Did you know I was pregnant when you left me?'

Like smashing glass, his expression shattered. All that remained was wide, transparent shock; you could see it in his blackened pupils, in the hang of mouth and chin.

'There you go. My gift to you. I mean the first time, when we were kids. We never had it, don't look so horrified. We don't have a secret love child – except Alice, that is. Now will you please do as I ask and look after my children until I get back? I mean guard them. Guard them and Rob the way you would if it was Cath or your kids. And don't tell any fucker where I am.'

The door swung open. She didn't wait for an answer. The days of waiting for anything had gone.

Chapter Fifty-One

There was a hands-free kit in the car – you ran it through the satnav. Anna plugged in her phone, turned the music down. She had been blaring Kings of Leon since she left Wester Ross. Jamie's CD had been in the player when she started the car, and it was ideal – if predictable. Would you ever grow up, Jamie? But she needed grunts and the heavy syncopation of drums to ripple and press on her. Driving very fast and listening, that was all she could cope with for the first hour. Instead of Laura crying, or the indescribable smell of Grace's head, the pull of Grace's mouth on her breast, she kept switching to Rob, to his stillness and the anger it engendered in her. Could feel her cheeks scarlet and tight, it was bursting in her. But the repetitive actions of driving helped; they conferred a sense of safety. In her car, Anna was in charge, she was driving forward and she was *doing*; she would not wait any more.

As she drove, her mind emptied, not seeing the majesty of the hills, the grazed neatness of moorland, the dip of the hawk, the banality of sheep. All these features sucked past her, swirling down the empty tunnel that was outside the car. Anna was compelled to drive, to keep driving as her rage built, forcing her to accept that this was how it was going to be. She *was* an automatic pilot, sweeping the car through twisting roads, overtaking the ubiquitous caravan wherever it appeared, observing the passive whoosh of trees and registering none of these things at all. As the roads levelled out, became wider, she dialled 121 on her phone.

  – Anna, it's Alex Patterson. I need you to phone me straight away . . .

– Hiya! Auntie Laney here. Just checking in. You made the Evening Times *by the way. Oh, and Alice sends purrs. My God that cat can eat. I thought they were meant to be dainty wee things …*

– Anna. Alex again. I can't stress how important it is that you call me. Please …

– Anna. Alex. What the fuck's going on? Do you want me just to phone your division? I'm gonny have to, because there's not a lot of time left – d'you understand what I'm saying?

She wiped a drip of sweat from her eyes. Alex, always so solicitous and polite. Careful not to incriminate himself, but she understood exactly. Francine's clothing had given up no ghosts. Somewhere in her head she'd hoped that they would trace Galletly through the garments, that they'd have pulled him in for interview and it wouldn't have mattered by now that Francine had been seen going into Cranstonhill. The fact that Alex was still hounding her meant he'd no other leads at all; he was determined not to let this thing about Francine go. *Too late, my love. It's all too late.*

The last message was the very man himself: Shelly, breathless and shrill with anguish.

Omagod Maddie. Gonny answer your fucking phone? For fucksake gonny pick up and tell me you're okay? I didny know where he'd went … and then Big – well, it disny matter who, but a friend of a friend tells me he's just after rolling intae town and saying that's it done and dusted. He's fucking joking about it. Phone me baby, please.

He was so weak, Shelly. Anna had little confidence in his ability to arrange flowers, let alone a meeting with Galletly. He had no influence there, had probably relayed everything he'd exchanged with Anna via a third party, and Anna was positive who that third party was. Andrew Semple, Shelly's brother. The fat skinhead who had run the loan-shark operation, very badly, until Galletly had been summonsed by those higher up the organisation to call in all the debts. Which he did in his own inimitable style. She should have realised then; a man who carves IOUs on the faces of his debtors is not a man to be subtle. He's not even a man who cares that much if he gets caught. Galletly exacted his missions with relish and tenacity; he was a businessman who got the job done, probably saw prison as an occupational hazard, accepted it (unless unfairly foisted upon him by a duplicitous cop) as part of the downtime of the job, but nothing that would interfere with his single-minded dedication.

Not that Galletly didn't enjoy the thrill of the chase. Those artistic little flourishes: stalking her stepdaughter, singling out the photo, depositing crime scene evidence at Anna's house – well, she'd done the right thing there. She hadn't torched the clothes, even though she'd wanted to. Christ, he must have tracked down another medal, he must have, because the Clyde's thickly shifting silt would never have relinquished it. All these elaborate brush strokes just to see what she would do, how far he could make her fall. And all of it simply window dressing. When he found out she was still extant, an annoying limpet clinging to the surface of her own life, he'd just come after her again. The payment Anna owed him was simple. Money or blood.

She filled her lungs with too-warm air. Anna had only wanted a small life. This gangster-canvas that had been painted round her was huge and gaudy and crass. She was just a Scottish cop, destined to deal with shoplifters and group disorders and Orange Walks. At first, even that had scared her. First time a ned had intimated that he 'knew where she lived', even though her neighbour had silenced him with a well-placed dunt, Anna had fretted that it might be true. Of course, it wasn't, it never was, so you got blasé, and you wound them up, the neds. You played God or little Hitler, and you swelled yourself up with your self-assured sense of right. But you were just a little person, same as them.

It was so hot in this car. She blinked, searching for landmarks. Passing Dumbarton now, with its sugarloaf rock bearing down on the Clyde. Nearly home. This was the Britons' ancient capital, where kings and monks had settled and where, legend has it, Saint Patrick was stolen from as a boy, and sent in a slave ship to Ireland. *Ah, see – maybe we invented the Irish, and not the other way round.*

Anna opened the driver's window. Heat like fever was on her, over her, sticky on the seat. She had turned the heater right down, but it offered no respite. Galletly had had enough blood already.

In addition to the fifty-five grand in the safe at Stewart Street, there was a quantity of heroin they'd seized, the street value way in excess of the ready cash. She'd give him that, too, as well as everything she had left in her instant access account. There was about ten thousand remaining from the sale of her flat, she'd just give him the card and the bloody PIN. Ask him if he'd take a cheque. Take the entirety of what she had to give, and just leave her her babies and her husband.

A small, hard impact. *Punch it harder, deeper that I did not marry him.*

The silver cables of the Erskine Bridge rose up to Anna's right, two vast Meccano uprights and an elegant double-dip of steel wire carrying the road across the Clyde. They had abolished tolls here a few years ago, so the journey had changed from a frustration of queues and booths to a smooth swift sweep. If she'd to stop and fumble for a handful of change, Anna would have gubbed someone. If, that is, she could have swung her right arm. The tissue in her breasts had become inflamed; it extended to her armpits and the tender weight of them was excruciating, churning thick with nowhere to go but pump harder and harder into the overfull ducts. Who knew milk could be so spiteful?

As she came off the bridge, Anna phoned Shelly again.

'It's me.'

'Where are you?'

'I'm back. Where's Galletly?'

'In his hoose, well, no his hoose, but where he's been staying, I mean, I don't know where that is, but ma contact assures me—'

'Shelly, shut up. Is he definitely in Glasgow?'

'Aye. I promise you. He's no went anywhere.'

'Okay. I want you to arrange to meet him. Today, tonight.' She glanced at the clock on the dashboard: 4.30 p.m. Her breasts were like rocks, distended and engorged. It was agony to move. 'He can decide where, I don't care. Tell him he'll get what he wants.'

'A hundred fucking grand?'

'More, if I can get it. But I want *you* to do it, Shelly; don't give the money to someone else to give to him. I want you to physically give it to him, so I know it's been done. Once you've sorted out when and where you're meeting him, phone me. Then I'll tell you where I am and how you can get the money.'

'Shit, I don't know doll. D'you no want to do it yourself? I don't really want to get up that close and personal, know? I know what Gilly's like – he'll want to see the whites of your eyes like. Enjoy the show.'

'Aye, take the money and then end me anyway.'

'But he could do that any time, doll.'

The corners of the road shrieked and thickened. She saw it alive, a beast of striped and intersecting lines, extending so much further than her blinkers allowed her to see. It was a flashback to childhood. Then, everything was alive. You saw faces in paintings of mountains, you saw dancers in the fire, even when you pretended not to. You didn't just see these things, you heard them too. When Anna was a little girl, they'd had a shed out the back. It was a lean-to, made of corrugated iron and, in her bed at night, if it was windy, the discordant clangs of its movement would drill through her. The gaps of it moaned and the bones of it clattered and she knew it was a trapped defeated creature that would never be free, no matter how much it struggled.

'What else can I do, Shelly? Who can I trust? I've got no one.'

She heard him sniff. Then his tongue clicked, or his jaw. 'It's alright hen. I'll sort it. Right? Leave it with me.'

From Erskine, Anna drove directly to Stewart Street. All her keys were kept on the same keyring: doorkeys, office, safe. You weren't supposed to do that, some keys were never meant to leave the office, but Anna figured these safe keys were hers, her responsibility, and if they were on her person, they were safe. The duty officers had their own keys; it wasn't as if no one else could get access. The fact it was a Sunday tea time was a blessing; there'd be hardly anyone about.

But as she pulled into the yard, she saw there were more cars parked there than on a weekday. She didn't understand it. All the gaffers' spaces were full too. She double-parked and went in the back door. The bar seemed quiet enough.

One station assistant at the back. He came out to see her. 'Hi ma'am. In for the briefing?'

'What briefing?'

'That Commonwealth barge thing's on the night, mind? With the Christmas light switch-on? We've got half of the cops from Crannyhill and Partick in for a briefing.'

'Oh yeah . . . No, I'm just in to get something. Left a cheque in the safe.'

In the tiny sharp spaces between the battering dark, she had planned this out. She would slip the drugs inside her coat and the money into her bag; then immediately, she would cry out, demand to see the duty officer and ask where the hell the money had gone. Shit, not just the money – was there not a load of drugs in there too? He (or maybe she, Anna didn't know who was on duty and it was probably best that way) would blanch, pick up the phone, they would scream at someone, anyone, to get down here now. And Anna would march out in high dudgeon. In the confusion, everyone would think that everyone else was pivoting competently in their own separate roles, doing whatever it was they were meant to do when a large sum of money had gone missing from the safe because they were trained to deal with crises, and Anna would be long gone. Available on request for whatever questioning and interviews were demanded later, of course.

She bent down. Her legs were unbearably stiff. The pad inside her pants was chafing. It felt damp as her breasts, and she thought of Grace's black-domed head and all the incubating hopes her baby had brought as she unlocked the safe. Bits of Grace were still inside her, and Anna was doing this. It took two goes. Her hands were slippery, her head, as it bent to the task, was light.

'Fuck.'

'What's up ma'am?'

'Why has this safe been emptied? Where's the money that was in here? Has someone stolen it?'

She dug through the safe again, hands in all the dark corners. There was nothing there. She couldn't believe it; there was really nothing there.

'Eh, I'm not sure.' He came over, so they could both peer into the empty space.

'You're not sure? Well what are you doing sitting in that uniform drinking fucking tea? There were thousands of fucking pounds in here, money and drugs—'

'Oh, *that*. It got taken up to Pitt Street this morning.'

'Why? Who authorised that?'

'I dunno. Do you want me to get Mrs Reekie? She's only in the muster room?'

'Christ no. Just forget it.'

'Ma'am are you alright? You don't look too good.'

'Just leave me alone.'

She ran blindly from the room, the fever of her breasts pushing up to meet the lighter sweat of stress. It melted her face, her body tumescent. There was still Cranstonhill. She'd check at Cranstonhill, the plainers were working on that music piracy over the weekend. Paul said it could run into thousands, please God let there be money there; if Galletly thought she was winding him up, if Shelly had arranged a meet and there was no money, and he knew exactly where Rob was, he knew Laura, he could simply pick them off one by one.

She scoured into Cranstonhill yard, colliding with the offside of a stationary van. It was parked too close, too close to the entrance, who would do that? She slowed, but the more she tried to ease herself past, the more the two wing mirrors scraped, grinding their reluctance at one another. She left the engine running, jumped out and battled with the rear door of the office. Brain so full of milk she could no longer remember the entry code. She buzzed and buzzed until the station assistant came. It was a face she didn't recognise, slim and clean-shaven; then she realised it was Whisky Mac.

'Evening ma'am. You alright?'

'Just let me past.' She barged through and into the bar. The safe at Cranstonhill was squat and dumpy, it didn't hold much but if there was anything, anything at all please dear Christ let there be something in it.

It was empty.

Anna slammed the safe door over. It was the clap of a closing book. Down like a shot, on her knees, she was on her knees weeping, the black spreading stain coming through her coat as well as her top.

'Ma'am. Here, here. Let me help you up.'

She felt Whisky raise her from the floor.

'Oh, Jesus. Did you know you're bleeding?'

Anna looked down at the vinyl tiles. Watery blood had pooled there, it was coming from her ankle. Whisky crouched to search for the wound, pushed the leg of her joggers up a little. The blood was running down her leg.

'Ma'am – I think you might be in labour.'

Tearfully, she shook her head. Opened her coat fully, so he could see.

'Can you get me some towels from the female toilets please? I don't think I can make it up the stairs.'

Wordlessly, he left the room. Anna curled back on to the floor, staring at the safe. The cold tiles were comforting, soaking up some of her heat. You didn't realise how uneven the floor was until your cheek was resting on it. They had only put a new roll of fake-tile vinyl down at the end of August and yet the shine of its surface was already pitted and frayed.

'Ahem ... there you go, ma'am.' Whisky Mac passed her a discreet little bundle of paper towels. She had meant sanitary towels. 'The um, your requirements are in there.' The heels of his boots clicked together. She could see the tips of them, the polished band of military bull that set him apart. 'And can I take this opportunity to congratulate you on the birth of your ... ?'

Anna's hands dragged vaguely on the floor, scooping up the emptiness of air. 'Daughter,' she said absently. 'I had a wee girl.'

'Well, my congratulations to you and Mr Cameron, ma'am.'

'Thank you.'

'So.' He knelt down beside her, one knee only, like a valiant prince. 'Can I get you anything? Tea, water?' He half smiled. 'Whisky?'

'I wish.' Anna sat up. There was a hole in her. It felt odd, not to take the weight of her belly and hold it with her, keeping the net of muscles on an even keel.

'This?' said Whisky. In his hand was a sealed envelope. 'It was handed in for you at the bar, ma'am. On Friday. I don't know if . . . well, I'm sure it's not the right time, but the lassie that left it was adamant it be delivered to you, directly and asap. She caught me outside actually, wouldny come in.'

'What did she look like?'

'Like a wee hairy actually. And she smelled of horseshit.'

'Ah.' Anna took the envelope from him. The shift of her body compressed her buttocks against the floor. The back of her joggers was wet. What had she become?

'Ma'am, are you in some kind of trouble? Naw, don't answer that. I can see you are.' Whisky sat beside her, their spines leaning companionably against the skirt of Anna's desk. It was an old-fashioned one, in the pale Fifties style beloved of teachers. Anna liked her desk. She hugged her knees in, sucking air as they brushed her breasts.

'I should be feeding my wee girl just now, you know? She needs me. And I'm splayed out here making puddles on your floor.' She tried to sigh away the pain. 'You got kids?'

'Two,' said Whisky. 'But they'll both be grown up by now. I . . . to tell the truth, ma'am, I wouldny know them if they came up and bit me on the nose. I've no seen them since they were wee.'

'I'm sorry.'

'Ach. I wisny the best of dads, put it that way.'

'Least you got a couple of years with them.' She put her hands up to embrace her head. It felt too heavy for her neck to support.

'Can I give you a piece of advice, ma'am?'

'Go for it.'

'In my opinion, you're the best senior officer this division has. Male, female, it disny matter to me. You really care about what you do. Aye, you're a bad-tempered besom, don't get me wrong, but you aye apologise after. So I'd hate to see you implode.'

'Is that what you think I'm doing?' Her voice came muffled from inside her arms.

'I know it is. But see – and you'll have to excuse the military analogy, it's all I know – see when the RPGs are flying in and they're shooting at you from all sides, you've only got the two choices. You either give up and die or you fucking fire up with everything you've got. Come out all guns blazing.'

'What if you've got nothing, Whisky Mac?'

'Then you end up like me.' He got to his feet, held out a hand to hoist her up. 'And I wouldny recommend that to anyone.'

Outside, in the car with the bloodstained upholstery, after she had been to the bathroom and tried to sort herself – and failed – Anna opened the letter Whisky had given her. It was written in slanting loops, how you would imagine a romantic novelist would write, except the paper wasn't pink. And it began with a perfect hook.

You don't know me. The man who is trying to hurt you is trying to hurt me as well. He killed my friend and I want to stop him. I will be at Kelvinbridge Underground on Friday, Saturday and Sunday. I will only be there between five and six o'clock each day. After that I am just going to go away. Please help me. If you don't help me, there is no one else I can try. If you bring other people with you, I will know. I will just run away then as well. I have left the same note at your house, so you have to get one of them.

The scribbles reared off the pages, touching at her face. Anna went back and read it again.

Chapter Fifty-Two

Ten more minutes. One hundred and seventy very fraught ones already wasted, Mary presenting herself out in the open, a sitting duck in a rather nice coat. Well, she'd been standing actually, hanging over the balcony rail of the bridge in Great Western Road. This way she could observe all the comings and goings from the subway station down below. And gob on folk if she got bored. It was true what they said about last-chance saloon: the closer it gets to the end of the road, the more desperate you become. She thought you would get more resigned, but no, it was completely the other way. You pace yourself at first, thinking something will come up, I've loads of time yet; and then, as the seconds tick down to your – admittedly self-imposed – deadline, your heart speeds up and you want to cry.

She had been sure that the blonde woman would come, had been willing to risk everything to go to the police station, go back to her fancy big house. Did people not care about anything except themselves? Mary cared about plenty, far more than she'd thought she did. She cared about Bernie, about Calder Riggs. She cared about her horses. Shit, she cared about her mother. And even though she didn't believe in it, a scrap of her cared about justice. But she couldn't live in limbo any more. Mary was cold, she was hungry. She was tired of living on her nerves and dodging the faceless threats, perceived or otherwise, that waited for her everywhere. She had saved up thirty pounds, it was enough to get her on a bus to England. London was the obvious destination, but it was passé, every shape-shifter drifted there. No, she was thinking somewhere in the countryside, by the sea. Devon or Cornwall, from whence the smugglers came. Holidaymakers, pony-trekking on the beach – there were bound to be plenty of stables.

Last night, she'd gone to say goodbye to the horses. A few of them had been sold already, but Autumn was still there, and poor old Gerry. No one would want Gerry. She had sunk her face into his sweet, dusty coat and his sigh had split her heart. Half the night she'd spent there, sleeping in with the horses and the hay. Calder Riggs was a sad place now. It had hung its head down, ready for the chop. There were surveyor's poles dotted in the paddock, greedy fingers coveting the unmade land. Mary wouldn't have been surprised if Fiona had moved out already, left the lassies to come in and feed the horses daily. There was plenty of hay in their nets, but the house was utterly dark. Generations of Fiona's family had grown crops on this land, and now it was going to grow houses – hundreds of crass wee boxes; the city claiming another chunk.

It made her so miserable, she probably wouldn't have stayed at all, but for the fact that she'd woken up the night before to find a man on top of her. She thought she'd been safe in her derelict tenement, just her and the stray cats and her cleverly concealed entrance via the loose metal board. All the windows had been encased with metal shutters, but one at the back had some rivets missing, and she'd pulled at it long enough until it swung like a hinge. Animal cunning and all that, but evidently she was not the only smart-arse in the homeless village. Imagine the guy's delight, though, when he realised that not only had he found a bed for the night, but a bedmate was thrown in for free. Aye well, he'd not even be attempting to get his dick out again for some time.

No, Mary was definitely for the off. It needn't be as far as Devon. She could go up north – there was that place Bernie said she learned to ride. An outward bound ranch was how she described it, in Perth. It was probably some home for wayward girls, but Mary would fit the bill fine. And in a year or so, she could get in touch with her mum and say: *Hi Mum. It's me. Fancy a wee holiday?* How far was Perth? Only a hour and a half in the car – bugger it, she could ride! She could take the horses and they could ride all the way, stopping in fields for grass and water.

It could happen.

The stair beneath her clattered with approaching feet. Another batch of travellers were being disgorged from the station. Not many. It was Sunday tea time, when all good folks were snuggled up with their roast chicken and *Songs of Praise*. Nope. The woman wasn't on that train either. Mary stood straight. That was it then. She turned to leave, the vast, grand length of Great Western Road stretching east as well as west. Which way would she go? *Hey sweetie, the world's your oxter*, as her dad used to say.

'Excuse me. Mary?' A low, female voice beside her.

'Jesus Christ, you nearly gave me a heart attack.'

The woman was jiggling like a junkie, like she had bare feet on needles. 'I'm Anna,' she said. 'You sent me a letter? You're Francine's friend?'

Mary nodded. 'Yes. How do you know my name?'

She'd only had quick looks at her before, but the impression Mary had gleaned was of a glossy long strip of caramel, baked hard. This had to be her evil – or more like her decomposing – twin. The policewoman, Anna, smelled of sour blood, and she looked like shit. Her eyes were red, hair all over the place, not the smooth bob of before. No make-up, only blotches, and a top, down which, it appeared from the bit Mary could see, she had been very sick. Her coat, mind you, was a cracker, a massive big quilted thing in the manner of an overdeveloped Parka. Mary could have lived inside it for weeks: a tent, sleeping bag and big warm cuddle all in one – but whatever she'd been up to, this woman had ruined it. It too, was all stained.

'How do you know me?' she said.

'I don't. But I know someone is watching you, trying to hurt you.'

She flinched.

'I've been following him,' said Mary.

'Why?'

'Because I think he killed my friend. I can't prove it though. I've tried everything – I've given his name to the newspapers and the police.'

Anna's brow crinkled; a wavy postmark of doubt. 'You have? How did you know his name?'

'Well, I don't know, but I do know that he works for a builder's. A guy called Robert Crilley.'

'I don't think so.'

'Yeah. I've seen the planning application they put in – to knock down our stables. I thought that was what this was all about, but then I realised he was after you as well, so then I got confused. But I figured if you were as shit-scared as I was, then . . .'

There was no reaction, no stepping up to the plate or running with the ball. This Anna was a blank bit of wood.

'Ach, I don't know, right?' said Mary. 'I actually don't know what the hell's going on, but I didn't know what else to do. I thought you might.'

Anna smeared her hand over her mouth, the way you do when you'd just had a great big drink. She looked really ill. Could you see straight if your eyes were that bloodshot? 'The guy you saw at my house is called Mark Galletly, and he doesn't work for a builder's, right? He's a very dangerous criminal, and he's murdered people before.'

'So why did he kill Francine then? Did he not kill her?'

'No, no, he did. I'm positive he did.'

'Well, you're a cop – why don't you do something about it?'

'Because you're right. He is after me too, Mary.'

'All the more reason to stop him then.'

'I know. But it's . . . complicated.'

'Christ, I don't see what's complicated about it. You know he killed her, I know he killed her, he knows he killed her.'

Hand fluttering at her face again. Anna's mouth was spilling over, there were actual dribbles running down her chin. Was she fitting? Biting her tongue? Withdrawal. That's what it made Mary think of. So much for the polis coming to save the day. This one was a care in the community shot if ever there was one. Mary's feeble surge of hope extinguished. That was it then. Everything gone.

She heard a rattle swell in Anna's chest. Looked at her again, properly this time, so that her eyes were drilling right through the shell, to the soft underside.

Mary could mould her. She could glamour and twist her so that Anna would never know who was truly helping who. Shit, she could probably blow on her and knock her sideways if she wanted to. This girl didn't know which way was up. But, if this worked, they would both benefit. Mary would gently take her by the hand and spoon-feed her until she got better. Once more, it was going to be down to the quick-witted resourcefulness of the Lady Mary. Oh here, this was great – seeing a woman in a worse state than you. Fair brought roses to your cheeks. *The Lady Mary brushed the fall of her fine new cloak. This peasant woman may have soiled it.*

'Look, I've got a proposition for you.' She folded her arms. Anna's wavering inconstancy made her want to stand stock-still.

'What?'

'What if I said I saw him kill her?'

'Did you?'

'No. But would it help?'

'You'd lie for me?'

Mary glimpsed a wild bead of hope in her eyes.

'No. I'd lie for Bernie – I mean Francine. I'd lie for you for money.'

'I'm not with you?'

Perhaps it *was* a leap too far, but to Mary it seemed an obvious, expedient exchange, all flying together like that old Channel 4 logo. Fast and bright and fitting. It was Mary's jigsaw picture, only so perfect you couldn't see the cracks.

'Okay, put it this way. Would it be in your interests to have this man arrested? Have an eyewitness say exactly what it was he did, stand up in court and say it, so that he gets put away in jail?'

Anna's face fell away; younger, light. 'You have no idea how much that would help.'

'Well, in that case, I'd need to know exactly where and when it happened.' The bridge of Mary's nose went tight. She moved her jaw from side to side to loosen it. 'What he did to her, too.'

'I can do that,' said Anna. 'I've got all that in my office already, notes and stuff from the investigation.'

'Okay, well, I want to see him in jail as much as you do. So I'm prepared to say I saw him, if you'll do something for me in return.'

'What is it? Anything.'

'I want you to get him on tape. I want to hear him say he killed her.'

The anguish returned to Anna's face. 'But why? We don't need that – if you come forward as a witness, and you can corroborate details of her injuries, what time it happened . . . I can get you all that. I'll make it easy for you too; I know Alex, the DI dealing with this. I can take you direct to him and—'

'Yeah, but I need it for insurance. No offence, but I don't know you from Adam, you look like a basket case and, as far as I'm concerned, the police still think I was involved in Bernie's death.'

Plus there was the lure of ready cash from the journalist at the *Evening Times*. If Mary provided him with a taped confession, he'd have to give her a couple of grand at least. Hell wap it into him when he realised that the information couldn't be used. He should have helped Mary right at the start.

'But I can't . . . Mary, I'm operating on my own here, I don't have access to wires and surveillance and stuff.'

'Bullshit. You could use a mobile. Or one of those wee diddy things for dictation.'

'And what do you plan to do with this confession?'

Mary's expression must have been less outraged and noble than she realised, or this woman actually was a half-decent cop in a very good disguise, because then she said: 'Is it money? Are you just doing this to get money? Because I can give you money. Here!' She flung a bank card at Mary. 'Here, take it all. There's nearly ten grand in there; you can have the fucking PIN number, it's no use to me any more. He'll laugh me out the fucking park if I turn up with ten grand.'

'Calm down, eh? Folk are looking at us. They'll be thinking we're two jakies having a love-tussle over a bottle of meths.'

'Coffee?' the policewoman said, suddenly bright.

'Pardon?'

It was one of those unearthly transformations, when the bipolar subject flicks from just mental to hypermanic.

'Let's go for coffee,' she smiled. 'I'm dying for a coffee.'

'Eh, I don't know if you've noticed, but I'm not exactly dressed for polite company. And neither are you, really.'

Anna swept her coat open to examine her attire. Without the cocoon of all that fabric, her belly was surprisingly flat.

'Hey, have you had your baby already?'

Anna stared across the road. 'Clothes first, then coffee.'

The only shop still open that looked remotely like it might sell clothes was Eurasia Crafts, full of hippy scarves and joss sticks.

'Could we not just go to your house?'

'Got to keep moving. Keep moving. He could be anywhere, could be watching us right now.'

Actually, there was a gorgeous crushed velvet coat in the window. Deepest purple, with a damson, frogged front. Lots of gathers and pleats; the swirl-factor on the skirt of it would be amazing.

'No,' Anna moaned out loud. Mary watched her slide against the dry, stone parapet of the bridge. Knees bent, her back ramrod like it was on a chair. She must have had right strong thighs.

'It's no good. Even if you do say you saw it, Galletly's still going to tell them about me.'

Jes-us. Was Mary getting the coat or what? She joined Anna at the parapet. 'What about you?'

And then the woman told her this extraordinary story, so extraordinary that they both knew it must be true. You couldn't make it up, even though they both had, and for the same woman too. How strange.

'She made you want to protect her, didn't she?' said Mary, after. A man tutted, picking his way around their clutter of their legs as they sat in their invisible chairs. It was reasonably comfy, though Mary wasn't sure how long she could keep it up; it was like doing the plank at yoga – a doddle at first, then the tremors started. They had used yoga in prison, as a meditative alternative to methadone. It didn't work.

''Scuse you,' called Mary at the man's retreating back. 'Ten pee for a game of Chinese Ladders, sir.'

He didn't oblige.

'She did,' said Anna. 'I just kept thinking that she'd never had a chance. If she could have just got a wee chance.'

'Well, she did, you know. For eight years, Bernie – sorry, Francine – had a brilliant life. She found someone that she loved, she went clean, built a home, a business, and she was happy. Really happy, Anna. You gave her that.'

Anna's head touched against the high side of the bridge, the most gentle of bangs. 'Aye. And the rest.'

'No. That's not your fault. The rest was Galletly and his fat-arsed pal.'

'I knew it!' said Anna. 'He's working with Shelly's brother, isn't he?'

'Who's Shelly? Who the fuck is Shelly? Is there three of them now? Is this going to be like *The Matrix* and they just keep multiplying?'

'No, you don't need to worry about Shelly, I promise. He's my mate. He's on our side – and he hates his brother's guts. But I think that might be how he's getting in touch with Galletly. Via his brother. This fat guy: really short hair, rolls of fat on his neck?'

'That's him.'

'Huh. I bloody knew it.'

Anna closed her eyes. With her head back and her eyes shut, she looked like a wee girl. One who hadn't slept in days. Mary's legs were beginning to quiver, a nice tight burn in them, licking from thigh to knee. She unfolded herself, put a hand on Anna's shoulder. Apart from sticking her heel in that night-marauder's balls, Mary hadn't touched another human being in days. People were always careful to avoid any actual physical contact when they deposited their coins in your hat or bag or shoe.

'Look, if you want, I'll say Galletly's lying about you too.'

Anna's eyes snapped open.

'I'll say Francine told me all about it, that Galletly was planning to fit you up – because he wanted to blackmail you. No, better, I'll say I heard him say it to Francine, just before he killed her. Yeah, I'll say Francine told me that she'd been there when Galletly killed

that old man, and she saw it all. In fact, that would make sense
– that's why Galletly *had* to kill her, because she knew the truth
about what he was going to do to you.'

'Mary, you've got a very fertile imagination.'

'Thank you. I like to cultivate it. Pulp fiction mostly, and fables.
I love a good fairy tale, don't you?'

They both burst out laughing. When she smiled, Anna's face
was beautiful, the kind of bone-built beautiful that would last
well into her eighties, a perfect scaffold to hang her skin high.
Lucky besom. Their hilarity – and it was hilarity, an untethered
thrill rising in it – was interrupted by Anna's phone ringing. She
checked the screen. 'Shelly,' she whispered. 'See. Told you he'd
come across.' Anna clicked her phone to speaker, but the voice
floating from it was so tinny and camp Mary could only catch
snatches. Mostly high-pitched tuts.

'Uh-huh. Right, okay. I understand.' Anna raised a thumb at
Mary. 'Yeah, but if he's insisting I meet him face to face, then I get
to choose the location, right?'

– *Fair dos*, crackled the phone. *Need tae clear it . . . but.*

'I want somewhere busy.' Anna rubbed her nose with the back
of her hand. See, if Mary did that, it would just look gross, but with
Anna, even in her squalid state, it had an air of decisiveness about
it. It was like she was regenerating herself, bits of her that had
been shattered away reforming. 'We'll meet in the McDonald's on
Maryhill Road.'

– *. . . right classy dame . . . don't fancy the Rogano?* Then it sounded
like *jazz with your oysters?*

'McDonald's,' reaffirmed Anna. 'One hour's time. It's busy,
bright with lots of windows. And there's only one way in.'

Here, the voice became much louder. *Fucksake . . . paint wir faces
green . . . some lovely camouflage shorts—*

'Shelly, just sort it, yeah?'

– *two tics doll . . . back to you.*

'There.' Anna flicked her phone shut. 'Now we just have to wait
and see.' Her eyes skimmed the length of herself. 'You're probably
right about the coffee. Why don't we nip back to my office and I'll

dig out that paperwork? There's bound to be a dictaphone kicking about there somewhere too.'

'So you'll do it?'

Quick back at her. 'Will *you*?'

Anna's phone rang again before Mary could answer.

'Christ, that was quick. Shelly – is he there with you? Are you pissing me—'

It wasn't on the speaker this time, but Mary leaned in close enough to hear the man's indignation. It was like a whiny child talking through tin.

'Naw! Fuck, no way José. Funny enough, Gilly does have a phone.'

'Don't suppose you'd like to give me the number?' said Anna.

'Don't suppose I would.'

She sighed. 'Well? Are we doing this?'

There was a chuckle. It made Mary think of a malevolent doll.

'The man from Belfastio, he say yes.'

Chapter Fifty-Three

From here, it was too close to read, like being pressed up against the *Hollywood* sign. Joe's mum had taken him there once, just him and her when Dad had been working in America, and he'd thought it was like concerts and football matches – far better seen artificially at one remove, where a bank of camera angles could give you the all-round experience lacking in real life. He closed one eye, surveying his work again. No, from up here, this was just wiry wooden lines and circles that he hoped would make sense from the ground.

Dusk was moving in, smudging lilac lines to grey. Little tips of light poking through in a tracery of pindots, offering the weakest hint of Via Lactea. City light pollution made it almost impossible to see, but on the coast, in places like Kircudbright, you could see the stars stretch for miles, a pale, hazed fall of light arching over sky. Wrong. Arching over the celestial sphere. There were two hundred billion stars in the Milky Way, bound in halos and clouds and logarithmic spirals. Joe could imagine the galaxy singing, was positive that's where they got the idea of angels from, with their hierarchies of seraphim and cherubim, their dominions and virtues and principalities. Nine orders of winged babies with oxen faces and conjoined wings. What was that all about?

The structure towered above him. Joe tightened the wooden struts that held it all in place. The big torch he'd taken from the garage washed the section he was working on, its false light weedy and one-dimensional under the waking stars. Being up closer to the sky, being in the fresh sharp air and doing this big and complicated creation, it made him feel almost human.

How could he go to school tomorrow?

He had spent Wednesday in bed. All day with the covers pulled over his head and the hot shame of his blood coursing up and down his body. His mother thought it was a hangover, and perhaps it was; never having had one before, Joe didn't know the sum of all its parts. But his torso would not stop trembling, rough stones clashed and clattered in his head and he had the thickest, driest tongue. Plus a thirst he could not slake. Even now, five days on from the party, he was still all dried inside.

All that time, he'd kept his phone off, fearful of who or what might intrude. Going to work on Thursday had only made it worse; he'd thought it would help, but he had to go off sick halfway through. Today was the only other time he'd ventured out of the house, and he'd been busy, so busy. Keeping busy, just busy busy busy.

He checked the cardboard tubes he'd filled this morning with their careful mixture of powders. Magnesium and aluminium, whisked with a good dose of rat poison to introduce the necessary calcium phosphide, that cathode white of fabled Greek Fire. How many enemy ships had the Greeks consumed with that?

How could he go on?

Yes, they were fine. The Araldite glue had set it all, keeping the fuses straight. Joe stuck a couple in his mouth, then swung his arm over the frame so he could reach the place where these last ones were to go.

The ball had ended on a high. Dancing, fireworks and a fight.

'You coming to the party, Joe?'

'Yesh, come and keep me company Jojo.'

'C'mon busman – you need to give us all a lift anyway.'

'Ding, ding. All aboard.' Joe had reached for the lever to open the coach door.

'Do you go *all* the way, Joe?'

'Fucking retard, in hish big red buss.'

Voices pecking. He'd kept his eyes fixed on the door, staring, just staring at it, but he'd known that last voice was Doug. There was a perpetual fury in Doug, in his pent-up posture, his choice of words, even when he hadn't been drinking. He wasn't evil, thought Joe, not in the sense the priests spoke of in church, but he was inculcated with a meanness of spirit which found its target in the everyday, choosing petty words and actions always – even when it brought him no advantage. Malice was his default, and that was that.

Joe kept looking at the door. Doug must know that he had him sussed; that was why he felt he had to be like this. That was it. For a brief minute, Joe had savoured his superior analysis of the situation – plus he had been desperate to find a use for the word *inculcated* since he had come across it in the big Chambers dictionary. Using it inside your head still counted as using it.

'Och leave him alone Doug, eh?'

'What was that, Ali Baba?'

'What did you call me?' said Ali, who was easily bigger and broader than Doug. They all were.

'Nothing.'

'No, if you've got something to say, come over here and say it, *prick.*'

'Comrades, desist.' Patrick had opened his hand to encompass all three of them, his eyes locked on Doug. Doug looked far more menacing when he was pished. That disconnect in his eyes, his face on fire. It felt to Joe like their audience was seeping away on all sides, until it was just the four of them trapped on their own wee island. In reality no one had moved.

'Well,' Doug paused, lifting his voice up a decibel or two: 'At least we don't go around trying to blow up Glasgow Airport.'

'Oh, for fucksake.' Ali took a step closer, his shoulders bulking up. 'I'm as Scottish as you are, you cretin.'

'You speak better English than he does anyway,' said Patrick. There was a swell of laughter. Doug shambled round to face him.

'And you, you, Pat-prick. I shought you were a Scottish Nationalist?'

The weight of him began to topple forward, a progressive totter as if Doug was gearing up to attack. The energy rose to

Joe's mouth; it was a glutinous speech-bubble bursting of its own volition:

'Scottish Nationalism is about being free. It's about growth and diversity, not about distilling folk down to their genetic juice and siphoning them off.'

'Who the fuck d'you think you're—'

'Well said, Slowjo!' someone shouted.

Poor Doug, all fired up and nowhere to go. But it wasn't funny; none of this was remotely funny. Joe's heart was bucking, the same way fish did when he pierced them from the river, dragging them drowning through air and grass. He wanted to run away, there were too many voices, all pecking and cawing in his eyes and ears and mouth. Then he thought it was him that was cawing, and he didn't meant to, but he heard himself yell out again: 'Och, this is a pile of shite. I've had enough,' as he grabbed the heads of both Ali and Doug, crashing them together once, like cymbals.

Heads and bodies, someone clipping him round the ear, then other fists began to fly. Guys shouting, an arm punching out and fresh sweet rain on his face, as he was running, running, Doug and Ali after him, then beside him. Patrick too. They were all running, then slowing. Stopping, his bum pressed against some jaggy wall, his belly doubled. Panting and laughing.

'Oh for fucksake, Slowjo. That was mental.'

'Did you mean for us to start a riot?'

'Of course he didn't. He's fucking thick.'

Joe straightened himself up. He was near double the size of Doug, he could probably lift him off the ground and smite him. That was a cracking word. *Smite.* Except Doug would just knee him in the balls then reach up and break his jaw. Instead, Joe had stretched, extending long arms, spreading fingers like a peacock would fan its tail. Ali was squatting, laughing still. Even Joe felt bubbles in his nose. There was a warm, shared element to the laughter; they had been compressed and expelled in a joint ordeal.

'Right,' said Patrick. 'Are we going to this party or what?'

It started well, a sharing of fags and beer. Though not of the money Joe had used to buy the beer. But there had been a sense of community, almost, of mutual joshing and affectionate shoves. Then a shove had become a casual arm, and the music had got louder and folk kept offering him drinks, green and blue liquids that you would wear gloves to pick up in a lab. Someone had brought a set of comedy dentures, the kind that clack when wound up, and they kept asking him to say it. *Say it again Joe. Say what you said about his teeth, Joe.* There'd been dancing too, much dancing, and he'd let his limbs go free, revelling in their jerkiness. Folk were laughing, clapping. They'd asked him to put his driver's hat on, could he kick his legs up higher?

The wind caught his face, and Joe reeled as he remembered, bumping against the frame. It wouldn't do to close his eyes, not up here. He took a long breath, straightened one of the lances he had knocked against, ensuring its link to the next one remained unbroken.

Lorna had joined in the dancing, squeezing closer and closer into him until he wasn't sure which flesh was hers and a dizzy creamy feeling guzzled into him. He had gone willingly with her into the bedroom, they had jointly pushed the pile of coats to the floor. All of it mutual, consensual, up until the clothes bit and then it was only him, and her clapping him as he kept dancing and he kept his hat on.

Get on the floor Joe.
Beg like a dog Joe.
Get on all fours Joe.

His penis had seemed enormous, ramming out from between his legs. He had stared down in amazement as Lorna climbed on to his back, watching it swing under the shadow of his peaked cap. Then Lorna had slapped his bum and it went even harder; he thought it would split its skin and what was he meant to *do* with it, aye. he knew the mechanics alright. but he was getting scared and then the door cracked open and they all piled in. All of them, just all of them, lassies and Doug and Brillo, Patrick too, with their mobiles high and snapping. Getting close-ups of his balls, his arse.

His stricken, ugly face beneath its stupid fucking hat. Sending the photos round, posting them Godknows where and it was ugh and it was he couldn't they wouldn't let him get away if he stood up they'd see him more and he was just staring, staring at the carpet, staring at the carpet and his dying flaccid penis then Lorna had slid off him and he'd got up and run away. Tugging a coat from the pile, he still had his socks on. Coat and socks and he'd run all the way home and he was there, lying there all night and day. Awake, but pretending when his mum came in.

And he wished all day that he was dead. Joe peeled off a strip of Sellotape. God bless Blue Peter. Sprinkled a little of the powdered metals on the loop of sticky side out tape. Not one person had challenged him, not since that policeman had shouted up from the road this afternoon. And Joe had told him flat. *It's for tonight.* The power a yellow jacket bestowed.

Chapter Fifty-Four

It was good that they only had an hour. Anna had done it deliberately, less time to think or make mistakes. Less time also to be away from Rob's bed and the warmth of Grace's skin. Already, her breasts were drying up. How long until it stopped altogether; when did it mean no going back, that your miraculous abilities had been absorbed and your body would produce no more milk? Or was it symptomatic withering? Would three witches be popping up soon, to offer tonics and advice?

'Back so soon, ma'am?' Whisky Mac nodded at Anna across Cranstonhill's front bar.

'You didn't see me.'

'Fair enough. You'll no be wanting to know they Citicard protesters are trying to hijack the Christmas Lights parade, then? I mean, impeding Santa's lawful progress; it's just not on.'

'Like I said, I'm not here. Never was.'

She'd gone from hot to shivery. Even with the duvet-coat swaddling her, Anna couldn't get warm. She smacked her open palms together, kindling some sensation, but there was a numbness to her, pervading every part. None of this was real. On rapid wheels, she had glided through Cranstonhill Police Office, a weight of nostalgia pressing on her. She found the dictaphone her predecessors would have used, in the days before downloads and PCs and voice recognition software. It was dusty, but the wee wheels still whirred, after she'd knocked two batteries from a wireless in the kitchen. Last Christmas Eve, that same wireless had crackled out carols as she and Stuart Barrowman prepared a turkey dinner for the nightshift, and she'd spilled hot gravy there, on that shiny mark on her thumb. She also unearthed the notes Alex had given her, detailing how Francine had died. Praying it would be enough. Anna was placing all her trust in the glimmer of Mary. Alex too. She had chosen McDonald's primarily for its proximity to Maryhill Police Office; it was past the Barracks if she remembered right, but still only two, maybe three minutes' drive. Quicker maybe, on a Sunday night.

Alex was the only cop she could think of who would come unquestioningly if she called – and might understand why. As soon as she had a confession from Galletly, she'd have to get out of there. She would have to hold it together long enough to convince Galletly that she had the money, just not *here,* not with her but close by. She would simply have to hold it together just to look at him.

Anna could not articulate, even to herself, how scared she really was. How deep, deeper than any other motivation, had been the imperative to make Galletly go away. That was a huge part of why she had done it. She'd thought if he was looking at her through sliced bars of light then he couldn't touch her; could reach no further than the confines of his cell. Anna had received several beatings in her career, it was an occupational hazard. But the atavistic, piss-yourself terror Galletly engendered was as raw now as the night he cracked her skull. She needed the reassurance of knowing Alex would be there if there was no other way out. And she needed to hear a friend's voice. She sat inside her office, in the dark, and phoned him.

'Alex? It's Anna Cam—'

His voice was thick with anger. 'Where the fuck have you been? What have you been playing at? I've been phoning you all weekend.'

'I know. I was in an accident.'

'Oh shit Anna. Are you okay? What about the baby?'

'I'm fine; I had her. A wee girl.'

'Anna.' His tone softened entirely. 'Oh man, that's brilliant. And she's alright?'

'She's beautiful,' said Anna.

'Just like her mum.'

'Rob was in the car too, Alex. He's . . . he's still in a coma.'

'Fuck . . . Oh Anna, I'm so sorry. Where are you?'

'I'm . . . here. I'm in Glasgow.'

'Do you need me to come over?'

'No. No it's cool. But thank you.' Shocked at how the gratitude hurt her, its impact tightening her chest and returning her to Plockton, to the fur of her baby's head and the coldness of Rob's pale hand and she had to focus. Seal them up in compartments as if the sea were pouring in. 'Look, you know I haven't been straight with you about this Fran—'

'Aye, aye. Trust nae bugger, Anna. Whatever you want to say to me, best not say it over the phone, eh?'

'I know. But Alex, I have to . . . I might need to see you later on tonight. You still at work?'

'For the next hour or so I reckon.'

'Right. Will you please keep your mobile on you, in case I call? Please?'

'Where are you though? Are you still in hospital? Look, don't you worry about anything else at the moment. Just you look after your husband and your baby the now, yeah? Work can wait.'

If Anna told Alex she was going to deliver him his suspect on a plate, he would prevent her from going. He would want to know all the details of why Anna was involved, why she was risking her own person in this way and how she knew Galletly was their man. Then he would take over, run this as a proper operation and intercept Galletly on sight. Ergo, Anna would be back to square one: no confession from Galletly, no statement from Mary and herself on a one-way trip to the fingerprint suite. But if all else failed and Galletly pulled a gun on her and Shelly, there had to be some cavalry in reserve. Indefatigable as they both apparently were, they weren't indestructible, and however much Shelly liked to flutter round the dark side, he was a delicate wee moth. Always had been, irrespective of the patina prison had given him. Her heart bucked as she checked her watch. Less than twenty-five minutes to go.

'I'm fine, Alex. I have to go now. Will you please just do what I'm asking? Then I can explain everything to you, yes? Just be ready in case I call.'

'Always.'

'I know. That's why I phoned you.'

There was one other person she had to phone. Had to, to prove that she was coming back, that this was not a just-in-case call, it was not the sealed letter left under the pillow.

This was not her legacy. It was a normal mum, checking in. If it was not, it was unbearable. If this is your life, Anna, here and now, it is as unbearable as the incipient tightness crawling up your chest.

She left the office by the back door, dialling as she went. Nobody there to see her go.

'Laura? It's Mum.'

A hard, gasping silence.

'Laura? Are you there?'

'Where are you?'

'I'm in Glasgow baby. I'm fine. How's Dad?'

'How could you leave us?'

'Darling, I didn't want to . . . I'm sorry. Please tell me how Dad is?'

'Just the same.'

Anna's neck bowed. 'And Grace?'

'She's doing good. Her hair's got blonder, definitely. It's like the gold tips are moving further up every hour.'

'Really?' Already, she was changing. The features Anna had imprinted behind her eyes were vanishing.

'They let me hold her hand today.'

'Did they? That's brilliant. I'm so proud of you, Laura.'

'Yeah, right. So proud you piss off and leave me to it. Fair enough Dad and me, but d'you not even care about your own baby? Your own blood?'

'You're my baby too. I . . .' Anna didn't want to scare her, but she owed her some fragment of the truth. 'You know the man that chased you?'

'Yeah?' Either tentative or disdainful; Anna couldn't tell, not through all this vast, crackly distance.

'Well, I'm frightened he might come after us again. So I've come down to Glasgow to stop him. To *stop* him, Laura, I promise, so he never comes back to hurt any of us again, right?'

'Did he hurt my dad?'

The girl was so clever. Her suspicion as accurate as it was fast.

'I . . . I think he might have.'

'And is this because of your stupid fucking work?'

'Please don't swear, Laura.'

'Who the fuck are you to tell me not to swear?'

'Laura, please. Would your mum want you talking like that?'

'Don't you talk about my mum. You have no right to talk about my mum—'

'Please baby. I don't have much time.'

Laura's anger faded into tears. 'Are you coming back?'

'I promise. Tomorrow. I'll be back tomorrow, and everything will be fine. What about you? Are you okay? Are Cath and Jamie looking after you?'

'Yeah.' Laura sniffed. 'Jamie's nice – he's really funny. Cath's nice too. Don't think she likes you much, though. She was pure shouting at Jamie when he told her you'd gone away. Saying it was bloody typical.'

Despite herself, Anna smiled. 'Cath's alright. I stole something of hers once. But I did give it back. You can trust her a hundred per cent, though. Anything you need, you go to her, right?'

'Mum?' A desperation entered Laura's voice, the spiralling blades of it higher than pain, higher than the ache of ice cream. 'Are you coming back? Please, please be coming back.'

'Of course I am, silly.' She made the words come out in steady drops. 'Give Gracie and your dad the biggest kiss, yeah? I love you. Don't ever, ever forget that.'

'Mum—'

Anna switched the phone off. Kissed it. Then placed it in the pocket of her coat. Beside the rolled-up sheets of A4 that told you how Francine had been tortured, how her head had been held under water for the optimum length of time, until her lungs began to drown themselves and then the air burst in again. And again. Letting you suck in just enough to give you that plaintive glimmer of hope, which is worse than no hope at all. Alex had recorded each stage of Francine's death dispassionately, methodically listing what he knew of her journey and when it had finally ended. But nothing of the why.

Mary looked like she was good at embroidering tales; all she'd need was a framework of plausibility. She was a funny wee thing; had refused to come into the police station, insisted on being dropped off round the corner in Kent Road. Anna half expected her to be gone when she returned, but the girl was still there, loitering in a doorway and chewing on her thumbnail.

'Are we right?' said Anna, opening the passenger door.

'Did you get it?'

'Here.' Anna passed her the cone of paper, held with a red elastic band. Mary's index finger stretched beneath the band, loosening the papers.

'Why don't you leave it just now?' said Anna. 'The light here's no good anyway. Leave it until after we've got him on tape.'

'Why?'

'Because it will upset you, and if I don't get this confession then you don't need to do it, do you?'

Mary shrugged. 'I guess not. Did you get a tape recorder then?'

Gingerly, Anna tapped her left breast. 'Yup. Tucked up beside my mammoth mammaries. Which seem to have stopped oozing for the moment, so fingers crossed we'll not end up with the thing rusting. I've a ton of tissues between me and the dictaphone anyway. Just as a precaution.'

Mary clicked her seatbelt in place. 'When did you have your baby?'

'Today. Or maybe yesterday – it's a bit hazy.'

'Bloody hell! Are you mental?'

'Totally. Now, are we ready? We have less than fifteen minutes to get to Maryhill.'

'And do we have a plan exactly?' asked Mary.

'I'll tell you when we get there.'

'Do you not trust me? Why not tell me now?'

Anna swung on to North Street, with the motorway dropping down to her right and the shimmering, erudite fatness of the Mitchell Library illuminated on her left.

'Because I've still to make it up yet.'

Neither of them spoke much as Anna drove through Charing Cross and turned left on to Maryhill Road. It wasn't the night for first-date exchanges. They both looked instead at the statue of dragon and knight perched incongruously at the truncated junction of St George's Cross, forever chewed by the intersection of the motorway, and they watched the busy headlights shine above them on the bridge. They noticed the men outside pubs, sucking on pale-blue smoke and the graceful angular rise of Queen's Cross Church, a lesser-known Mackintosh masterpiece which Anna always meant to visit but never had. As Maryhill Road progressed, it became darker, pools of yellow light becoming white. They had done studies, those boffins who did such things, and it was proven that white street-lighting made folk feel safer than the dusty buzzing yellow of before, but Anna couldn't see why. The white was too stark. It was unforgiving, setting bright monochrome sureness against firm black relief. Fine if you were bathed directly in the whiteness, which blazed your eyes like night-sun, but the shadows were decidedly darker. They drove on in silence. And here was happy yellow again. Yellow and red, the cosy steaming gobbling light of McDonald's. Anna pulled into the side street before the restaurant. Handed Mary the keys.

'Can you drive?'

'Kind of. I did pass my test, but it's been a while.'

'Well, hang on to these – and be ready to put the boot down if needs be, right?'

'If needs be what? Do we have a plan yet?'

'Have you got a mobile?'

'Yeah. But it's deid. Not been charged in two weeks.'

'But you still have it?'

Mary rummaged in her rucksack. 'Somewhere . . . yup.' She extracted a wee red oblong. 'There you go. But it's useless.'

'I'll take it anyway.'

Anna swapped it with her own phone. 'You take mine, okay? Now, what I want you to do is give it seven minutes – no more, no less. If I'm not out in seven minutes, you phone this number.' She scrolled down to Alex's number.

'Why seven minutes?'

'It's my lucky number.' Anna pretended to grin. She'd read you should do it to trick your brain. If you were about to give a presentation and your nerves were threatening only gibbering stutters and long, blank blinks, you should smile, not hyperventilate. The physical act of doing set up a psychosomatic reaction of feeling. Thus, by smiling, your brain would think you were relaxed, and would release happy, confirmatory endorphins in response. Maybe Anna wasn't grinning hard enough.

'Mary, are you looking? This number here, see? No matter what happens, do not phone anyone else. This is the DI I was telling you about at Maryhill. He's waiting for us to call.'

'And what do I tell him when I phone?'

'Just say you're with Anna Cameron, tell him where we are and say I need him to come now.' Anna pinged the button on her seatbelt. It shot back on its inertia reel. Two minutes to go. 'But this is just as a final, final measure. I'll be out before then, don't worry. And when I am out, you be ready to drive your arse off, okay?'

Mary was unbuckling her own seatbelt. 'D'you not want me to come with you?'

'Fucksake, no! No way. Mary, whatever happens, you make sure you keep out of sight, d'you understand? Galletly doesn't even know you and I have spoken. Apart from Shelly, who will squeal like a girl at the least sign of trouble, Galletly thinks I'm totally on my own. You are my get-out-of-jail card.'

Was making bad-taste jokes also part of the psychological armoury? Anna blew stale air from her mouth, felt her fringe lift, then land, sticky, on her brow. The feverish ague had become part of her; she could not recall feeling comfortable any more, or what constituted a normal heartbeat – and time, other than the ticking immediacy of the second hand on her watch, had lost its power to anchor. Yesterday. The hills. Her body opening up in birth. When was that? She exhaled once more, sought the handle of the door. The curve of it was nicely cold inside her hand.

'See you Mary.'

'Got your tape on?'

'Oh, shit.' Anna fumbled inside her bra.

'Can I ask – why there?'

'Closest I could get to his head – he's only wee.'

Keep telling yourself that. He's a tiny, vicious nothing.

'See you in five then,' said Mary. 'I mean seven.'

Anna nodded, got out of the car. She went round the corner to the big gold M and pushed the glass and plastic door. Inside, the restaurant was painfully bright, scattered with people. A small queue meandered at the two open tills, diners deliberating on the various delights with slow, bovine stares. A young man in a red baseball cap wiped crumbs to the floor with a blackened cloth, yawning, and two youths went in tandem to the toilets, their wide-eyed eagerness and shrunken shoulders suggesting the one thing on their minds – a quick score. *You want fries with that, bud?* Anna searched the room in vain for Shelly and Galletly, moving her eyes from left to right. Dreading what she might see. And then she heard Shelly's familiar caw.

'Maddie! Over here, doll.'

She turned, saw a man sitting alone, close to the door through which she'd come. He was wearing a long green coat, and all his curls were hidden, tucked inside a red beanie. The glittering earring should have given the game away though. It was a diamante question mark, twinkling at her. How could she have missed him? But the man Anna had been looking for was skinny, and this Shelly was definitely not. She went over to him, almost running.

'Hello beautiful.' He pre-empted her embrace, standing up and offering outstretched arms.

'Oh Shelly, pal. It's so good to see you.' Her head on his collar, synthetic fur tickling her nose and she thought of Alice. Wanted desperately to cuddle her cat and be quiet by a fire in a soft-lit room.

'Here you. Don't be getting ma mangy minge all soggy.'

Anna stood a little back from him, still holding his fleshy arms. 'I'm sorry. My head's up ma arse – I didn't recognise you when I came in.'

'Aye, so I seen. Ach well, I canny really blame you since I've went and done a Boy George, eh? Fae Queen of the World tae Fat Nan the Boxer. Who ate all the pies indeed?' He held up an emphatic hand. 'And naw, don't go all, "Ooh Shelly, I'd hardly of noticed if you'd no of said". It's too late now, doll,' he pouted, tossing his wool-clad head.

'Are you wearing eyeliner?'

'Fucking aye. There's just mair of me to be gorgeous now.'

She wanted to kiss those rosy lips, wanted to mark all the ways that made them similar and connected. 'Me too.' She indicated her belly, but of course, Shelly wouldn't have known she'd been pregnant.

'Oof. You havny half piled on the beef, doll.'

'I know. Alice says hi, by the way.'

Strangely, Shelly didn't respond. A heaviness entered his eyes, just briefly, and then he picked up his newspaper. He waved the tabloid at her. 'Wisny sure how long I'd have to wait.'

Anna's nails were digging into her hands, her nervous adrenalin becoming impatience, conscious that Mary was on a clock. At least two of their seven minutes had ticked away. 'When's he getting here then?'

'He's not. Don't freak – we're going tae see him.'

'Oh, now, wait a fucking minute, Shelly. You promised me . . .'

Shelly took her by the elbow, nudging her towards the door. 'Cool your jets doll. It's just roon the corner. He didny want tae be seen in such a public place.'

'But I *did*, Shelly. That's the whole point.'

'Christ, Anna. You canny argue with a man like Gilly. I've got us this far, alright?'

Outside, with the heat of anger and warm, vent-borne grease on her cheeks, the air bit brutally. It was good; cold sky slapping her awake.

She let the cold enter into her, welcoming it until there was only cold. No fear, no frustration, simply an awareness of the deep and constant air and how it moved around her; stretching over ambivalent planes of roof and lamppost, parting for each stride of anxious leg, each twist of spine. Going with them down the side street, not the one in which Mary was parked, but its parallel, leading them behind the McDonald's and across one other road. Three minutes gone at least.

'He's in here,' said Shelly, nodding towards a tall, thin building which stood in a yard of its own. It was clad in darkness; you could just catch the faint painting running in a vertical banner down the building's side: *Bilsland's Bakery* in curly, peeling white on brick. An iron fire-escape ran adjacent to the lettering, its black spindles conjuring a sharp image of the Applecross Road and how it doubled back on itself in angry, climbing spikes. A warp of sickness cut through the cold.

'Shelly. I'm not going in there. No fucking way.'

'Then you canny see the man, doll. That's the way it goes. He's probably watching us the now. Which reminds me. I'm gonny have tae frisk you.' Shelly raised an eyebrow. 'Doctor's orders.'

With powerless lassitude, she lifted her arms, allowing Shelly to run his hands up and down her body. When he came to her breasts, she flinched.

'What the hell do you think you're doing?'

'He said tae make sure I got your moby. It's no in your coat, it's no in your joggers, so it's either up your fanny or down your tits. Which are all crinkly, by the way.'

'Are you for real? Whose fucking side are you on?'

Shelly lunged in tight to her ear. Anna jerked away. From a distance, it would look as if he had struck her. 'Whose d'you fucking think, ya stupit mare?' he hissed. 'But he'll no entertain us if I don't go through the motions.'

Anna delved inside her bra. Threw Mary's mobile to the ground. 'Satisfied?'

'And the rest.' You'd think he was appearing on stage, the big open gestures and the sotto voce. 'What's all the padding for? Nae way do you have tits as big as that, Anna Cameron.'

'It's the money, duh? Sorry, did you want me to bring it in a big bag marked swag?'

'Oh, aye, right enough.' He pretended to pat her breasts in confirmation.

'Shelly. Get tae. I'm warning you.'

'Don't worry about the phone, gorgeous,' Shelly whispered. 'I've still got mine, alright?' Then, in a louder voice, he said, 'Thank fuck I'd no tae plunder your nether regions, doll. I'd of had tae get psychological counselling. And a job-lot of steri-wipes, too. Right, that's us. M'oan.'

Together, they walked into the shadow of the building. The front door had been forced, clean new wood showing in the gash beside the lock. As your head goes under water, you gulp all the desperate air you can. Francine would have done it. Anna regulated her breathing, taking only that which she required. Tasting sumps of saliva and cold, clean air.

'Shelly.' She grabbed his hand. 'Tell me this is going to be okay.'

'I swear to you, Anna. On ma big brother's life.'

Which she thought, as they were walking in, was an odd thing to say.

At first, Anna could see nothing, as she was meant to, every aspect of this little pantomime designed to unnerve and disconnect. You could hear the night move through this place, hear the gentle murmur of roosting birds. Refocusing, recalibrating until she could make out the full vastness of the building. No floors remained intact, just the dusty shell, with a kind of gantry running on one side.

'Evening all.'

Galletly's diminutive frame was silhouetted ten times larger than life. Small-man syndrome writ large and black. He was positioned on the gantry, an open space behind him. A broken window maybe? It was the sole source of light, fingering its way in.

'Grand night for it, don't you think?'

Anna couldn't bring herself to speak.

'Eh, Gilly. That's us here then.'

'Indeed, it is yourselves, Michael. I can see that. But, here, this is no way to conduct a conversation. C'mon up to my office and we'll do the necessary.'

'No,' Anna shouted. 'You come down here and stop fucking me about. You want your money, you come and get it.'

There was a pause, and underneath that, the pitch and toss of wings as the pigeons flurried. She could hear Galletly clear his throat. Deliberately or otherwise, he leaned forwards into the beam of light, adopting a casual pose. His nose and chin were the muzzle she remembered, eyes still concealed. He placed his toecap on the bottom rail of the gantry, his fingers neatly clasped and draped over the top rail. Then he flung his words down like solar wind.

'You want a fucking deal, you will do it on my terms or not at all.'

Chapter Fifty-Five

From her corner of the abandoned street, Mary had watched them go inside. *Rather you than me, doll.* The place looked like a Hammer House of Horror – derelict buildings always had that sense of loss about them. You could screw your eyes up and see thin shapes of workers in their flour-dust clothes, the trays and vans and bustle of it. What was once a chirpy, necessary place had gone, and in its place, a black hole of negative energy which made it seem darker than the living buildings round it. Lucky for Anna, Mary was a free spirit. If a person told her not to do something, then you were guaranteed she would. By going after Anna, she was merely protecting her investment – that woman was not at all stable. Plus if Mary was following them, rather than sitting in the motor like a big fat stooge; well, there was no way some bastard could creep up behind her. She'd only just caught the two of them going in: Tweedledum and Tweedledee, a bizarre confection of elaborate coats and two, let's be frank, big waddlers. From the rear, Anna could have been any old jakey, and that Shelly was a total state too, with his lurid coat and his big daft hat. But where was the Irish tosser; where was Shelly's brother? Presumably the reception committee was waiting inside.

Mary looked at the time on Anna's phone. Did the seven minutes start from now, or from when she'd left the car? Anna hadn't been at all clear. Should she try and get closer then? You couldn't see or hear a thing from here. But what if they were right behind the door, and big saft Mary ran headlong into a delicate discussion? It wasn't right, though. They'd said they'd meet Anna in McDonald's, and now the parameters were shifting. Perhaps if

she just went *over* to the door. For once, Mary would have liked
to have been at the centre rather than drifting on the periphery.
But that was apt, wasn't it? For the Lady Mary was nothing if not
a drifter.

She was about to make a run for it, darting over the shadowed
yard and into the doorway, when a grating noise that culminated
in a thump made her look up high. Figures, no, a single figure at
the top of the iron fire-escape, then two more figures coming out
the bakery, moving out of the building and round, towards the
bottom of the stair. It was very dark, almost pitch-black, but in the
borrowed light from the street outside, she could make out Anna's
pale, tight face, could see the supportive arm of Shelly behind her,
who passed to the outside as they turned into the staircase. She
saw him pull off his hat, scratch the surface of his close-cropped
head. For one stark moment they were directly facing, Mary and
the man called Shelly who could not see her.

Her stomach flipped, a run of cold air inside her.

She could see him, though. Scalpel-sharp.

Shelly. It was the face of the Fat Man.

No other. No doubt.

Chapter Fifty-Six

A sparse row of metal treads, swaying as she put her foot down. Mounting the scaffold, him standing at the top, she could feel his leer. Head reeling at the thought of the height and how flimsy it was, how his stare could knock her off, just from here. When was the last time Anna had eaten? Shelly's hand steadied her. 'It's alright, doll. I've got your back.'

Two minutes. If she had not come back in two minutes, Mary would phone. Another three minutes and Alex would be here, she had five minutes, five minutes to hang on and make him speak and then she did not care.

'An interesting choice, eh?' he's saying, with an accent that grates and prises its way into your head. 'Maryhill. Did you think I'd not come back to the scene of the crime then?'

'So you admit you killed Francine Gallagher then?'

Surely it couldn't be that easy? Anna gripped the handrail of the fire-escape. She was about four steps away from him, Shelly tucked up behind her. It wasn't so far to look up now, but she wouldn't. Could just make out the tips of his feet. Black leather Docs, his speciality.

'Me? I'll admit to nothing. Will you?'

She had to get a little closer. The night air was very still, but all it needed was a passing car or a gust of wind and the tape would fill with fuzz.

'I want to hear you say it,' she said. 'I know there's nothing I can do, but I need to know. Why did you have to kill her? Francine did nothing, not to you.'

'Did she not? Did the bitch not see me rot then? Did she not wonder why no one came after *her*?'

The wail in his voice made her brave. Anna found she could look at him. He was just as sparse and weedy as before. A nothing person, an insipid, transparent creature with barbed fronds.

'Is that why you tortured her first?' she said.

'Ah no, see. That would be your doing, Anna Cameron. All I wanted was a name, and the cow would not provide one. There's always a chain of command in these affairs, you see. Francine is grunt material, not a leader. I knew that as soon as I smelled the rankness of her.' His stare wavered briefly, floating past Anna and on to Shelly's wee red hat. 'Here, d'you think that's where rank comes from? What do you think, Michael me lad?'

'Eh, I wouldny know, Gilly.'

'No. No you wouldn't know fuck all if it wasn't draped in sequins and riding you from behind.'

Anna took one more step, so she was almost level. 'Leave him alone. Leave him alone, leave me alone and leave my bloody family alone.'

Galletly showed his teeth. 'How is the good doctor by the way?'

'You shut your mouth.'

'Ah, here. Can we do it now, Michael? Ah, go on, go on go on go on.'

His tongue was running under his upper lip, stretching the pink-gummed slevery mass away from yellow teeth. A small man with a massive ego, the thick-entwining shivers of his neck a nascent pounce. Anna prepared to start moving backwards. Her bum nudged against Shelly's chest, but he didn't take the hint.

Almost whispering, Galletly carried on. 'Tell Anna why you phoned her, Michael.'

You could hear the night moving in this place. Measured frequencies of sigh and spoor, of dust and starlight and small creeping things. You could feel Shelly at your back, hard and solid and pressing tighter than he needed to. You could make out words, and a voice that seemed to be his.

'To find out if you were still alive.'

'I know,' you say, not turning. 'You told me that.'

'Ah, yes. But did he tell you why?'

'I don't ...' Anna just kept looking at Galletly, fixing on his bleak and bitter eyes.

'Ach, I was getting bored with you, Anna. And the cheek of you, haring off like that. No, bugger the money. Enough is enough, says I. What if you got ideas, really did slip off somewhere? So off I went – and, I have to say, Wester Ross is just beautiful at this time of year. But Michael here, ach he's a mercenary, so he is. Wants blood from a stone – then her life savings too.'

Anna reached out behind her.

'Shelly?'

He was still warm and soft. Still Shelly. Didn't sound like Shelly though. There was no light about him.

'It's aye about fucking you, isn't it Maddie? Your life, your family. Who you can pick and drop to suit your fucking self.'

Each syllable expelled with a dreadful, lowering spite. Anna braced herself against the handrail, half turned. Found herself beyond the fear that was dispassionately bricking her in. He wore no hat, and his hair was shorn. Brutal.

'What about ma life, but? Mind my big brother, Maddie <i>doll</i>? Aye well, he never made it out the fucking jail. The Handymen ended him, because he was a grass. And who made him that grass? You did.'

'How can you say that? I only—'

'You fucking used him to suit yourself. They Special Branch wankers said he'd get protected status – well, did he fuck. Did you check? Did you care? Did you even know if <i>I</i> was alive or fucking deid?'

Galletly clapped his hands. 'Oh Jee-sus, this is magic. I think I have a hard-on. I do! I have a big stiff willy and a—'

Whatever else he had was consumed by the pounding roar of an explosion and over that, the sound of Mary screaming up at her.

Chapter Fifty-Seven

'Did yous catch that? M'oan!' The Tube spun through the double doors of the mess room. The heavy doors swung back on themselves, a clash of in and out, in and out and at first you couldn't hear what he'd been saying. Alex turned the sound down on the telly no one was really watching. He'd only come through to use the vending machine – a refreshing wee Snickers bar to contribute to his five-a-day (peanuts were a vegetable, he'd decided), and a can of juice, but then this programme was on about crop circles, so he'd pulled up a chair. Couldn't concentrate all the same, even when the man was saying about the Aztecs and *remarkable parallels*. Anna phoning had unnerved him – on several levels – and now he was jittery, aye checking his watch, then fiddling with his phone. A callow youth waiting for the girl of his dreams to throw him a bone.

He couldn't wait here all night, Sandra had phoned him twice, telling him that dinner was ready; then, the second time, that dinner was ruined, yabbering on for ages and him thinking, *get off the bloody phone woman*. But every time he tried to speak, she ploughed on through him, drilling down another layer of STUFF THAT WAS WRONG and WAYS THEY COULD TRY HARDER.

Anna had said she needed him. He'd got the sense they might actually meet up, and then it would be fine to hold her, to do this thing his body was crying out to do. And she'd tell him what was going on because she wanted to, not because he'd made her or threatened her, and it would be honest words, pouring from her mouth, and he'd take those words and give them back to her. Alex

would say to her, *Anna, baby. It's okay. I knew it all along.* Which of
course he hadn't, didn't, but he knew enough. There was Galletly
stalking her, and Francine needing her, and Anna's voluminous
silence. All speaking of subterfuge and revenge.

But it doesn't matter, none of it matters, he'd say. *We've got Galletly's
DNA – thanks to you. Aye, I know it was you who left those clothes,
and he's going to jail as soon as we can track him down. Man can say
any old shite he likes, but he canny prove it. I can keep you safe, Anna,
if you'll let me.*

By doing that, she would love him again, the way they first were,
mates and muckers before sex got in the way. Alex wasn't quite
sure how that worked, a man and a woman who were asexual
friends, but he would give it a try. Anything to get back what
they'd lost.

'Boss! Boss! Are you coming, then?' The Tube's head was
wobbling good-style. Alex wished it would just roll from his
shoulders and give them all peace. He'd sent most of his team
home; they had assembled as much of the case as they could
pending an interview with their suspect. It was only a couple of
uniform cops in the mess room with him, quietly engaged in a
game of Noms. They looked up, barely hiding their amusement at
the Tube's weird, lolloping jig.

'Coming to what, Terry?'

'The bomb!'

'Oh fuck aye!' One of the cops pressed the volume on his
Airwave set, and the dispatcher's voice filled the room. 'Listen.'

'Repeat. Reports of a fire and explosion on Gairbraid Bridge,
directly above Maryhill Road. Urgent request for all available
stations to attend—'

As the dispatcher was speaking, the phone on the wall began to
shrill. Alex picked it up. It was the duty officer. 'Who's that?'

'Alex Patterson.'

'Right, I need anyone who's anyone to get down to Garloch
Bridge now. It's utter chaos – we've a double-decker bus on fire
directly beneath the bridge. Many's up there?'

'Four of us.'

'Tell them to make their way to the bar immediately and the van'll run them down.'

Alex waved his arm towards the door. 'Bar, now, the lot of you. Full kit, the works.' He spoke into the phone again. 'How bad is it, Eric? The Tube said it was a bomb?'

'Aye, well the fire appears to have exploded or detonated some device, which is now reacting with the water in the canal above. And we've that bloody barge full of school weans and celebs bang in the frigging middle. Mind that Commonwealth crap the boss was banging on about?'

'Shit.' Alex shrugged on his jacket as he was speaking. 'Should the road no have been closed then, for security? How the hell did a bus get wedged underneath?' He swiped his mobile from the table. Bloody thing was trilling again. Glanced at the screen. *Anna*.

'Good question,' said the duty officer. 'Ask A Division. Apparently they did the risk assessment for the entire route. *Arseholes*. Now mind and tell everyone to switch off any mobiles or electrical equipment, in case of further explosions. Get them to do it now, before they leave the office. We've no idea if there's other devices.'

'They're en route already, pal, so you can tell them yourself. I'm just coming, okay? Get the van to wait.'

'Time and terrorists wait for no man.'

'I'll be there right now.'

'You mind and switch off your moby and all. Seriously. Do it now.'

'Aye, aye. I'm minding it.' Alex hung up, ran towards the stairs. His mobile had gone quiet anyway. 'Sorry Anna,' he said, switching the thing off. He'd check his messages later. There'd still be time, later.

Chapter Fifty-Eight

Mary was frantic. They had Anna on the fire escape, trapped. The instant she had seen that bastard's face, before she even saw how it was going to pan out, she'd been phoning and phoning. The detective's number was constantly engaged, and then, when it had finally rung, he'd never even answered.

Bugger it, she was dialling 999. Before she could do anything, the place erupted. It was a massive whoomph and the sky lit up. An orange mushroom, billowing headache-bright. Up there, on the stairs, they'd all flinched and stopped. It was like kids having someone shout at them and Mary had just let her lungs rip, screaming at Anna to get away.

'He's not Shelly. He's the Fat Man.'

'Well fuck you, ya cheeky cow,' he screamed, belting it down the stairs.

Never offend the sensibilities of a vain old queen who knows he's overshared the biscuits.

'Mary!' yelled Anna. 'Take the tape.' She plunged her hand down the top of her jumper, lobbed the dictaphone high into the air. At least Mary supposed it was the dictaphone, but the object never made it to the bottom, striking and bouncing open on the second landing and she had no opportunity to run up because the Fat Man was bearing down, his lurid coat flapping as he ran.

Anna, still screaming at her. 'Mary, just get out of here.'

'I'll get help,' she shouted up, picking up her speed as the Fat Man advanced. She had hammered down two streets before she remembered the fucking car. Too late, too late, just keep powering down this road.

First a fire engine, then a police car. She tried to flag them to stop but they screeched on down the long fast street, Mary after them. Constantly pressing redial, pressing redial. Unable to hear if it was answered, her feet breaking on to stone, his girth crashing behind her; she could smell his meaty sweat. She knew she was running *to* something. Getting close to the confusion, you could feel it before you saw it. A rain of fire, the shrillest blue light. She could smell burning, could hear it sizzle. There was a chaos of horns and engines, cars latticing the road, a mass of people churning. Mary ran to a policeman, there were dozens of them, running like ants, and two of them holding on to a boy who was weeping. 'Tell them not to use water – it's phosphine gas.' He stared, distraught, at Mary. 'I didn't know about the water.' She ignored him, grabbed the policeman nearest to her.

'Help me! Please help me!'

The officer frowned, yanked her to one side as another fire engine powered through. Furious red whipping past her, Mary turning to see where Fat Man was, but he had gained, had passed her in the confusion. She saw him legging it into the crowd spilling over the embankment, saw the burning arc of bridge.

Saw bright dancing fire. A row of flaming stakes, fastened above the bridge. The stakes were massive fireworks, shaped in letters.

And they spelled out: *F R E E D O M*, emblazoned red and orange on a velvet band of sky.

Chapter Fifty-Nine

To the west, Maryhill was burning. A great streak of orange with no sun behind it, the sweet song of sirens calling distantly. Anna needed them here.

Alex wouldn't let her down.

Galletly wasn't going to use a gun, that would be too clinical. He had taken a knife from his inside pocket, a long, slim blade. Was rubbing it down with impeccable slowness. An artist, honing his craft.

'Just you and me then, Anna my darling. Did you bring me my cash?'

'All I've brought you is to the finish.'

Absurd, papery words, disintegrating before impact. He knew it and she knew it, and in the grim, relentless midst of an ache to which she could see no end, Anna remembered her first day out alone. This ned, laughing at her when she opened her handbag to retrieve her notebook, and a spare pair of tights had come out with it, snagged on the lid of her pen.

'Oh, very profound. And did you stand in front of your bathroom mirror rehearsing that, did you? Ach, it's a damned shame to waste it, because you really are a fine-looking woman. But you know what happens now, don't you?'

Deliberately slowing her speech, stretching every last second into minutes. There was no sensation below her waist. If she tried to run down these stairs, she would fall and break her neck.

'Yup. Like I said. It ends here.'

He tapped the tip of his tongue with the blade. 'Ah well, no. Not really. Because once I'm done with you, then I think I might go back to Plockton. I mean, I have the taste for it now, you know? The man, he's just a big plate of vegetable soup, I reckon, otherwise he'd be here, he'd've stopped you. Foolhardy little shite that you are.'

She felt a muscle taut in her spine. Her body's lack of mobility did not extend to her brain. 'The police will be here in fifty seconds.'

He widened his eyes. 'Is that right? Well, this should only take about ten.'

'Maybe less,' she replied.

It nestled in her hand, had been ever since she tugged it out along with the dictaphone. A six-pointed star, enamelled. It had a quickness about it, alive and on fire, hot metal dancing the way Laura juggled pancakes when she snatched them from the pan. In her head, she kissed them all goodbye.

Anna had no compunction about holding the star. She knew it was not Ezra's. Some other brave man had won and lost this medal and now it had come to her.

It had come to this and there was no more time. As he lunged forward, Anna met him dead on. Not feinting, not dipping, but rising in a counter-attack, her right arm behind.

Let it draw, let it draw.

Then you fire. You fire with the force of all the love in you, driving your hand over and up, up into the soft drape of his eyelid, the point of the medal glittering as it judders through fibrous twine. That is what it feels like, it feels like a ball of twisted elastic bands and the glittering point pops through, spilling red, which is unctuous and deeper than any red you've ever seen. Him gulping; he does this ventriloquist turn, face tight and shiny towards you, with a patch of gore which spatters on your face, a warm-shock beside the chill that is moving in regular bars. This is what it feels like, it feels like when your mobile finds its signal, cold moving in steady long chunks across your skin. You are shedding your skin, all the skins and layers you never got to be and it is only

Ever

It is only ever.

For ever and ever, world without end. His weight is crushing her backwards and then it is a feather; it is spinning and tumbling but her feet her feet she cannot find her feet you know that feeling when your dad goes fast over the brow of a hill but her hands are tight on him, persistent as a comet tail and he is coming, weightless too. Both moving through the night, and the night and the sky, it spreads so rapidly this wavering whipping air, fast and slow – boom, fast and slow – boom and a long fine hand and the world rushing by.

And it is . . . bright

And it is . . . not sore

Words form on her lips, but the air whips them away.

And all the stars are turning. Stars and tiny hands.

Chapter Sixty

TUESDAY 27 NOVEMBER

– *Bravo Echo Three. Are you available to deal with a call on Maryhill Road?*

– *Bravo Echo Three. Ah, that's a negative. Two forty-five a.m. and it's chocolate time.*

– *Repeat, Bravo Echo Three?*

– *Is it urgent?*

– *That's a negative Bravo Echo Three.*

– *Aye well, would you note, we are currently on our piecebreak. Tuesday night is croissants and hot chocolate, mind? And you canny really reheat a croissant.*

– *Ah Roger. Area Control to any station free to attend report of a woman riding a horse down the middle of Maryhill Road. Described as early twenties, long dark hair, wearing a purple velvet coat. Reporter states she is also leading another horse behind her. Any stations to attend? Anyone?*

– *Yee-ha! Telt you Hairymill was the Wild West.*

GLASGOW FAIR

Parade! ParADE – ATTENTION!

The sharp spatter of hundreds of segs shifting in a chorus line. Rigid tap dancers, with their eyes snapped centre, desperately trying to avoid their loved ones' waves and glittering teeth, feart lest the virus of grinning infected the ranks as well. She shivered in the sun. Amazing, how familiar this place felt. The tatty canteen, the crenellated turrets of the castle. The stone urn marking the last few hundred metres of the five-mile run, where the whole class assembled to cheer stragglers over the line.

Tulliallan. The Scottish Police College. She had made it.

Her family were all there, watching. There was Grace right at the front as usual, Anna in every facet of her, from the blonde hair bright in the sunlight to the determined scowl as she pushed ever-nearer to the dais reserved for the VIPs.

One final stomping of feet, a right wheel, a shuffle. And then the parade was done. They were marching off the square, to applause and spouses and proud parents rushing over.

Not him. He couldn't rush, but he'd insisted on standing there, on leaving the chair at home. She could see his stoop, and the people either side of him. Liz – of course – and Cath, taking his other elbow and waving for them both. Her heart lifted on seeing Cath. She knew Jamie wouldn't have come, he never went to police things, but it meant a lot that Cath had travelled down. She had been so good to them over the years, so kind with the sharing of herself and her family.

Here it comes – the blonde explosion. Grace had fled the herd the second the band stopped playing, was streaking towards her across the drill square. They had made her wear a dress which, on the hanger, was every girl's tulle-lavished dream. On Grace, it was an encumbrance.

'Look,' she demanded. 'I made a daisy chain.'

'Were you not watching all that marching?'

'Yeah, a bit. Then I got bored. You all kept sticking your hands up and I thought you were going to ask some questions.'

'No. We were doing saluting and stuff.'

'Why?'

'Good question. Because it looks impressive?'

'What's himpressive?'

'Nice.'

'No it didn't. It looked stupid.'

Laura laughed. 'You're probably right. As usual. C'mon, titch. I want to show you something.'

She led her sister away from the tumult of the drill square, and the clusters of families kissing and snapping their young. They walked round to the front of the castle – which everyone thought was the back. Nobody came in through this façade; it sat in splendid isolation, presiding over a broad swathe of lawn. In moments of genteel madness, you could play croquet on that lawn. Probationers never did, but you saw the old boys occasionally, the CID guys up for a course maybe, stooping and swinging to make elegant awkward thwacks.

Further down the lawn were three slim black tablets, set seven feet high in earth and stone. She took Grace over, so they could read the surface.

'What does that say?'

Mouthing slowly, then more confident as she picked up the shape and depth of the letters.

'S.E.M.P.E.R. V.I.G.I.L.O. What's that mean?'

'Always vigilant. It's the police motto. But look. Whose name's that? See the one below the Chinese man's name?' Laura pointed to the end stone, its polish so high that it mirrored the sunlight back at them. You could see them both reflected there, the kid and the cop, framed like a corny recruitment poster.

Grace frowned. 'A. N. N. A. C. A. – Mum's? Is she *in* there?'

'No, silly. It's a kind of monument. You know how she was a policewoman too?'

'Yeah. I'm not stupid.'

'Well, this is to remember all the police officers in Scotland who died on duty. You know, when they were helping folk.'

And it had been on duty, Uncle Alex had been very clear about that. One day, Laura might show her sister the *Evening Times* article she had torn out and kept. It was very speculative, done in a tawdry 'truth behind the headlines' style, with a mystery woman known only as 'M', but it did offer some colour to shade the blanks they'd been left with. Uncle Alex wouldn't talk about it, neither would Dad. He'd talk about Mum of course, all the time. But not how they'd lost her.

'D'you miss her?' asked Grace.

'Yeah. Loads.'

'Me too. What was she like?'

What was Anna like? Laura screwed up her eyes against the sun. 'Well, she was clever, and . . . she loved animals – especially cats.'

'So do I.'

'I know. You won't remember Alice, you were only a baby, but that was Mum's cat.'

'I do so remember cos she used to sit on my bed and growl at folk.'

Wee fibber. She couldn't possibly have recollected Alice. Laura could see her dad, still standing, over by the cars. Where had everyone else gone? He couldn't stand for long like that; it was a miracle he could do it at all. She needed to get him comfy again.

'C'mon you. We'd better get back.' She started to walk away from the memorial. Didn't feel in any sense like a goodbye; it was only words. Nice, proud words, but words all the same.

'What else about Mum?' persisted Grace.

'Och, I don't know, Grace.'

'Well you know more'n me.'

Briefly, Laura touched her sister's hair before she jooked away. 'Get off.'

'Well, everyone says Mum was brave, but you know that. Dad's told you enough.'

'Yeah,' Grace rolled her eyes. 'How she killed a bad man and the bad man killed her back.'

'Woah – he said that? Why? When?'

Grace rearranged the daisy chain around her neck, smoothing it so all the flowerheads ran one way. 'When you joined the police. Don't shout at him. I was crying cos I thought the police meant you got killed.'

'And what d'you think now?'

She shrugged. 'I don't know.'

'I promise you, Grace – I will not get killed.'

'Okay.' She sighed. 'Was Mum pretty?'

'Yeah! She was beautiful. Even when she went all grumpy; her eyes would go dead big and bright. Bet Dad hasn't told you that. No *way* would she let you away with the stuff Dad and I put up with. She was a right bossy-boots.'

'Well, one day I'm going to be a policewoman too. And I'm gonny be the boss of all you lot.'

'I bet you are.'

Grace wriggled free of Laura's hand, began to tread on the flowerbed.

'Get back here, you. You're not supposed to stand there.'

Paying her no heed, Grace crashed through the jaggy rose bushes until she made it back to the memorial. Tongue protruding, she stood on tiptoe and draped the daisy chain over the top of the middle stone. Came back laughing, with scratches on her knees.

Laura held her by the wrist. 'I told you: you're not supposed to do that. Now, here's Dad coming. D'you want to get into trouble?'

She shrugged. 'So? Did she like flowers?'

'Eh . . . I'm not sure. She wasn't really a flower person, I don't think.'

'But what was she *like* then?' tutted Grace, her lithe quick frame already tugging to break in some other direction.

'She was like you.'

Grace laughed, a clear high ring of crystal, took a skipping step back and launched herself like a spinning-top, turning starwheels towards her father. For a moment, Laura watched his broken face go whole.

THE END